The

BARBARA CARTLAND

Collection

Also available in one volume from Chancellor Press

Two Hearts in Hungary
A Theatre of Love
Too Precious to Lose

The BARBARA CARTLAND Collection

Volume 2

Stand and Deliver your Heart
The Magic of Paris
The Scent of Roses

CHANCELLOR
PRESS

Stand and Deliver Your Heart first published in Great Britain
in 1991 by Mandarin Paperbacks
The Magic of Paris first published in Great Britain
in 1991 by Mandarin Paperbacks
The Scent of Roses first published in Great Britain
in 1991 by Mandarin Paperbacks

This collected volume first published in Great Britain
in 1992 by Chancellor Press
an imprint of
Reed International Books Limited
Michelin House
81 Fulham Road
London SW3 6RB

ISBN 1 85152 210 7

Printed in Great Britain by The Bath Press

CONTENTS

ABOUT THE AUTHOR

Barbara Cartland, the world's most famous romantic novelist, who is also an historian, playwright, lecturer, political speaker and television personality, has now written over 540 books and sold over 600 million copies all over the world.

She has also had many historical works published and has written four autobiographies as well as the biographies of her mother and that of her brother, Ronald Cartland, who was the first Member of Parliament to be killed in the last war. This book has a preface by Sir Winston Churchill and has just been published with an introduction by the late Sir Arthur Bryant.

"Love at the Helm" a novel written with the help and inspiration of the late Earl Mountbatten of Burma, Great Uncle of His Royal Highness The Prince of Wales, is being sold for the Mountbatten Memorial Trust.

She has broken the world record for the last sixteen years by writing an average of twenty-three books a year. In the Guinness Book of Records she is listed as the world's top-selling author.

Miss Cartland in 1978 sang an Album of Love Songs with the Royal Philharmonic Orchestra.

In private life Barbara Cartland, who is a Dame of Grace of the Order of St. John of Jerusalem, Chairman of the St. John Council in Hertfordshire and Deputy President of the St. John Ambulance Brigade, has fought for better conditions and salaries for Midwives and Nurses.

She championed the cause for the Elderly in 1956 invoking a Government Enquiry into the "Housing Conditions of Old People".

In 1962 she had the Law of England changed so that Local Authorities had to provide camps for their own Gypsies. This has meant that since then thousands and thousands of Gypsy children have been able to go to School which they had never been able to do in the past, as their caravans were moved every twenty-four hours by the Police.

There are now fourteen camps in Hertfordshire and Barbara Cartland has her own Romany Gypsy Camp called Barbaraville by the Gypsies.

Her designs "Decorating with Love" are being sold all over the U.S.A. and the National Home Fashions League made her in 1981 "Woman of Achievement".

Barbara Cartland's book "Getting Older, Growing Younger" has been published in Great Britain and the U.S.A. and her fifth Cookery Book, "The Romance of Food" is now being used by the House of Commons.

In 1984 she received at Kennedy Airport, America's Bishop Wright Air Industry Award for her contribution to the development of aviation. In 1931 she and two R.A.F. Officers thought of, and carried the first aeroplane-towed glider air-mail.

During the War she was Chief Lady Welfare Officer in Bedfordshire looking after 20,000 Service men and women. She thought of having a pool of Wedding Dresses at the War Office so a Service Bride could hire a gown for the day.

She bought 1,000 secondhand gowns without coupons for the A.T.S., the W.A.A.F.s and the W.R.E.N.S. In 1945 Barbara Cartland received the Certificate of Merit from Eastern Command.

In 1964 Barbara Cartland founded the National Association for Health of which she is the President, as a front for all the Health Stores and for any product made as alternative medicine.

This has now a £650,000,000 turnover a year, with one-third going in export.

In January 1988 she received "La Medaille de Vermeil de la Ville de Paris", (the Gold Medal of Paris). This is the highest award to be given by the City of Paris for ACHIEVEMENT – 25 million books sold in France.

In March 1988 Barbara Cartland was asked by the Indian Government to open their Health Resort outside Delhi. This is almost the largest Health Resort in the world.

Barbara Cartland was made a Dame of the Order of the British Empire in the 1991 New Year's Honours List, by Her Majesty The Queen for her contribution to literature and also for her years of work for the community.

Stand and Deliver your Heart

AUTHOR'S NOTE

It was in the 18th century that the Highwayman became the greatest menace so that no main road was safe for a traveller.

But he was also thought romantic.

In actual fact, however, few of them were anthing but the very worst type of criminal, who would murder or torture their victims.

There were, as I have told in this novel, a few wellborn Highwaymen, who came from respected families, and had been educated at Public Schools.

William Parsons was a Baronet's son, who was educated at Eton and was commissioned in the Royal Navy.

Simon Clarke was a Baronet in his own right, but became a Highwayman.

But they behaved better than Dick Turpin, the most romanticised of the Highwaymen, who was both brutal and unscrupulous.

Some Highwaymen escaped the gallows, but the majority were hanged at Tyburn which, until the end of the 18th century was the most uncivilised sight.

There would be thousands in the crowd assembled to witness the hanging: the Gentry sitting in the expensive seats which were close to the gallows.

The mob who could not afford the closest view, fought fiercely for the best places.

Spectators often had their limbs broken and some were even killed in the crush.

Apart from this, Tyburn was a Fairground with side-shows and street vendors offering their wares.

In 1789 the gallows were moved from Tyburn to the courtyard of the Old Bailey.

But a hanging was still open to the Public, and matters were not very much improved.

Chapter One

Vanda rode through the woods thinking it was the loveliest day they had had for a long time.

There were primroses and violets peeping through their leaves under the trees, and the birds were singing.

She always enjoyed being able to ride in the great Park which encircled Wyn Hall.

Mr. Rushman had been the Manager of the Estate during the war.

He had given her permission to go there whenever she liked.

The old Earl of Wynstock was bed-ridden and his son was fighting Napoleon in the Peninsula.

"It would be nice to see someone young about the place," he said, "and there will be no need to take a groom with you."

That to Vanda was more important than anything.

Her father had insisted that she was always accompanied when she rode elsewhere.

They lived on the border of Wyn Park at the end of the village.

She had really only to cross the road under the trees to be, as she told herself, free.

She was thinking that it would be very frustrating now that the war was over.

When the Earl returned she could no longer use his grounds as if they were her own.

The young Earl, whom she hardly remembered, had come into the title three years ago.

He had distinguished himself at Waterloo and received the medal of gallantry.

He had then joined the Duke of Wellington's staff to serve him in the Army of Occupation.

Soldiers were demobilised and thousands began to return to England.

There was no sign however of the Earl.

"Perhaps he will never come back," Vanda thought happily.

She rode on towards the centre of the wood where she knew no one but herself ever went.

There closely surrounded by trees was the remains of an old Chapel.

It had once been used by a Monk who retired from the world to minister to the birds and wild animals.

He was a very holy man and there were all sorts of legends in the countryside of the animals he had healed.

Foxes which had been caught in a trap would have died had he not placed his hands upon them.

Cats and dogs that were injured and birds with a broken wing or leg were taken to him, usually by children.

He prayed over them and gave them his healing touch.

They left, so the legends said, stronger and better than they had ever been before.

The tiny Chapel he had built for himself had fallen into disrepair.

The villagers believed he haunted the wood and were afraid to go there.

"How can you be afraid," Vanda asked one old woman, "of someone who was holy?"

"'E were holy right enough," she answered, "but it be creepy-like aseeing th' dead."

No one in the village would put a foot inside Monk's Wood, however often they went in the others.

Vanda knew the boys went there to poach!

She thought personally they did very little harm.

With the Earl away at the war there was no one to shoot the pheasants and pigeons.

Nor for that matter the magpies and jays which the Game-Keepers thought of as vermin.

For Vanda the woods were therefore very much more enjoyable.

She loved being alone so that no one could disturb her.

She listened to the buzz of the bees, the rustle of the rabbits in the undergrowth, and the chatter of the red squirrels searching for nuts.

Sometimes too she thought she could hear music which came from the trees themselves.

She tried to compose it into music that she could play on the piano.

Her mother had been an exceptionally good pianist and Vanda had tried to emulate her since she was a child.

She was thinking now that she should compose a song of Spring.

She knew that the trees were giving her inspiration.

The wind moving the green leaves was creating a melody that she must try to remember.

Then suddenly she heard a strange sound.

It interrupted her thoughts and somehow seemed alien and coarse in the beauty around her.

There was another sound and she drew in her horse.

Her father always had exceedingly good horse-flesh in his stable.

The horse Vanda was riding was called *Kingfisher* and was her favourite.

Kingfisher responded immediately to her pull on the reins and came to a stand-still.

Vanda realised that ahead in the very centre of the woods, where she had never seen anyone before, there were men.

The sound she had heard was a coarse laugh.

Now listening she could hear voices and she knew immediately that they did not belong to local men.

The inhabitants of Little Stock – as the village was named – spoke with a slow but distinct Wiltshire accent.

Sometimes she laughed with her father at what they said and the way they spoke.

But she thought actually that it was quite attractive.

Whoever they were ahead in the wood were talking harshly.

Their accent was quite different and there was something about the sound of their voices that she did not like.

In fact she felt unaccountably afraid.

Who, she asked herself, could possibly be making so much noise in the one place in the wood that many people thought was holy?

She supposed they must be village hooligans, but from what village?

How dare they trespass in the private estate of the Earl of Wynstock?

These were unanswerable questions, and she knew it would be a mistake to try to find out the answer.

The laughter came again, then a chatter of coarse voices.

She could not understand what was said, but she was sure there were three or perhaps more men speaking.

She turned *Kingfisher* round and went back along the moss-covered path by which she had come.

When she could no longer hear the strange sounds behind her, she felt angry that the privacy of the wood was being violated by strangers.

She wondered what they could be doing there and why they found it so amusing.

"I shall never know the answers to those questions," she told herself. "But I hope they will go away and never come back."

It suddenly struck her that they might do damage to the great House itself.

Wyn Hall was a magnificent example of the work of the Adam Brothers.

It had been completed in the middle of the last century on the site of a much older house.

The Earls of Wynstock dated back to Henry VIII.

They had grown more important down the centuries and each one had improved the house in which they lived.

They had also bought more land.

Having been brought up in the shadow of Wyn Hall, Vanda had a deep affection for it.

In the same way she loved the old Earl.

He was a distinguished man who enjoyed the company of her father who was nearly the same age as he was.

The Earl had never been in the Army, but he liked to hear of the life Vanda's father, General Sir Alexander Charlton, had lived.

He told him about the years he had spent with his Regiment in India and how well it was doing under Wellington.

When the Earl died, Vanda knew that her father felt lost without him.

He had been shattered by her mother's death and when she was no longer there he was like a man who had been crippled.

He was however able to forget his unhappiness when he had a friend of his own age to talk to.

Now she thought sadly he only had her.

14

Although she tried to fill the gap in his life, it was difficult to do anything but listen when he talked.

Fortunately "The General" as the village called him, was now writing a book.

It was taking him a long time because he had so much to remember and so much to record.

At least, Vanda thought, he had reached the year when she was born.

She was certain that when it was finished it would be of great interest to the public.

She had actually had great difficulty in persuading her father to write down the stories he told so amusingly.

Her mother had loved them all.

"Tell Vanda," she would plead, "how you quelled a mutiny among your sepoys."

Or else she would say:

"Describe the beauty of the Palace belonging to the Maharajah of Udaipur and the pink one you liked the best in Jaipur."

Vanda adored her father's tales.

She knew that the task of writing his reminiscences was making all the difference to his life.

He had been writing when she left the house, and he would not realise how many hours she was away.

It was only for the last eighteen months that he had been unable to accompany her on horseback.

At first she felt guilty, knowing how much he enjoyed being on one of his well-bred horses.

Sir Alexander's legs were however swollen with rheumatism and it hurt him to walk, let alone ride.

Vanda reached the end of the wood.

She wondered if she should go home and tell her father about the strange men in the centre of it.

Then she had a better idea.

She would ride up to the Hall and tell the Caretakers to be on their guard.

If the hooligans were intent on making trouble, they might stone the windows.

Or, perhaps, try to break some of the stone statues in the garden.

"I will warn the Taylors," she decided.

15

She rode *Kingfisher* quickly through the Park under the ancient oak trees, across the bridge which spanned the lake and into the stables.

She was so used to going there that it was almost like coming home.

As she reached the Yard the Head Groom, who had known her since she was a child, came out of the stable.

He smiled a greeting before he said:

"Aft'noon, Miss Vanda, t'be a sight fer sore eyes t' see thee."

"Thank you, I hope you are feeling better and that the cut on your hand has healed," Vanda replied.

"It 'ealed immediate after yer tells Oi wot t' do with it," the Head Groom replied.

He took *Kingfisher* from her and led him into a stall.

Vanda walked along the path through the big banks of rhododendrons which led to the kitchen-door.

She did not knock, but went along the flagged passage to the kitchen.

It was a very large room with a high ceiling.

There was a large beam on which there had hung in the past game and dried hams.

Now there was nothing on the beam but one small rabbit.

The Caretakers were sitting at the large deal table drinking tea.

Taylor would have got up when Vanda appeared, but she said quickly:

"Do not move, I only came in to tell you something."

"Now ye sit doon, Miss Vanda," Mrs. Taylor said, who was a large rosy-cheeked woman. "I'm sure ye could do with a cup o' tea an' Taylor an' me were ajust having one."

"I would love a cup of tea," Vanda replied.

She knew it was what they expected to hear.

Although she did not really enjoy the strong, dark Ceylon Tea, they would have been disappointed if she had refused.

When it had been poured out and the cup was beside her she said:

"Such a strange thing has just happened. I was riding in Monk's Wood, and what do you think was right in the centre where no one ever goes except myself? There were men!"

She paused. Then as Mr. and Mrs. Taylor did not speak she went on:

"They were strangers and they certainly did not come from Wiltshire. There were quite a number of them, laughing in what I thought was an unpleasant manner."

It was then that she was aware that Mr. and Mrs. Taylor were looking at each other.

She felt, though it seemed incredible, they were not surprised at what she had just said.

"They be in Monk's Wood?" Taylor said at last very slowly. "Now what do ye think they'd be adoing there, Mother?"

He looked at his wife as he spoke.

She did not answer but seemed to be busying herself pouring more tea into her cup.

Although it was already nearly full.

Vanda looked from one to the other and then she said:

"Have you heard of these men before?"

"No, no," Mrs. Taylor said quickly. "We knows nothin' about 'em."

She was obviously agitated and spoke in a way which was not in the least like her.

Vanda looked at Taylor.

She did not speak, but he was well aware she was asking him a question.

"I knows o' nothin' us can tell ye, Miss Vanda," he said at length. "They 'as nothin' t' do with us."

"But you are aware they exist," Vanda insisted. "Have they been here causing trouble?"

Mrs. Taylor put down the tea-pot and laid her two hands palm-down on the table.

"Now listen t' me, Miss Vanda. Go home an' say nothin' of what ye've heard. There be nought ye can do about it an' us wants no trouble."

"Trouble?" Vanda asked in a bewildered tone. "What sort of trouble are you talking about, and how can it possibly affect you?"

Mrs. Taylor looked helplessly at her husband.

"We be alone 'ere, Miss Vanda," he said, "except for the grooms, an' Goodrid be an old man while Nat an' Ben be high on a horse but small on th' ground."

Vanda would have smiled at the description of the two younger grooms, who did in fact look rather like jockeys, if she had not been worried.

"What is going on?" she wondered. "And why are the Taylors so mysterious about it?"

When she thought about it there was really no one to tell.

Mr. Rushman, the Manager, was over seventy and could no longer ride a horse on the estate, but drove a gig.

He was not in good health and in the winter was laid-up with bronchitis.

It kept him in his house week after week.

She pulled her chair a little nearer the table and resting her chin on her hands she said:

"Now tell me what is troubling you both. You know I will help if I can and, if you want me to remain silent, I will say nothing to anybody."

Taylor looked at his wife.

Mrs. Taylor gave a big sigh which seemed to shake her whole fat body.

"We'll tell ye," she said at length, "but I be too 'fraid t' speak o' them."

"Speak of who?" Vanda asked.

Taylor cleared his throat.

"It be like this, Miss Vanda. We be 'ere as ye knows to look after th' 'ouse till 'is Lordship comes 'ome."

"No one could do it better," Vanda said encouragingly.

It was true that with the help of three women from the village the house was as well looked after as when the old Earl was alive.

Granted there were not four Footmen in the Hall or a Butler in charge of them.

Nor was there a Chef in the Kitchen, the equal of the one employed by the Prince Regent, and three scullions under him.

When the Earl died, Mr. Rushman had appointed the Taylors as Caretakers.

They had lived up to that name and had taken the greatest care of Wyn Hall.

They had always in the past told Vanda how much they enjoyed their job.

She could not understand what could have occurred now to make them frightened and reluctant to talk of their fears.

"Go on," she prompted Taylor.

"They comes first about two weeks ago," he began.

"They?" Vanda asked. "Who are they?"

"That's what we ain't supposed to know," he replied, "but they be men."

Vanda knew that from the voices she had heard. She did not interrupt and Taylor continued:

"They asks for water an' they says t' the Mrs. an' I: 'ye keep yer eyes t' yerselves an' yer lips closed, an' no harm'll come t' ye.'"

"They said that!" Vanda exclaimed. "And what did you reply?"

"They be not th' sort o' men t' who ye'd make a reply," Taylor said.

"Then what happened."

"Don't tell 'er, don't tell 'er," Mrs. Taylor said in an agitated manner.

"I had much better know the whole truth," Vanda said, "and then if anything happens I will be able to help you."

"Nothing'll happen, nothing!" Mrs. Taylor said. "They promised that if us said naught."

"I do not count," Vanda said with an encouraging smile, "and I do not like to see you so upset."

"Us be upset right enough," Taylor said, "but there be nothin' us can do aboot it. Nothin'!"

"So where are the men?" Vanda asked.

There was a pause.

Then lowering his voice to little more than a whisper Taylor said:

"They be in th' West Wing, Miss Vanda."

Vanda looked at him in astonishment.

The West Wing had been shut up for a long time before the Earl died.

He had decided the house was too big and the West Wing contained a number of rooms which were never used.

In the East Wing there was the Picture Gallery, the Ball-Room, and a few bedrooms on the top floor.

The West Wing was just an accumulation of rooms of no particular historic interest.

Vanda thought the architects had built it merely to balance from the outside the other wing of the house.

At the same time it was definitely a part of Wyn Hall.

She could not imagine anything more horrifying than having hooligans, or whatever the strangers were, living in the house.

It seemed extraordinary that the Taylors had not gone to

see Mr. Rushman and demanded that the men were turned out.

She knew, however, it would be a mistake for her to criticize their behaviour.

She therefore said:

"If they have threatened you it must have been very frightening. But surely they do not intend to stay for long."

"Us don't knows aboot that," Mrs. Taylor replied. "We just keeps ourselves t' ourselves an' pretends they bain't there."

"But they are trespassing," Vanda said quietly.

"Us knows that," Taylor said, "but they be dangerous, Miss Vanda, an' us 'ears tales o' things that 'ave 'appened which might 'appen 'ere."

"What sort of things?" Vanda enquired.

Again he lowered his voice so that she could hardly hear.

She was really reading the movements of his lips as he said:

"Murders."

"I do not believe it!" Vanda exclaimed. "And if these men are murderers, then how can we allow them to be here in the Hall and near the village?"

Taylor glanced over his shoulder because he was afraid that they were being overheard.

"Not so loud, Miss Vanda," he begged. "If anythin' 'appen t' thee we'd ne'er forgive ourselves."

"No indeed," Mrs. Taylor agreed. "Now ye say nothin' aboot it, Miss Vanda, an' per'aps they'll go away."

"And if they stay?" Vanda asked.

The Taylors looked at each other and she realised how frightened they were.

She wondered what she could say to comfort them.

At the same time she was trying to think quickly who could turn out these trespassers.

They had taken possession of an empty house with no one to protect it but two elderly people.

"I suppose," she thought, "it would be foolish to believe that something like this could never happen, especially after a war."

Men after risking their lives in fighting for their country had been turned out of the Services without a pension.

Even those who had been wounded or had lost a limb had no compensation.

Her father had been told what was happening in the Coastal areas.

Sailors dismissed from the Navy roamed the countryside in search of food and demanded money from quite humble householders.

"I can hardly blame them," Sir Alexander had said bitterly. "They won a war, but no one is concerned about them now that there is peace."

"Surely the Government should do something," Vanda had said hotly.

"They should," her father had replied, "but I doubt if they will."

They had gone on to talk about how the men who had fought came back to find their jobs had been taken by those who had stayed at home.

Many were lost altogether.

Now that hostilities had ended there was no longer the desperate need for food that there had been over the last fifteen years.

Farmers could not now sell their crops.

Also, a great many aristocratic land-owners had suffered financially from the war.

They could not employ the large numbers of staff they had been able to do before it began.

Tenants needed their houses repaired, but the landlords did not have the money to spend on doing it.

It was difficult to know where England could find purchasers of what goods were available.

"There must be somebody who could make these men behave," Vanda was thinking.

She felt she could hear again the sharpness of the voices and the rough way they spoke.

But she knew there were few men available in the village who could stand up to them.

Finally she decided it was something that she must discuss with her father.

He would know if there were any military in the vicinity.

If the worst came to the worst, they could get soldiers to turn out the intruders who were causing trouble.

"That is what I must do," she thought.

But at the same time she knew it would be a mistake to tell the Taylors what she intended.

"I can see you have been very brave," she said gently, "but at the same time it is something that cannot continue."

"Now don't ye be doin' anythin' aboot it, Miss Vanda!" Taylor said hastily. "If ye do, they might 'urt thee an' th' General."

"I doubt that," Vanda answered. "They can hardly come into the village, bursting into people's houses and beating up or murdering ordinary citizens."

"That be exactly what they will do," Taylor said stubbornly.

Vanda stared at him.

"Now you are a sensible man, Mr. Taylor," she said, "and you know as well as I do that we cannot have rough people taking the law into their own hands."

"This lot," Taylor said with the jerk of his thumb, "be abo'e th' law."

Vanda shook her head.

"No one is above the law and no one has the right to interfere with or to threaten ordinary citizens . ."

"Ye don't understand," Mrs. Taylor interrupted.

She looked at her husband and said:

"Ye'd better tell wh' they be."

"It'd be a mistake," Taylor replied sharply. Then he added:

"Well, as Miss Vanda knows s' much, 'er better understan' that unless 'er keeps 'er lips closed us'll be in trouble."

Again Vanda was staring from one to another.

She was trying to understand why they were so frightened and why they were so determined that she should do nothing.

She was suddenly afraid that these men might break into the rest of the house.

Wyn Hall was so beautiful inside.

She felt as if every piece of furniture, every picture, every book in the Great Library belonged in some way to herself.

She had known and loved them ever since she was old enough to appreciate such exquisite possessions.

Wyn Hall had become as familiar to her as her own home.

She knew that if any of it was damaged, it would break her heart.

Now she thought with horror of the miniatures which hung on the walls in the Drawing Room.

The portraits of the Wyns which hung on the beautifully carved stairs, the pictures in the Gallery which had been added to by every Earl.

She clasped her hands together.

"We must protect the Hall from these terrible people," she said. "Supposing they ransack the State Rooms, supposing they set the whole place on fire?"

"They'll not do that, Miss Vanda," Taylor said, "so long as us give them shelter. But if us turns 'em out anythin' might 'appen."

"They cannot stay here indefinitely," Vanda said.

"They'll go when it suits 'em," Taylor said. "They just want somewhere t' rest an' 'ide their 'aul."

"Hide their haul?" Vanda repeated. "What do you mean by that? What can they have to hide?"

They were questions that once again seemed to leave the Taylors silent and frightened.

In fact Vanda began to think that it was ridiculous.

Taylor was a well-built man. Why should he be shaking in his shoes when he thought about a few riotous young men who so far had done no harm?

"Now what I want you to let me do," she said in a soft voice, "is to talk to my father. You know how clever he is, and he has been a soldier all his life."

Mrs. Taylor suddenly gave a scream.

"Soldiers!" she cried. "If soldiers come 'ere they'll kill us. We'll both be dead, that's what we'll be, Miss Vanda, an' it'll be ye who's done it."

Vanda reached out to put her hand on Mrs. Taylor.

"Please do not upset yourself," she said. "The soldiers will not come if it frightens you, but we have to do something."

"There be nothin' we can do, an' that be th' truth," Taylor asserted.

"Just you go away an' forget us," his wife begged. "We be all right so long a' us do nothin'."

Vanda felt as though she was up against an insurmountable obstacle.

After a moment she said:

"Tell me where these men come from and who they are. Surely you must know that."

"Yes us knows that," Mrs. Taylor said in a whisper.

"Then tell me so that I can understand why you are so frightened," Vanda pleaded.

23

She looked at Taylor.

Once again he glanced over his shoulder towards the door as if he thought someone might come through it.

He then leant across the table and said:

"They be 'ighwaymen!"

Chapter Two

Riding home, Vanda wondered what she could do about the Taylors.

They were obviously terrified of the Highwaymen.

They had begged her almost on their knees not to tell anyone about them.

Nor to try to remove them from the West Wing.

Thinking over what she knew about Highwaymen, Vanda could understand their fear.

She had often made her father tell her about the terrible menace the Highwaymen had been when he was a young man.

The most famed Highwaymen were a fraternity called "Knights of the High Toby".

A number of them, Hawkins, Maclean, Rann and Page, had all been in liveried service.

They therefore modelled themselves on their erstwhile masters and liked to be thought of as "The Gentlemen of the Road".

There were also, Sir Alexander had said, men who actually were gentlemen and had found it the only way to earn money.

"It must have been very dangerous, Papa," Vanda said.

"They nearly all ended up on the gibbet," her father replied.

"Were there real gentlemen who would do anything so outrageous?" Vanda enquired.

Her father thought before he said:

"Maclean was of good Highland stock and his father was a Minister. William Parsons was a Baronet's son, educated at Eton and commissioned in the Royal Navy."

"How could they have sunk so low!" Vanda exclaimed.

"Sir Simon Clarke was a Baronet in his own right," her father continued.

"It seems incredible that they should do anything which would make them outlawed completely from society."

"They certainly were that," Sir Alexander smiled. "But some of them retained the manners of their class."

"Who in particular?" Vanda enquired.

"James Maclean really deserved the title of a "Gentleman High-wayman," Sir Alexander replied. "He accidently fired his pistol and wounded the famous Horace Walpole in Hyde Park."

Vanda was surprised, but she did not say anything and her father went on:

"He was profoundly apologetic and sent Mr. Walpole two letters of regret."

"He at least was a decent sort of man," Vanda said.

"There were unfortunately a great many who were the exact opposite," Sir Alexander stated.

He thought for a moment before he said:

"Perhaps two of the worst were Captain James Campbell and Sir John Johnson, who abducted an heiress. She was only thirteen, but had a fortune of £50,000."

"What happened?" Vanda asked.

"They compelled her to marry James Campbell against her will."

"How terrible for her!"

"It was!" Sir Alexander said grimly. "Sir John Johnson was hanged for his part in the abduction, but James Campbell escaped to the Continent."

Thinking of these stories now, Vanda wondered what sort of men they were in the West Wing.

From what she had heard of their voices they might be as murderous and as terrifying as the Taylors thought them to be.

On the other hand, they might be led by someone better born and not so violent.

'Perhaps I am just being optimistic,' she thought.

They had certainly appeared very ferocious to the Taylors.

As she drew nearer to her home she decided that she must tell her father what was happening.

She must swear him to secrecy.

But she was quite sure that, however horrified he was by the situation, there was nothing that he personally could do about it.

Suddenly it occurred to her that if the Highwaymen were as bad

26

as they were reputed to be, she and her father could also be in danger.

Theirs was the largest house in the village.

From a Highwayman's point of view, they were certainly wealthy.

Against a gang of armed men they had no defence whatsoever.

Besides her father and herself, there were in the house only Dobson and Jennie who acted as Butler and Cook.

Also Hawkins, who had been her father's batman.

Although he was getting on in age, he was indispensable.

Two women came in to do the cleaning.

But at night, now she thought of it, with the exception of herself every one in the house was old.

"If I do not tell Papa, whom can I tell?" she asked.

She felt she was carrying too heavy a burden.

Having gained the confidence of the Taylors she must try to help them in some way.

The difficulty was how to do so.

She took her horse to the stable where the two grooms, both over fifty, were looking after her father's horses.

They took *Kingfisher* from her and led him into a stall.

Vanda walked slowly to the house.

She was still undecided.

At the same time every instinct told her that she could not sit back complaisantly and just hope the Highwaymen would go away.

"I must discuss it with papa," she decided finally.

She walked into the Study and to her surprise her father was not at his desk.

Instead he was seated in one of the comfortable arm-chairs in front of the fire-place.

There was a book he had obviously been researching on his knees.

He was lying back with his eyes closed and Vanda realised that he had fallen asleep.

She stood looking at him.

Although he was still a very distinguished and good-looking man he was beginning to show his age.

His hair was almost white.

In repose there were lines from his lips to his chin that she did not remember noticing before.

"I cannot upset him," she thought. "It would be unkind. I shall have to think this out for myself."

She went very quietly out of the room shutting the door behind her.

Then she remembered Mr. Rushman. After all he was the Manager of the estate.

Although he too was old, in his position he could take action to preserve his Master's house.

Now she thought of it, she was certain that Mr. Rushman could appeal to the Lord Lieutenant.

Alternatively he could write to the Officer in charge of the Barracks which were not far away at Melksham.

"That is the solution," Vanda told herself triumphantly.

She knew she must go to Mr. Rushman at once.

There was no need to ask for *Kingfisher* again.

Mr. Rushman's house was inside the wall which encircled the Park.

She could walk there in under ten minutes.

Without bothering to change from her riding-habit, she went out of the front-door.

She entered the Park through the side gate she always used.

Hurrying along under the oak trees she came in sight of The White Lodge.

It was not really a Lodge, but had replaced one which had guarded a different entrance to the Park.

The Lodge had become a very attractive and comfortable house.

Mr. Rushman had lived in it with his wife since he was first appointed Manager of the estate.

Now his wife had died and he was alone.

Yet he seemed to be quite happy and there were always a great number of callers at The White Lodge.

There were villagers with their grievances over a leaking roof or a broken window.

There was also a number of people like the Doctor, the Vicar and Members of the Hunt who looked on Mr. Rushman as a friend.

The General was very fond of him and so was Vanda.

She thought now she had been very foolish in not realising that she should have gone to Mr. Rushman immediately.

Also she should have advised the Taylors that was what they should have done.

Mr. Rushman's Housekeeper, who was a very superior middle-aged woman, opened the door.

"It's nice to see you, Miss Charlton, and I'm sure Mr. Rushman'll be delighted."

She hurried across the hall without waiting for Vanda's reply.

Only when she reached the door into the Estate Office where Mr. Rushman usually sat, did she turn to say in a whisper:

"His legs are hurting him today and it's all the worse for him because, as he'll tell you himself, something important's happening."

"Important?" Vanda longed to question.

The Housekeeper had already opened the door.

"Miss Charlton to see you, Sir," she announced.

Vanda walked in.

Mr. Rushman was not at his desk, but sitting upright in a high-backed arm-chair with his legs raised on a stool.

He had a great number of papers and account-books arranged beside him.

He was writing with a large quill pen.

He looked up and smiled as Vanda walked towards him.

"You are just the person I want to see, Miss Vanda," he said, "and actually, I was just going to send a message to your father."

"What about?" Vanda asked as she sat down in a chair near him.

"I have news," Mr. Rushman said, "good news. But at the same time it would come when it is difficult for me to move."

"And what is your news?" Vanda enquired.

Mr. Rushman replied almost dramatically:

"His Lordship, the Earl, is coming home!"

. . . .

The Earl of Wynstock arrived in London.

It was a long time since he had been in England and everything had changed.

Not, he thought, for the better.

The streets were more crowded and there appeared to be a great number more beggars than he remembered.

He had not missed after landing at Dover the numbers of demobilised soldiers and sailors who were to be seen in every town at which he stopped.

They were lounging about with obviously nothing to do.

Or, in many cases, sitting despondent by the roadside, hoping against hope that somebody would take pity on them.

The Earl had heard, while he was still in France, that this was happening in England.

Now he saw it for himself, it made him very angry.

After fighting for five years against Bonaparte no one appreciated more than he the courage and the endurance of the British Soldier.

He had heard the same story from his friends who had been in the Navy.

It seemed appalling that the men who under Nelson and Wellington had saved England should be treated so shabbily.

He was determined he would speak about it as soon as he had the opportunity in the House of Lords.

He was, however, aware there would be a great deal for him to do once he arrived home.

First he must open Wyn House in Berkeley Square and Wyn Hall in Wiltshire.

The Duke of Wellington thought him one of the most able of his Officers in that he had a genius for organisation.

The Earl was sensible enough to be aware that was something he would certainly need in reconstructing his own life.

At twenty-nine so many of his years had been concerned with war.

He knew it would be difficult to readjust to a very different existence.

He had, in fact, found the gaieties of Paris almost overwhelming after the hardship and the danger of the battle-fields.

He had gone there with the Duke of Wellington from Cambrai, where the Army of Occupation was billeted.

He had felt at first dazzled by the notorious extravagant and fascinating Courtesans.

He was amazed by the way in which the French had adjusted themselves overnight to peace after the defeat of Napoleon Bonaparte.

Paris was once again a city of pleasure, and the Earl would have been inhuman if when he was off duty he had not enjoyed it.

He indulged in several exhilarating and fiery affairs with the most sophisticated and experienced women in Europe.

Then he became involved with Lady Caroline Standish.

She was beautiful, exotic, and had stalked him as if he was a stag from the first moment she set eyes on him.

A widow since the age of twenty-one, she made the most of

being related to a number of the greatest aristocratic houses in England.

It was influence that enabled her to reach Paris very shortly after hostilities ceased.

Because she was rich, the parties she gave for every attractive man in the British Army were much sought after.

They rivalled those given by and for the Courtesans.

The Earl was not quite certain how it happened, but he found Lady Caroline was with him wherever he went.

Without meaning to he met her practically every day.

It was on her insistence that it became every night.

It was only when it was almost too late that he realised that she was seeking not only amusement, but marriage.

One thing he had determined during the war was not to get married until he was very much older.

He had heard too much, not only from his friends, but also from the men he commanded, of unfaithful wives.

"I trusted her," a brother Officer told him bitterly, "not only with my house, my money and my children, but also with my heart."

He went on to tell the Earl exactly what had happened.

It was inevitably one of his relatives who had informed him in the first place of his wife's infidelity.

Because the Earl was a good Officer and his men trusted him, he learnt of their troubles also.

"Gone off with th' Inn Keeper, her 'as," his Seargeant-Major told him, "and me mother writes to tell Oi 'er has stripped th' house o' everythin' Oi bought for it."

There were innumerable men who had been cuckolded by their closest friends, besides the Carrier, the Landlord or the GameKeeper.

It was then that the Earl began to wonder if all women were untrustworthy.

He felt that a woman who took lover after lover was not a particularly admirable specimen of her sex.

He had never known his mother, whom he had adored, being concerned with any man except his father.

He told himself that, when he did marry, it would be someone who would love him and him alone.

He would kill his wife rather than share her with another man.

31

He would, however, have been inhuman if he had resisted Lady Caroline's experienced blandishments.

She entwined herself like clinging ivy.

It was only when there was talk of his returning home that he realised he stood on the brink of a very dangerous gulf.

"I hope I shall be able to get away next month," he had said to Caroline.

They were having dinner in the house he had rented with another brother Officer while they were in Paris.

It was a bore to stay at the British Embassy with the Duke.

Hotels were practically non-existent and uncomfortable and sordid.

The house his friend had found had belonged to one of Napoleon's social upstarts.

They had been disdainfully ignored by the French of the *Ancien Régime*.

It was expensively furnished.

The servants who were in charge of it were delighted to have regular wages from two Englishmen who paid them punctiliously.

The Earl's friend was seldom in the house.

He therefore found himself continually having dinner alone with Lady Caroline.

He had to admit she looked very alluring.

As the daughter of the Duke of Hull she had taken London by storm the moment she appeared as a débutante.

She had made a good marriage in marrying a man who came from a family which was as blue blooded as her own.

He was also extremely rich.

When he was killed it did not perturb her unduly.

She had already found him dull, and before he was dead she had amused herself with several lovers.

Caroline Standish was wise enough to realise that her beauty would not last forever.

Her extravagance both in England and France had considerably eaten into her fortune.

She was, therefore, looking for a husband who was both rich and distinguished.

Who better than the Earl?

Her golden hair gleamed in the candle light.

Her gown which was in the high-waisted style, originally set by the Empress Josephine, was very revealing.

After the announcement that he would be going home, the Earl said casually:

"Will you be staying here?"

Lady Caroline's large blue eyes looked up at him in surprise.

"Surely, Neil," she said softly, "you know that I will be coming with you."

The Earl stiffened.

He had found Caroline extremely attractive.

But he had no intention of arriving in London with her as part of his baggage.

He knew that not only his houses were waiting for him, but his family.

He was well aware how much she would shock his Grandmother, Aunts, Cousins and all their friends.

There was silence.

Then Caroline said in a low seductive voice:

"I love you, and if I cannot live without you, I am quite certain you cannot live without me."

The Earl thought it was not the sort of conversation one should have at the Dinner Table.

When he had taken Caroline back to her house, he had very unwisely, he thought later, stayed with her as he usually did.

She had been far too experienced to continue the conversation which she was aware had been a shock to the Earl.

Instead she used every wile she knew to arouse his passion.

As she was very experienced and he was very much a man, it was not a difficult thing to do.

Later they were lying closely in the big canopied bed.

There was only a faint light from a cupid-fashioned candelabrum behind the curtains.

Caroline drew a little nearer.

"How could anyone," she asked, "have a more wonderful lover? My darling, we shall be very, very happy together."

The Earl who was practically asleep was suddenly aware of the danger.

He had been aware of it in the same way when he was on the battle-field.

He knew that Caroline had chosen this moment when he was at his weakest to press her suit.

With an effort he yawned.

"I must go back," he said. "The Duke wants me to breakfast with him."

Caroline's hands were touching him and her lips were very close to his.

"I want you to stay with me," she whispered. "I find it hard to lose you even for what is left of the night."

The Earl got out of bed.

"One thing I dislike," he said conversationally, "is having to discuss political strategy at breakfast."

"You are not listening to me," Caroline said petulantly.

"I am sorry," the Earl replied, "but I really am tired."

He dressed quickly.

Caroline watched him.

Lying back against the pillows, she looked as beautiful as a translucent pearl in a velvet-lined box.

The Earl moved towards the door.

"Good night, Caroline."

She gave a little cry of protest.

"You have not kissed me good night! How can you be so cruel?"

She stretched out her white arms.

The Earl was well aware this could be a trap which had caught many men unawares.

If Caroline were to put her arms around his neck, he would lose his balance.

He would fall on top of her which was exactly what she wanted.

He took her hands and kissed first one and then the other.

"Thank you for making me happy," he said.

Even as she cried out to prevent him from going, he shut the door behind him.

His carriage was waiting outside.

He drove back to his own house where he was staying.

He was wondering frantically how he could avoid being married to Caroline Standish.

He was quite prepared to admit it was his own stupidity which had made him so involved.

Already, and this was of course engineered by Caroline, people linked their names together in Paris.

Doubtless the gossips were also talking about them in London.

Too late he saw he should have prevented her from being always at his side and of course from talking.

What woman did not talk?

Caroline was clever enough to use public opinion when it suited her.

When he got into his own bed he was still asking desperately what he should do.

The question turned over and over in his mind.

His valet called him early the next morning and after a cold bath he dressed himself in uniform and hurried to the British Embassy.

To his relief he was alone at breakfast with the Duke.

They discussed several propositions which had come from the French.

They were doing everything in their power to reduce the size of the Army of Occupation.

Suddenly the Earl had an idea.

"I wonder, your Grace," he said, "if you would consider sending me back to London as soon as possible."

The Great Man looked at him penetratingly.

The Earl was aware that he knew he had an ulterior motive in the request.

"You want to go home?" the Duke asked.

"If it is possible for you to spare me."

The Duke considered this for a moment and then he said:

"I shall miss you, of course I shall miss you."

He smiled and went on:

"But I appreciate, Wynstock, that you could easily have refused to stay with me this last year, having an unanswerable excuse in the necessity of attending to your own affairs."

The Earl inclined his head and the Duke continued:

"I think I can guess your reason for wishing to be gone, and if you take my advice you will leave without fond farewells, recriminations or tears."

With a slight twist of his lips, the Earl knew this was what the Duke often suffered himself.

Aloud he said:

"That is extremely kind of Your Grace. If I can do as you say, it will make it a lot easier."

"Very well," the Duke replied. "I order you to go to-morrow."

35

"Thank you," the Earl murmured.

"I will give you certain letters for the Prime Minister," the Duke said shortly, "and as they are of course secret, you can arrange your leaving so that no one is aware of your departure until you have gone."

"Thank you, thank you a thousand times," the Earl said again.

It was all much easier than he had anticipated.

Keeping secrets from the French had been well drummed into the members of the Duke of Wellington's Staff. As one wit said:

"I am afraid of my own shadow."

The Earl dined with Caroline.

Fortunately there were a number of other men present.

She was at her very best, holding everyone spell-bound by her charm and wit.

She flirted outrageously with every man from the oldest to the youngest.

It was, the Earl appreciated, a glittering performance.

He was quite certain from the way she looked at him under her eye-lashes and pouted her lips provocatively, that it was all done for him.

She was demonstrating how she could entertain his friends.

If she could shine against an alien background, how much better at Wyn Hall?

Caroline had once been to Wyn with her father and had never forgotten it.

The Earl was aware that more than anything else she wanted to become its Chatelaine.

To sit at the end of his table wearing the Wynstock Jewels.

He left the party at nearly one o'clock.

He knew that Caroline was perturbed that he did not stay until the rest of her guests had gone.

"I have to be up early," he said truthfully.

He was aware that she thought it a parade.

Or that once again he was breakfasting with the Duke.

"Come to me as soon as you are free," she whispered.

Her eyes told him exactly what that meant.

When their relationship first started, he had found her exciting to the point when it was hard to think about anything else.

He had on several occasions, at her invitation, called on her in the morning.

She was certainly alluring with her golden hair falling over her naked shoulders.

She usually wore little except a necklace of emeralds or one of black pearls which enhanced the whiteness of her skin.

The Earl did not pretend for a moment that he had not been infatuated with her.

But an *affaire de coeur* was one thing, and marriage was another.

He could not imagine his wife, the Countess of Wynstock, receiving a man in her bed-room while the servants sniggered about it downstairs.

As he left Paris for Calais he knew he was running away.

However he told himself it was a wise General who knew how to withdraw in the face of superior odds.

He would live to fight another day!

As soon as he arrived in London, the Earl found there were a thousand things to do.

He took the secret papers to the Prime Minister.

The Earl of Liverpool wanted to hear a great deal about the Army of Occupation that was not in the reports he had received.

The Earl then decided he must call on the Prince Regent.

If he did not do so he would certainly be in the Black Book at Carlton House.

The Regent was delighted to see him.

The Earl was new and interesting, something which His Royal Highness was always seeking.

He insisted on his lunching, dining, and meeting his friends.

He asked the Earl to accompany him to the Race Meeting at Epsom, to a meal on Wimbledon Common, to a display of swordmanship at Gentleman Jackson's Gymnasium.

In between these activities, the Earl engaged servants to run the House in Berkeley Square.

He also bought a number of horses at Tattersall's Sale Rooms.

Invitations poured in as soon as the great Social Hostesses of London realised he was back.

There were, of course, also a number of old friends to meet at White's Club.

They too had suggestions for what he should see and who he should meet.

They told him of the pretty new ballerinas at Covent Garden.

The pleasures of the White House, which he had not enjoyed before he went abroad.

Who were the latest Incomparables whom he would be very stupid to ignore.

It was rather like Paris, but at the same time he found the Regent witty and undoubtedly amusing.

The soirées and the receptions were somewhat dull. The Incomparables not so fantastic or so fiery as Caroline.

Even to think of Caroline made him wonder if he had really escaped, or if she would follow him back to England.

When he had heard nothing for nearly a week, he thought optimistically that she had found Paris too exciting to leave.

Then, as he walked into his Club, one of his closest friends said:

"I have just been told a friend of yours is back in London."

The way he spoke and the expression in his eyes made the Earl draw in his breath.

"Who are you talking about?" he asked.

There was no need to listen to the answer.

"Caroline Standish."

The Earl instantly made up his mind.

"I will go to the country," he told himself, "and I will leave first thing to-morrow morning."

Chapter Three

Vanda stared at Mr. Rushman in surprise before she exclaimed:

"The Earl is coming home? When?"

Mr. Rushman looked down at a letter which was beside him.

"His Lordship says," he replied, "that he will be leaving London on Wednesday which is today. That means he should be here on Friday."

Vanda made a little murmur before he went on:

"His Lordship asks that I send a pair of the best horses to the '*Dog and Duck*' at Gresbury."

He looked at Vanda and added:

"You know, Miss Vanda, as well as I do that we have nothing in the stable which His Lordship would consider worth driving."

Vanda knew this was true.

When the old Earl died, the horses were already getting on in years.

Gradually most of them were put out to grass.

What remained were only useful for the grooms to ride to the village to collect provisions.

She saw the worry in his face and said quickly:

"I know Papa would be delighted to send a pair of our horses to carry the Earl on the last leg of his journey."

"That would be extremely kind of you," Mr. Rushman replied, "as I am sure his Lordship wishes to arrive with a flourish."

He smiled as he spoke.

Vanda had the idea that he was thinking of the Earl as they had last seen him.

A young man of twenty-two, full of enthusiasm and a magnificent rider.

"There are a great many other things to do," Mr. Rushman went on, "for I expect His Lordship has forgotten that the House has been closed and the staff either dismissed or retired."

"Buxton is living in the village," Vanda said.

She was thinking of the Butler who had always been a very impressive, pontifical figure.

In the past the whole House had seemed to revolve around him.

"I have remembered that," Mr. Rushman said, "and thank goodness Mrs. Medway is alive."

"Do you think they will come back?" Vanda questioned.

"I am sure they will if you beg them to do so," Mr. Rushman replied. "They will at least be willing to oblige until we can get younger people to take their place."

"Me?" Vanda enquired. "You want me to ask them?"

Mr. Rushman made an eloquent gesture with his hands.

"When I received this note from a groom who had ridden post-haste from London, I was wondering who would help me and how I could reach Buxton and Mrs. Medway."

He paused before he added:

"I can, of course, try to crawl there!"

"You know I will do anything you want," Vanda said, "and it will be very exciting to have Wyn Hall full and the Earl in charge."

"I am afraid things are not like they used to be," Mr. Rushman said sadly, "but the Taylors have done their best."

Vanda realised that in the excitement of hearing about the Earl's return she had for the moment forgotten the Taylors.

And in particular the reason why she had called on Mr. Rushman.

Knowing how much he now had on his mind, she felt she could not add to his difficulties.

After all, she thought to herself, if the Highwaymen refused to leave, there was nothing that he personally could do about it.

The Earl was returning and it would be up to him to protect his own property.

She rose to her feet.

"I will go and talk to Buxton and Mrs. Medway. I suppose they can employ anyone they wish from the village."

"Everyone on two legs as far as I am concerned," Mr. Rushman replied. "I can only pray that the house is not as dusty as I fear it may be."

"Do not worry about that," Vanda said. "The Taylors have been wonderful and the women who clean the rooms every week have kept it looking exactly as it did when the Earl's father was alive."

Mr. Rushman gave a sigh of relief.

"That is one burden off my mind, Miss Vanda."

Vanda smiled.

"Dare I ask you," he continued, "to see if Mrs. Jacobs is capable of taking over the kitchen until I can find a Chef."

"She is very old," Vanda answered, "but she could sit down and tell the others how things should be done."

She considered a moment then went on:

"Mrs. Taylor is quite a good cook and there are several women in the village who could help them."

"You are an angel from Heaven when I was almost in despair!" Mr. Rushman exclaimed.

"I expect that is where I will get my reward," Vanda laughed. "I will go and see the three important people concerned with His Lordship's comfort, and report to you later what they say."

"Thank you, thank you," Mr. Rushman cried. "And tell your father also how grateful I am."

Vanda hurried away.

She knew better than anyone else how much there was to do.

If the Hall was to be as comfortable and the Earl as well served as he remembered, they needed time.

She was only a little girl of ten when, after he had left Oxford, he had gone into the Horse Guards.

It was always known as the family Regiment.

He had come home perhaps twice the following year.

Then he left England and no one had seen him again.

He had, of course, written to his father who showed the letters to Sir Alexander.

Both men knew that the young Viscount, as he was then, was in the thick of the fighting.

When there were so many casualties it seemed almost a miracle, Vanda thought, that he had survived.

Yet he had, and she knew he would be horrified if he returned to find the House still closed, the Taylors almost incoherent with fear and Highwaymen in the West Wing.

While Vanda was thinking, she had been walking quickly towards the village.

She soon came to a small, attractive cottage to which Buxton, the Butler, had been retired.

It was, of course, a cottage which belonged to the Wyn estate.

41

It was in good repair and had been recently painted.

The garden was bright with Spring flowers.

As she walked up the path to the front-door, she wondered if Buxton would feel too old to do what was asked of him.

He opened the door.

She thought, although his hair was dead white, he looked in good health.

"This be a surprise, Miss Vanda," he said, "but, a very pleasant one. Will you come in?"

"Thank you," Vanda said.

She walked into a small room which was a kitchen and where Buxton habitually sat.

On the other side of the entrance passage there was a very small parlour.

It was kept for important occasions, and could hold no more than four people.

Vanda, because she knew Buxton would expect it, sat down in an armchair in front of the stove.

"I have news for you," she said. "His Lordship has returned to England and will be arriving home on Friday."

"Friday!" Buxton exclaimed.

"Yes," Vanda answered, "and Mr. Rushman, who is too ill to come and see you himself, has asked me to beg you to get the House ready for him."

She was watching the old Butler as she spoke.

For a second she thought he was going to refuse.

Then as he smiled she thought there was a light in his eyes that had not been there before.

"Be Mr. Rushman giving me a free hand, Miss Vanda?" he enquired.

"You can have anybody and everything you want," Vanda assured him, "and you know as well as I do that nobody could get the place ready but you."

"Very well, Miss Vanda, I'll do my best," Buxton said, "but I'll need a lot of help."

"Mr. Rushman's actual words were that you could have 'everyone on two legs'," Vanda replied.

Buxton laughed.

She knew she had won this battle at any rate.

Almost the same conversation took place in Mrs. Medway's

cottage which was identical to Buxton's.

But being a women she needed more coaxing and of course more flattery.

"Who else but you," Vanda asked, "would know what sheets to put on the bed and make sure they are properly aired?"

She paused before she added:

"What is more, if you say no, I think Mr. Rushman will worry himself into the grave."

"Well I'll do what I can," Mrs. Medway said at last rather reluctantly. "I'm too old now to cope with them young girls who think they know better than I do."

This was an old cry that had echoed down the ages.

Vanda agreed with her that the young were uppish and not as respectful as they should be.

By the time she left, Mrs. Medway was calculating who in the village she would need to help her.

Vanda knew that with Buxton and Mrs. Medway at the Hall the Earl would be comfortable when he arrived.

Then she had seen Mrs. Jacobs.

She agreed to go to the Hall if she could be taken there in a carriage.

It was only as Vanda walked home that the problem of the Highwaymen returned to her mind.

She wondered what she should do about it.

Then just before she reached her own home, she recalled a frightening story her father had told her many years ago.

A Highwayman, who she thought was called Watson, had tortured a Diamond Merchant into giving him half his fortune.

Watson and his accomplice had captured the merchant when he was returning to his house on the outskirts of the City.

They had taken him to an empty barn in the countryside.

There they forced him at knife and pistol-point to write them a cheque for many thousands of pounds.

Because Watson could make himself look quite presentable, the Bank had handed over the money without querying the size of the sum involved.

They had then decamped, leaving their prisoner tied up and helpless in an isolated spot.

It was only by chance that he had been discovered by some children.

He was alive but practically dead from starvation.

The tortures he endured affected his health to the point that he died two years later.

Both the Highwaymen had already been caught and hanged for the theft.

Vanda now remembered hearing that story among a number of others, and thought it was very frightening.

She had forgotten it until this moment.

She wondered if the same treatment could possibly happen to the Earl.

Granted, there would be a great number of servants in the Hall, and their mere arrival might drive the Highwaymen away.

Yet as well as being in the House, the Earl would want to ride over the estate.

He could hardly do so with enough grooms to out-number the Highwaymen.

She thought now she had been rather remiss in not asking the Taylors how many of them there were.

However they were likely to have seen only two or three at any one time.

There might be any number of others with them in the West Wing.

"The Earl could be riding into a trap," she told herself and wondered what she could do about it.

She had now reached the Manor House.

She went first to the stables where she found the two old grooms.

She told them they were to take her father's two best carriage-horses to the "*Dog and Duck*" at Gresbury.

The grooms were obviously pleased.

"Our 'orses need exercise, Miss Vanda," the senior groom said.

"We's exercised them 's ye know," the other chimed in, "but we were only saying th' other day they be gettin' fat, an' a fat 'orse 's a lazy 'orse."

"I am sure as His Lordship wants to get home quickly, when you put them between the shafts at Gresbury, they will have to stretch themselves."

"That's what'll be good for 'em," the groom replied.

Vanda ran into the House.

Her father was working on his book and he was delighted to hear the news.

"I was wondering when that young man would be coming home," he said. "I shall look forward to talking to him."

"It will be all about the war!" Vanda protested. "You know, Papa, there is a great deal for the Earl to do on the estate, and the farmers have been asking for a long time when he will be back."

"Neil was always a good young man," Sir Alexander said, "and he proved to be an excellent soldier. I have no fears for the future."

Vanda wished she could say the same thing.

After they had finished dinner she went up to bed.

Alone she asked herself again how she could warn the Earl about the Highwaymen, and what he would do about them.

It would certainly be foolhardy for him to confront them personally.

She supposed he would think the right thing would be to contact the Barracks.

He could ask for soldiers to arrest the Highwaymen for trespassing on his estate.

She had the frightened feeling that this might end in a shooting match.

If it did, undoubtedly men would be wounded if not killed.

Then she thought that the Highwaymen would hardly be so foolish to stay in the West Wing.

As soon as they were aware that there was a great deal of activity in the Hall itself they would leave.

This meant that they might take to the woods, especially Monk's Wood, where she had first heard them.

Then the story of the Diamond Merchant returned to her mind.

Once again she felt sure that the Earl was running into danger.

"There is only one thing I can do," she decided finally, "and that is to warn him before he reaches home."

She wondered why she had not thought of that before.

If the horses were going to Gresbury, so could she.

The grooms would take them tomorrow, so that they would have a night's rest at the "*Dog and Duck*" before the Earl drove them home.

If she left on Friday as soon as it was dawn on *Kingfisher*, she could be at the Inn by breakfast-time and before the Earl left.

She thought it over carefully.

She then decided, just in case she missed him, she would ride along the side of the road for the last five miles.

He could not then pass her without her seeing him.

Early the following morning, she went up to the Hall to see what was happening.

She found Mrs. Taylor trying to organise what seemed almost an army of women.

They had arrived from the village on Mrs. Medway's instructions.

They were all gossiping excitedly about the Earl.

Vanda knew as soon as she moved among them that the Taylors had not mentioned the Highwaymen to them.

She walked round the different rooms.

Now the shutters were open, the windows cleaned, and the sunshine seeping in made the House look lovely.

She found Taylor alone in the Larder sorting out the food that was coming in from the farms.

Two young lambs, half a dozen fat ducks, a dozen chickens and a mountain of eggs!

In a low voice, just in case someone might be listening, Vanda asked:

"Have they . . gone?"

There was no need to explain who she meant.

"They be there last night, Miss Vanda," Taylor said in a conspiratorial tone.

When Vanda left him she walked to the back of the West Wing.

Moving silently through overgrown rhododendron bushes.

The lower windows were shuttered.

She stood outside one in the centre of the Wing which belonged to the principal Sitting Room.

She listened intently, thinking that if anyone moved or talked inside she was bound to hear them.

There was no sound and she prayed that the Highwaymen had taken the hint and gone.

She was not really sure if that made things better or worse.

If they were in the woods waiting for the Earl to appear, what chance would he have against armed men?

She went home more determined than ever that she must warn him before he reached the Hall.

Perhaps he would change his mind and go back to London.

Alternatively he might go first to the barracks for assistance.

She could not bear to anticipate what his reaction would be.

Yet she knew she would be doing the right thing in warning him so that he was prepared.

Sir Alexander talked about the Earl all through luncheon.

He was delighted to have lent him his horses.

He reminisced about his friendship with the old Earl and the things they had discussed when he was alive.

She thought the Earl had been very sensible in deciding to stay the last night of his journey at a Posting-Inn.

It would have spoilt the excitement of the homecoming if he had arrived late in the day.

However it made it more difficult for her to reach him.

She felt guilty in keeping her knowledge of the Highwaymen secret.

But what could her father or Mr. Rushman do themselves without help?

The answer was nothing, and she therefore felt she was entirely justified in tackling the problem on her own.

"If I save the Earl, they will all agree I have done the right thing," she told herself.

Then she sent up a little prayer to God for help.

. . . .

The Earl found it was not as easy to leave London quickly and secretly on Wednesday as he intended.

He had planned to leave for the country after breakfast.

He was however woken to be told there was a message from the Prime Minister.

It was too urgent to be ignored.

The Earl of Liverpool wished him to explain personally to several members of the Cabinet the latest demands of the French regarding the Army of Occupation.

Also to tell them of the Duke of Wellington's decision to send home ten thousand men.

It was impossible for the Earl to refuse such a request.

He therefore went to Downing Street, hoping he would not have to stay long.

He was over-optimistic.

The meeting went on until luncheon time and it was impossible to refuse to eat with the Prime Minister.

By the time he returned to Berkeley Square he knew he would have to postpone his departure until the following day.

It was annoying, but there was nothing he could do about it.

He therefore went to White's, to find, as he expected, several of his friends there.

"Are you going to the Devonshires' to-night?" one of them asked. "It is only a small Ball, but I always enjoy anything which is arranged by the Duchess."

"I have not made up my mind," the Earl replied evasively.

"Then someone will be very disappointed," his friend answered pointedly, "because you are sitting next to her at Carlton House."

The Earl remembered somewhat belatedly that the Prince Regent had invited him to dine with him before the Devonshires' Ball.

He had accepted.

He now decided that it was something he must refuse.

Caroline would contrive in her usual way to make people around them aware that he was her property.

To go to Carlton House would only add to the gossip which he knew was becoming dangerous.

A man could easily be pressured into marriage by social opinion.

The gossip could easily fetter him in a way that made escape impossible.

"What can I do?" he asked himself frantically.

He wished he had been able to follow his plan of leaving early that morning for Wyn Hall.

He went quickly home from White's and sat down to write a very apologetic letter to the Regent.

He had, he said, been suddenly afflicted with an extremely heavy and infectious cold.

This made it impossible for him to attend a Dinner Party.

"I am not only suffering myself," he wrote, "but I should be very remiss if I infected Your Royal Highness, when you have so many calls upon your time."

The Prince Regent was extremely fussy about his health.

The Earl knew this would ensure that his refusal to dine would be taken as an unselfish act and not an insult.

He sent a groom with it to Carlton House.

He then dined alone, having given orders that he was to be called at six o'clock next morning.

His Phaeton drawn by the best looking pair of horses he had just bought at Tattersall's was to be ready by half past.

His Valet and the luggage had already gone ahead in a Brake.

The grooms with four horses had left first thing in the morning for the Posting-Inn, where he would change horses.

Travelling with his Valet was a third groom, who was also an excellent cook.

He would see that what his master had to eat was palatable, and the Brake also carried his own wine.

The Earl thought he would be at Wyn Hall by Luncheon time the next day.

He was woken by the door of his bed-room opening, and he thought it must be a servant coming to call him.

Then as he half opened his eyes, he was aware that some-one standing by his bed was lighting the candles in a silver candelabrum.

To his astonishment it was Caroline!

She had a candle in her hand which he thought must have come from one of the sconces in the passage.

"Caroline!" he exclaimed. "Why are you here at this time of night?"

She turned her face to smile at him.

He saw that she was wearing a very elaborate evening-gown and a necklace of diamonds.

"When you did not turn up at Carlton House, or at Devonshire House," she answered, "I felt I had to see you."

The Earl sat up in bed.

"You must be crazy coming here at night!" he said. "Think what the world will say when they hear about it."

"The only person who knows where I am," Caroline replied, "is your night-footman."

"And your coachman?"

Caroline shrugged her shoulders.

"They are paid not to talk, and what do servants matter?"

The Earl did not reply, but merely looked at her.

"Go away, Caroline," he said at last, "and behave yourself. You may do this sort of thing in Paris, but not in London."

"And who is to stop me:" she asked.

As she spoke he realised she was undoing the back of her gown. While doing so her eyes were on his.

"You are behaving abominably, Caroline," he said. "You have no right to come to my house in this way and I insist on your leaving immediately."

Caroline laughed.

It was a happy sound and seemed to echo through the shadows.

Then as the Earl wondered what he could do to make her behave sensibly, she made a little movement with her body.

Her gown slithered down onto the floor.

For a moment she just stood there naked and looking in the light of the candles like a statue of Aphrodite.

Her skin was dazzlingly white and her necklace glistened iridescently.

Then before the Earl could speak or move she flung herself against him.

Her arms were round his neck, her lips on his and he felt the fiery passion of them seep through his body.

. . . .

It was nearly dawn before the Earl persuaded Caroline to leave him.

He watched her put on her gown.

He made no effort to rise himself or escort her down to the front-door.

"Will you give me luncheon?" she asked as she tidied her hair in one of the mirrors.

"I am going to the country."

"The country? Then of course I will come with you"

"No, Caroline," the Earl replied. "That is impossible."

"Why? You know I am longing to see Wyn Hall."

"I doubt if you would enjoy it, having been shut up with only Caretakers to look after it since my father died."

"We will – be together," Caroline said softly.

"There is a great deal of dust," the Earl went on, "ceilings that are leaking, beds that are damp, and of course the squeaking of mice to keep you awake."

He knew as Caroline gave a little cry that she disliked mice.

"It cannot be as bad as that!" she exclaimed.

"I expect it will be worse. When I have made everything look as it did before I went to the war, then I might consider giving a house-party."

Caroline turned to the mirror with her eyes alight.

"A house-party! I will be your hostess, darling Neil. That is a splendid idea and we will ask the Prince Regent as one of our guests. He was saying to-night at dinner it was something he would look forward to."

The Earl stiffened.

He knew exactly what Caroline had intimated when speaking of "our" guests.

If she had done so to the Prince Regent, he would believe that their engagement was just about to be announced.

His lips tightened in a hard line.

As if she was suddenly afraid she had gone too far, Caroline said:

"I did not actually say to His Royal Highness that we were engaged, but I think he suspected it."

"We are not engaged!" the Earl asserted. "As I have already told you, Caroline, I have no intention of marrying until everything I possess is as perfect as I wish it to be."

"And then I will make you the perfect wife," Caroline replied.

She moved towards the door.

"I shall expect to hear from you, darling, before the end of next week. If not, I shall come uninvited and, perhaps, bring the Regent with me."

She did not wait for the Earl's reply, but slipped out of the bed-room, closing the door behind her.

He threw himself angrily back against his pillows.

He was asking himself for the hundredth time what he could do about Caroline.

She was, the Earl knew, using every possible weapon against him.

He was not certain how he could prevent himself from being annihilated.

To use the Prince Regent as an intermediary on her behalf was, of course, a trump card.

The Regent liked to be in the know, he loved to play "cupid".

He might even, if Caroline charmed him and he was feeling generous, offer to have the Reception at Carlton House.

A wedding was just the sort of festive occasion he enjoyed.

The Earl groaned and shut his eyes.

He could see the claws of the trap, and God knows it was a man-trap, closing around him.

It would only be a question of time before he would be captured and imprisoned and there would be no escape.

Caroline would be his wife, and her lovers would eat his food, drink his wine, and sleep in his bed.

Thinking as they did so that they were fooling him.

"I cannot bear it," he murmured furiously.

He wished with all his heart he was still fighting Napoleon and the war had never ended.

Chapter Four

Sir Alexander went to his Study.

Vanda walked to the stables to speak to the grooms before they left for Gresbury.

She knew they would take the horses slowly.

She calculated that if they left at about one-thirty, they would be there soon after five.

They would go across country.

The journey took much longer by road because there were many narrow twisting lanes.

The horses were ready, looking well-groomed and, she thought, outstanding enough to please the most fastidious horse-lover.

She remembered how well the Earl had ridden as a boy.

Although she was very much younger than he was, she used to watch him admiringly.

She had a feeling that when he arrived home he would be only to glad to borrow her father's horses.

That was until he had filled his stables with his own.

The grooms touched their forelocks respectfully.

"Us be jes' off, Miss Vanda, an' us got a letter from Mr. Rushman to 'and to 'Is Lordship.''

"Do not lose it," Vanda smiled.

"Us jes' 'eard a strange thing, Miss," the other groom chimed in.

Vanda turned towards him to listen and he said:

"T'boy as works in t'garden o' White Lodge tells us that early 'smarnin' 'e sees seven men on 'orseback goin' into Monk's Wood."

Vanda was suddenly still.

She knew only too well who the horsemen were.

She thought she had been very stupid.

She had not remembered when she was thinking of the Highway-men in the West Wing that they would have horses.

This meant that they must have stabled them at the Hall.

There were a large number of empty stalls because the stables were built to hold at least fifty horses.

Now she knew, and she had never suspected it before, that the grooms also had been terrorised just as the Taylors had been.

They had therefore said nothing about the Highwaymen.

"I should have anticipated this," she thought.

Furthermore, she was horrified at learning there were more Highwaymen than she had supposed.

Seven men, all fully armed, were a formidable number for any man to encounter.

What would the Earl do about it?

She was aware that the grooms were looking at her.

They were surprised by her silence, and she asked quickly:

"I wonder who the horsemen could be?"

"Tha's wot us bin a-wonderin', Miss Vanda," the older groom said.

"While you are away, I will try to find out if anybody else has seen them," Vanda managed to say lightly, "although it seems to me the boy was dreaming."

"'E be a truthful lad," the groom said.

He was aware that Vanda was waiting for them to go.

He swung himself into the saddle of one horse and took the leading-rein of another in his left hand.

"Take them slowly," she admonished.

"Us will, Miss Vanda," the other groom replied, "'an' Jake's lookin' after t'other 'orses 'til us gets back."

Jake was his son, and nearly as experienced as his father.

Vanda watched them out of sight.

It was then she knew she must give the Earl the information where the Highwaymen were hiding.

She must also give him time to think what he could do about them.

As she walked into the house she realised that if she reached the *Dog and Duck* at Gresbury only in time to pass on her information hurriedly before he drove off on the last stage, he might run into great danger.

The Highwaymen might be planning to hold him to ransom as soon as he arrived at the Hall.

54

They could walk into the house when he was not expecting them. He would certainly not be armed.

Old Buxton and the boys from the village he had taken on as footmen would have no chance of stopping them.

And the women under Mrs. Medway would merely be hysterical.

By the time Vanda reached the Drawing-Room she had decided what she should do.

It was very daring, and if anyone knew of it, it would cause a great deal of gossip.

"All that really matters is that the Earl's life is at stake," she told herself.

She went upstairs to her bed-room and selected a few things she would want for the night.

She included a light muslin gown into which she could change for dinner.

She rolled them up in a long, light bag which could be attached to *Kingfisher*'s saddle.

She changed into her best riding-habit which was a very attractive one.

Then carrying the bag and her riding-hat she went down the stairs.

She laid them down on a chair in the hall.

Then slowly, because she was nervous, went into her father's study.

Sir Alexander looked up impatiently.

He disliked being interrupted.

"I am sorry to disturb you, Papa," Vanda said, "but I have just had a message from Miss Walters. She is not at all well, and I think I should go and visit her."

Miss Walters was an old Governess who had taught Vanda for some years until she retired.

She had a cottage in a village about a mile from Gresbury.

The General knew that Vanda visited her from time to time.

"She is not well?" he exclaimed. "Well, I suppose you will have to go to her, but take Jim with you"

Jim was one of the grooms who had already left.

Vanda knew her father had forgotten for the moment that the Earl was borrowing his horses.

"I will try to be back before it gets dark," she said. "But if she keeps me too long, I will stay the night."

"I do not like your gallivanting all over the country!" Sir Alexander said crossly. "But I suppose if she has sent for you, there is nothing you can do but help her."

"It would be unkind not to, Papa," Vanda said.

She kissed her father lightly.

"Do not work too hard, and do not forget to take your medicine!"

"There is nothing wrong with me!" the General retorted.

Vanda went from the room.

She knew that once he was immersed in his book he would forget all about her.

Jake saddled *Kingfisher* and she set off.

She made a short detour so that she would not encounter the two grooms who in fact by this time were half-an-hour ahead of her.

They would be aware of how angry her father would be if he knew she was going such a long way alone.

She had no wish to tell anyone else that there were Highwaymen in the vicinity.

She knew the country over which she was riding so well that she might have been in the Park at Wyn.

She had hunted over it in the Winter, and had ridden to Gresbury dozens of times with her father.

It was quite an attractive little village.

It boasted one of the few good Posting-Inns in the County.

It was therefore not surprising that the Earl had arranged to stay there on his way home.

It was a warm, sunny day, and *Kingfisher* was enjoying the ride as much as she was.

To begin with she gave him his head.

Then they settled down to a comfortable pace which would ensure that neither of them would be too tired by the time they reached Gresbury.

They passed Savernake Forest.

It just crossed her mind to wonder whether there were more Highwaymen lurking there.

She wished the seven "Gentlemen of the Road" in Monk's Wood had preferred the vastness of Savernake to where they were at the moment.

She was, however, convinced that they would not leave Monk's Wood until they had a good haul.

Either in money or valuables from the Hall.

Once again she was thinking with horror of the miniatures, the objets d'art, the silver and gold ornaments.

They would all be easy to carry away and would fetch a good sum in a Thieves' Market.

Without really meaning to, she quickened her pace.

It was only just after five o'clock when she turned into the yard of the posting-Inn.

An Ostler came hurrying towards her, and she asked:

"Have four horses arrived belonging to General Sir Alexander Charlton?"

"No, Ma'am."

"They are not far behind," Vanda said as she dismounted, "and when the grooms arrive they will look after this horse as well."

She inspected the stables and found five stalls which she thought were superior to the others.

She ordered fresh straw and went into the Inn.

The Landlord, who was a large, burly man, bowed to her politely.

"Good-day to ye, Ma'am, and let Oi welcome ye t' the '*Dog and Duck*'."

"Thank you," Vanda replied. "I have just been explaining to your Ostler that four horses belonging to my father, General Sir Aleander Charlton, will be arriving very shortly."

The Inn-keeper looked suitably impressed as Vanda went on:

"Two of them are for the use of the Earl of Wynstock, who is, I understand, staying here to-night."

"That's right, Ma'am," the Proprietor agreed, "an' we're very 'onoured t' have 'is Lordship as our guest."

"As I have a very important message for His Lordship," Vanda said, "I wish to wait until he arrives, and I should be grateful if you would allow me to do so in your Private Parlour."

The Landlord agreed immediately.

He took Vanda down a passage which lay behind the public Dining-Room.

He showed her into a small but comfortably furnished Parlour where there was a fire burning in the grate.

A table by the window was already half-laid for dinner.

Vanda thanked him and asked if she could wash away the dust of her ride.

She was shown upstairs by a mob-capped maid.

Because her hair was slightly blown about by the wind, Vanda took off her hat with its gauze veil.

She carried it in her hand when she went downstairs.

She hoped the Earl would not be long, so that she could ride home before it got really dark.

Otherwise she would have to stay, as she had told her father, with Miss Walters.

That would be rather trying, as her Governess had become very deaf in her old age.

Almost every word had to be repeated.

Vanda had found this very exhausting the last time she had seen her.

Nevertheless she had it all well planned.

The important thing was that the Earl should know of the menace which was waiting for him when he arrived home.

. . . .

The Earl woke and realised that though it was seven o'clock he had not been called as he had ordered.

He got out of bed and rang the bell furiously.

It was always the same: when his Valet was away his orders were not carried out as precisely as he wished them to be.

Then he told himself that Croker, who had been his Batman, was a soldier.

The new servants who had just been engaged had not yet got into his ways.

A footman came hurrying in response to the bell.

The Earl demanded to know why he had not been called at six o'clock.

"I peeped in, M'Lord," the man answered, "and as Your Lordship were sound asleep, I didn't like t' trouble ye."

The way he spoke and the expression in his eyes told the Earl he was aware why he was so tired.

The rest of the household must be aware of it too.

His lips tightened.

He damned Caroline under his breath.

But he knew it was no use losing his temper and he merely said: "Another time when I say six o'clock, I *mean* six o'clock!"

"Yes, M'Lord!"

The footman helped him dress.

There was another delay because he was quicker down the stairs than the kitchen had expected him to be.

He had therefore to wait for his breakfast.

By the time that was finished, and his Phaeton brought round from the Mews, it was after eight o'clock.

The Earl knew that to reach Gresbury that evening, he would have to drive faster than he had intended to do.

It was not that Wyn was so many miles distant from London.

It was that the roads, the Earl remembered from the past, were very bad.

It was one thing for the Prince Regent to break records when driving to Brighton.

Quite another to use the twisting, narrow lanes which had to be negotiated to reach Wyn Hall.

It was Spring, and the hedges and the banks of grass beneath them were beautiful with buds, primroses and violets.

The Earl however was concentrating on his horses.

He was too good a driver to push them and he would certainly take no unnecessary risks.

His horses were excellent and, to his relief, well-trained.

That was what he had been assured when he bought them at Tattersall's.

At the same time, it was easy when dealing with horses to be deceived.

To find, after they were delivered, that the Vendor had over-boasted his goods.

The Earl, however, was delighted with his team.

By this time he knew they were worth every penny they had cost him.

He had the good manners to stop at the Posting-Inn where he had intended to stay the first night.

He cancelled his booking, but he generously paid for it.

He had learned in France to pay for everything the British Army requisitioned from the local inhabitants.

This had astounded the French.

They had never expected to receive so much as a *cent* for their pigs, chickens and ducks from the enemy.

"Ye're a great gentlemen, M'Lord!" the Landlord of the Posting-Inn said as the Earl put a number of golden guineas down in front of him.

The Earl smiled.

Then he had driven on.

It was infuriating for one mile to be held up by a farm-cart, which it was impossible for him to pass.

It was however a very long day, having only stopped half-way to eat a very hurried meal.

He was therefore tired and extremely hungry when he turned in at the "*Dog and Duck*" at a quarter after eight.

There were two Ostlers waiting for him, and the Landlord was standing in the doorway, beaming a welcome.

"Ye've 'ad a good journey, M'Lord?"

"Not too bad," the Earl replied. "Your roads, however, are disgraceful, and something ought to be done about them!"

"Oi agree with Yer Lordship, an' every traveller says th' same," the Landlord replied, "but there be nothin' we can do."

The Earl decided he would make a very strong protest to the Lord Lieutenant.

He would make it quite clear there was no reason why the roads should be so neglected.

He was sure some of them were completely impassable in Winter when there was snow or torrential rain.

He was at the moment, however, more interested in his own comfort.

The Landlord himself took him up to a bed-room, which was the best and largest in the Inn.

A small trunk which he had carried on the Phaeton was already being unpacked by the groom who had travelled with him.

As he had ordered beforehand, there was a bath set ready on the hearth-rug in front of the fire.

"Cans o' hot water'll be up in a few minutes, M'Lord," the Landlord said respectfully.

He turned to leave the room.

Then, as if he suddenly thought of it, he added:

"There be a Lady waiting for Yer Lordship downstairs. She arrived several 'ours ago."

The Earl stared at him.

He could hardly believe that Caroline could have got here before him.

"A Lady?" he questioned.

"Miss Charlton, M'Lord. Th' daughter o' General Sir Alexander Charlton, whose horses are waiting for Yer Lordship in th' stable."

The Earl relaxed.

"I understand," he said, "and of course I will apologise to the Lady for being so much later than I intended. Perhaps she will do me the honour of dining with me."

"I'll tell th' Lady wot Yer Lordship says."

The Landlord went from the room.

The Earl thought it was in fact a damned nuisance that he should have company at dinner.

It was the last thing he wanted.

He suspected the daughter of the General would be getting on in years.

She was obviously one of those tiresome, hard-riding women, who thought they knew more about horses than a man did.

However it seemed that he was borrowing the General's horses.

It struck him for the first time that if there were any horses left after his father's death, they would be too old to be of much use.

There would have been nobody to order Rushman to buy in new stock.

He was quick-witted enough to understand that in the circumstances Rushman had procured a team from a neighbour.

As he got into his bath the Earl was remembering the General, and that he had been a close friend of his father.

"He must be getting on in years by now," he told himself, "but his wife was a very pretty woman!"

Then he began to think once again about Caroline, and what he should do about her.

She had occupied his thoughts almost the whole way from London.

He resented that she was spoiling his home-coming to which he had been looking forward with such anticipation.

He felt rather like a small boy who had been deprived of a very exciting present.

He hated her, he told himself.

To be truthful, he had known long before he left Paris that she was everything he really disliked in a woman.

At the same time he had been weak enough to be unable to resist the fire she aroused in him.

"I have made a fool of myself," he said as he put on his evening-clothes.

He took a quick glance at himself in the mirror, then walked down the somewhat rickety oak stairs.

The Landlord was waiting for him at the bottom of them.

"Dinner'll be ready in a few minutes, M'Lord," he announced.

"I admit to being very hungry," the Earl replied.

The Landlord went ahead.

He followed him down the oak-panelled passage with its heavy beams overhead into the Parlour.

Vanda, who was waiting for him, rose as he entered.

When the Earl looked at her he was astonished.

. . . .

When she had received the Earl's invitation to dine with him, Vanda had collected her bundle from *Kingfisher's* saddle.

She had then been taken up to a bed-room where she could change.

She was glad she had brought an evening-gown with her.

It was a very simple one, which she had intended to wear at Miss Walters'.

Its high waist revealed the curves of her breast.

The hem with two simple flounces accentuated the perfection of her slim figure.

She had brought with her no adornments of any kind.

But the Earl looking at her was thinking he had never seen hair of such a strangely beautiful colour.

It was very pale, the colour of the dawn when it first appears in the sky.

As if the simile was apt, there were touches of silver like moonlight among the gold.

Because Vanda was so slim her eyes seemed to dominate her face.

They were not the blue that might have been expected with the colour of her hair.

Instead they were green – the green of the buds that the Earl had seen in the hedgerows as he drove past them.

There were also little flecks of gold which might have come from the sunshine.

He had expected a middle-aged woman, but instead he found himself face to face with a young, and very lovely girl.

Suddenly he smiled.

"Now I remember," he exclaimed. "You are Vanda!"

"I thought you would have forgotten me."

"I remember you as a very pretty child who used to ride horses that were far too big for you, and swim in the lake like a small fish!"

Varda laughed.

"And I have always remembered you taking jumps which Papa said disapprovingly were too high!"

The Earl laughed.

"My father said the same thing, but I still tried to make the impossible possible!"

They were both laughing as the Landlord hurried in with a bottle of champagne.

Vanda accepted a glass and raised her hand.

"To your Home-coming!" she said. "We have waited a long time for you."

"I, too, thought the years would never pass," the Earl said solemnly.

They sat down at the table. While the food was plain, it was well cooked.

Because the Earl was hungry, he enjoyed every mouthful.

He asked questions, and Vanda talked while they ate.

She told him how the house was in perfect repair, how Buxton and Mrs. Medway had come back.

"It may not be in quite as perfect order as it was when your father was alive," she said, "but they are doing their best with very little notice."

The Earl heard the reproachful note in her voice, and he said:

"I know it was inconvenient. At the same time, I wanted to leave London at short notice. As it was, I was delayed at the last minute, and only left this morning."

"Then you have been travelling all day!" Vanda remarked.

The Earl nodded.

"You were very lucky. During the winter months it sometimes take three days for anyone to reach us."

Once again the Earl was talking about the roads.

The last course was served and the Earl had accepted a glass of brandy.

It was so good he was certain it had been smuggled.

The servants withdrew and they were alone.

They moved from the table to sit in two arm-chairs in front of the fire.

Large logs were burning cheerfully, and it was very warm and inviting.

However it was growing late.

Vanda knew she must hurry and tell the Earl why she had come.

Otherwise by the time she reached Miss Walters' cottage, she might be asleep.

"What is worrying you?" the Earl asked.

"I was thinking that I must talk quickly, otherwise my old Governess, who lives in the next village and is not expecting me, will not hear me knocking."

"You mean – you are not staying here?"

"Of course not!" Vanda said. "I came to see you because it was urgent. If you had not been so late, I had expected to ride home before it was dark."

The Earl looked at her. Then he asked:

"Why did you have to see me, apart from bringing me your father's horses?"

"They were coming without me."

The Earl put down his glass.

"Then what is it that you have to tell me?" he enquired.

He was aware perceptively that, unlike most women, she had not been waiting for him just for the pleasure of his company.

"Things are happening at Wyn Hall which are very serious," Vanda said.

She instinctively lowered her voice as she spoke.

The Earl looked at her, but he did not speak.

She went on:

"It is going to upset you and spoil your home-coming. At the same time, I have to warn you."

"To – warn me?"

"That you may be in grave danger!"

The Earl looked bewildered.

"Why – and from whom:"

Vanda drew in her breath.

"For some days now the West Wing has been occupied by a band of Highwaymen!"

The Earl sat upright and his expression was incredulous.

"Did you say – Highwaymen? In the West Wing? I do not believe it!"

"It is true," Vanda said. "They have terrorised the Taylors, who are your Caretakers, and I think, although I have not spoken to them, that they have also threatened the grooms."

"Why has no one done anything about it?" the Earl asked. "Surely, Rushman . . ?"

"Mr. Rushman does not know," Vanda interrupted. "'Nor does my father. In fact, I am the only person, apart from the servants concerned, who are aware that they are there."

"It seems extraordinary that they should go into the house!"

"The house has been empty," Vanda pointed out, "and I have been terrified lest they should ransack the many precious things that it contains."

"Why do you think they have not already done so?"

Vanda hesitated, then she thought the Earl had better hear the truth.

"What I fear," she said, "although I have no foundation for it, is that they need money and intend to extort it from you, if you return!"

"*If* I return?" the Earl repeated. "Are you seriously suggesting I should not do so?"

"I think it might be dangerous, unless you have Military protection."

"I have never heard such nonsense!" the Earl said scornfully. "And I can assure you, Vanda, I am not afraid of a couple of Highwaymen!"

"There are seven of them," Vanda said quietly, "and from the terror they have evoked in the Taylors, I think they must be very dangerous men!"

"This is certainly something I did not expect," the Earl said. "Do you really think they might injure me?"

"Years ago Papa told me how a Highwayman called Watson extorted money from a Diamond Merchant, who subsequently died as a result of the rough way he had been treated."

"I had forgotten that story," the Earl said, "but that was in the last century, and actually I did not think of Highwaymen being Kidnappers."

"Then you have forgotten Captain James Campbell and Sir John Johnson," Vanda replied.

"What did they do?"

"They abducted a girl of thirteen who was an heiress and James Campbell forced her to marry him."

"Good Heavens!" the Earl exclaimed. "Did she escape?"

"The Highwaymen were caught," Vanda replied, "and Sir John was hanged but Captain Campbell escaped by going abroad."

The Earl did not speak and Vanda went on:

"I am sure there are just as many Highwaymen, robbers and thieves now as there were then, especially with so many men being demobilised, without money and without work."

The Earl knew this was true, and was what he had seen for himself.

There was silence until he asked:

"What do you suggest I do?"

Vanda smiled.

"I came to warn you to be prepared, not to make decisions for you. After all, you are the soldier!"

"At least I knew where my enemy was," the Earl said.

"I told you . . at the moment they are in Monk's Wood."

"And you think they will stay there?"

"I cannot be sure, but I think it very likely as they know you are coming home."

"I suppose that is the obvious thing to think," the Earl agreed. "But what can I do?"

"I have already suggested you should go to the Barracks, and ask the Officer in Charge to send a Company of men to Wyn Hall."

The Earl considered this for some seconds.

Then he said:

"I suppose, really, I dislike having to admit that I am helpless. Are there no able-bodied men on the estate?"

"There are a few," Vanda admitted, "but most of them, as they have not been in the war, do not know how to shoot, and a pitchfork is not very efficient against a bullet."

The Earl slapped his hands down on the arms of his chair.

"It is intolerable!" he exclaimed. "The situation is as bad as it was fifty years ago! I remember my grandmother telling me that the streets were so dangerous when she was a girl that when she and her mother moved to and from Court in sedan chairs they had to be escorted by servants carrying blunderbusses to protect them from the robbers!"

Vanda laughed.

"At least you can move quicker than that!"

She paused before she said:

"I cannot help thinking that if your horses had been better than theirs, they would have taken yours with them!"

"I suppose you are right," the Earl agreed rather reluctantly. "But I have to admit it is humiliating that I cannot protect myself and my staff and am obliged to ask help from the Military."

"It would be far more humiliating to be tied up and forced to give them an enormous sum of money!" Vanda said practically.

"That is true. Very well, I will not go straight home, as I had intended, but drive to the Barracks."

Vanda clasped her hands together.

"I am so glad you think that is a sensible thing to do. Now I must go!"

She rose to her feet, and the Earl said:

"Do not be stupid, Vanda! Look at the time!"

There was a clock on the mantelpiece, and when Vanda looked at it she was horrified to find that it was after eleven o'clock.

She stared at it, thinking it must be incorrect, but the Earl said:

"Stay here. I am sure you are not nervous at being with me."

"No, of course not!" Vanda replied. "I am only thinking of my reputation . . and of course . . yours!"

The Earl laughed.

"No one would be surprised to hear I was accompanied by a beautiful Lady, and you are in fact very beautiful!"

She blushed, and he thought she looked exceedingly lovely as she did so.

"Thank you," she said. "That is the first compliment I have had for a long time."

"Is everybody blind in Little Stock?" the Earl enquired.

Vanda's eyes twinkled.

"No, My Lord, they are old!"

"I never thought of that," the Earl said. "Of course, all the young men, like myself, must have gone to the war."

"All of them!" Vanda said softly. "And some will never come back."

There was a little tremor in her voice.

"Well, you shall listen to my compliments," the Earl said, "and as

67

soon as the house is livable, I will produce my friends from London, who can be far more eloquent than I am."

"Your Lordship is very kind," Vanda replied, "but at the moment I am more concerned with Highwaymen!"

"If you call me 'My Lord' again, I think I shall spank you!" the Earl said. "We were brought up together, and my name, in case you have forgotten it, is Neil."

"I am well aware of that," Vanda said, "but I thought it would be a mistake to presume on a childhood friendship."

Before he could speak she added:

"No, that is the wrong word – childhood adoration. I thought you were all the heroes in the History Books, besides undoubtedly being the reincarnation of a Greek god!"

The Earl threw back his head and laughed.

"Until I became the age you are now, I thought all girls were a nuisance!"

As he spoke he thought they still were, if they were anything like Caroline.

She was certainly beautiful.

Yet at the moment he was thinking that Vanda outshone her in a very different way with a beauty that was unique.

Aloud he said:

"Now be sensible, and take a room here for the night. You will have to come with me to-morrow to the Barracks to explain exactly what is happening at Wyn Hall. As I have never been there, they may not listen to me."

"I think that is unlikely," Vanda smiled. "Everyone in the County knows how important you have been to the Duke, and the medal you received after Waterloo."

"Oh – that!" the Earl exclaimed.

"Yes, that!" Vanda echoed. "You will find even in peacetime it counts for a great deal!"

"Then by the authority I gained during the war," the Earl said, "you will, Vanda, take your orders from me!"

He smiled at her beguilingly and added:

"I will explain to the Inn-Keeper that my being so late has prevented you from going on to where you were staying. I will tell him you need one of his best rooms with a maid servant next door in the dressing room."

"I think no one could object to that," Vanda said.

"The important thing is for no one to know about it," the Earl remarked. "We will leave early in the morning and, as you suggested, go straight to the Barracks."

He thought for a moment, then said:

"Perhaps it would be a mistake for us to ride into the village together. We must therefore tell the grooms who will be riding my horses to wait at a place where I can drop you before I go on to the Hall."

Vanda looked at him approvingly.

"Now you are taking charge!" she said. "And that is exactly what I wanted you to do!"

"And now, as we are both tired," the Earl said, "we will go to bed as soon as I have seen the Landlord."

He walked from the room as he spoke.

Vanda felt as if the burden she had carried on her shoulders ever since she had spoken to the Taylors had lightened.

She was afraid, desperately afraid, that the Highwaymen would rob the house or injure the Earl.

But at least she had been able to persuade him to ask for assistance.

She was saying a little prayer of thankfulness when he came back into the Parlour.

"Everything is arranged," he said, "so now you can stop worrying about me."

He stood looking at her in a manner which made her raise her eye-brows enquiringly.

"I am wondering how I can thank you," he said, "for taking such good care of me."

He knew exactly how any other woman would have responded.

But Vanda merely said quickly:

"Keep your fingers crossed! We have a long way to go before you are really safe, and I can only go on praying that you will be clever enough to outwit the enemy."

The Earl took her hand in his.

"Thank you, Vanda," he said, "I need your prayers."

Because he was grateful to her, and also because he had been in France, his lips touched the softness of her skin.

He saw the surprise in her eyes.

He also felt the little quiver that went through her.

69

Chapter Five

The Earl came down to breakfast early to find Vanda already in the parlour.

She was looking very smart in her riding-habit wearing a hat which had a gauze veil trailing behind it.

"Good-morning, Vanda!" he smiled. "Now I know you really are a country-girl!"

"Because I am up so early?" Vanda asked. "I like riding when the world is fresh."

"So do I," the Earl agreed, "and I wish I was riding this morning."

As the Landlord and the waitresses came hurrying in with their breakfast he said:

"As I want to talk to you on the way to where we are going, I have told my groom to ride your horse."

He thought Vanda looked as if she was going to refuse, and added quickly:

"He is a very experienced rider, and I promise you, you can trust him."

"I am sure I can," Vanda said, "and actually Papa's grooms with your team have already left."

"I thought they would have," the Earl said, "and if they have to wait for you so that you can ride home with them, I am sure that will present no difficulties."

Vanda had already told the grooms to take the Earl's superlative horses as gently as possible.

They were to meet her at the crossroads.

It was about a mile from the village, and she doubted if there would be any people about to notice them.

She knew her father, when they arrived home, would be extremely interested in the Earl's new horses.

She thought with a little feeling of excitement that it would be wonderful when the stables at the Hall were filled with horses to equal them.

Now as they went on with their breakfast the Earl asked:

"Did you sleep well?"

"Very well, thanks to you."

There was a question in his eyes and she explained:

"I have been worrying about you, riding blithely into danger. But now that you are going to the Barracks, I am no longer afraid."

"I am longing to say," he answered, "that the whole situation is exaggerated! I cannot really believe that English Highwaymen, however many there may be, are anything like as intimidating as Napoleon Bonaparte!"

Vanda laughed. Then she said:

"One is a National problem, the other a personal one."

The Earl liked the quick way she managed to reply to him, and he said:

"After what you told me last night about the distressing lack of compliments paid in this part of the country, may I tell you that you look very lovely, and very smart!"

"You are making me feel as if I were deliberately asking for compliments," Vanda replied, "but now they are here, I am definitely enjoying them."

The Earl laughed.

Vanda could not help feeling that it was very exciting to be with him.

When breakfast was finished, the Earl paid the Inn-Keeper so generously that he bowed almost to the ground in appreciation of what he had received.

Outside the Earl's Phaeton was waiting.

When his groom had handed him the reins he started to move out of the yard.

The groom mounted *Kingfisher* and followed them.

Vanda knew the way to the Barracks, but the Earl, having been away for so long, was not certain.

He could not go very fast, owing to the lanes twisting and turning.

Or places so narrow that if they met a cart or a wagon one of them would have to go back.

To Vanda's delight the Earl was ready to talk about his experiences in France.

71

Best of all, he told her how brilliant the Duke of Wellington had been.

"No one else," he said positively, "could have succeeded in defeating Bonaparte."

"That is what we all felt," Vanda said.

"He is the hero of all Europe," the Earl went on, "and when he comes home for good next year, I am only hoping this country will show its appreciation."

"I hope so, too," Vanda replied. "He is a very great man!"

"And I am extremely lucky to have been associated with him this last year," the Earl said.

Vanda liked the way he spoke almost humbly.

He was obviously reluctant to talk about his own achievements.

Then the Barracks loomed ahead of them.

She thought sadly that perhaps never again would she have a chance of such an intimate conversation with the Earl.

They drove up to the gates.

He said who he was and informed the sentry that he wished to speak to the Officer in Charge.

"That'll be Major Lawson, Sir," the sentry replied.

He pointed the way to the centre building and the Earl drove his horses up to it.

There they had to wait until the groom who had been riding *Kingfisher* could find a soldier to hold him.

When he did the man went to the head of the team.

The Earl helped Vanda to alight.

They walked in through an imposing door with two sentries at attention as they did so.

When the Earl again said who he was, he was taken immediately to Major Lawson's office.

He was a middle-aged man, looking smart and efficient in his uniform.

He greeted the Earl enthusiastically.

"This is a very great honour, My Lord!" he said. "In fact I did not know that you had returned to England."

"I have only just got back," the Earl answered.

"Then I can only say how very glad we are to see you:" Major Lawson replied.

"Thank you," the Earl said, "and now may I introduce you to

Miss Charlton, who I think you may be aware is the daughter of General Sir Alexander Charlton."

"I do not think we have met," the Major said to Vanda as he shook her hand, "but I know your father, and have a great admiration for him."

"Thank you," Vanda said.

"We have come to see you on an important matter," the Earl said, "and I should be obliged, Major, if we could talk to you in private."

The Major looked surprised, but he said:

"Of course!"

He turned to the young Lieutenant who was working at another desk in the room and said:

"See that we are not disturbed."

"Very good, Sir!" the Lieutenant replied.

He walked from the room closing the door quietly behind him.

The Earl and Vanda sat down on two chairs near the Major's desk.

As they did so Major Lawson asked:

"Now, what can I do for you, My Lord?"

"I think Miss Charlton can explain it better than I could do," the Earl replied.

He looked at Vanda as he spoke who said:

"When I learned that the Earl was returning to Wyn Hall, I contacted him very early this morning to warn him of the danger . . "

"The danger?" Major Lawson asked in surprise.

"Seven Highwaymen have been occupying the West Wing, and are terrorising the Caretakers and the grooms."

For a moment the Major stared at her in astonishment before he exclaimed:

"So that is where the Baker Gang are hanging out!"

"The Baker Gang?" the Earl repeated. "Do you mean you have been looking for them?"

"For the last two months," Major Lawson replied. "We were warned by the Barracks in Warwickshire that they were on their way, and we thought they were in Savernake Forest."

"And you have been trying to capture them?"

"So far they have managed to conceal their exact whereabouts," Major Lawson replied. "But they are very dangerous and a menace to the countryside. In fact their criminal record is the worst of any Highwaymen I have ever encountered."

The way the Major spoke made Vanda give a little exclamation of horror.

The Earl bent forward to say:

"Tell me about them."

"The leader," Major Lawson said, "a man called Baker, was once a Pastry Cook. He had a shop in Mayfair and was patronised by the aristocracy – who bankrupted him:"

The Earl looked surprised, and the Major explained:

"His clients ran up large bills and eventually, when they did not settle them, he could carry on no longer."

The Major paused for a moment. Then he said:

"As you can imagine, this gave him a grudge against society, and he vowed he would avenge himself."

"So he took to the road!" the Earl exclaimed.

"Exactly:" Major Lawson agreed. "He and his Gang have not only murdered a great number of people, but also tortured them!"

"Oh, no!" Vanda exclaimed involuntarily.

"I am afraid it is true, Miss Charlton," the Major said. "Baker prefers cash to valuables, and in several instances, having sent a ransom note to his victim's relatives, if the money is not forthcoming immediately, he has sent them a finger, a toe, or an ear, to speed up the payment!"

Vanda drew in her breath and clutched her fingers together.

She was looking not at the Major, but at the Earl, and after a moment he said:

"You were quite right, Vanda, in making me come here!"

"This is Miss Charlton's doing?" the Major asked. "Then I can only assure Your Lordship that you are not dealing with Story-Book 'Gentlemen of the Road', but a monster, and the world will be a better place once he is out of it!"

"I can understand that," the Earl said.

"Baker and those who follow him also have an unpleasant habit when they have taken a prisoner of putting out his eyes so that he cannot identify them."

Aware that what the Major was saying was upsetting Vanda, the Earl said:

"You have told me enough, Major, to assure me that I was right in coming to you for protection, and Miss Charlton can tell you where the Gang are at the moment."

The Major picked up his pen and Vanda said:

"They have left the West Wing at Wyn Hall now and were seen by a boy, who told my father's grooms, going into Monk's Wood."

"It is a long time since I was at Wyn Hall," the Major said, "but I think I am right in believing that Monk's Wood is a little South of the house."

"That is right," Vanda said. "It is a large, rambling wood and no one in the village will go there, which I am sure is why they have chosen it."

She thought the Major looked puzzled and explained:

"Monk's Wood was named after a Priest who left his Priory and settled in the wood to pray and minister to the animals who came to him when they were injured."

"Now you mention it," Major Lawson said, "I seem to remember hearing the story."

"In the very centre of the wood, which is where I think the Gang will be, are the remains of the Chapel he built, and where it is said he administered the Mass not only to any traveller who happened to find his way there, but also to the deer, the foxes, the hares, the rabbits and the birds who trusted him to mend their injuries."

"So that is the story!" Major Lawson exclaimed. "Then the sooner we can get those fiends out of such a Holy place, the better!"

"I agree with you," Vanda replied. "I have always loved riding in Monk's Wood because it has an atmosphere which I believe lingers on, even though the Monk has been dead for two hundred years."

She spoke with a touching sincerity and the Earl smiled at her as if he understood.

"Now, what I suggest," Major Lawson said, "is that His Lordship stays here to-night."

"To-night?" the Earl asked sharply.

"It is extremely unfortunate," Major Lawson explained, "but at the moment practically every soldier in the Barracks is out on manoeuvres. Some of them will be returning at about five o'clock to-day, but the rest will not report in until to-morrow morning."

The Earl's lips tightened, but Vanda, knowing there was nothing else he could do, said quietly:

"You must stay. It would be madness to go back to the Hall now we know what those men are like."

75

"I agree with you, Miss Charlton," Major Lawson said, "and I can assure you, M'Lord, we will make you as comfortable as possible. My wife and I will be very honoured if you will stay at our house, which I hope would be more comfortable than the Barracks!"

He gave a little laugh before he added:

"All the same, you are certainly used to them."

"I am indeed," the Earl replied, "and I was looking forward to being in my own house."

"Of course you were," Major Lawson replied, "but I cannot stress too strongly how dangerous it would be for you to go there alone. I am sure Miss Charlton is right in thinking the Baker Gang are only waiting for your return."

"Very well," the Earl agreed reluctantly, "I must do as you say."

"What you and I will do, My Lord," Major Lawson said, "is to work out the best plan of attack, which means, I think, approaching the wood simultaneously from every angle so that there is no possibility of their being able to escape."

"If it comes as a surprise, it will, I hope, prevent a lot of bloodshed," the Earl said.

"That is what I hope," Major Lawson said, "and, My Lord, as you are far more experienced than I am in fighting a battle, I shall certainly bow to your superior judgement in anything we do."

"Thank you," the Earl said quietly.

There was a little pause. Then Vanda said:

"I will go home and tell everybody that His Lordship has been delayed in London. The only people who will know he spent the night at the '*Dog and Duck*' at Gresbury are my father's grooms, who are absolutely trustworthy."

"If you will do that, Miss Charlton," Major Lawson said, "it would be a very great help, and give us a chance to take these felons off their guard."

Vanda rose to her feet.

"My horse is outside," she said, "and I will leave at once."

Then she hesitated and said to the Earl:

"I had better put your horses into Papa's stable, where no one will see them. If they go to the Hall your grooms will know that you are not still in London, and the Highwaymen will get to hear of it."

"That is sensible of you," the Earl agreed.

Vanda held out her hand to Major Lawson.

"Good-bye, Major," she said. "I only pray that all this horror will soon be over, and His Lordship can enjoy his home-coming in peace."

"I promise you, Miss Charlton, that my men will do their best," Major Lawson answered, "and I shall be looking forward to seeing your father again."

Vanda smiled at him.

Then the Earl said:

"I will see Miss Charlton off, then return, Major, to go into our plans in detail."

The Major nodded his agreement, and did not leave his desk.

The Earl escorted Vanda outside to where a soldier was holding *Kingfisher*.

"For God's sake, Vanda," he said in a low voice, "take care of yourself, and do not take any risks."

"No, of course not."

She knew he was thinking of her telling him how she had first become aware of the Highwaymen.

He lifted her into the saddle and arranged her skirt neatly over the stirrup.

When he had done so he looked up at her and their eyes met.

"There is no need for me to tell you that you have been wonderful!" he said quietly.

"All that matters is that you are safe," Vanda replied.

They were looking into each other's eyes, and somehow it was very difficult to look away.

Then with an effort Vanda lifted the reins and turned *Kingfisher*'s head towards the gate.

She was aware as she went that the Earl was watching her, but she did not look back.

She was already praying that he would work out a plan by which as few men as possible would be in danger.

She had, however, the uncomfortable feeling that if there was going to be a battle with the Highwaymen, the Earl would be in the thick of it.

It was some distance to the crossroads from the Barracks, but the grooms were there waiting.

As she drew nearer to them Vanda thought it would be impossible to find finer horses anywhere than those the Earl had recently purchased.

As she drew up beside them the grooms touched their forelocks.

They were obviously pleased to see her.

"These be real foin 'orses, Miss Vanda!" one of them said. "We're 'opin' the Master, when he sees 'em, will be lookin' for somethin' like 'em for our stables."

"We will show them to him," Vanda said, "because we are taking them home with us, and not to the stables at the Hall."

The two grooms looked at her in surprise.

They started to ride slowly in the direction of the village.

Then Vanda told them about the Highwaymen in the wood and that the Earl was in grave danger.

"That be roight terrible news, Miss Vanda!" the older groom said.

"I know," Vanda agreed, "and we have to play our part in keeping the secret until the Highwaymen are all captured."

She then told them that they had to make everybody in the village believe that the Earl had stayed in London.

He had not met them as they had expected him to do, at Gresbury.

"You set off with four horses and came back with four," Vanda insisted so that the grooms would get the story into their minds, "and unless anyone looks into our stables, they will have not the slightest idea that two of the horses are not the Master's."

"Oi sees wot ye mean," the younger groom said. "An' we're t'tell everyone as asks uns that 'Is Lordship be still in London."

"That is right," Vanda said in a tone of relief. "And it is very, very important that everybody in the village believes you."

"An' wot 'bout them up at t' 'All?" the older groom enquired.

"I will tell Buxton and Mrs. Medway exactly the same tale," Vanda replied.

. . . .

Vanda and the grooms arrived home having been careful not to go through the village.

They had approached the Manor from the far side so that no one saw the horses.

Vanda gave *Kingfisher* to Jake, who was waiting for them.

Then she went into the house.

Her father, as she expected, was already in his Study.

He looked up with a smile when she entered the room.

"You are back, my dear!" he said. "I worried when you did not return last night."

"I was afraid you might, Papa," Vanda replied, "but something very, very important has happened about which I must tell you."

She shut the door and pulled off her hat.

Sitting down in front of him she told her father the whole story of the Highwaymen.

Sir Alexander listened in astonishment.

"Why did you not tell me before?" he asked.

"Because, Papa, it would have worried you, and there was nothing you could do about their being in the West Wing, and it was for the same reason that I did not tell Mr. Rushman."

"I think we should both have known!" Sir Alexander asserted. "I should have sent to the Barracks immediately."

"They might somehow have got away," Vanda said quietly. "But now the Earl is in charge, and I am sure they can be captured, which Major Lawson has been trying to do for several months."

"It is absolutely disgraceful that this sort of thing should be happening!" Sir Alexander said angrily. "And the Army so incompetent that they have been unable to bring these felons to justice!"

This was the sort of attitude, Vanda thought, that her father would take.

At the same time, there had been few soldiers left in the country.

Also in a County like Wiltshire, where there were so many forests, it was not really difficult for a few men on horseback to be able to hide themselves.

Aloud she said:

"You do understand, Papa, that no one is to know anything about this except yourself until after to-morrow? I am going up to the Hall to tell them that you have had a message from London to say that the Earl has been detained, and will be returning later in the week. Somehow I expect the Highwaymen will hear of it."

"I blame the Taylors," Sir Alexander stormed, "for being too chicken-hearted to inform anyone in authority what has been going on."

"The Taylors are absolutely terrified," Vanda said, "and now we know what monsters these particular Highwaymen are, one cannot really blame them."

Her father was silent, and she added:

"You have never told me stories of Highwaymen who were cruel

79

enough to put out their victim's eyes, or to send fingers and toes to those from whom they were demanding a ransom!"

"It is not the sort of thing one would tell a child!" Sir Alexander replied. "And I agree with you, my dear, the sooner the Baker Gang are hanged at Tyburn, the better!"

"That is true, Papa," Vanda said. "But you have forgotten that Highwaymen are no longer publicly hanged at Tyburn as they were in the past. It was a horrible and barbaric practice with the whole place looking like a Fairground, with side-shows and street vendors!"

"It was disgraceful," Sir Alexander admitted, "and I remember as a boy hearing gruesome tales of the society women who waited there as if the place was a Playhouse!"

"Now the gallows are in the court-yard at the Old Bailey," Vanda said. "The procession and the Fairground have been done away with, but the hanging is still open to the public."

"Where criminals are concerned I agree with that as a deterrent," Sir Alexander said firmly.

Vanda picked up her hat and walked towards the door.

It was justice, and certainly the Baker Gang deserved to die for their crimes.

Yet she did not like to think of any man however bad being hanged by the neck until he was no longer breathing!

After lunching with her father, and they were very careful what they said in front of Dobson, Sir Alexander returned to his Study.

It was then Vanda decided to go to the Hall.

Kingfisher was saddled for her, and she entered the Park by the gate she always used.

Then she trotted under the oak trees towards the lake.

She was thinking of the Earl.

She knew how frustrated he must feel having to stay in the Barracks, and not being able to come home until to-morrow.

She had realised that every instinct in his body rebelled against Major Lawson's decision.

At the same time, his brain told him he would be very foolish to do anything else.

'The Earl is too good a soldier to take any unnecessary risks,' Vanda thought.

She rode up to the front-door of Wyn Hall.

Buxton must have seen her approach for a footman came running down the steps to hold *Kingfisher*'s head.

Another footman helped Vanda to dismount.

It was something she could easily have done herself.

But she appreciated that Buxton was teaching the footmen the correct way of behaving when guests arrived.

He greeted her as she walked up the steps and she said:

"Good-afternoon, Buxton. The General has asked me to bring you some news, which I am afraid you will find disappointing."

"Disappointing, Miss Vanda?" Buxton enquired.

"Yes, a messenger arrived from London to tell my father that His Lordship has been detained, I think by the Prime Minister, and he will therefore not come to-day, as was expected, but as soon as he possibly can."

"Oh, dear!" Buxton exclaimed. "Chef'll be disappointed! He's got everything ready for a special dinner to-night for His Lordship!"

"That is what I expected would happen," Vanda said, "but of course, as His Lordship has just returned from France, it is understandable that many important people wanted to see him as soon as he got home."

"I suppose we'll just 'ave to wait our turn," Buxton said. "I only hopes it's not for long!"

"From what His Lordship wrote to my father," Vanda replied, "he is as disappointed as you are, but we think in fact he may turn up to-morrow."

"Then that's what we'll look forward to," Buxton said.

As if he wanted Vanda to appreciate the improvements that had been made at the Hall he said:

"I wonder, Miss Vanda, if you'd just take a look at the silver I've got out of the safe. It's taken a lot of cleaning, but I hopes you'll think it looks like it did when the old Master, God rest his soul, was alive."

"I would love to see it!" Vanda exclaimed.

The silver was certainly worth looking at.

There were beautiful examples of de Lamerie and Paul Storr besides the cutlery which had all been purchased in the reign of George II.

As Vanda knew, Buxton had a way of cleaning silver that made it shine like a diamond.

As most of it was laid out on the Pantry table, she looked at each piece with interest.

Afterwards, she went upstairs to see Mrs. Medway, who was just as eager to show off as Buxton had been.

Vanda inspected the linen cupboard, where everything had been ironed and re-arranged.

It all smelt of lavender which was in bags inserted between the sheets and pillow-cases.

She was then taken to the Master Bed-room which had always been used by each successive Earl of Wynstock.

The furniture had been cleaned and polished until it shone as brightly as the mirrors and the silk hangings on the great four-poster bed.

The Wyn coat of arms embroidered on the velvet backcloth looked extremely impressive.

There were also Spring flowers in vases on the chests-of-drawers.

Vanda thought that after years of War, the Earl would appreciate the comfort, luxury and grandeur of being in his own home.

It was getting late in the afternoon when she left the Hall.

She thought she might talk to the Taylors, then decided it would be a mistake.

They had kept their word to the Highwaymen and had obviously not said anything about them to anyone.

That was how it should be until the Baker Gang were behind bars.

The shadows were growing long in the Park as Vanda rode under the trees towards the gate she had come in by.

She was thinking of the Earl.

She wondered if he was feeling restless at having to stay in the Barracks.

Then suddenly unexpectedly *Kingfisher* reared up.

As he did so Vanda was aware of a man on horseback directly in front of her.

Then she realised that two other men were closing in on her on either side.

Her hands tightened on the reins as she gave a frightened gasp.

The man in front prevented *Kingfisher* from going any further.

Vanda looked at him and saw that he wore a mask.

"If yer makes a sound," he said in a common voice, "ye'll suffer fer it!"

As he spoke the men on either side of her took the reins from her hands and started to lead *Kingfisher* forward.

Vanda held onto the saddle.

At the same time she bit her lip to prevent herself from screaming.

The man in front moved swiftly and the two men holding *Kingfisher* quickened their pace.

They were out of sight of the house and she knew there was no one to see where they were taking her.

But she herself knew exactly where it was.

It was only a few minutes before the man ahead of her passed between the trees at the beginning of Monk's Wood.

As the path narrowed the men on either side of her fell back.

They did not speak.

Vanda lifted up *Kingfisher*'s reins which had been taken from her.

There was no escape with one Highwaymen ahead of her, and two behind.

She was their prisoner and completely helpless.

Chapter Six

When they reached the centre of the wood where the little Chapel was, she saw Baker.

There was no mistaking that he was in command.

He was standing waiting for her while the other three Highwaymen were lounging on the grass.

Baker had the air of authority she had expected.

She brought *Kingfisher* to a standstill and he bowed mockingly to her saying:

"Let me welcome you, M'Lady, to my humble abode!"

She did not reply.

Baker made an imperious gesture to one of the other Highwaymen to come and take hold of *Kingfisher*.

Vanda suspected he was going to lift her down.

She slipped quickly to the ground before he could do so.

"I suppose," she said in what was an admirably controlled voice, "I need not ask why you have brought me here."

"I imagine," he replied, "you're clever enough to guess that as the Earl hasn't honoured us with his presence, you must take his place!"

Vanda drew in her breath.

She could not force herself to ask the question which trembled on her lips.

Baker was not wearing a mask.

She thought he must have been a decent-looking man when he was attending to his shop in Mayfair.

Now there was something hard and cruel about him.

There were lines on his face which she thought did not come from old age, but from debauchery.

She did not wish to think about it.

"If you're curious," Baker was saying as the men on the horses moved away and *Kingfisher* followed, "a note demanding your ransom has been left at your father's house."

Speaking in a voice which again did not tremble, Vanda enquired: "How much have you asked for me?"

"How much d'you think you're worth?" Baker retorted.

He was looking at her in a way which she knew was not only impertinent, but also lewd.

She raised her chin higher as she replied:

"I would be interested to hear, Mr. Baker, what you have demanded."

"So yer know my name!" he said quickly. "How might that be?"

"You must be aware that you are famous in the countryside," Vanda replied evasively.

"Too famous!" he said harshly. "And if you've told those damned soldiers about us, I'll kill you!"

He spoke menacingly.

Vanda felt as if her heart had missed a beat.

Then she said:

"I heard a long time ago that the soldiers were searching for you in Savernake Forest, but they could not find you."

Baker threw back his head and laughed.

"We fooled 'em!" he boasted. "It's something we'll do again, and we won't be hanging around here once your father pays up."

"I only hope you have not asked more than he can afford," Vanda replied.

"He can afford for you the same price as those accursed Magistrates have put on my head!"

He spoke violently, and Vanda now was really frightened.

Her voice quivered as she asked:

"How . . how much is . . that?"

"A thousand Jimmy o' Goblins!" he replied.

Vanda gave a little gasp and he went on:

"And the longer he takes, the less of you'll be returned to him!"

Vanda knew exactly what he meant, and felt she must faint at the horror of it.

Then she told herself that the Earl and the soldiers would be here to-morrow.

What she must do was to play for time.

"I suppose, Mr. Baker," she said as she made an effort at self-control, "I should be flattered that my value is the same as yours!"

It was impossible for him to miss the sarcastic note in her voice.

He laughed before he said:

"I like your pluck, and I hope we won't have to chop too many pieces off you!"

"It is of course something you are very good at doing!" Vanda retorted. "Do you ever miss your Pastry Shop?"

Baker stared at her.

"So you know about that too, do you? Well, it's people like you, and that damned Earl who can't keep his appointments, who cost me my living."

"Which I think is very sad." Vanda answered.

"Now don't you start feeling sorry for me!" Baker snarled. "I enjoy what I'm doing, and if I have to torture some blasted aristocrats to pay my way, it's what they deserve!"

He spoke in a manner which would have terrified Vanda if she had not known that help would come eventually.

She was only praying that what would happen in the meantime would not be too humiliating.

She had hardly looked at Baker's confederates but she was sure they were very much rougher and commoner than he was.

There was a neatness about him and he spoke in almost an educated manner.

It was obvious that he came from a better class than the Highwaymen he led.

She only had a quick glimpse at the men lying on the grass.

Those who had brought her here into the wood wore masks.

But she knew instinctively that they were out of the gutter.

Or rather, the over populated, filthy and disease-ridden slums of London.

They would never have known anything but privation, cruelty and crime.

The men who had brought her into the wood had hobbled the horses so that they could not wander off.

Now they returned and seeing their leader was unmasked removed theirs.

"Wot d'ye think o' 'er?" one of them asked Baker crudely. "Pretty litt'e piece, ain't she? 'Er can keep Oi warm 'til th' money comes!"

He took a step towards Vanda as he spoke.

Seeing the look in his eyes, she backed hastily away from him.

"Leave her alone," Baker said. "If she belongs to anyone 'til the cash arrives, it's to me!"

Vanda felt she could breathe again until he went on:

"If it doesn't, you can have your turn later!"

She was so frightened at what he had said that she felt her knees quake.

"May I sit down?" she asked quickly. "I have been busy to-day, and as you will appreciate, Mr. Baker, I have missed my tea."

"That's something I can't remedy," he replied, "but you can have a swig of brandy, if you're thirsty."

"No, thank you," Vanda replied.

She looked towards the ruins of the Chapel.

It was behind the grass on which the men were lying.

Baker's eyes followed hers.

"That's where we're shutting you up for the night," he said harshly, "and if you think you're going to escape, you're mistaken!"

"I am not so foolish as to try to do that," Vanda answered.

"That reminds me," Baker went on. "I hear your father has some decent horses, which is more than the Earl's got!"

"Most of them are getting old," Vanda replied.

"There's nothin wrong with the one you're riding." Baker remarked. "So I might as well have him, as well as the thousand quid your father'll cough up for you!"

Vanda wanted to scream.

How could she let *Kingfisher* be taken away from her by men like these?

Then she told herself the Earl and the soldiers would save her, and *Kingfisher* as well.

Whatever happened, she must keep her head.

She knew almost instinctively that if she screamed or protested they would use it as an excuse to handle her in some way.

It could be very roughly.

She did not like to think that it might also be something very different.

She was wondering whether she should sit down on the ground.

Then she saw that just by the entrance of what had once been the Chapel there was a fallen tree.

Slowly, in case the Highwaymen thought she was trying to escape, she moved towards it.

Then she turned and sat down facing them.

She held her back straight and her head high.

Baker, who was still standing, was watching her with a smile on his lips.

"You've got class," he said, "as I know, having talked with the Beauties, as well as the old hags who chaperoned them!"

"I am only sorry I did not have the opportunity of patronising your establishment," Vanda said.

"If you had, you'd probably have left your bills unpaid, like all the other rubbish who call themselves the 'Gentry'!" Baker said rudely.

"That is not true!" Vanda retorted. "My father always pays what he owes, and so do I!"

"Then you're the exception of the rotten crowd who swank about London calling themselves the '*Beau Ton*'!"

He mispronounced the French words but Vanda knew what he meant.

"The *Beau Ton*!" he repeated furiously, and spat. "Man-eating Reptiles is what I call them, and that's what they are!"

Before Vanda could think what to reply a Highwayman came up to Baker.

"'Tis gettin' dark," he said, and his hoarse tone sounded as if he had been drinking, "an' our stomachs be empty!"

"Then light a fire," Baker said. "There'll be no one about to see it at this time of night!"

He spoke to the man who was standing beside him, then turned his head towards Vanda.

"That's true, isn't it?" he asked. "There are no spies watching us? If there are, I'll strangle you with my own hands!"

"Why should there be spies watching the wood," Vanda enquired, "when no one ever comes here for fear of the ghost?"

"Th' ghost? Wot ghost?" one of the Highwaymen asked.

"The ghost of the Priest who lived in this Chapel," Vanda replied. "He was a Holy man, and the villagers believe he can be seen at night praying with the animals who came to him for help when they were injured."

She spoke very softly.

Not only Baker but also the Highwaymen were listening.

"Oi don' loik ghosts!" one of them said. "Fair gives me th' creeps, they does!"

There was something in the way he spoke which made Baker say sharply:

"Well, you won't have to stay here for long. Light the fire, and let's hope for the lady's sake that her ransom is on Papa's door-step at dawn."

Vanda drew in her breath.

She was wondering as the Earl was not coming until to-morrow how her father could find a thousand pounds by dawn.

He never had much money in the house and Mr. Rushman might perhaps have £50 for wages.

She supposed her father would send his grooms into Trowbridge to wake up the Bank Manager.

He could provide the money, even if it meant opening the Bank.

When she thought of this, she was sure that the demand for ransom would include the threat that if her father should inform the Magistrates or the soldiers why the money was necessary, she would die.

As one of the Highwaymen began to light the fire, she wondered if it could be seen outside the wood.

Then she remembered that they had been here some time.

Yet no-one but herself had the slightest idea they were there.

The wood was so thick, with no Game-keepers and the villagers afraid to go into it, that it was isolated from all human contact.

When the fire was burning, the Highwaymen erected some posts over it on which Vanda saw they intended to roast a young doe.

They must have killed it in the Park and it had already been gutted and skinned.

They set it up in such a professional manner that Vanda knew Baker must have taught them how to do it.

Some of the Highwaymen had other contributions to make for their dinner.

Large potatoes were set round the fire to cook in the embers.

There was a pot which was also hung over the flames which Vanda learned later contained a soup of hare, rabbit and pigeon.

Each man had a tin plate and a mug that he carried in his saddle-bag.

They set them down on the grass and Vanda realised there was nothing for her.

"Because you're my guest," Baker said in a mocking tone, "I'll share my mug with you."

"I suppose if I behaved correctly, I should refuse disdainfully," Vanda replied in much the same tone as he had used to her, "but as it happens, I am extremely hungry!"

Baker laughed.

"You've got grit," he said, "and I'll tell you later what else you've got!"

There was an unmistakable innuendo in the way he spoke.

Vanda felt a streak of fear run through her like fork-lightning.

She knew she was walking on a tight-rope.

It was even more frightening than if she was imprisoned and alone.

The soup was poured into the mugs and was, she had to admit, very palatable.

It was a relief to realise that Baker's mug was clean.

She could not say the same of those belonging to the other Highwaymen.

Also the way they ate made her look away from them in disgust.

As soon as the doe was roasted, they hacked at it with knives which they produced from their belts.

Vanda had the unpleasant feeling that they were stained with human blood.

They thrust huge pieces into their mouths, spitting out what they did not want.

They also talked with their mouths full.

Some of the food trickled down their chins onto their clothes.

These were already dirty, stained and torn.

It was almost a relief to look at Baker.

He ate as fastidiously as she did herself, his hands were clean, and his chin shaved.

She longed to ask him how he could bear to associate with men who were so uncouth.

She could understand why Major Lawson had said he wanted only money and was interested in nothing else.

She knew that what Baker spent his money on would be vastly different from what the other Highwaymen desired.

As they finished the soup, each Highwayman put his mug upside-down on the grass beside him.

Vanda was wondering if it was a custom that had some significant meaning.

Then when they had gorged themselves on the doe, she understood.

Baker produced a bottle of rum and it was passed round, each man filling his mug.

"Do you want some?" Baker asked Vanda.

He filled his mug first and also, she noticed, cleaned it out with grass.

She shook her head.

"Have a sip," he urged, "it'll do you good and warm you. I like my women warm!"

Again she felt a streak of fear from the way he spoke.

He turned away from her to pass the bottle to the other men.

She began praying frantically, both to God and to her mother.

She called to the Earl to save her by a miracle from having to stay in the wood for the night.

"Help me . . help me," she prayed.

She felt as if her silent plea winged its way towards the Earl like a bird in flight.

She looked up at the sky.

While they had been eating, the stars had come out and the moon was rising.

Already the first of its rays were touching the tops of the trees turning them to silver.

She knew the moonlight was also illuminating what was left of the ruins of the Chapel behind them.

"Help me . . help me!" she prayed to the Monk.

Her body was tense.

She thought even the Highwaymen must realise that she was beseeching God who was greater than them all to come to her rescue.

The men were drinking the rum and whispering amongst themselves.

She knew that what they were saying concerned her.

If what she feared happened, the only thing she could do was to kill herself.

She was not at all certain however how she could do so.

There was a pistol, and she thought it was loaded, in every man's belt.

They also carried the sharp pointed knives they had just used for hacking pieces of flesh from the carcass of the doe.

Would it be possible, she wondered, to get hold of one of those instruments of death?

Then as the fire began to flicker as it was dying out and the moonbeams became stronger she knew it was very late.

Baker poured the last drop of rum that was left in the bottle into his mug and raised it to his lips.

Then he put down his mug and rising to his feet held out his hand to Vanda.

"Now," he said, "you'll come with me, and leave these gentlemen to sleep alone."

It was then Vanda opened her lips to scream.

Even as she did so, there was a sound in the forest – a sound that was different from those made by the animals moving in the undergrowth.

Different from the sounds the birds had made in the branches of the trees all the time they had been eating.

The sound came again, and now the Highwaymen turned their heads towards the direction from which it came.

. . . .

"Well, we can certainly do no more now," Major Lawson said.

"I feel we have considered everything," the Earl agreed.

The two men had planned during the whole afternoon, consulting maps, drawing up plans, and thinking out every aspect of a campaign which would ensure the Baker Gang would be unable to escape this time.

"We can only hope," Major Lawson said a dozen times, "they will not have moved on elsewhere before we get there."

"If they are waiting for me, I think it is unlikely." The Earl replied.

"I can think of no other reason why they should have stayed for so long," Major Lawson agreed.

The Major stretched himself as if he felt cramped after having been sitting for so long.

The Earl felt the same.

"We will go to my house," the Major said, "and I am sure, My Lord, you need a drink! I know I do!"

The Earl was just about to reply when there was a knock on the door.

The Major had given orders that they were not to be disturbed.

There was a pause while he collected his papers together.

Then he said sharply:

"Come in!"

The door opened and a Sergeant-Major marched into the room, clicked his heels together and saluted.

"'B' Company reporting back for duty, Sir!" he said.

Major Lawson smiled.

"It's good to have you back, Sergeant-Major. I trust our men distinguished themselves?"

"They did indeed, Sir! We received a commendation from those directing the exercise."

"Then I congratulate you!" the Earl said.

"How many men have returned with you?" the Major asked.

"My Company are all back, Sir. The rest should be here in about an hour."

"That is good!" Major Lawson said.

He dismissed the Sergeant-Major and said to the Earl:

"I know you will be glad to hear that we can leave first thing to-morrow morning."

For a moment the Earl did not speak.

Then as Major Lawson looked at him in surprise he said:

"I think it essential that we leave to-night."

"To-night?" The Major echoed. "But it will be dark, and difficult for the men to find their way."

"On the contrary," the Earl said, "there is a full moon to-night, and it was a blessing last night as I only reached Gresbury after darkness had fallen."

"The rest of my men will not be here for another hour," Major Lawson said. "They have been on manoeuvres all day, and will be both hungry and tired."

"When he goes into battle," the Earl replied, "a soldier often has to go for several nights without sleep."

The Major flushed.

"I apologise, My Lord," he said. "I realise I spoke like a 'peacetime soldier'."

The Earl took charge.

"This is what I intend to do," he said, "and your men must follow me as quickly as possible."

The Earl's trunk had been carried to the Major's house and unpacked by his own groom.

His evening-clothes were laid out on the bed.

It took the Earl four minutes to change from what he was wearing into his riding-breeches, and to put on a grey whipcord jacket.

By the time he came downstairs the horse which Major Lawson had ordered for him was standing outside the house.

An Orderly was holding the bridle.

It was what the Earl had asked for – the fastest horse in the Barracks.

It was not the equal of the horses he had bought in London.

But he knew it would go faster than those in the team he had borrowed from the General.

Major Lawson did not see him off.

He was busy giving orders and telling the soldiers, who had assembled on his instructions, what was expected of them.

The Earl set off at a gallop, moving across country.

He found his way easily in the remaining day light.

By the time he neared Little Stock it was dusk and the first evening star had appeared in the sky.

He arrived at the Manor House.

As he was not expected, there was no groom to take his horse.

He therefore rode into the stables.

An elderly groom appeared to look at him in surprise.

"Why, it's Yer Lordship!" he exclaimed as the Earl dismounted. Wot's 'appened to our 'orses?"

"They will be coming on later," the Earl replied.

He did not say any more, but walked round to the front-door.

He did not knock, but finding it unlocked he opened the door and walked in.

He imagined that as it was nearly time for dinner, Vanda would be downstairs.

He opened the door into what he thought would be the Drawing-Room, only to find it empty.

Walking a little further down the passage he opened the door of the General's Study.

As he entered he saw the General, whom he remembered, and sitting at a large desk beside him was Mr. Rushman.

Both men had their feet raised on stools. They stared at him in astonishment.

The Earl was about to speak when Sir Alexander exclaimed:

"It is Neil! Thank God you are here, boy!"

He spoke so fervently that the Earl asked:

"Why? What has happened?"

"Your Lordship may well ask," Mr. Rushman answered. "Forgive my not getting up, but . ."

"Never mind about that!" the Earl said quickly. "Where is Vanda?"

"That is what I was going to tell you," the General answered, "but she told me you were not coming until to-morrow."

"Where is she?" the Earl repeated.

The General held out a piece of paper.

Even as the Earl took it he had an idea what it contained.

He had not admitted it to himself, but he had had a presentiment she was in danger.

All the time he was riding toward Little Stock he knew that something had occurred which made it imperative for the troops to move in to-night.

On the piece of paper the General had handed him was written:

"We have taken your daughter prisoner.

If you don't leave £1,000 on your doorstep at dawn to-morrow morning, we will send you one of her fingers, then one of her toes, every two hours until the ransom is paid. Inform no one of this or she will die!"

The Earl was aware that the note had been written by Baker.

It was in the same type of handwriting as the pastry maker would have used for rendering his accounts.

"What do you mean to do?" the Earl asked.

"Mr. Rushman and I between us can produce only a little more than fifty pounds," the General replied. "We have sent Hawkins on the fastest horse available to the bank at Trowbridge to get the rest."

He looked worried as he went on:

"We can only pray that it will be obtainable from the Manager, although the Bank will be closed."

"At what time do you expect him back?" the Earl asked.

The General made a gesture of helplessness with his hands.

All three men were aware that Trowbridge was at least seven miles from Little Stock.

There was little likelihood that Hawkins, after arousing the Manager, would be back before midnight.

"We cannot wait so long," the Earl said. "The soldiers will be coming as soon as possible, but as you are very well aware, General, it takes longer to bring them here by road than to travel across country."

There was no need to explain that the soldiers at the Barracks were Foot Soldiers.

The General knew that as well as he did.

"What I am going to do," the Earl said quietly, "is to join Vanda!"

Both men stared at him in sheer astonishment.

"We all know what these Devils are like," the Earl said brusquely. "Even if they do not torture her, she is very pretty!"

The General clenched his fingers together, but he did not speak.

"Is there a woman in the house?" the Earl asked.

"There is a Cook called Jennie," the General replied.

Without making any explanations the Earl turned to walk across the hall to where he knew the kitchen would be situated.

Jennie was standing at the stove in the kitchen.

Dobson had brought in the soup tureen and the silver entree dishes and put them on the kitchen table.

They looked around in surprise when the Earl entered.

He walked towards Jennie.

"I want you to make me a mask," he said, "as quickly as possible."

"A – mask, Sir!" Jennie exclaimed.

"My Lord!" Dobson corrected.

" . . My Lord," Jennie said dropping a curtsy.

"Miss Vanda is in danger," the Earl explained, "and there is no time to be lost. Please make me a Highwayman's mask."

Jennie gave a little cry of horror.

She pushed the saucepan she was holding to one side, and ran to the dresser at the end of which lay her sewing-basket.

"Now, where have I got some black material?" she asked.

"You've got a black petticoat," Dobson volunteered.

"Get it!" the Earl ordered. "I will replace it with one far better!"

The Earl returned to the Study.

"What I intend to do, General," he said, "is to find Vanda who is in Monk's Wood."

Before the General could speak, the Earl went on:

"When the troops arrive, Major Lawson will contact you immediately."

He was just about to say something more when he exclaimed:

"I have forgotten something!"

He left the Study and ran back to the kitchen.

Dobson had just returned to hand Jennie the black petticoat.

"Listen," the Earl said to him, "I want two bottles of red

wine from your Master's cellar, a bottle of Gin, and another of Burgundy."

"We've got all those, M'Lord," Dobson replied.

"Then fetch them quickly. Open the bottles, mix all the drinks together and return them to the bottles. Do you understand?"

He paused to say: "I think I will make it two bottles of Brandy."

"Very good, M'Lord."

Dobson had also been in the Army at one time.

He was therefore used to obeying orders without question.

As he hurried to the cellar, the Earl went back into the Study.

He told the General briefly what he and Major Lawson had planned during the afternoon.

He explained also that Major Lawson would come first to the Manor House in case the Earl had learnt anything new.

"What you have to impress upon the Major, General," he said, "is that they move so silently that the Highwaymen have no idea they are there until they are surrounded."

"I understand, my boy," the General said, "and I commend you on an excellent idea."

"What I did not expect, and what you will have to tell Major Lawson," the Earl said, "is that Vanda is with them."

Before he could do any more, Dobson came into the Study with the mask in his hand.

Jennie was a good sewer and the slits for the eyes were wide enough for the Earl to see clearly.

The mask covered a great deal of his face.

It would be difficult, even for somebody who knew him well, to identify him.

"That is exactly what I wanted," the Earl said with satisfaction, looking at his reflection in the mirror.

He turned back to the General.

"Wish me luck," he said, "I can only hope that I am in time to prevent Vanda from suffering at the hands of those fiends!"

The General put his hand on his arm.

"God go with you, my boy," he said.

Then the Earl was running out of the house and back towards the stables to collect his horse.

He gave the elderly groom, who was startled by his appearance, certain instructions he had not mentioned to the General.

"Go at once!" he ordered.

"Oi will, M'Lord," the groom replied.

He was saddling another horse as the Earl rode away.

By now the moonlight was turning the garden into a scene of exquisite beauty.

It seemed impossible there should be evil lurking in the darkness of Monk's Wood.

The Earl found the path which ended in the Park and led into the centre of it.

The moonlight flickering through the branches of the trees cast patterns of silver on the ground ahead of him.

Everything seemed very silent, except for the sudden flutter of a bird that had gone to roost.

As the Earl rode on he began to think despairingly that after all the Highwaymen had moved away.

If so their plan would be useless.

Then in the distance he thought he heard a voice.

A moment later he saw a flickering light.

He knew it came from a fire.

Unless the Highwaymen had already injured or imprisoned Vanda, in a few seconds he would find her.

He could only pray that if she recognised him she would not cry out to him to save her.

If she did it would endanger both their lives.

They would be at the mercy of men who showed none to their enemies.

A minute later he reached the clearing in the centre of the wood.

One glance showed him that six Highwaymen were seated round a dying fire while the seventh was standing.

Seated on the trunk of a tree behind him was Vanda.

Quickly, because he was afraid she might speak, the Earl said:

"Good-evening, my brothers! I hope I may join you, and it's with the greatest respect that I bow to your Leader, Bill Baker!"

He rode his horse over the grass right up to the Highwaymen.

He was aware as he did so that several of the men put their hands to the pistols in their belts.

"Who are you?" Baker demanded.

"John Garrat, at your service! And, naturally, a 'Gentleman of the Road'!"

The Earl spoke with such a flourish that one man laughed.

A second later several others followed him.

"Ye're certainly well pleased wi' yerself!" one of them said.

"But not as pleased as you must be," the Earl replied looking at Baker. "I congratulate you on capturing an heiress. She is, in fact, someone I was looking for myself!"

"An Heiress?" Baker exclaimed.

The Earl looked at Baker in astonishment.

"Do you mean to say you do not know?"

"Know what?"

"That she," the Earl said pointing his finger at Vanda, "has a fortune of between ten and fifteen thousand pounds!"

"I knew her father was wealthy," Baker said, "but . ."

"She has her own money, inherited from her mother," the Earl informed him.

Baker scratched his chin.

"That makes things a bit different," he said. "If what you're saying is true, I've not asked enough."

"Not enough?" the Earl exclaimed incredulously. "What have you demanded?"

"Same as what they put on my head," Baker replied. "A thousand golden goblins."

The Earl threw up his hands in horror.

"You are cheating yourself! I have a much better idea than that where an heiress is concerned."

"And what's your idea?" Baker asked.

He was resenting this new man, who he thought looked as smart as he himself did, interfering.

The Earl looked at him through his mask and stroked his chin reflectively.

"Now what would you say," he asked in a slow, quiet voice, "if I told you how each one of you could make a thousand quid, and leave the rest to me?"

"I don't believe the Old Josser could find that kind of money in a thousand days," Baker retorted. "And we're not waiting that long!"

"No, of course not," the Earl agreed scornfully. "I'm leaving at dawn, and if you are not interested in my idea, then I will not press it on you."

"I *am* interested – of course I'm interested," Baker said irritably. "I just don't believe it's possible."

"Let's 'ear wot it is," one of the other men said.

There was a chorus from all the others.

99

"That's roight! Let's 'ear wot 'e's got to say! 'E might be as smart as 'e looks."

There was a snigger at this, and Baker said:

"Well, come on, out with it! Tell us how we can each make a thousand pounds."

"In exactly the same way as Captain James Campbell did."

"Campbell?" Baker repeated reflectively.

"And Sir John Johnson," the Earl prompted.

"Now, what did they do ?" Baker asked who obviously did not know.

"I'll tell you what they did," the Earl replied. "They abducted an heiress, and Campbell married her!"

Chapter Seven

Vanda had been so shocked by what Baker had said that she was almost paralysed by fear.

She was wondering frantically how she could kill herself.

Suddenly a man came into the clearing on horse-back.

Seeing that he was a Highwayman she relapsed into her thoughts.

But when the Earl began to speak she stiffened, looked up and thought she must be dreaming.

She knew his voice.

But she could not believe it had come from a man whose face was covered with a black mask.

The Earl went on speaking and she knew it really was him.

She wanted to jump to her feet, to run to him and beg him to save her.

Every nerve in her body seemed to spring towards him.

Then her brain told her that if she did anything so foolish she would destroy him.

He was one man amongst seven dangerous criminals.

If they had the slightest idea that he was deceiving them he would die.

Clenching her hands together, she began to pray that his disguise would not be penetrated.

She realised soon that he was talking as if he wanted to keep the Highwaymen interested.

She knew he was afraid they would move somewhere else.

She suspected the plans he had made for the soldiers to arrive in the morning had been changed.

Then he spoke of James Campbell and of his marriage to an heiress.

She remembered that was the tale she had told him.

She was aware that he was trying to save her from the Highwaymen in a very subtle way.

She heard Baker say:

"I don't believe you can do this."

"I can and I have," the Earl replied.

"Then where's your wife now?"

The Earl gave a little chuckle before he replied.

"Now you are asking questions I am not going to answer."

Baker laughed.

"You are certainly a cool card," he said, "and we could do with a
few thousands, couldn't we, boys?"

There was a murmur of assent from the Highwaymen.

They were listening intently to everything that was said, almost
as if the Earl had mesmerized them.

He walked to his horse.

"To show you that I am in earnest," he said, "I have something
for you which speaks louder than words."

He drew something from his saddle.

Watching, Vanda saw it was a small bag of the type Mr. Rushman
used when he was paying the wages.

The Earl opened it and tipped its contents into his hand.

They glittered for a moment in the moonlight.

"Catch!" he shouted.

Then dramatically he threw what he held up into the air.

Golden sovereigns soared above the heads of the Highwaymen to
fall amongst them.

They scrambled for them like small boys at a Fair.

They snatched up the coins, several men biting them to see if they
were real.

"That is my wedding-present to you," the Earl said. "Now two of
you be off to fetch the parson."

"And how do we know," Baker said as the others watched
in silence, "that when you marry the wench, we'll get her
money."

"You have to trust me," the Earl replied. "At the same time I will
give you my written assurance that each one of you, if alive, will
receive one thousand pounds."

"Tat be fair en'ugh," one of the Highwaymen shouted, as if he
thought Baker might refuse it.

"You will get nothing, if you don't hurry for a Parson," the Earl said. "He lives in the house next to the Church which is only a short way down the road on the left-hand side."

Two men walked towards their horses.

"Make him ride here," the Earl said. "It will be quicker."

"You're certainly good at giving orders," Baker said sarcastically. "How do you know all this?"

"I have been planning to abduct this particular heiress for some time," the Earl replied. "But you came along and queered my pitch."

Baker smiled.

"Too many of us in the same place," the Earl went on. "So I thought we had better join forces."

"There's something in that," Baker answered.

The Earl drew a piece of paper from his pocket.

He walked towards Vanda and sat down on the same fallen tree on which she was sitting.

He did not look at her.

But she felt her whole being vibrate towards him and was sure he understood.

He did not write anything and she wondered how he could do so without a pen.

Instead, he read to himself what was already written on the paper.

Then he rose and handed it to Baker.

"I guessed this was what you would want before I came," he said.

Holding it up so that it caught the moonlight, Baker read what was written.

"Seems fair enough," he said, "but, I'm still wondering how you'll manage it."

"Once the woman is my wife, the Law says her fortune is mine."

Baker nodded.

"And what I do with it," the Earl added, "is my business."

Baker was still scrutinizing the paper as the Earl continued:

"It will be safest to go to a Bank in London and you must tell me where we can meet, say three or four days from now."

Baker was obviously not keen on going to London.

The two men discussed other places.

Each having some objection to anything suggested by the other.

Only Vanda knew that the Earl was playing for time.

She was also listening for the sounds of the Highwaymen returning.

It was not far to the Vicarage and she was sure they would hurry there as quickly as possible.

Then, she thought, the Parson, who was an elderly man, would be in bed.

He would have to dress and it would surely be impossible for the Earl to keep Baker talking all that time.

The Earl appeared to come to some arrangement with him and he said:

"Now all we have to do is to wait for the Vicar, and that reminds me, I brought you something in which you can drink to my happiness."

There was laughter at this from the men who had been listening.

Several made remarks which Vanda did not understand, but she knew they were crude and vulgar.

The Earl went to the side of his Charger.

The horse who had been well trained had not moved away, but stood where he had been left.

Only bending his head to crop the grass that was in reach.

The Earl pulled the bottles out of the saddle-bags.

He carried the first two to Baker, putting them down at his feet.

Then he returned for the other two.

"I may tell you," he said lightly, "that the wine merchant from whom I procured these was very reluctant to part with them."

He spoke in a way which told the Highwaymen that he had taken them at pistol-point.

They laughed and joked about it.

"I could not carry more," the Earl said. "There is more than half a bottle for each of us and we will leave one bottle for the boys who are fetching the Parson."

"They'd 'ave th' skin off yer back if ye 'ad forgot 'em," a Highwayman jibed.

The Earl opened the first bottle and handed it to Baker.

He took a long swig then as he handed the bottle back to the Earl he seemed to be gasping for breath.

"In God's name!" he exclaimed when he could speak. "What the Hell have you put in the wine . . Dynamite?"

"The very best French Brandy amongst other things," the Earl replied, "and there was no duty paid on it!"

The bottle was being passed from hand to hand.

The Highwaymen had drawn in closer and someone had thrown a few sticks on the fire.

It had made it leap again into flame.

The first bottle was passed around twice before it was empty.

Vanda thought in the light of the moon the men's eyes seemed to glitter.

They smacked their lips after they had drunk.

It was as if they relished every drop that had passed down their throats.

The second bottle had been started when Vanda heard the sound of hooves.

She could hardly believe that the Highwaymen could have been so quick.

A moment later the horses came into the clearing.

The elderly Vicar was riding beside his captors.

He was wearing his Cassock.

When he dismounted he lifted down his surplice which had been hung over the front of his saddle.

As if he was determined to assert his authority, Baker went forward.

"Good evening, Parson," he said. "I see you have agreed to join a man and a woman we have here in Holy Matrimony."

He was speaking in his usual mocking tone.

The Vicar replied quietly:

"I had no choice, but I am here."

It was then the Earl said:

"If you stand just inside the Chapel you will be on consecrated ground."

The Vicar did not look at him but put on his surplice.

Walking past the Highwaymen who were lying on the ground, he reached the Chapel.

The two men who had escorted the Vicar put their horses with the rest.

Then the other men gave them the bottle which had been kept for their return.

The men were drinking thirstily.

But Vanda realised that their voices were low.

It was as if they were slightly overawed by what was happening.

The Vicar had gone inside what was left of the Chapel.

Part of the Altar was still there.

But the roof had fallen in and there was nothing left of the windows.

The Vicar knelt down amongst the broken stones.

The Earl took off his hat.

Then he put out his hand to Vanda and drew her from the fallen tree.

They stood in front of the Chapel.

As if the Parson was aware they were there, he made the sign of the cross and rose to his feet.

First he spoke to Vanda.

"Is it your wish," he asked, "that this wedding should take place."

"Y . . yes."

Her voice was hardly audible and she suddenly felt shy.

It all seemed like a dream yet at the same time her heart was singing.

The Earl was saving her, saving her from Baker and his brutal men.

Or, if she had been capable of it from having to kill herself.

He was still holding her hand in his and she felt the strength of his fingers.

Although she was desperately frightened that he might be unmasked, she felt a little thrill run through her.

The Vicar spoke to the Earl:

"John," the Earl replied.

"The Vicar had no Prayer Book with him, but he knew the Service by heart and shortened it.

He said a prayer then told the Earl:

"Repeat after me: 'I, John, take thee, Vanda, to my wedded wife."

The Earl repeated the words slowly and seriously in his deep voice.

And finally: 'till death us do part'.

Vanda wondered if he thought this was all a mockery and therefore a sacrilege.

Then she found herself saying very quietly:

"I, Vanda, take thee . . John to my . . wedded . . husband."

The Earl pulled off his signet-ring and put it on the third finger of her left hand.

He felt her tremble when he touched her, but he knew it was not with fear.

They both knelt and the Vicar blessed them.

When he had done so he turned back to the Altar.

He knelt down in front of it as he had before.

While the actual Service was taking place, the Highwaymen had all been quiet.

Now they started shouting:

"Kiss th' bride, kiss 'er, or Oi'll do it fer yer."

They were all yelling at once, but Vanda knew they were slurring their words.

She was sure that the wine which the Earl had brought them must have been very potent.

She looked at them nervously.

Then she felt the Earl put his arm around her and drew her close to him.

With his other hand he tipped her head back and his lips found hers.

Because he was aware how frightened she was, it was a very gentle kiss.

At the same time, she felt as if the moonlight touched her lips and invaded her breast.

She loved him and, whatever happened next, as he kissed her she had given him her heart.

For a second the Highwaymen were silent and then they shouted again.

Vanda had no idea what they were saying.

She only felt as if the stars had fallen down from the sky to cover them and she and the Earl were alone in a world of their own.

It was then as she looked at him and the moonlight haloed her head there were sounds of men moving through the trees.

Baker, who was more sober than any of the other men, heard it at the same time as the Earl.

Swiftly he pushed Vanda onto her knees with the fallen tree behind her.

He placed himself in front of her.

Baker drew the pistol from his waist and fired into the darkness.

His bullet struck a tree.

Another shot rang out, he staggered and fell to the ground.

Even as he did so, the Highwaymen gave a shout of warning.

Soldiers appeared on all sides of the clearing.

They were pointing their guns at the Highwaymen.

Befogged by the wine, they were unable even to pull their pistols from their belts.

As the soldiers converged upon them, Major Lawson came towards the Earl.

"We came as quickly as we could My Lord," he said with a smile.

"At exactly the right moment," the Earl replied, "but I am afraid you have lost the chief culprit."

Both men looked at the limp body of Baker.

His coat had fallen open and there was already a crimson stain on his shirt.

"There's a price of one thousand pounds on his head," Major Lawson said, "which of course, My Lord, belongs to you."

"I suggest," the Earl replied, "that I double it and the money is divided between your men who managed to get here so quickly, despite the fact that they have had a long day on manoeuvres."

Major Lawson's eyes were twinkling.

"That is very generous of Your Lordship," he said, "and this manoeuvre will keep them happy for a long time."

He turned from the Earl to shake hands with the Vicar who was standing in the entrance of the Chapel.

The Earl was suddenly aware that he had not removed his mask.

Now as he pulled it off his face he said:

"Thank you, Vicar, you played your part brilliantly. Miss Charlton and I will talk to you more about it to-morrow. Now I shall take her home."

"I know the General will be waiting very anxiously to learn what has happened." the Vicar replied.

The Earl was aware that Vanda was feeling it was impossible to talk normally to anyone.

He drew her towards the horses.

He lifted her on to *Kingfisher's* back. Then as if he felt she was unsteady he sprang up behind her.

She felt his arm go around her, holding her close.

She thought it was the most wonderful thing that could ever happen.

The Earl turned *Kingfisher's* head.

As they passed Major Lawson, who was still talking to the Vicar, he said:

"Thank you for the loan of your charger. I will leave it to you to take him back to barracks."

As Major Lawson saluted, the Earl rode slowly through the wood.

The soldiers and their prisoners had already disappeared towards the brakes which had carried them from the barracks to Monk's Wood.

It did not take the Earl long to reach the gate of the Park which Vanda always used.

To her surprise, the Earl pulled *Kingfisher* to a standstill.

He spoke for the first time since they left the clearing.

"Are you all right?" he asked.

She had been resting her head against his shoulder and now she looked up at him.

"How could .. you be so .. wonderful as to .. save me?" she asked.

"I ought to be shot for not realising sooner that you were riding into danger," the Earl replied. "How could I suppose that when I did not turn up those scoundrels would turn their attention to you?"

"You saved .. me when I was .. wondering how I .. could kill .. myself."

His arm tightened around her.

Then as if there were no words he could say to reassure her, he bent his head and his lips found hers.

He kissed her until once again she was touching the stars.

Her terror and fear had faded away and she was trembling with the wonder of it.

Only when he raised his head did she say in a voice that seemed to come from the stars.

"I .. love you, I love .. you."

"And I love you, but I might have lost you!" the Earl answered.

. . . .

Vanda woke and saw it was very late in the morning.

It had been difficult to go to bed last night when there was so much to tell her father and Mr. Rushman who were waiting for them.

She realised how worried they had both been.

It was only when the Sergeant-Major had returned from manoeuvres that the Earl had suddenly become aware of the danger Vanda might be in.

It had never crossed his mind that she would do anything so foolhardy as ride about the Park alone.

Nor had he anticipated that because he had postponed his arrival the Highwaymen might take Vanda in his place.

After she had gone and he and Major Lawson were sitting down to work out their plans of attack, the Major said:

"I, of course, did not say anything in front of Miss Charlton, but Baker and his gang have created the most appalling havoc in some of our small villages."

He saw the Earl was listening and went on:

"There was not much money to be found there, and Baker prefers money to anything else."

He paused before he said:

"Those brutes raped all the young women and murdered any men who tried to prevent them from doing so."

"I am not surprised that you are making every effort to capture Baker, as he is the Ringleader," the Earl remarked.

They went on working until the Earl suddenly knew, almost as if someone had said so, that Vanda was in danger.

He had found her enchanting, amusing and very beautiful.

Perhaps because they had known each other since she was a child, there was a kind of affinity between them.

It made it possible to read her thoughts and to feel in some way which he did not analyse that they were a part of each other.

While he was riding as fast as he could towards the Manor, he remembered the story Vanda had told him of Captain James Campbell.

How he had married the girl he abducted.

The Earl was suddenly terrified.

If the soldiers were delayed for any length of time, Baker might storm the village or the Manor House - if he did either he or his men might rape Vanda.

When he learnt from the General that Vanda was actually Baker's prisoner, he knew he had to save her or die in the attempt.

As always in the face of the enemy he appeared cool and in control.

It was almost as if a power greater than himself directed him.

He had sent the groom to the Vicar telling him to be ready when the Highwaymen called to collect him.

Then he had left the General to convey his instructions and warning to Major Lawson.

Vanda had learnt last night from her father that it was the Earl, and the Earl only, who had any idea of how he could bring her to safety.

But she was obviously so exhausted that the Earl had insisted that she went up to bed, while her father and Mr. Rushman were still asking questions.

He had taken her to the top of the stairs and opened her bed-room door.

Then pulling her into his arms he kissed her until she felt as if the whole house was spinning around them.

"Go to bed, my precious," he said. "You are safe and no one will hurt you. We will talk about ourselves to-morrow."

He kissed her again and put her gently through her bed-room door and shut it behind her.

She heard him walking down the stairs.

Then the tears filled her eyes, and as she undressed she was saying over and over again:

"Thank You, God, thank You!"

Now the sun was shining, and she knew she was happier than she had ever been in her whole life.

She dressed quickly, putting on one of her prettiest gowns so that the Earl would admire her.

Then she wondered if she should perhaps have worn her riding-habit and gone to meet him at the Hall.

She began to question for the first time if they were actually married.

Was what had happened last night just a pretence to deceive the Highwaymen?

"I love him," she told herself, "but at the same time why should he love me when we have seen so little of each other?"

She felt as if she had been wakened from a dream.

A glorious, magical one, but still a dream!

Then there came a sudden blow to her heart.

She remembered that the marriage between Captain James Campbell and the heiress he had abducted had been annulled by Royal Proclamation.

The sunshine seemed to fade into darkness.

She had assumed both that their marriage was legal, and that the Earl had kissed her because he loved her.

Any man, she now thought, would have kissed her because she was safe.

He was congratulating himself on being so clever.

The more she thought of it, the more she decided she had been impulsive and in fact presumptuous.

She went downstairs slowly.

It was too late to ask for breakfast and anyway she was not hungry.

The house seemed very quiet, but she was sure that her father was in the Study.

She went into the Drawing Room.

The sun was shining through the bow window.

Yet she felt as if her world was suddenly thick with a fog through which she could not find her way.

"What shall I do, what shall I say to him?"

She thought the most important thing was not to make the Earl feel tied.

She was sure there were hundreds of women for him to marry if he wished for a wife.

The stories of the gaieties of Paris once the war was over had trickled back to England.

She was certain, because he was so handsome, the Earl had enjoyed them.

"I must make it very clear to him," she decided, "that I will not hold any in any way and that if he wishes to be free, I will agree to anything he suggests."

. . . .

At the Hall the Earl, who was used to having very little sleep, had awakened at his usual hour.

When he had gone back there last night, he had ridden *Kingfisher*, because the horse was saddled.

When he entered his own house for the first time in seven years, the Night-footman had hurried to fetch Buxton.

He had got out of bed, dressed in a matter of a few minutes, and his usual self-composure was unimpaired.

"I deeply regret, M'Lord," he said, "that I was not here to welcome Your Lordship, but as you were so late we were not expecting you until to-morrow."

The Earl held out his hand.

"I am aware of that, Buxton," he said. "It is a long story which you will doubtless hear a thousand times in the future, but I have just helped the Army to capture the Baker Gang, who I understand have been hiding in the West Wing."

It was impossible not to tell Buxton a little more.

Then Buxton realised the Earl must be hungry, having had no dinner.

The Chef was aroused and two of the footmen.

It was therefore nearly three o'clock before the Earl finally lay down in the bed of his ancestors and fell asleep.

Now, as he came downstairs, he was thinking of Vanda and deciding he would ride over to see her.

He would return *Kingfisher* and arrange for his own horses to be taken to his own stables.

He was walking towards the Breakfast Room, when he was aware a Post-Chaise had drawn up outside the front-door.

A footman ran down to it and came back with a letter.

One glance at the writing told the Earl who it was from and he carried it into the Breakfast Room.

He helped himself to the dishes that were waiting on the side-board.

Buxton had poured out his coffee before he finally opened Caroline's letter.

He wondered why Caroline should send it by post-Chaise.

It was a considerable expense unless there was some urgent reason for it.

He soon learnt the answer.

Caroline informed him that she had arranged a House party at Wyn Hall for the following weekend.

As she had already mentioned, the Prince Regent would be delighted to be his guest.

She continued:

"I hope You will not be Angry with me, Dearest Neil, but I told the REGENT that we were Secretly Engaged. He has promised NOT to SPEAK of it."

For a moment the Earl stared at what she had written, his eyes darkening with anger.

Then unexpectedly he laughed and threw the letter down on the table.

He knew he had found the answer to his own problem when he solved Vanda's.

Now he was free!

Yesterday in his terror at what might happen to her, he was concerned only with how he could rescue her.

It had never struck him that Caroline was no longer a menace to his life or his happiness.

He had in fact never given her a thought.

Today he was in love and married.

There was no question of his having a House Party until he had finished his Honeymoon.

He would write to the Regent immediately and tell him what had happened.

His Royal Highness would be thrilled to be the first in the know.

Although the Earl disliked personal publicity, he knew it would be impossible for the news of the capture of the Baker Gang not to be a sensation.

He would, whether he liked it or not, be a National Hero.

What was more the romance of how he married Vanda in the ruined Chapel would captivate every woman's heart.

Whatever Caroline might say no one would listen.

He went from the breakfast-table to his Study.

He sent his letter to Carlton House in charge of two grooms on fast horses.

Then he mounted *Kingfisher* and rode through the Park to the Manor House.

He had always loved his home, but he had forgotten how beautiful it was.

The sunshine was dazzling.

The Spring flowers, the ducklings on the lake, and the rooks feeding their young in the tree-tops, were all telling him that he was starting a new life.

It would be very different from the one he had lived in the recent strenuous and dangerous years.

Having left *Kingfisher* in the stables, he found the door to the Manor House was open and walked in.

He had a feeling that Vanda would be in the Drawing Room.

That was where he found her.

She was standing at the window and the sunshine illuminated the exquisite colour of her hair.

For a moment she did not hear him as he walked across the room.

Only as he reached her did she turn around.

He thought the stars were caught in her eyes.

Then quickly her eye-lashes flickered and she curtsied.

"Did you sleep well?" he asked in his deep voice.

"I was very . . tired, as . . you must . . have been."

"I was also very happy," the Earl said. "You were safe and that was all that mattered."

Vanda looked away from him.

"I am very . . grateful to you for . . saving me," she said, "but, I am sure it would . . be a mistake for . . anyone to . . know how you . . did it."

"A mistake?" the Earl questioned.

"I am not . . thinking of how you . . captured the Highwaymen," Vanda said quickly, "but of . . our . . marriage."

She stammered over the words and the colour rose in her cheeks.

"You are ashamed of it?" the Earl asked.

"No . . of course not . . it is just . . that it was a . . very clever way of . . protecting me . . but it was not . . legal."

"I do not know why you should say that," the Earl replied. "The marriage took place on consecrated ground. My first name is John, and as we are both residents in this Parish there was no need for a Special Licence or for the banns to be called."

Vanda drew in her breath.

"But . . but you . . want to be . . free."

The Earl smiled.

"I have not said so."

"You hardly . . know me."

"I have known you for, let me think, eighteen years," the Earl answered, "and I know something which is more important than time."

"What . . is . . that?" Vanda asked curiously.

"That you are exactly the wife I want to take my mother's place in looking after Wyn, and of course me."

She raised her eyes to his as if she could not believe what she had heard.

Then he put his arms around her.

"Are you really anxious to get rid of me so quickly?"

"I love . . you," Vanda whispered, "but . . at the same time I am . . sure there are many . . other women whom you would . . rather marry . . than me."

The Earl laughed very gently.

"Are you really so modest?" he said. "I thought when I saw you – could it really be only the day before yesterday? – at the Inn, that you were the most desirable woman I had ever seen in my life."

"Is that true . . really . . true?" Vanda asked.

"I swear to you on everything I hold sacred."

He pulled her a little closer and went on:

"I fell in love with you although I was not certain that it was . . love . . until I thought I had . . lost you."

"Oh, Neil!"

Their eyes were held by each others.

Slowly, for there was no hurry, the Earl found her lips.

He kissed her very gently until the sweetness and innocence of them excited him in a way that he had never been excited before.

His kisses became more insistent, more demanding.

Only when they were both breathless did he say:

"If you try to escape from me, I swear I will think out a plan to keep you my prisoner and never set you free."

"That is . . what I . . want," Vanda murmured.

"I am now a Highwayman, my darling," the Earl said, "and at pistol-point I order you to stand and deliver your heart."

"It is . . yours," Vanda cried. "It has . . always been yours since I . . worshipped you . . as a child."

"Then go on worshipping me," the Earl said. "I need you and I know that I cannot go on without you."

He kissed her again until they sank down together on the sofa.

Vanda put her head against the Earl's shoulder.

"What I really came to say," he said, "is that now that you are my wife, I am taking you to the Hall, and as soon as you feel well enough, we will go and inspect the other Houses I own which I have not seen for such a very long time."

"Can . . we go . . alone?" Vanda asked.

"We are on our Honeymoon, my precious. No one – and I mean no one – is going to interrupt or bother us until we come back to Wyn."

"There is a . . great deal for . . you to do . . here."

"I appreciate that," the Earl replied, "but, there is also a great deal for me to learn and discover about my wife, and she comes first."

Vanda laughed. Then she said:

"I am afraid your family will be very . . disappointed that you are not marrying . . someone more . . important than . . me."

"On the contrary," the Earl said, "they will be delighted. So many of them admire your father and loved your mother."

He kissed her forehead before he added:

"What could be better than that you and I should produce exactly the right sort of family to carry on the Earldom?"

Vanda blushed and hid her face against his neck.

"I often . . thought," she murmured, "it was sad that you were a . . lonely child, as . . I was."

"We will have a large family," the Earl said, "and we will turn the West Wing into an enormous Nursery, so that there will be no Highwaymen lurking there to terrify anyone."

Vanda thought of something.

"Taylor said, when he told me about the Highwaymen, that they went there to have somewhere to put their haul."

"We will look for it," the Earl said, "but, I think from what Major Lawson said, Baker was not interested in anything but money."

He pulled her a little closer as he said:

"Nevertheless, my precious, if there is anything worth having we will give it to the Soldiers and Sailors who suffered injuries in the war and who have been left with no pension."

"I knew you would be upset about that," Vanda said.

"It is something I intend to raise in the House of Lords," the Earl replied.

He kissed her straight little nose before he went on:

"And I am sure, my darling, you can think of ways of raising money to help the really desperate cases."

"You are so clever," Vanda said, "and you know I will do anything you want. So please, when you are working out plans for this and that, let me help you."

"You will help me, you will be with me, and you will love me," the Earl said. "That is my plan for the future!"

Vanda laughed and put her arm around his neck.

"That makes it very easy," she said, "because I love you, I love you, and I want to go on saying so."

"You cannot say it too often to me."

Then he was kissing her, kissing her not gently, but demandingly.

His kisses grew more insistent and more passionate as he drew Vanda closer and closer.

He knew he had ignited in her a little of the fire which burnt fiercely within him.

At the same time it was very different in every way from what he had felt with any woman before.

She was perfect and she was sacred.

He would murder any man who tried to spoil her innocence and her purity.

"You are mine – mine!" he said.

His kisses grew more demanding still, but Vanda was not afraid.

She knew this was love and it was meant to be.

The merging of two people who were so much a part of each other that they became one.

"I love you, I love you," she said in her heart.

It was a love that would not die, but would grow greater month by month and year by year.

It was a love against which they had no defence. They could only surrender to it unconditionally, knowing it was given them by God.

The Magic of Paris

AUTHOR'S NOTE

On 2nd September 1870 the Emperor Napoleon III of France, surrendered to the Prussians at Sudan.

It was the end of the Monarchy and the beginning of the Third Republic.

The Second Empire, had been proclaimed on the 2nd December 1852, at the Hotel de Ville and the new Emperor rode into his Capital through the Arc de Triomphe.

The Second Empire was his creation and it was Louis Napoleon who moulded the social and political character of it.

For eighteen years France enjoyed a glittering, brilliant Imperial Regime.

The wild extravagance of the Courtesans, their jewels, their luxury and their arrogance astounded all Europe.

At the same time it all contributed to French History.

The ultimate disaster was partly the Empress Eugene's fault, who declared openly that their son would not reign unless the Emperor destroyed the military supremacy of Prussia.

It was she, combined with the Foreign Minister, the Duc de Gramond, who pressured the Emperor who was ill and suffering from acute pain as a result of a stone in his bladder into declaring war.

Bismark, on the other hand knew the French Army was completely unprepared for modern warfare, whilst he had trained an enormous fully equipped Army.

The Royal Family escaped to Britain where the Emperor suffered two operations.

He seemed to survive them and the third had been arranged in 1873.

That morning while the doctor was with him the Emperor murmured:

'We were not cowards at Sudan.'

They were his last words. he died before the operation could take place.

He had planned to return to France, hoping it would lead to his restoration on the throne.

The death of his son, the Prince Imperial, six years later, deprived not only the Bonapartes of any future, but France of a Monarchy.

Chapter One

Eva looked helplessly round the room in which she was sitting.

It was a very attractive room, furnished with the exquisite inlaid and gilt furniture which only the French could design.

There was an Aubusson carpet on the floor.

The pictures while not by great artists, were French and very attractive.

When Eva had first seen the house she had exclaimed to her father:

"It is like an adorable dolls'-house! Oh, Papa, how lucky we are!"

"We are indeed!" Sir Richard Hillington replied.

He was thinking not only of the house, but also that he was in Paris again.

He had always loved Paris more than any capital City in the world.

When, six months ago, he had learnt that his wife had been left a house in Paris by her grandmother the *Comtesse* de Chabrillin he was elated.

Unfortunately, Lady Hillington had already contracted the disease which was to kill her very quickly.

Her husband always thought it was because they had visited the Alps.

He had bought her a fur coat and wrapped her up as warmly as he could.

But the treacherous winds from the snowy peaks had affected her lungs.

She had died four months after she learned that she owned the house in Paris.

It was said that she had not been strong enough to cross the Channel to see it.

Sir Richard Hillington adored his wife.

He had given up the prospect of early promotion in his Diplomatic career in order to marry her.

They had in fact run away.

He had been in Paris when he had met what he thought was the most beautiful girl he had ever seen.

She was engaged when she was very young, as was usual amongst the French aristocratic families.

The Bridegroom to be was a Frenchman a little older than she was and whose blood was as blue as hers.

The marriage had been arranged, and the gifts were already beginning to arrive.

Then Lisette de Chabrillin ran away with Richard Hillington.

It was the sort of thing, the French said, which might occur in England, but not in France.

Lisette's parents thought their daughter had behaved disgracefully.

How could she jilt a French nobleman to whom she was already betrothed?

They were also not impressed with the Englishman she had chosen in his place.

Lisette did not hear from her family for years.

In fact it was only when her father-in-law died.

Her husband then came into the title, and became the 5th Baronet.

After that, there was a somewhat cool communication between the Hillingtons and the Chabrillins.

But there was no invitation to visit France.

Lisette sometimes longed to see her family.

Actually she was completely content with the husband she adored, and their beautiful daughter who was very like herself.

Eva had inherited her mother's figure and large dark, eloquent eyes, but her father's fair hair.

It was a strange but compelling combination.

Sir Richard was well aware when she made her début that his daughter would become an acclaimed Beauty overnight

This should have been at the beginning of the year, but Eva was in deep mourning for her mother.

What was worse, her father had only just discovered that they were very short of money.

He had given up his Diplomatic career after his father died and had never reached the rank of Ambassador.

He had to cope with a large, unwieldy house in Gloucestershire.

The estate which required a great deal of money spent on it.

He had always thought his father was reasonably well off.

But the farms, which were let, had deteriorated over the years.

Sir Terence had apparently not been a good administrator.

Nor did he have any knowledge of finance.

He had invested in Companies which had gone bankrupt and lent money to friends who forgot to return it.

Sir Richard tried to save his home which had been in the family for two-hundred years.

It was an impossibility.

Finally, when his wife died, he realised that the only possible thing he could do was to sell the house in Gloucestershire.

He and Eva would then move to Paris.

There at least they would have a roof that did not leak over their heads.

Eva was delighted because it meant her father was happy.

He had been so miserable after his wife's death, that she thought he would never smile again.

She also knew it was impossible for him to go on living in the wilds of the country without decent horses.

He could not afford servants to run a big house.

Certainly he could not spend money on entertainment or hospitality.

"We will go to Paris, Papa," she said. "I am sure everything will be cheaper there."

Sir Richard was rather doubtful about this.

At the same time he knew that Gloucestershire was making him despondent.

Also it was also not the right place for his daughter.

He was well aware how beautiful she was.

He lay awake at night wondering how he could best present her to the Social World.

Only there would she meet the right sort of men she could marry.

He had no intention of forcing her into marriage.

He wanted her to be as happy as he had been with her mother, but without the scandal.

He had never counted the cost of marrying Lisette de Chabrillin because he was so ideally happy with her.

He knew however, that if he had not caused a scandal, he would have become an Ambassador.

The French had been very vehement in their denunciation of him.

Otherwise he would have been in a very much more important social position than he was now.

Nevertheless, no one could query the antecedents of the Hillingtons.

Yet he thought a little cynically they might be more appreciated in France than they were in England.

Eva was still suffering from the shock of her mother's death.

They had finished disposing of the house in Gloucestershire and everything they possessed.

Then she found that she and her father were as excited as two School-children going off on an adventure.

Eva had never been to Paris.

But Sir Richard had gone there once or twice since his marriage on his way to other Capitals in Europe.

His wife had not been with him.

She had however, talked to her daughter about the land to which she belonged.

She had made Paris seem a Fairy Tale City.

Eva arrived with her father late one evening.

When they had inspected the little house in the Rue St. Honore she knew her mother must have guided them there.

The house, which had belonged to her grandmother through her family and not the Chabrillins, was small but exquisite.

It had been built between two much larger houses

It was Eva thought, a part of her dreams, and she would wake up to find it had vanished.

The *Comtesse* had decorated every room as if it was a marvellous jewel.

Everything seemed to have been specially made or designed for the place in which she had put it.

The bedrooms with their canopied beds of silk and muslins were only fit, Eva thought, for Royalty.

"Now my dearest," her father had said, "we will enjoy together the most civilised and the most exciting City in the world."

He took her to dine at the *Café Anglais*.

It was, he told her, the smartest place in Paris.

It was patronised by everyone who was of any importance

It was certainly full, and a great many of the other diners remembered her father.

From that moment, Eva thought, he was swept away from her, so that she felt as if she had lost him.

He arranged for them to ride in the *Bois* and took her to see one or two of the traditional sights of Paris.

But after that, almost every evening he said:

"Will you forgive me, dearest, if I dine out tonight and leave you on your own?"

"But of course, Papa, but why cannot I come too?"

Sometimes the answer was that the party was for men only.

But often her father was far more evasive and said:

"It is a party at which your mother would not wish you to be present."

"Why not, Papa?" she queried.

"Because, my dear, the ladies, who I admit are very attractive, would not be accepted by your grandmother the *Comtesse* or, for that matter, by any of your Hillington relatives."

He did not say anything more about the friends to whom he went alone.

Eva was naturally very curious about them, and thought perhaps they were some of the ladies she had seen driving in the *Bois*.

They were certainly spectacular.

But the clothes they wore and their horses and carriages appeared to be more suited to the Theatre than to ordinary everyday life.

Then a week ago had come disaster.

It was so terrible that Eva could still not believe it had really happened.

Her father had sat with her while she ate her own dinner at the English hour of seven-thirty.

He had talked to her while she ate.

But he had already told her he was dining later with some of the mysterious friends who she was not allowed to meet.

She thought, as he sat with her in the small beautifully furnished Dining-Room, that he looked very elegant.

He had always seemed rather dashing.

Even though now he was nearing fifty he was still exceedingly handsome.

The few grey hairs appearing at his temples made him look more distinguished than he was already.

He still had a slim, athletic figure.

His evening clothes made in Savile Row fitted him without a wrinkle.

He was wearing, Eva noticed, on the front of his stiff shirt a single pearl surrounded by several small sapphires.

Her mother had given it to him for his birthday three years ago.

Lady Hillington had saved for a whole year to buy it.

It had delighted Sir Richard, not only because it was something he enjoyed wearing.

It was also an expression of his wife's unchanging love.

Eva could remember all too vividly how her father had opened his present, and stared at it incredulously.

He had then put his arms around his wife.

"Thank you very much, my darling," he said. "But how could you give me anything so delightful and so perfect that I can only thank you like this."

As he spoke he kissed her mother passionately.

Eva knew she was forgotten and tactfully crept away to leave them alone.

"You look very smart, Papa," she said as she put down her knife and fork.

"I am glad you think so," he replied, "because I am up against a lot of competition."

"Competition?" Eva enquired.

There was a twist to his lips as he said:

"The lady who is dining with me has already had a dozen other invitations!"

There was a sparkle in his eyes as he spoke.

Eva thought that he was excited at having defeated the other competitors, whoever they might be.

When her father left her she had picked up the book she was reading and gone up to bed.

She read until after midnight, then fell asleep.

She was wakened by the French man-servant who, with his wife, looked after them saying:

"Wake up, *M'mselle*! Wake up!"

Eva did so with a start.

"What is it?" she asked. "What has happened, Henri?"

"It's *Monsieur, M'selle,* he has been brought back, and he is ill, very ill!"

Eva scrambled out of bed and put on her dressing-gown.

Quickly she ran down the stairs to find her father had been carried into the house by two men dressed as coachmen.

They were standing in the Sitting-Room looking at him where he lay on a sofa.

Eva rushed to his side.

He looked as if he was asleep.

Yet at the same time there was something about the pallor of his face and the coldness of his hand.

When she touched it she was terrified.

She sent the coachmen for the Doctor.

By the time he came she knew before he confirmed it that her father was dead.

He had died of a heart-attack.

It was all the more poignant because Eva had never known there was anything wrong with him.

He had always seemed so strong, so well and, as he often said himself:

"I have not a pain in the whole of my body!"

Two days later he had been buried in the Cemetary of the British Embassy.

When the Service was over the British Ambassador, who was present, had said to Eva;

"I expect, my dear, you will want to return to England, and of course, I shall be only too willing to help you in any way I can."

"I thank Your Excellency," Eva answered.

"Well, you know where you can find me," the Ambassador said, "and I shall be expecting to hear from you."

She had come home alone.

Apart from the Ambassador whom she had never met before, she thought despairingly, there was no one she could consult about herself.

She was alone.

She supposed the Ambassador was right in thinking she should return to England.

127

There were a number of her father's family who she felt would offer to look after her.

But it would definitely be as a duty rather than something they wished to do.

She always had the feeling when she was with her father's relatives that they thought it rather odd of him to be so in love with her mother.

Although they had been very pleasant they were not really friendly to a foreigner.

Eva knew her mother had in return found them dull and dowdy.

"*Les Anglais*," she had exclaimed often enough to her small daughter, "have not the gaiety of the French. They seem to take the sparkle out of the air, and even the sun shines less brightly when they come to see me."

"Why is that, Mama?" Eva had asked.

"Because the English are very, very serious, *ma petite*," Lisette Hillington replied. "They are too much concerned with things that are wrong, and not with those that are right."

She had laughed as she spoke.

But, on thinking over what she had said, Eva came to the conclusion that it was true.

Her father's relations nearly always started their sentences with:

"I am afraid this will distress you . . " or "I think you ought to know . . "

One of their favourites was:

"Of course, it is no business of mine, BUT . . "

"I am glad I am half-French, Mama," she had said to her mother.

Lady Hillington had laughed, and kissed her.

"So am I," she had replied, "but you are also your father's daughter, and I thank *le Bon Dieu* there is always a smile on his lips and a twinkle in his eyes."

"That was true," Eva thought.

Because her father had laughed when they had so little money she had laughed too.

"Something will turn up!" he said.

Then, when he saw the pretty little house in Paris, he exclaimed:

"How can we be so lucky as to have anything so lovely all to ourselves? It makes me feel as if your mother was with me because it is so like her."

Looking at the small Salon now, Eva knew exactly what he meant.

"I am here in Paris with Mama," she told herself, "and why should I return to England? Why should I live with Papa's relations in one of those dull, gloomy houses where the furniture is of dark mahogany and the curtains shut out the sun?"

She walked round the room looking at the pictures, the Louis XIV chairs, and a beautiful commode with its gilded handles and feet.

'I could sell some of this,' she thought, 'but instead I will work so that I can keep it just as it is.'

Even to take away one picture or one chair from any of the rooms would make her feel as if she was committing a crime.

She was however, practical enough to know that the small amount of money her father had transferred to the Bank would soon be spent.

Then there would be nothing to pay the servants' wages.

Besides there would be the inevitable question of food.

"But what can I do?" she asked herself.

It was then she remembered something she had not thought of since her father had died.

He had been taken upstairs and undressed before the Doctor arrived.

It was then that Henri the man-servant had noticed that the shirt-stud he had been wearing was missing.

It was the pearl and sapphire one which her mother had given him.

Eva thought when he had his heart attack it must have fallen from his shirt.

She had asked Henri if he knew with whom her father was dining.

She remembered how that he had said, as if he was reluctant to tell her:

"It was *Madame* Leonide Leblanc, *M'mselle*."

In her grief and while she was seeing to all the preparations for the Funeral, Eva had not thought of it again.

Now she decided she would call on *Madame* Leblanc.

She would ask her if she had found her father's shirt-stud.

It would give her something to do, and it was a mistake to sit in the house trying not to cry.

She put on her black bonnet.

Because she had bought it in Paris, it was a very becoming one.

She flung a silk shawl over her shoulders. As it was a warm day it was all she needed.

Her gown, although it was black, revealed the perfection of her figure.

She had never given it a thought, but it showed off the clarity of her skin which was very English.

Also the gold of her hair which she had inherited from her father.

As she came down the stairs she found Henri, who was a middle-aged man in the hall.

He and his wife, who was a little older than he was, ran the whole house.

"You're going out, *M'mselle*?" he enquired.

"Yes, Henri, and I want you to tell me the address of *Madame* Leonide Leblanc."

Henri looked at her in astonishment before he replied.

"Why should you want to know that, *M'mselle*?"

"I intend to call on her to ask her if she has found Papa's pearl shirt-stud. I feel sure it must have fallen off when he collapsed."

Henri looked worried.

"I'll do that for you, *M'mselle*," he said.

"There is no need, Henri," Eva replied. "Just let me have the address."

"It is in the *Rue d'Offemont* but it is not correct, *M'mselle* for you to go to the house of . . ."

Henri paused for the right word, and Eva said:

"But I want to go and I think the lady, who was a great friend of my Father's, would like to see me."

Because Henri seemed incapable of it, she opened the front door herself.

Before he could say any more she had walked out into the street.

If she had looked back she would have seen he was looking after her with a worried expression in his eyes.

She had studied the map of the part of Paris where they were living and she realised that the *Rue d'Offemont* was not far.

It was a sunny day and she felt her spirits lifting above the grief and misery which had encompassed her since her father's death.

As she walked along she had no idea that almost every man who passed her turned to look back.

Nor that there was an expression of admiration in their eyes.

No Frenchman could resist a beautiful woman, and Eva was very lovely.

She reached the street and a *gendarme* told her which house it was.

She raised the very elaborate, highly polished knocker on the door.

It made a loud rat-tat.

The door was opened almost immediately by a servant dressed in what she thought was a very spectacular livery.

"Would it be possible," Eva asked in her perfect French, "for me to speak to *Madame* Leonide Leblanc:"

"I'll ask *Madame* if she's receiving," the servant replied. "Who shall I say is calling?"

"I am Miss Eva Hillington, daughter of the late Sir Richard Hillington."

The servant showed Eva into a room.

It was at the side of what she thought was the rather over-furnished hall.

The furniture was certainly valuable, but there was rather too much of it.

She thought too that the room was somewhat over-crowded and the curtains trimmed with too many tassels.

But what surprised her most were the flowers.

There were huge baskets, vases and bowls of them everywhere.

They were, she noticed, all the most exotic and expensive blooms.

There were orchids, tiger lilies, carnations and Parma violets which could only have come from a different part of France at this time of the year.

The servant reappeared.

"*Madame*'ll see you, *M'mselle* if you'll come upstairs."

The man went ahead and Eva followed him.

When she reached the landing he opened a door and she walked in.

To her surprise, she was in a bedroom, and *Madame* Leblanc was in bed.

It was not like any bedroom Eva had ever seen before.

Apart from the bed which was hung with blue silk curtains from a corolla of gold cupids, the whole place was full of orchids.

There were orchids on tables, and huge vases of them on the floor

It made the place a bower for the striking appearance of its owner.

Leonide Leblanc was much younger than Eva expected.

She was not beautiful, nor even lovely.

But she had a fascinating face. Eva thought it would be very hard to forget her.

Her dark hair fell over her shoulders, and a lace nightgown barely concealed two perfectly rounded and rose pointed breasts.

She held out her hand on which there were several glittering rings and said:

"I am so desperately sorry about your dear father! It must have been a terrible shock for you!"

"It . . it was," Eva replied.

"He was a charming man," Leonide Leblanc went on, "and it would be difficult for a woman to refuse him anything!"

"I know that the night he died, he was delighted with the idea of dining with you, *Madame*."

"I have never known him in such good spirits," *Madame* Leblanc said. "But do sit down."

She pointed to a chair near the bed and, as Eva sat on it, she said:

"*Alors*, but you are very lovely, and that is what I would expect of your father's daughter."

"Thank you," Eva said, "but it will . . never be the same . . without him."

"That I understand," *Madame* Leblanc replied, "but you must be brave. What are you going to do with yourself?"

"Perhaps that is . . something I could . . ask you," Eva said.

"Ask me?"

The idea obviously astonished Leonide Leblanc.

"What I really came for, Madame," Eva said, "was to ask you if you have found my father's shirt-stud. It was a pearl surrounded by several small sapphires, which my mother gave to him."

Madame Leblanc gave a little cry.

"So that is who it belonged to! I wondered who could be the owner when it was found under the bed."

Eva's eyes widened for a moment.

Then she told herself that *Madame* Leblanc had obviously received her father as she was receiving her.

Perhaps he had sat on the very chair on which she was sitting now.

"I will return the stud to you," *Madame* Leblanc said. "In the meantime, tell me what you meant by saying that perhaps I could help you."

She sounded so friendly that Eva bent forward to say:

"I do not know whether or not Papa told you, but we have inherited a little house in the *Rue St. Honoré*. It is so pretty and so charming that I cannot bear to think of leaving it and going back to England as the Ambassador advised me to do."

"You want to stay in Paris?" Leonide Leblanc asked.

"I am half-French," Eva said, "and I know I would be happier here than in England with Papa's relations."

Madame Leblanc smiled as if she could understand that, and Eva continued:

"I have been wondering what I could do, and perhaps you could advise me. If I could find a position, perhaps teaching children, or doing anything, I could stay where I am, and earn enough money to afford it."

Madame Leblanc stared at her.

"Are you saying that your father has not left you any money?"

"Very, very little," Eva replied, "and what there is will not last for long."

"Then I must think," *Madame* Leblanc said.

She was looking at her, Eva thought, in a strange way, almost as if she was appraising her.

She could not help wondering if her appearance was an asset.

It might prove to be the opposite.

Eva was too intelligent not to realise that if she worked for a Lady as a Governess she might be considered too pretty.

Her employer might be jealous of her.

She looked at Leonide Leblanc anxiously.

She was thinking she had never seen anyone who managed to look so fascinating, even though she was in bed and her hair not arranged.

It was then that there was a knock on the door.

"*Entrez!*" *Madame* Leblanc said.

It was the man-servant who had let Eva in and he held in his hand a small gold salver on which lay a card.

Leonide Leblanc read it, then she said:

"Escort *Mademoiselle* Hillington to the Salon, and tell Chef to provide her with English tea. Then bring Lord Charles upstairs."

She said all this very quickly to the man-servant, in what was almost an aside.

Then she said to Eva:

"Listen my dear, I want to continue our conversation and to think how I can help you, but I have an important visitor whom I cannot refuse."

"I understand," Eva said, "and of course I could go and come back another day."

"No, no, that would be a mistake," Leonide Leblanc replied. "Go downstairs and wait until I can see you again. I sometimes have English visitors, so my Chef knows exactly what they always desire at four o'clock!"

She laughed, and because her laughter was so infectious, Eva laughed too.

"Now, run along," Leonide Leblanc said, "and I will not be longer than I can help."

Eva obeyed her, and followed the servant downstairs.

They crossed the hall into a different room from where she had been before.

It was larger and again there seemed to be too much furniture and too many flowers.

Here they were almost overwhelming.

Eva remembered that when she had passed through the hall there had been a number of baskets of orchids and lilies standing just inside the front door.

They had not been there when she first arrived.

"I think *Madame* Leblanc must be an actress," she told herself. "That is why she has so many bouquets, and she must be a very famous one!"

She seated herself on a velvet-covered sofa.

As she did so she wished she had been more inquisitive and made her father tell her more about his friends.

One thing was obvious! *Madame* Leonide Leblanc was very different from anyone she had met before.

Yet she could not help being somewhat shocked.

Madame was receiving her next visitor, who was called Lord Charles, in her bedroom.

Chapter Two

When Eva had left the room Leonide Leblanc got out of bed and went to the dressing-table.

She powdered her nose, touched her lips with salve and sprayed herself with an exotic perfume.

It had been made specially for her.

Then she got back into bed and waited for Lord Charles to be brought upstairs.

Although Eva had no idea of it, Leonide Leblanc was one of *La Garde*.

They were the twelve most famous Courtesans in Paris.

While she was still young, she had already gained the name of '*Madame Maximum*'.

No one was quite certain whether it was due to her fees, her accoutrements or her extravagance.

More likely than anything else it was the number of her lovers.

Leonide had come to Paris with her father when she was five.

He was a shoe-maker in Burly, a small hamlet in the Loire *Département*.

He decided to take his daughter to Paris.

As they had no other means of travel, they had walked there.

A heavy shower of rain just before they reached the Capital of France had made Leonide's shoes unwearable.

She had therefore entered Paris bare-footed.

Her father who was ambitious, wished her to become a Governess and sent her to School.

There she was so clever that she won a number of prizes.

Her intelligence was acclaimed by the teachers.

Leonide, however, had no intention of being anything but an actress.

At fourteen, she ran away and got herself a part on the stage of the *Belleville Theatre* which was on the outskirts of Paris.

From there she moved to the *Théâtre des Variétés* where she was a great success.

But her fascination for men soon made it unnecessary for her to be an actress.

As she was to be described later:

"She was not only very witty, very intelligent, and very ambitious, she was also voluptuousness itself, in flesh and blood."

Leonide's ambition made her bring *La galanterie* up to a fine art, and she soon had the most distinguished lovers in Paris.

Her most important was Henri d'Orleans, Duc d'Aumale.

The Grand Seigneur of Chantilly provided her with the most exquisite furniture and objets d'art that were the envy of everyone who saw them.

Leonide soon became not only one of the sights of Paris, but at Baden-Baden and Homburg.

At the latter, she won half-a-million *francs*.

'*La Vie Parisienne*' and the other magazines and newspapers of France, seldom went to press without mentioning her.

When she was twenty-six she was recognised as the most fascinating woman in the whole of the country.

Now, as she lay back against her pillows, she was thinking of Eva.

She wondered what she could do for Sir Richard Hillington's daughter.

She had found him charming, attractive and she enjoyed being with him without being paid for her favours.

She felt, because he had his fatal attack in her arms that she owed his daughter something.

Although what she could do for the girl she had no idea.

The door opened and Lord Charles came in.

The brother of the Duke of Kincraig, he was an extremely handsome young man with an infectious *joie de vivre* which made him popular wherever he went.

He had pursued Leonide relentlessly every time he was in Paris.

Finally she had succumbed to his importuning.

Even though he was in no position to give her the money or presents which her other lovers lavished on her.

She liked him because he was an aristocrat.

She found him very accomplished in bed and very amusing out of it.

He burst into the room now, walked across to Leonide, put his arms round her, and kissed her.

Then he sat down on the bed and said:

"*Ma Belle*, I am in trouble!"

"Not again!"

"This is worse than usual."

"How?"

"Because, my adorable Siren, I cannot see a way out unless you can think of one."

"Then I will try,Charles," Leonide said, "although I have no intention of paying your debts."

"It is not my debts," Lord Charles replied, "but it is a millstone round my neck, and fetters that I cannot remove from my legs."

Leonide settled herself more comfortably against her
pillows.

"Now, start from the beginning," she said, "so that I can understand what you are saying."

She was speaking French.

Lord Charles was speaking in the same language, with a decided British accent.

At the same time, he was surprisingly fluent, and he began:

"When I was here a month ago the Millionaire Banker Raphael Bischoffheim asked me to find him some horses."

Leonide gave a little cry.

"I had heard that Bischoffheim had started a racing stable" she said, "and of course, English horses have so far done very well in France."

"That is why he asked me to buy him six or eight outstanding animals," Lord Charles replied, "and from the top owners in England."

"And you obliged?"

"They are arriving tomorrow."

"Then – what is wrong?" Leonide asked. "I am quite sure you will make Bischoffheim 'pay through the nose' for them!"

"That is what I intend he shall do," Lord Charles said, "although actually, because they are the most superb animals you will ever have seen, he will be getting a bargain however much he pays for them!"

"I believe you," Leonide smiled, "although a lot of people would not!"

"I arrived, as you know, yesterday," Lord Charles went on, "and came to see you; then, before I visited Bischoffheim, I went to the Club to hear the latest gossip."

"I am sure that was most informative," Leonide remarked a little sarcastically.

Lord Charles drew in his breath.

"I was told by a friend of mine that Bischoffheim, while looking forward to owning the horses, has also decided I would make an excellent husband for his eldest daughter!"

Leonide stared at him.

"I cannot believe that is true!"

"I can," Lord Charles replied. "The ambitious Banker not only intends to set up one of the best racing stables in France, but he also wishes to shine in England."

There was silence. Then Leonide said:

"It seems incredible, absolutely incredible! But what can you do?"

"That is what I came to ask you," Lord Charles replied.

He thought for a minute. Then he added:

"You can imagine what my brother would say if I suggested bringing Bischoffheim's daughter into the family. Besides, as you are well aware, I have no desire to marry anyone!"

"Do you really think," Leonide asked after a pause, "that if you refuse to do as he wishes, he will tell you to take your horses back to England?"

"I am fairly certain that is exactly what he plans. He knows I am heavily in debt, which is nothing new: he knows I have bought these horses on credit, and quite frankly, Leonide, I am in a tight corner with not the slightest notion of how to get out of it!"

"But you have to!" Leonide cried.

She looked at the handsome young man sitting opposite her, with his fair hair, blue eyes and clear complexion.

Then she saw Raphael Bischoffheim.

He was small, dark, a large nose, and a dazzlingly brilliant brain, but absolutely no breeding.

The aristocrats with whom Leonide associated, both French and English, had made it clear to her how much breeding mattered to them.

She was aware that Lord Charles was in what he had said himself, a 'very tight corner'.

"Come on," he was saying, "you have the reputation of being the cleverest woman in France. For God's sake, Leonide, save me! Think of what I can do, and what I can say."

"Bischoffheim is a hard man," Leonide said slowly. "If he has set his heart on marrying his daughter to an aristocrat, I will wager every *franc* I possess that somehow he will do it!"

"But not to me!" Lord Charles replied. "I am damned if I will marry a French girl who has nothing to offer except her father's money."

"You could do with it!" Leonide remarked.

"Not at the price of my freedom, and frankly, I would not soil the Family Tree with the name of Bischoffheim!"

"That is something you cannot say to him!" Leonide remarked.

"That is what I will have to say if he presses me, and what is more I will then have to take the horses back to England."

Lord Charles got off the bed and walked restlessly across the bedroom and back again.

"I had to go on my knees to get the horses I wanted," he said. "I even bought one from the Royal Stud!"

There was silence. Then he said:

"For God's sake, Leonide, tell me what I am to do! What *can* I do?"

There was another silence, then Leonide gave a little cry.

"I have it!" she said. "I have the perfect solution!"

Lord Charles went back to the bed to sit where he had sat before.

"What is it?" he asked.

"You must tell Raphael Bischoffheim before he tells you what he desires, that you are engaged to be married!"

"Engaged to be married?" Lord Charles asked. "But to whom? He is unlikely to believe that I have a *fiancée* in England if it has not been announced in *'The Gazette'!*"

"You will produce your *fiancée*," Leonide said slowly, "here in Paris!"

Lord Charles stared at her. Then he said.

"Leonide, you are a genius! But you will have to produce the girl, and she will have to look the part. Bischoffheim is no fool!"

"I am aware of that," Leonide replied, "and what you are saying is that she must be a Lady, and look like a Lady."

She saw the look in Lord Charles' eyes and added:

"It is all right. She will know she is acting a part, and you do not really wish to marry her, but you will have to pay her."

"I would give her the Crown Jewels, if she will get me out of this mess!" Lord Charles said impulsively.

"Be careful," Leonide said. "You have to make a profit on the deal."

Lord Charles laughed.

"Leonide, I adore you! Tell me exactly what you have planned."

Leonide hesitated, and he thought she was choosing her words.

"I know of a girl," she began, "who is definitely a Lady, but needs money so that she can stay in Paris."

"If she is good looking, I should not think there as any difficulty about what she can do!" Lord Charles said.

"I have told you she is a Lady," Leonide said sharply, "and if you are going to treat her as a *jolie poule* you can find your own solution to the problem."

Lord Charles flung up his hands.

"I am sorry, I apologise! Go on, I am listening."

"I will produce her," Leonide said, "on one condition and one condition only."

"What is that?"

"That you do not touch her, you do not try to make love to her, and you leave her exactly as you find her: a very pure and very innocent young girl."

Lord Charles stared at her.

"And you are going to produce her for me? Come on, Leonide, as you know, I adore you, but that does not sound as if she is likely to be a friend of yours or entrusted to you by her parents as a counsellor."

"That is my business!" Leonide said. "Do you, or do you not promise what I have asked you?"

"I promise! Cross my heart, and on the word of a gentleman!"

"Very well, this is what you must do."

She was obviously thinking out the programme ahead of him and Lord Charles waited in silence.

He was thinking as he looked at Leonide that there was no other Courtesan who could manage to be a friend to her lovers.

Nor was there one to whom he could have gone for help.

Leonide was different, and he was well aware that to some of her lovers she talked Politics and to others Art.

Quite a number of men visited her whenever they came to Paris, just because they admired and liked her.

After he had waited for some time, Leonide asked:

"When are you getting in touch with Bischoffheim?"

"He has asked me to luncheon tomorrow, and I planned that afterwards we would go straight to his stables where the horses would have been delivered during the morning."

"Good!" Leonide exclaimed. "Now, what you have to do is to write him a note saying how much you are looking forward to seeing him, and to showing him what you have purchased on his behalf."

At the thought of the horses Lord Charles's lips tightened, but he did not interrupt.

"Then you will add that you are bringing with you someone you are anxious for him to meet."

"I do not say who it is?" Lord Charles questioned.

"No, not if the person is male or female. When you arrive you introduce her, at the same time swearing Bischoffheim to secrecy because your engagement has not been officially announced since your *fiancée* who is half-French, has not yet met your brother."

"It sounds too good to be true," Lord Charles said. "The only thing is – what is she like?"

"She will look the part, she will act the part, and you will keep your promise to me," Leonide said.

"All right," Lord Charles agreed. "At the same time, you had better fill in the gaps."

"I will do that tomorrow, when you collect her here at twelve noon," Leonide replied. "Now we have to decide how much you will pay her."

"What she gets will entirely depend on whether Bischoffheim coughs up, but at the moment my pockets are 'To Let'!" Lord Charles said.

"That is what I expected," Leonide replied. "And because there will be no reason for him not to buy the horses after he has asked you to procure them for him, you will receive a cheque. I think my little *protégée* should receive – now, let me think . ."

"For God's sake, Leonide!" Lord Charles exclaimed "Leave me a few *francs* with which to enjoy myself. I might even buy you some orchids, as you seem so short of them!"

He was speaking facetiously, but Leonide paid no attention.

She was in fact calculating *francs* into pounds.

"I propose £500," she said.

Because Lord Charles had been frightened that it might be more, he held out his hand.

"Done!" he said, "but if she is not perfect in her part and Bischoffheim 'puts the boot in', she gets nothing!"

"Agreed!" Leonide said, and put her hand in his.

His fingers tightened and he kissed it, then bending forward he said:

"As usual, I find you irresistible!"

. . . .

Downstairs, Eva began to think that *Madame* Leblanc had forgotten her very existence.

She had eaten a large tea, in fact the *pâtisserie* were so delicious that she had been greedy and eaten two.

Then she inspected the Salon.

She found there was a collection of snuff-boxes that she was sure her father must have admired.

They were ornamented with diamonds, pearls and other precious stones.

Some of them also contained miniatures of the French Kings.

There was a beautiful collection of pink *Sèvres* on the mantelpiece which was very rare.

There were ornaments in jade and pink quartz which she was sure were extremely valuable.

Even while she was admiring such a wonderful collection of treasures she kept wondering what she should do.

How would it be possible for her to earn some money?

Perhaps if *Madame* Leblanc was on the stage she could find her a small part in the Theatre.

She was quite certain, however, that her mother would have been horrified at the idea.

"Why did I not discuss it with Papa before he died?" she asked herself.

She knew that if she had done so her father would merely have said in his happy-go-lucky way that 'something would turn up'.

She tried not to think that his Funeral had cost her a great deal, and that food in France seemed far more expensive than in England.

Of course at home they had had their own chickens and ducks.

In the winter, her father had shot the birds in the woods.

While the goods they had bought in the village shop had not seemed as expensive as those which Marie, who was Henri's wife, bought in the market.

"There must be something I can do!" Eva said to herself despairingly.

They were the same words that had echoed in her mind last night and the night before.

She was wondering whether she should go into the hall and ask if *Madame* Leblanc had really forgotten her.

Then a servant appeared and she was told she could go upstairs again.

She thought that *Madame*'s visitor, Lord Charles, had certainly been very long-winded.

However she hoped that *Madame* Leblanc had had time to think of her as well as of him.

She entered the bedroom and thought as she had before how attractive its owner looked.

There was a faint flush on her cheeks and her eyes seemed to be shining.

Although it might have been the sunshine coming through the windows.

"I am sorry to have been so long, *Ma cherie*," *Madame* Leblanc said, "but I know you will excuse me for having kept you waiting when I tell you that I have found employment for you."

Eva clasped her hands together.

"You have? How very, very kind of you! I have been praying that you would somehow find a solution to my problems."

Leonide Leblanc smiled a little wryly.

"I seem to have had quite a number of problems today," she said. "But I have solved yours, at least for the moment. Now sit down and let me tell you what you have to do."

Eva obeyed her and *Madame* Leblanc took a sip of what looked surprisingly like champagne, from a glass that was standing on a table by her bed.

Then Eva thought she must be mistaken.

She could not imagine anyone would drink champagne in bed.

At home her father and mother would occasionally open a bottle to celebrate a birthday or an anniversary and of course, at Christmas.

At other times it had been too expensive.

Then her father drank claret or white wine, while her mother preferred lemonade.

Leonide Leblanc took another sip. Then she said:

"Now, what you have to do is to act a part."

Eva gave a little cry.

"I was thinking," she said, "that because you must be on the stage and a very, very clever actress, that perhaps you could find room for me in the Theatre."

"It is not in the Theatre," Leonide replied sharply, "and as your father's daughter, I would not think of sending you on the stage."

Eva looked at her wide-eyed.

Then she flushed and said:

"I know Mama would not have . . approved . . but . . I thought perhaps it was the . . only thing I could . . do."

"It is something you should not do!" Leonide said, "and when I said 'act a part', this is something for which you are very well qualified."

Eva looked at her enquiringly, and *Madame* Leblanc went on:

"My last visitor, who has just left, was Lord Charles Craig, and he is in a difficult situation."

Eva had now heard his surname for the first time.

Although it sounded somewhat familiar, she did not remember any of her father's friends having the name of Craig.

"Lord Charles," Leonide Leblanc continued, "is a charming young man who has never been married and has *no wish to be.*"

She spoke slowly, accentuating the last four words as if she wished to impress them upon Eva.

"He has, however," she went on, "become involved in an unfortunate situation through no fault of his own."

"What is it?" Eva asked.

"I do not suppose you have heard of the most influential Banker in Paris whose name is Raphael Bischoffheim?"

Eva shook her head.

"He has decided, and no one could afford it better, to have race horses which will outrun and beat those belonging to the members of the Jockey Club."

Eva smiled.

She could understand his ambition.

Her father had told her about the Jockey Club and how important its members were.

"*Monsieur* Bischoffheim asked Lord Charles to procure for him a number of horses from England, from the very best stables."

Leonide Leblanc threw out her hands as she finished and laughed.

"Now Lord Charles has found an obstacle that he had not foreseen."

"An obstacle?" Eva asked.

"*Monsieur* Bischoffheim wants Lord Charles to marry his daughter!"

Eva looked surprised.

"But . . surely . . ?" she began.

"Exactly!" Leonide Leblanc replied. "It is impossible for Lord Charles to marry *Monsieur* Bischoffheim's girl, however attractive she might be. And his brother, the Duke of Kincraig, would be furious at the idea!"

"I can understand that," Eva said.

She was wondering as she spoke how she came into the story.

"There is only one way," Leonide Leblanc went on, "by which Lord Charles can obtain the money he has expended on the horses, without offending *Monsieur* Bischoffheim by refusing to become his son-in-law."

Eva did not have to ask the question which trembled on her lips.

Leonide Leblanc added dramatically:

"If Lord Charles produces a *fiancée*!"

"Oh!" Eva exclaimed. "Then he is already engaged to be married!"

"I have already said that he has no intention of marrying anyone!" Leonide Leblanc replied.

"Then . . how . . how . . can he . . ?"

"Do not be stupid," Leonide Leblanc said. "Lord Charles will produce *you* as his *fiancée*!"

"Me?"

"You have to pretend that you are the girl to whom he is engaged to be married!"

She paused a moment and then continued:

"When Lord Charles receives the cheque for the horses, which will amount to quite a considerable sum, you will discreetly disappear."

Eva looked bewildered.

"B . but . . suppose . . ?" she began.

"It is quite an easy thing for you to do," Leonide Leblanc said sharply. "You just have to be yourself, but you will of course have a different name, and even Lord Charles must not be aware of your real identity."

"Why not?" Eva asked.

"Because, my dear, it would embarrass him. Besides, if it was known in England that you had pretended to be engaged to a very distinguished young man, it would ruin your reputation, and certainly your chances of marrying the type of man your father would wish you to marry."

"Yes . . of course . . I understand," Eva said nervously. "Then . . who am I to . . be?"

Leonide Leblanc smiled.

"What is more important, and what you should be asking is how much is he going to pay you for doing this."

"But . . surely . . I do not . . have to . . ask him?" Eva said quickly. "I . . I would find that . . very embarrassing!"

"Of course you would! And that is why I have arranged it all for you. If you act your part convincingly and *Monsieur* Bischoffheim gives up his ridiculous idea of Lord Charles marrying his daughter, you will receive £500!"

Eva gave a gasp.

She knew that the average Governess in England received about forty pounds a year!

If she was careful £500 would enable her to let in her little house for quite a long time without worrying about money.

Because she was so surprised she said the first thing that came into her head.

"It . . it is . . too much!"

Leonide Leblanc laughed and held up her hands.

"Never refuse money, *ma Cherie*! Never say any sum is too much when you have to work for it, and in this case accept with gratitude what the gods are giving you."

"I think really I should be . . thanking you," Eva said. "How can you be so kind to me? I am so very . . very . . grateful!"

"I was fond of your father," Leonide Leblanc replied, "and I am repaying him for many hours of happiness we spent together."

"Then I am sure Papa . . wherever he is now . . is also very grateful to you," Eva said in a soft voice.

There was a little silence.

Then, as if Leonide Leblanc was afraid of becoming sentimental, she said:

"Now, let us get to work. I presume you have some clothes that *Monsieur* Bischoffheim will think suited a young English Lady, engaged to the brother of the Duke of Kincraig?"

"They are . . not very smart, I am afraid," Eva said apologetically, "but I have some of my mother's gowns with me which I can wear, but of course . . they are not black."

"You are not to wear black!" Leonide Leblanc exclaimed in horror. "You have to look happy, and who would not be happy if they were marrying Lord Charles?"

She thought for a moment. Then she said:

"I will send my maid back with you to your house and she can iron and tidy up what you have and perhaps add a ribbon trimming or lace to a gown if it looks too dull."

"That would be . . very kind," Eva said.

"And now we have to decide what you will call yourself."

"My name is Eva."

"That would be suitable as you have an English mother and a French father."

Eva laughed.

"The reverse is the truth."

"Of course, but you have to explain why you are in France, and not in England."

"And what is to be my French name?"

It flashed through Eva's mind that she might call herself 'Chabrillin' which had been her mother's name before she married.

Then she thought that might be dangerous in case *Monsieur* Bischoffheim knew any of the family.

"You will be Venarde," Leonide Leblanc decided. "'Eva Venarde'. It is very attractive, and you will not wish to talk a great deal about your family, so *Monsieur* Bischoffheim will not know."

"It would be embarrassing if he . . asked questions," Eva said.

"Then you must just be clever enough to speak gaily about something else."

"I will . . try . . I will try to do everything you tell me," Eva said humbly.

As she spoke she knew that her heart was singing.

£500 would mean that she could stay in Paris!

She could live in her own exquisite little house, and for the moment she was not afraid of the future.

Then as if Leonide Leblanc was looking at her for the first time, she said:

"You are very lovely! In fact beautiful, so perhaps I could give you a little advice, which I hope you will follow."

"You know I will do anything you say," Eva said. "I am so very grateful for your kindness to me."

"You can keep your thanks until the £500 is in your hand, and Lord Charles can leave Paris a free man."

"I am only . . afraid I shall . . make a mistake," Eva said.

"Why should you?" Leonide Leblanc asked. "You just have to be yourself, but remember, you are a very correct, prim and proper little English girl and you are embarrassed by fulsome compliments."

She paused for a moment before she said:

"And you quite understand – you do not allow any man to touch you."

"Touch me?" Eva exclaimed in surprise. "You mean . . they must not hold my hand?"

"I mean they must not kiss you!"

"I cannot imagine anyone would want to do that unless they knew me well," Eva said.

"No, of course not, and they would not have the opportunity if your mother was there to chaperon you."

Eva looked at her with frightened eyes.

"I . . I did not think of that . . and surely . . *Monsieur* Bischoffheim and Lord Charles would think it . . strange of me to be staying alone in my house in the Rue St. Honoré without a chaperon?"

"That is just what I was going to say to you," Leonide Leblanc said. "You must never reveal to either of them exactly where you are staying, or that you are living alone."

Eva's eyes widened and she went on:

"You are intelligent enough to say convincingly that you have your Aunt with you, but she is at the moment in bed with a bad cold and therefore cannot receive visitors."

She paused before she added:

"Neither can you, so if any man suggests coming to your house, you explain very politely that it would not be correct as your Aunt is ill."

"Yes, of course . . I understand," Eva said, "and it was very stupid of me not to think of that before."

She thought as she spoke that it was something of which in future she should certainly be careful.

She could not however imagine she would meet many men who would indicate that they would wish to call on her.

If they did, that was the answer.

Leonide Leblanc took another sip from her glass.

Then she said:

"I will ring for my maid Josie and tell her what I wish her to do, and also give you your father's shirt-stud."

She rang the bell by her bed as she spoke.

A few seconds later the door opened.

A maid dressed in black with a tiny lace-trimmed apron came into the room.

She was not young, in fact she was a woman of nearly forty.

She looked at Eva in what seemed to be a surprised fashion.

"This, Josie," Leonide Leblanc said, "is the daughter of Sir Richard Hillington, whom you will remember was taken ill here a week ago."

"Yes, indeed, *Madame* the poor gentleman! I was so sorry for him."

"Well, apparently it was his shirt-stud we found later," Leonide Leblanc said. "I want you to give it to Miss Hillington, and also, Josie, to go back to her house with her, to look at her clothes."

Now the maid was definitely surprised, and Leonide Leblanc said:

"I have set Miss Hillington a little task which will oblige me, and it is important that she should be correctly dressed for what she has to do."

Josie looked curiously at what Eva was wearing at the moment as her mistress went on:

"She requires something smart and very ladylike to wear tomorrow for luncheon. You understand, Josie. She is a *jeune fille*, and must not in any way be flamboyant."

"I know exactly what *M'mselle* needs," Josie replied. "When I was with the Ambassadress I was in England for three years and *Oh là* the English *jeunes filles* are dowdy, drab and dull!"

She was speaking in French, thinking perhaps that only her mistress would understand.

Then Eva burst out laughing.

"*Mademoiselle* speaks perfect French, Josie," Leonide Leblanc said.

"*Pardon, M'mselle,*" Josie said. "I did not mean to be insulting!"

"What you said is true," Eva said. "I understand because my mother was French, and often said the same thing!"

Then as she thought she had been indiscreet she looked at Leonide Leblanc.

"A slip of the tongue," Leonide said, "but remember in future to be very careful. Your mother was English, and your father was French."

"I . . I will remember," Eva said.

"Now, hurry, Josie, and put on your bonnet," Leonide Leblanc said, "for I shall want you back because you must help me dress."

"*Mais oui, Madame* I shall be very quick."

She went from the room and Eva rose to her feet.

"What can I say?" she asked.

"You will thank me by doing exactly what I have told you," Leonide Leblanc replied. "Lord Charles is a dear friend of mine and I wish to please him. I also want to help you because of your father. And as it is, everything is very satisfactory!"

"Very . . very . . satisfactory!" Eva agreed.

She took Leonide Leblanc's hand, then impulsively bent forward to kiss her.

For a moment the Frenchwoman seemed surprised. Then she smiled.

"You are very sweet," she said, "and I hope, one day, you will marry somebody as nice as your father, and be very, very happy."

"That is what I have always wanted," Eva replied.

Chapter Three

Josie was on the whole quite complimentary about Eva's clothes.

They were very simple, but as she said, correct for a *jeune fille*.

However, as a Frenchwoman, she could not resist adding little touches of *chic*.

Eva thought they made all the difference.

A bow on the shoulder, lace round the sleeves and a few silk flowers on the hem of the skirt.

They transformed what had been a very ordinary gown into something which might easily have been worn by a young French girl.

"Thank you, thank you," Eva said.

Looking at the clock Josie said she must return to *Madame* Leblanc.

She had obviously been impressed by the elegance of the house.

Now she looked round her and said in the voice of a disapproving Nanny:

"You should not be living here alone, *M'mselle!*"

"But I am very happy, even though I miss my father," Eva protested.

"*Vous êtes très belle*, and you need a chaperon."

"I have already promised *Madame* that I will behave in a very circumspect way," Eva said defensively. "I will pretend that my Aunt, who is very strict, is in bed with a cold."

Josie laughed.

"*M'mselle* is clever, but you are very young."

"I will get older," Eva said, "and if things are too difficult, I will go back to England."

She was not quite certain what she meant by "too difficult".

It must somehow involve men who would want to kiss her.

The men whom Leonide Leblanc had warned her against.

"Once I have done what Lord Charles requires of me," she told herself consolingly, "then I shall not be meeting any Social people. I shall visit the *musées* and try to paint a picture which will be saleable."

On thinking it over she thought that was the only way she could make money.

It would now prevent her from becoming involved with men.

Her mother had praised her water colours.

When she had tried her hand at oils, she had, after many mistakes, produced quite a good portrait.

It was of one of her father's horses.

She wondered if she could afford to have lessons, knowing there must be many artists in Paris who could teach her.

Then she knew that to be concerned with Artists, Poets and Writers who were to be found on the Left Bank might be dangerous.

More so, she felt than being involved with the Social World which her father had enjoyed.

"I shall just have to be like Papa and hope that 'something turns up'," she told herself philosophically.

She was, however, so excited by the idea of earning so much money that she found it hard to sleep.

Only when dawn was breaking did she fall into a heavy slumber.

She dreamt that she was riding a fast horse.

She was being pursued round a race-track by a lot of strange men who were also on horse-back.

She woke up and laughed at her dream.

As she dressed she knew she felt elated, as if something very exciting was about to happen.

At the same time, she felt very nervous in case she did anything wrong.

She sent up a little prayer to her father saying:

"Please . . Papa . . help me! You will know what Lord Charles is like, and also *Monsieur* Bischoffheim. You must prevent me from saying . . anything which will . . spoil *Madame* Leblanc's plans."

She arranged her hair very carefully and put on the gown that Josie had pressed.

Although she was not aware of it, it made her look very young and innocent.

It was white with a full skirt, and a bodice which just showed the curves of her figure.

Josie had added a little bow of blue ribbon on the shoulder.

There was another on the opposite side of her waist.

A little round hat sat on the back of her head like a halo, with blue ribbons trailing down her back.

She was getting ready to walk, as she had yesterday, to Madame Leblanc's house in the *Rue d'Offemont*.

Henri came upstairs to knock on the door.

"*Entrez*," Eva called out.

Henri came in.

"There's a carriage arrived for you, *M'mselle*," he said.

"For me?" Eva exclaimed in surprise.

Then she realised who had sent it, and added:

"How very kind of *Madame* to think of me!"

She drove off feeling very grand in the most elaborate and spectacular carriage she had ever seen.

It was only then that she remembered she should not have walked alone through the streets yesterday to visit *Madame* Leblanc.

Her mother had told her that when she went to London to shop, or if she walked in the Park, she would have to be accompanied by a house-maid.

"How tiresome, Mama!" Eva had exclaimed at the time.

"I agree with you," her mother said, "but it would not be at all *comme il fait* for a *jeune fille* to wander about alone."

When they had first come to Paris her father had accompanied her everywhere.

It had therefore never crossed her mind that she should not walk about the streets without somebody being with her.

This created a problem for the future.

Marie was getting on in years.

Eva was quite certain that having already been to market, she would not wish to venture out again.

The horses trotted quickly through the streets.

Eva found herself thinking despairingly that, once she was alone, there would be a great many difficulties

The carriage drew up outside *Madame* Leblanc's house.

The footman on the box opened the door with a flourish.

The Butler whom she had seen yesterday smiled at her.

"*Bonjour, M'mselle!*" he said. "*Madame*'s expecting you if you'll go upstairs to her bedroom."

Eva walked up the stairs, knocked on the door and heard Leonide Leblanc call out: "*Entrez!*"

153

She went in, expecting to find her in bed, as she had been yesterday.

But she was dressed and, while Josie was arranging her hair, she was putting the finishing touches to her face.

She had looked fascinating yesterday.

But now Eva saw she was very smart and very elegantly dressed.

It would be impossible, she thought, for anyone who saw her not to stare at her in astonishment.

Her gown was certainly too flamboyant to be worn by any Englishwoman.

Not only was her face powdered and painted, but she had added mascara to her eye-lashes, and her lips were crimson.

What was more, she was wearing a necklace, ear-rings, and bracelets of rubies and diamonds.

They glittered in the sunshine.

They made her whole appearance not only striking, but also theatrical.

"*Bonjour*, Eva!" Leonide Leblanc said.

She turned from the dressing-table at which she was sitting.

She was looking at Eva's appearance, and now she said:

"*Tres bien*! You look exactly as I would want you to do, and I can see that Josie had added French *chic* to your shoulder and your hair."

"She was very kind and helpful," Eva said.

As they were talking, Josie brought from another room a hat which Leonide Leblanc was going to wear.

It was the same colour as her gown.

It was covered with ospreys which shimmered with every move.

It was so fantastic that Eva stared at it and Leonide Leblanc said with a smile:

"I am going for my drive in the *Bois*. The carriage which brought you here will be open. Every day I appear in a new *toilette* and generally with a new livery for my servants!"

"You look marvellous!" Eva exclaimed.

Leonide Leblanc laughed.

"Now perhaps you understand why,when you leave here with Lord Charles, you must never admit to knowing me."

"But, why?" Eva asked.

"Be sensible, my dear," Leonide Leblanc replied. "Can you imagine your mother or your mythical Aunt who is in bed with a cold being seen dressed like this?"

Because the way she spoke was so funny, Eva laughed.

"No, *Madame*, and if they did so in London they would stop the traffic!"

"That is what I try to do in Paris," Leonide Leblanc said complacently. "In fact, there are quite a number of people who go to the *Bois* specially to see me!"

Josie put the hat on her head.

"I do not think this outfit is as smart as the one I wore the day before yesterday," Leonide Leblanc complained.

"I like it better, *Madame*!" Josie said firmly. "And you said yourself that the black coachmen in a white livery were a mistake."

To Eva it sounded fantastic, but she said nothing.

She was aware that Leonide Leblanc shrugged her shoulders.

Josie pinned the hat to her hair with long hat-pins which were encrusted with diamonds.

She rose, still looking at her reflection in the mirror.

"I am bored with these rubies," she said. "Send them back to my jeweller and tell him to re-set them."

"Very well, *Madame*," Josie said in a resigned tone as if this was something she did frequently.

"Tell him to send the bill to the *Duc* or, better still, I will get him to give me a necklace of emeralds. I am tired of the one I possess already."

Leonide Leblanc did not wait for an answer.

She merely walked towards Eva saying:

"Lord Charles is downstairs and we have kept him waiting long enough. Now remember, you are a girl who has fallen on hard times. You need money, but you are a Lady, and outside this house you know nothing of women like myself."

She spoke with a mocking note in her voice, but Eva said:

"I know that you are very kind, *Madame*, and that I shall always remember you in my prayers."

For a moment Leonide Leblanc was still.

Then she said quickly:

"Come along, come along! I have to drive in the *Bois* and you and Lord Charles must have a little talk before you go to visit *Monsieur* Bischoffheim."

They went down the stairs, and a man-servant opened the door into the Salon.

Leonide Leblanc swept in.

155

Lord Charles, who had been sitting on the sofa reading a news-paper, rose to his feet.

"I thought you had forgotten me," he said.

"How could I do that?" Leonide Leblanc replied.

As she spoke, Eva thought there was a different note in her voice from the way she had been speaking to her.

She could not describe it, but it was somehow, for want of a better word, 'Caressing', and Eva thought, "inviting".

Leonide Leblanc gave Lord Charles her hand and he raised it to his lips.

For a moment Eva thought they were speaking to each other without words.

Then Leonide Leblanc said quickly:

"Now I want you to meet Eva Venarde, who has promised to help you and will, I know, do exactly what you require of her."

Eva had walked in somewhat slowly behind Leonide Leblanc.

Lord Charles had not even glanced at her.

Now he stared at her.

She thought it was in a somewhat insulting manner before he exclaimed:

"Leonide, you are brilliant! I called you a genius, but now I know you are a Genie, and can magic up everything a man could desire!"

Leonide Leblanc smiled at him before she said:

"You are not to frighten Eva. She has never done anything like this before, and you have a great many things to explain to her."

"You are leaving?" Lord Charles asked.

"Why do you think I am dressed like this?" Leonide enquired. "My public is waiting, and I must not disappoint them!"

"I will see you to your carriage."

He put his hand under her arm and drew her across the room.

Only when she was alone did Eva think that he had in fact, been rather rude to her.

Undoubtedly he was very good-looking in a typically English manner.

At the same time, he frightened her.

As she waited for his return she wished she did not have to do anything so complicated to earn £500.

Then she told herself she was being very ungrateful.

What other girl would have had such a splendid opportunity?

"I can stay in Paris," she said beneath her breath, "and live in my perfect little house so I must be sensible and not complain whatever happens."

Lord Charles came back into the room and she was still standing where he had left her.

He smiled at her pleasantly, then said:

"Let me compliment you or shall I congratulate Leonide ? You look exactly as I wanted you to look!"

"Thank you!" Eva said. "And I hope I will not make any mistakes."

"Suppose we sit down and talk about it?" Lord Charles suggested. "I have ordered a bottle of champagne, and I think a drink is what we both need."

Eva looked at him in surprise.

She supposed that gentlemen like Lord Charles started drinking early in the day.

She was certain it was something of which her mother would not approve.

The servant must have had the champagne ready.

He came into the room with a bottle and poured out two glasses.

He handed one to Eva from the gold salver, then another to Lord Charles.

Eva took it because she thought it would be a mistake to refuse.

She only took a tiny sip.

Then she set the glass down on a small table near the sofa.

When they were alone again Lord Charles said:

"I suppose Leonide has told you why you are doing this to help me?"

"I am pretending .. to be your .. *fiancée*," Eva said a little hesitatingly, "but I think you should .. tell me how long we have known each other .. and if we met in France .. or in England."

"In France!" Lord Charles said firmly. "If Bischoffheim talks about you to any of my English friends, they will think it strange they have not heard of you before."

"Oh, I understand," Eva exclaimed, "and *Madame* Leblanc said I was to say that my father was French."

"That I think would account for the fact that according to Leonide, you speak French perfectly, which Bischoffheim would not expect of an English girl."

"You make it much clearer for me to understand," Eva said.

"What I want to do," Lord Charles went on, "once we have

established the fact that we are engaged to be married and Bischoffheim has coughed up what he owes me, is to make certain there will be no more difficulties."

"I . . I hope not," Eva said.

"You sound doubtful," Lord Charles exclaimed. "What is worrying you?"

"Nothing really," Eva replied, "except that my mother always said I was a very bad liar, and I am afraid of . . letting you down."

Lord Charles laughed.

"I am sure you will not do that, and Leonide, who is an excellent judge of character, assured me that you would be perfect in the part."

He drank some more of the champagne. Then he said:

"You look stunning! How on earth did Leonide find anyone like you at such short notice?"

Eva was just about to say that she had called on her, then thought perhaps it would be a mistake.

Instead she said:

"I think it would be wrong for me to remember anything except that I am your *fiancée* and we are looking forward to being married."

Lord Charles looked at her sharply. Then he laughed.

"So you are being evasive! You are quite right! Of course, keep your secret and, as you say, we must stick to the script."

He glanced at the clock on the mantelpiece.

"Bischoffheim asked us to be there early," he said, "so I suggest we drive to his house which, as you can imagine, is very luxurious and important, and is in the *Champs Elysées*."

"Is he so very, very wealthy?" Eva asked.

"He is as rich as Midas, and everything he touches turns to gold," Lord Charles replied. "It is said the whole Empire would collapse without him, and certainly the members of the *Bourse* grovel at his feet."

"You sound as though you do not like him," Eva said.

Lord Charles smiled.

"I have a great affection for his money," he replied

He said it in a way which made Eva laugh.

Then as Lord Charles rose to his feet he remarked:

"You have not drunk your champagne!"

Eva was about to say that she did not want it so early in the morning, but instead she replied:

"I do not think your *fiancée* My Lord . . would drink, except on special occasions."

"You are quite right," Lord Charles agreed. "At the same time, you need not keep up this pretence when we are alone."

He paused a moment and then went on:

"I find you very interesting and lovely, and I want to hear the true story of why, looking like you do, you are not as rich as Leonide."

Eva did not understand what he was implying, so she merely said:

"I expect the real answer is that I am not as clever as she is."

As she spoke she walked out of the Salon and therefore did not see the look in Lord Charles's eyes.

The carriage waiting outside for them could in no way be compared to Leonide's.

The roof was open and the coachman driving it was properly dressed.

But Eva thought it was just the kind of vehicle which might have been hired from a superior Livery Stable.

The two horses which drew it were certainly not to be compared to those owned by Leonide Leblanc.

Eva, however, thought it was a mistake to ask questions.

As they drove along she realised that while Lord Charles seemed at his ease, he was in fact slightly nervous.

Because she was curious, she could not help asking:

"If *Monsieur* Bischoffheim is really angry because you will not marry his daughter, what will happen about the horses you have bought for him?"

"He could refuse to pay for them," Lord Charles replied, "in which case, I shall have to look for another buyer, or find myself bankrupt, unless my brother rescues me."

He spoke violently, and Eva knew it was a very real fear.

Because she felt sorry for him, she said:

"I am praying, I am praying very hard that does not happen. I am sure, because it is wrong for *Monsieur* Bischoffheim to thrust his daughter on you, that my prayers will be heard."

"I certainly hope you are right," Lord Charles said, "and it is very kind of you to take so much interest in my affairs."

"I am also thinking of myself," Eva said honestly.

Lord Charles looked at her curiously.

"Can £500 really mean so much to you?" he asked, "when you

look as you do? There must be dozens of men wanting to give you that amount of money, and a great deal more besides!"

Eva's eyes opened until they seemed to fill her whole face.

Then she said:

"I do not know many men . . and I certainly could not . . accept money from one . . unless I earned it."

She sounded so shocked at the idea that Lord Charles thought, if she was acting, she was certainly a brilliant performer.

"Where the devil did Leonide find her?" he asked himself, "and how can she look the part, besides talking as she does?"

He, however, had no more time for introspection for they had arrived at Raphael Bischoffheim's house.

It stood among the trees in a large garden.

It had formerly belonged to a French aristocrat of the *ancien régime*.

He had been unable to afford to keep it up and had therefore retired to his *Château* in the country.

Bischoffheim had bought for a bargain one of the most outstanding houses in Paris.

They entered through the iron gates which were heavily tipped with gold.

Eva thought that everything she looked at seemed to portray wealth.

The red carpet that ran down the stone steps was thicker and softer than any carpet she had trodden on before.

There were six footmen in the hall.

They wore a fantastic livery, decorated with gold braid.

The Major Domo was even more brilliantly attired.

He escorted them across the hall, and having asked Lord Charles their names, opened a door.

"*M'mselle* Eva Venarde and Lord Charles Craig, *Monsieur!*" he announced in stentorian tones.

Because she was frightened, for a moment Eva felt the room swing in front of her eyes.

Then she realised that what was dazzling her were the enormous crystal chandeliers, the gold-framed chairs and sofas, and the mirrors.

These were set in gold carved frames.

The pictures which would have graced any Museum were also framed in gold.

Raphael Bischoffheim, who had been standing by the mantelpiece walked towards them.

When she could focus her eyes on him, Eva saw that he was short, with shining dark hair and heavy eye-brows.

He must have been over fifty, but he was slim and moved quickly.

He put out his hand to Lord Charles saying:

"It is delightful to see you, My Lord, and of course, I am ready to welcome your friend?"

There was, although Eva did not realise it, a question-mark after the word 'friend'.

There was also a suspicious expression in *Monsieur* Bischoffheim's eyes, as if he thought that Lord Charles had brought with him a young woman who would not be welcome in his mother's Drawing-Room.

Lord Charles, understanding the implication of his words merely replied:

"And it is delightful to be here, *Monsieur*. May I introduce to you *Mademoiselle* Eva Venarde?"

There was a confidential note in his voice as he added:

"We will let you into a little secret, which you must promise not to reveal to anybody for the moment. It is that *Mademoiselle* and I are engaged to be married!"

Raphael Bischoffheim was too good a businessman to show any surprise.

Yet Lord Charles, who was watching him closely, was aware that it was something he had not expected.

It took him a second or two to adjust himself to an entirely new and unexpected situation.

Then he said, and his quiet voice did not sound anything but sincere:

"I am extremely gratified that you have taken me into your confidence, and of course I will not speak of your engagement until you allow me to do so."

"You have to understand," Lord Charles explained, "that I have not yet broken the news to my brother, or to the rest of my family."

He smiled at Eva before he added:

"As soon as they know, we shall be arranging our marriage, and of course, sending you an invitation."

"Which I shall be delighted to receive!" *Monsieur* Bischoffheim replied. "Let me be the first to congratulate you and of course I must drink to your health!"

They moved towards the fireplace.

At the moment, and Lord Charles knew it had been planned in that way, *Mademoiselle* Jael Bischoffheim came into the room.

She was, as it happened, quite a good-looking girl, even though she resembled her father.

Her rather big nose was off-set by two very large dark eyes in a small oval face.

"Ah, here you are my dear" Raphael Bischoffheim said in an over-hearty tone. "I want you to meet Lord Charles Craig and a friend of his, *Mademoiselle* Eva Venarde."

They all shook hands.

A somewhat stilted conversation followed until luncheon was announced.

Because they were only a party of four Lord Charles realised that Raphael Bischoffheim had been contriving very cleverly how he would meet his daughter.

Then when luncheon was over and before they left for the stables, he would put forward the proposition that he should marry her.

As it was, Lord Charles talked to his host about the horses he had purchased for him.

He told him from which stables they had come, emphasising not only their breeding, but also that of their owners.

Eva realised she must talk to Jael Bischoffheim.

But she found the girl was shy.

She was also obviously terrified of saying anything which would incur the wrath of her father.

Before any answer she made to a question she glanced at him to see if he was listening, or to evoke his approval.

By the end of luncheon Eva was convinced that *Monsieur* Bischoffheim was a bully.

Just as he extorted money from those outside his home, so he demanded obedience inside it.

The food was excellent, and the wine the best and most expensive a French *Vignoble* could supply.

When luncheon was finished, Lord Charles told Raphael Bischoffheim that the horses would be waiting for them in his stables.

"Then we must go to see them," *Monsieur* Bischoffheim said. "I suppose, if they wish, the young women can stay here."

162

Before Lord Charles could speak, Eva said:

"Oh, please, let me come with you. I love horses, and I have heard so much about those that have come to France for you."

"Then of course you must accompany us," *Monsieur* Bischoffheim agreed. "And what about you, Jael?"

"I have a Music Lesson, Papa," his daughter replied.

She spoke convincingly, but Eva felt she had already been told that she was not wanted.

They left Lord Charles's vehicle behind and set off in a swift, well-sprung carriage belonging to their host.

Everything about it was shining and it was almost as spectacular in its way as Leonide Leblanc's.

Eva longed to ask if the accoutrements; the lamps, the bridles, the door handles and everything else, had been made of real gold.

She thought, however, this might sound impertinent and annoy *Monsieur* Bischoffheim.

They reached the stables which were just on the outskirts of Paris.

Once again they were luxury personified.

Eva had the feeling that even the horse-rugs were made of thicker and better wool than those in other stables.

Certainly the stalls were as luxurious as a room in the Tuileries Palace!

Monsieur Bischoffheim already had a number of horses.

None of them compared however with those that Lord Charles had brought from England.

He might be annoyed that his plans for his daughter's marriage had come to nothing.

But he could not disguise his delight at becoming the owner of such outstanding animals.

They were in the stall of the stallion which Lord Charles had bought from the Royal Stud when the Head Groom said:

"You've got visitors, *Monsieur*!"

Monsieur Bischoffheim turned round and at the same time Lord Charles glanced over his shoulder.

Then he exclaimed in English:

"Hello, Warren! I did not expect to see you here!"

"I heard you were in Paris, Charles," the newcomer replied.

An extremely handsome man, he was over 6' tall with broad shoulders and athletic hips.

Eva thought he would have been recognised as an Englishman wherever he went.

There was something vaguely familiar about his face.

Then Lord Charles said:

"I do not think, *Monsieur* Bischoffheim, that you have met my brother the Duke of Kincraig!"

"No, indeed," *Monsieur* Bischoffheim replied, "and I am delighted to make Your Grace's aquaintance."

"And I am anxious to see your horses," the Duke replied. "The *Comte* tells me you have one of the most outstanding stables in France."

"That is what I hope to have," *Monsieur* Bischoffheim replied.

The Duke looked back to where the Gentleman who had accompanied him was giving orders to one of his servants

Now he came forward to say:

"Forgive me, Bischoffheim, how are you? It is nice to see you again."

"And delightful to see you, *Monsieur*!" the Banker replied.

The Duke looked to his brother:

"I do not think, Charles, that you have met the *Comte* de Chabrillin with whom I am staying!"

"No, but I have heard of him!" Lord Charles replied holding out his hand.

As the Duke spoke, Eva started and stared at the newcomer.

He was a man of about fifty, very distinguished and at the same time obviously French.

"So this," she thought to herself, "is Mama's brother, and my Uncle!"

Then she was aware that the Duke was staring at her, and Lord Charles said slowly:

"Let me introduce my brother, *Mademoiselle* Eva Venarde!"

Eva curtsied and *Monsieur* Bischoffheim said:

"This is a momentous occasion, and something I did not expect to take place in my own stables!"

The Duke looked surprised.

"Momentous?" he questioned.

Monsieur Bischoffheim put his fingers to his lips.

"*Tiens!*" he exclaimed, "now I have made a *faux pas*! How tiresome of me! You must forgive me, Lord Charles, but I had completely forgotten that you told me your engagement was a secret!"

As he spoke, Eva was quite certain that he had not forgotten what he had been told.

He was however deliberately and because he was annoyed, making trouble for Lord Charles.

She was sure now that he would buy the horses.

At the same time, his plans for his daughter's marriage had gone awry and he had no intention of letting Lord Charles get away with it.

"Engaged?" the Duke repeated. "Why have I not been told about this, Charles?"

It was quite obvious that he was annoyed, and Lord Charles replied quickly:

"I have not yet had time, and in any case, I had no idea you were in France."

"Well, now that the 'cat is out of the bag'," the *Comte* de Chabrillin interposed, "of course we must celebrate."

He paused to smile at his brother, before he went on:

"As I am sure you would wish your *fiancée* to become better acquainted with your brother, let me invite you to dine with me tonight."

There was nothing Lord Charles could do but say that they would be delighted.

Then, as if he thought he had stirred up enough trouble, *Monsieur* Bischoffheim began to praise volubly the horses which had come from England.

Eva followed the gentlemen round with no one paying any attention to her.

She had therefore the chance of looking more closely at her Uncle.

She could only feel it was a strange quirk of Fate, but one which undoubtedly would have made her father laugh.

While she was pretending to be somebody else she had met the Head of her mother's family!

Chapter Four

Driving back from *Monsieur* Bischoffheim's house to her own, Eva was alone with Lord Charles.

"How could *Monsieur* Bischoffheim behave so badly," she asked, "in telling your brother of our engagement when he had promised he would not?"

"He was getting his own back!" Lord Charles replied. "He is known to be a hard, vindictive man, and he certainly has made things difficult for me!"

Eva gave a little sigh.

"Perhaps I should not . . dine with the *Comte* tonight," she said.

As she spoke, she knew it was something she wanted very much to do.

It was fascinating to see one of the mother's relatives.

She had always been curious about the whole family.

Lord Charles thought for a moment, then he said:

"I think that would be a mistake."

"Why?" Eva asked.

"Well, first of all, my brother would think you were avoiding him, and secondly, as Bischoffheim will be there, he might be suspicious about our engagement."

"I did not realise that the *Comte* had also invited *Monsieur* Bischoffheim," Eva remarked.

"I heard him do so when he was saying goodbye," Lord Charles replied. "After all, he could hardly be the only one of the party to be left out."

"No . . of course not," Eva replied.

"The *Comte* has a house near the *Bois*," Lord Charles said, "so I will call for you at about a quarter to eight. We are not dining until half-past."

He spoke in a somewhat disagreeable voice.

Eva knew he was upset that his brother should have been told of his 'engagement'.

There was silence until Lord Charles said:

"Damn Bischoffheim! This is sure to be embarrassing, and as he has not yet given me the cheque, there is nothing either of us can do but make ourselves pleasant."

"But surely he cannot refuse to pay you now?" Eva asked in a frightened tone.

"Bischoffheim is so rich that he is a law unto himself," Lord Charles replied, "and as you have already seen, we cannot trust him; so for God's sake, do not make any mistakes!"

"I will try . . not to," Eva replied.

At the same time, she was nervous.

One of the gowns which Josie had altered for her had belonged to her mother.

While it was in a more sophisticated style than her own, it was in a very pale shade of Parma violet.

Of soft chiffon in a simple style, it had a *chic* about it which her own gowns did not have.

As she put it on, Eva thought that it might have belonged to Leonide Leblanc.

But she would doubtless have had magnificent amethysts to wear with it round her neck, and also in her ears.

Then she laughed and thought that jewellery was not important.

She had her own perfect little house and would have enough money to keep it going for a long time.

She had to arrange her own hair.

Then she found some velvet ribbon amongst her mother's belongings which were the same colour as the gown.

She tied it in a bow round the curls that she had arranged at the back of her head.

She thought that she had achieved the same style that Josie had created on *Madame* Leblanc.

There was a wide scarf of the same velvet to wear over the gown.

When Lord Charles arrived she stepped into his carriage.

"You look lovely," he exclaimed as they moved off, "as I expect all the men at dinner tonight will tell you, with the exception of my brother!"

"Do you . . think he . . disapproves of me?" Eva asked.

"I am sure he does," Lord Charles replied. "I saw the expression on his face when Bischoffheim said we were engaged, and I am quite certain he is going to be difficult."

He spoke in such a worried tone that Eva said:

"I . . I am sorry."

Then Lord Charles laughed.

"It will be all right," he said, "and as soon as Bischoffheim pays me, I can tell Warren the truth and force him to admit that I did the only thing possible in the circumstances."

Eva had the feeling as he spoke that the Duke would be very difficult to force into doing anything.

There was something commanding about him.

She did not say anything, and Lord Charles remarked as if to himself:

"There is nothing else we can do."

They were driving in the same carriage which Lord Charles had used during the day.

But Eva had noticed that the coachman was different and was certain she was right in thinking it came from a Livery Stable.

They drove up the *Champs Elysées* and had almost reached the *Bois* when the horses turned into a small drive.

It was in front of what to Eva appeared to be a large attractive house.

Her mother had told her a lot about the *Comte*'s *Château* in the country where she had lived as a girl.

But Eva could not remember her mentioning a house in Paris.

She was, however, for the moment more interested in the *Comte* than in his possessions.

He was waiting for them in a large Salon.

It over-looked the gardens at the back of the house.

It was beautifully decorated, Eva thought, and very French.

The *Comte* looking smart in his evening clothes, which were a little different from those worn by the Duke and Lord Charles, held out his hand.

"I am delighted you are here, *Mademoiselle*," he said. "I have always admired your fiance's knowledge of horses, and no one is better informed than your future brother-in-law."

While he was paying these compliments, Eva was aware that the Duke was scowling.

There was certainly no admiration in his eyes as he looked at her.

"I am very fortunate this evening," the *Comte* went on, "in having another expert on horses whom I think you all know, as my guest."

As he spoke a man came into the room.

He looked distinguished, middle-aged, and had an air of authority about him.

Eva was not surprised when he was introduced as the *Marquis* de Soisson.

He was obviously on very friendly terms with the Duke.

"Congratulations, Jacques!" the latter said. "I see that two of your horses won last week, and I suspect you are already thinking of winning the Gold Cup at Ascot."

The *Marquis* laughed.

"Dare I aim so high?"

"Why not?" the Duke asked, "and, quite frankly, I think you have a very sporting chance!"

"In which case I shall certainly try," the *Marquis* replied.

He had shaken hands with Lord Charles and *Monsieur* Bischoffheim before the *Comte* said:

"And now, *Mademoiselle* Venarde, I must introduce you to one of our most important 'Patrons of the Turf' – the *Marquis* de Soisson!"

Eva curtsied and the *Marquis* put out his hand, and she lay her fingers in it.

As she did so she found he was looking at her as if he was surprised by her appearance.

When they went into dinner, she was seated on the *Comte*'s right.

The *Marquis* was on her other side.

To her annoyance, because she wanted to listen to what her Uncle was saying, the Marquis did his best to monopolise her.

He paid her compliments, and there was a look in his eyes which she felt was definitely impertinent.

The *Comte* was exchanging a joke with the Duke.

While he did so the *Marquis* said in a voice that only she could hear:

"With whom have you come, and when may I see you again?"

Eva looked at him in astonishment and was silent.

"I suppose you came with Bischoffheim!" the *Marquis* went on. "He has a *penchant* for very beautiful young women!"

It was then Eva realised that there was no other woman at the dinner-table.

This had therefore given the *Marquis* entirely the wrong idea about her.

Perhaps he thought she was an actress.

Or else like Leonide Leblanc, she could defy the conventions because she was not really a Lady in the full sense of the word.

She could not tell him she was engaged to Lord Charles in case he should spread the falsehood further.

At the same time, she knew that she should answer his question.

"I . . I came here with Lord Charles Craig," she said coldly.

"*Nom de Nom!*" the *Marquis* swore. "This is not the first time that Charles has 'pipped me at the post'!"

A burst of laughter from the other side of the table concealed his next words which were:

"I suppose you know he has no money?"

Eva did not know what to do.

Then quickly, she turned towards the *Comte* saying:

"I am sure that was a very amusing joke, but the *Marquis* was speaking to me, so I did not hear it!"

The *Comte* smiled.

"You have missed nothing that would be suitable for your young ears," he said, "and now, *Mademoiselle*, you must tell me about yourself. Does your family live in Paris?"

Eva shook her head.

"No, I am only staying here for a short time, and I live in the South near Vence."

She had thought while she was dressing what she should say if this particular question was asked.

She remembered reading a book about Vence and how beautiful it was.

"Then you do not often come North?" the *Comte* said.

"This is really the first time," Eva replied.

"Then you have never visited any of the *Châteaux* South of Paris?"

"It is something I would love to do," Eva replied.

"Lord Charles will tell you that mine in particular is very attractive," the *Comte* smiled.

"Oh, do tell me about it!" Eva pleaded.

She was anxious to hold him in conversation. She knew that if he turned away from her she would have to listen to the *Marquis*.

"My *Château* was built at the same time as Vaux-le-Vicomte," the

Comte said, "of which doubtless you have read about in the History Books."

"Yes, I have," Eva said eagerly.

In fact, it was her mother who had told her about Vaux-le-Vicomte.

It was when she had been describing the *Château* belonging to the Chabrillins.

"Then of course you know that it was Le Vau who designed the *Châteaux* which set the fashion for the Courtiers of Louis XIV to own fantastic *Châteaux* within reach of Paris."

Eva was listening intently, and he said unexpectedly:

"I can see you are interested, so instead of listening to me, why do you not come to see my *Château* for yourself?"

Eva gave a little gasp.

"I would love to do that more than anything else in the world!" she exclaimed.

"Then it is something you must certainly do," the *Comte* replied.

He looked down the table at Lord Charles and said:

"As your brother is staying with me, Lord Charles, and this charming lady is very anxious to see my *Château,* I suggest you bring her down tomorrow and stay for at least two nights before returning to the gaieties of Paris."

Watching Lord Charles, Eva saw him hesitate.

Then as if he thought it would be a mistake to refuse, he replied:

"That is very kind of you, *Monsieur* and I am sure it is something we will both enjoy."

Because she had been willing him to accept, Eva gave a sigh of relief.

Then as she turned her head she realised that the *Marquis* was looking at her in astonishment.

"What is all this about?" he asked, "and what will *Madame la Comtesse* have to say?"

"I hope, *Monsieur*, she will be pleased to see me," Eva said primly.

The *Comte* was continuing his conversation with her.

There was no chance for the *Marquis* to say any more.

In French fashion, they all left the Dining-Room at the same time.

Soon after they had moved into the Salon, *Monsieur* Bischoffheim said he had promised to look in on a party that was being given by one of his friends.

As he said goodnight to Lord Charles he said:

"I am afraid I shall not be in Paris tomorrow, but if you will call on me as soon as you return from your visit to the *Comte* we can conclude our business transaction."

Listening, Eva knew that Lord Charles was annoyed.

Once again Bischoffheim was delaying paying him the money he owed.

There was nothing he could do, however.

She thought as *Monsieur* Bischoffheim walked jauntily away that he was enjoying keeping Lord Charles on tenterhooks.

They did not stay very much longer, and as Lord Charles drove Eva home, he said:

"Why on earth did you get the *Comte* to invite us to stay with him? If we had remained in Paris, I could have received the money the day after tomorrow."

"I . . I am . . sorry," Eva replied, "he was talking about his *Château* and I really . . did want to hear . . about it."

Lord Charles did not say anything, and to excuse herself she went on:

"The *Marquis* de Soisson was interested in the reason why I was at the party when there were no other ladies present."

Lord Charles looked at her in surprise.

"Why? What did he say?" he asked sharply.

"He asked me if I was with *Monsieur* Bischoffheim and said he wanted to . . see me again."

"I can understand what he was thinking," Lord Charles said, "but if you will take my advice, you will have nothing to do with him. He has a nasty reputation."

"That is . . what . . I thought," Eva murmured.

"Of course, he is rich," Lord Charles went on, "and, as you well know, that covers a multitude of sins, but there must be lots of other men waiting for you who are far better than him!"

Eva did not understand what he was saying.

Because she did not wish to talk about the *Marquis* any further, she changed the subject.

"It may be very annoying for you," she said, "but I am very anxious to see the *Château* of the *Comte* de Chabrillin, and we need stay only one night."

"Yes, of course," Lord Charles replied, "and I have no intention of staying any longer, as we will have to cope with my brother."

"Perhaps it would be .. wiser to tell him .. the truth," Eva suggested in a small voice.

She was thinking that if Lord Charles did so, he might then think it unnecessary for them to stay with the *Comte*.

In which case, she would not be able to see the *Château* where her mother had lived.

Lord Charles considered this for a moment, then he said:

"No, I think that would be a mistake. Warren is the type of man who will never tell a lie if he can possibly avoid it, and if by some mischance Bischoffheim should learn that we have been deceiving him, the 'fat would be in the fire'!"

"Then we must be very, very careful!" Eva said.

"We will be," Lord Charles agreed, "and we will leave my brother in ignorance, but for God's sake, be careful what you say."

"Then .. please .. do not leave me .. alone with him," Eva begged.

"I will do my best," Lord Charles said, "but you know what these French households are like – too many people with too much to say!"

Eva laughed.

She could not reply that she had never been in a French household.

She therefore had no idea what it was like.

. . . .

The following day, Eva woke up with a feeling of excitement.

By the sheer hand of Fate, she was going to visit her mother's home.

It was something she had never expected to be able to do.

When she thought about it, she was sure that the Family Chabrillin would have been annoyed that her mother had been left a house in Paris by her grandmother.

They had never made the slightest sign that they wished to meet her father or, for that matter, her.

"It is really very strange that I should enter their house under a false name," Eva thought.

She felt a little shiver go through her in case she was exposed.

That would not only make her Uncle the *Comte* angry but also Lord Charles and his awe-inspiring brother the Duke.

"Please .. Mama .. help me," she prayed.

173

She knew that her mother was the one person who could do so.

She thought she ought to tell Leonide Leblanc that she was going away, but there was no chance of her doing so.

Before Lord Charles said goodnight he arranged to collect her at eleven o'clock the next morning.

Eva knew she had to pack her clothes.

She also had to make sure that she had all the right things to wear in the country.

It was no use expecting any assistance from the old servants.

She managed by getting up early to press the country clothes that had been packed up since she arrived in Paris.

Then she repacked them.

By the time she had finished she only just had time to tidy her hair and put on a pretty gown.

It was one which was not too smart for the country and she found a hat to match it.

Remembering what Leonide Leblanc had said to her, she was waiting in the hall when Lord Charles arrived.

When he appeared she said a little breathlessly:

"I am sorry I cannot ask you in, but my Aunt, who is staying with me is not very well, and has had breakfast in bed."

"Your Aunt!" Lord Charles exclaimed.

She thought his eye-brows were raised.

But he did not say any more.

Nor did he seem to think it strange that she had spoken to him in English.

This was because she did not wish Henri to overhear what she said.

He had been standing in the hall, and he now carried her trunk outside.

Eva saw that instead of the carriage they had used yesterday, Lord Charles had a very smart Curricle.

She wondered if he had hired it or bought it.

It certainly had two well-bred horses to pull it.

When they set off with the groom sitting up behind, Eva was aware that he drove very well.

He did not seem to have much to say to her.

They therefore were silent until they were out of the traffic and Eva was thinking how lovely the countryside was.

Driving beside the Seine, they passed fields already green with the Spring crops.

"It is lovely!" Eva exclaimed involuntarily.

"That is what I always think when I come to France," Lord Charles replied. "You should however, be used to it as you live here."

"But every part of France is different," Eva said evasively.

"Yes, of course," he replied, "and I understand why Artists come here in their droves!"

He made what he said sound so funny that Eva laughed and said:

"When they see the *Comte's Chateau* they must either paint a picture of it or write a poem."

"Personally, I am more interested in a piece of paper called a cheque!" Lord Charles remarked. "We shall have had quite enough of the *Comte* and his *Château* by midnight tonight, and I intend to leave early tomorrow morning, so do not over-sleep."

"I will be ready at whatever time you wish," Eva replied.

She spoke so gently that Lord Charles looked at her as if for the first time.

"You are a very accommodating young woman!" he said. "It is only that things are not working out exactly as I intended. I nearly had a stroke yesterday when my brother walked into Bischoffheim's stables!"

"You sound as if you are frightened of him!" Eva remarked.

"Of course I am!" Lord Charles replied. "You would not under-stand, but in England the Head of a family like yours holds the title, the estate and all the purse strings!"

"Do you really mean '*all*'?" Eva asked.

"I depend on my brother for every penny I possess," Lord Charles replied savagely. "And at the moment, I possess nothing but a mountain of debts!"

"It sounds very . . frightening!"

"It is!"

He drove on a little way before he said:

"Warren is obviously annoyed at my getting engaged without telling him, to somebody who has nothing to recommend her except her looks!"

It made her sound of so little worth that Eva said ten-tatively:

"Perhaps it would be better if we pretended that I was an heiress until we can tell him the truth."

Lord Charles laughed, but there was no humour in it.

"That would be too dangerous," he said. "The French, who love money, are well aware who has it and who does not. My brother would know that, if Bischoffheim had been aware you were hung with golden shekels he would have mentioned it."

Eva was silent, and after a moment Lord Charles said:

"We just have to sit it out until tomorrow, and once I have cashed that all-important cheque, we can breathe again."

"Then I can only repeat," Eva said in a small voice, "please do not . . leave me alone with the Duke. If he cross-examines me . . he will guess that I have not told him the . . truth."

"That is something he must not do!" Lord Charles said sharply, "and, incidentally, what you are paid to prevent, so watch your words, and do not get us into any more of a mess than we are in already!"

There was nothing Eva could say, and they drove on in silence. But she felt depressed.

It was only when the *Château* finally came in sight that she felt better.

It was exactly as she had expected it to be with its towers, fountains and formal gardens.

As they drove up to the front door she felt as if her mother was with her telling her that in a way she had come home.

They arrived just before luncheon-time and the *Comte* greeted them effusively.

A servant brought them aperitifs.

While the men were talking, Eva went to the window to look out at the garden.

It was just as her mother had said a French garden would look like, but words were inadequate beside the beauty of the reality.

There was a huge fountain playing in the centre.

There had been smaller fountains at the approach to the house.

The one in the garden was exquisitely carved and the water gushed from a huge cornucopia held by a cupid.

As it rose iridescent into the sunshine, Eva held her breath.

"I hope my garden, and also my *Château* come up to your expectations, *Mademoiselle*!" she heard the *Comte* say beside her.

"It is lovely . . perfectly lovely!" she exclaimed. "Just how I knew it would be!"

He raised his eye-brows.

"You have heard of my *Château* before, or were you just anticipating your visit?"

"Both," Eva answered, "and it is lovely to think that anything so beautiful survived the Revolution and must be today just as it was when it was first built."

After she had spoken she thought perhaps she had been indiscreet.

It was her mother who had told her that, strangely enough, the *Château* was not devastated during the Revolution

"I think the truth was," she had said, "that the people in the village were so fond of the *Comte* who lived at the time that they not only spared his life, but also his house."

"There is a great deal more for you to see," the *Comte* was saying, "and now, here is my wife. I know she is looking forward to meeting you."

Eva was then introduced to a charming woman whom, she learned later, came from a distinguished family, the equal of the Chabrillins.

The *Comtesse* sat at the top of the large table in the Dining-Room, and the *Comte* was at the other end.

They both looked very aristocratic and distinguished.

Eva could understand why the family had been disappointed when her mother, who was so beautiful, had run away.

Especially as it was with a man who, at the time was an unimportant Englishman.

As her mother had told her to expect, there was a number of relatives staying in the house.

There were also the six children of the *Comte* and *Comtesse*.

Three of them were grown up, and the ages of the others ranged from twelve to eighteen.

They were all, Eva thought with satisfaction, extremely good-looking.

They all had dark hair.

Although she thought somebody might have noticed the resemblance to her mother in her face and eyes, her hair and complexion was certainly different from that of her cousins.

At luncheon they all chatted away to everybody in the delightfully informal manner characteristic of the French.

Eva found it charming.

At the same time, she was aware that the Duke was staring at her in a somewhat hostile manner.

When they arrived he had greeted both her and his brother coldly.

After the meal was finished, the *Comte* said:

"Now I want to show you my horses, and I am hoping, Lord Charles that *Mademoiselle* Venarde will not find them too inferior to those magnificent animals you have brought from England."

"I scoured the country for the best!" Lord Charles replied.

"That was obvious," the *Comte* said, "and I only wish I could afford anything as good, but unfortunately, I do not have Bischoffheim's reserves!"

The two men laughed as if that was a joke.

The they walked through the garden towards the stables.

Eva wanted to linger and inspect the fountain, but she also wished to see the horses.

She was accompanied by one of her older Cousins, who was telling her unasked the history of the family.

She was sure it was something strangers always wanted to know.

"And what do you do?" Eva asked when he paused for breath.

"I intend to be a Politician," he said, "but do not tell Papa! He thinks that Politics are a bore, while I find them intriguing."

Eva laughed.

"I will keep your secret, and I agree with you that politics are always exciting."

"If you are interested in History," her Cousin said, "I must tell you about the cannon which you see at the end of the garden."

They walked on.

Eva longed to tell him that she knew the history of the cannon as well as he did.

The *Comte's* horses were good, very good.

Yet they certainly did not equal those which they had seen in Raphael Bischoffheim's stables.

"If you have made certain he will win every race, Lord Charles," the *Comte* said, "there will be no point in us poor owners competing for the *Grand Prix* or any other race!"

"I think you are being very pessimistic," Lord Charles replied. "After all, while Bischoffheim may be able to buy the best, he does not know a great deal about horses. It is the right training and choosing the right Jockey that win races."

The *Comte* put his hand on Lord Charles's shoulder.

"That is very wise of you, young man," he said, "and I am sure your brother appreciates how much you know about the 'Sport of Kings'."

"Charles is undoubtedly an expert in his own field," the Duke said rather grudgingly.

'He is unpleasant in more ways than one!' Eva thought indignantly.

She was being very careful to keep as far away as possible from him.

There was a great deal to see during the afternoon.

Then, accompanied by Pierre, who was the same Cousin who had escorted her before, she went into the Library.

Unexpectedly the Duke joined them.

"Your mother is looking for you, Pierre," he said.

"I said I would try to find you. She is in the *Salon Bleu*."

There was nothing Pierre could do but go to his mother.

With a sinking of her heart, Eva realised that although she had tried to avoid it, she was now alone with the Duke.

"You are interested in books, Miss Venarde?" he asked.

"Very!" Eva replied. "But I have never before been in such a magnificent Library."

"I would rather, at the moment, talk about you," the Duke said.

"I . . I wonder where . . Charles is?" Eva asked quickly.

She remembered only just in time that Lord Charles had said as they neared the *Château*:

"Do not forget to call me by my Christian name! You would hardly address the man to whom you are supposed to be engaged as 'My Lord'."

"Charles is at the moment with our host," the Duke said, "and you cannot continue, Miss Venarde to keep running away from me!"

Eva blushed.

She was not aware that he had noticed her efforts to avoid him.

There were two sofas one on either side of the huge mediaeval fireplace, and the Duke said:

"Suppose we sit down?"

There was nothing Eva could do but obey him.

As she did so she glanced at the door praying that somebody would appear to join them.

"First of all," the Duke began, "tell me about your family. I feel my brother has been very remiss in not even informing me of your existence."

"He intended to do so when he returned to England," Eva replied.

"But I am here," the Duke said, "and it would make things far easier if you would tell me about yourself."

"I . . I do not think there is . . very much to tell," Eva said. "Both my parents . . are dead."

That, at any rate, she thought, was true.

"I am sorry! It must be very sad for you to be alone."

"I miss them . . both very much!" Eva replied.

"I believe, although I may be mistaken, that you are not wholly French?"

"No, my mother was English."

"English!" the Duke repeated. "And what was her name?"

Eva had already thought of this, and because she did not wish to tell more lies than was necessary, she replied:

"Hill. Her maiden name was Hill."

"There are a great many Hills in England," the Duke remarked. "It is, in fact quite a common name. Where did your grand-parents live?"

"In . . in Gloucestershire."

"You have been to England?"

"Yes"

"And did you like it as much as France?"

"I love both countries," Eva answered, "and after all, there is only the Channel to divide them."

The Duke smiled.

"That is a good way of putting it, but it is of course a division, and I am just wondering, Miss Venarde, or perhaps, as you are to be my sister-in-law, I should call you Eva, if you will enjoy living in England."

"I look forward to it!" Eva said defensively.

"I expect Charles has already warned you that it will be in somewhat straitened circumstances, unless of course, you have money of your own?"

Eva felt she was getting out of her depth.

She was frightened of what she might have to say next, and rose to her feet.

"I hope Your Grace will forgive me," she said quickly, "but I really must go to find our hostess. She promised to show me some of the . . State Rooms, and she will think it rude if I keep her waiting . . too long."

She did not wait for the Duke to answer.

Dropping him a curtsy she moved swiftly towards the door.

Even if he had called after her she would not have heard him.

When she reached the passage she ran towards the hall and up the stairs to the First Floor.

Only when she reached the bedroom into which she had been shown on her arrival did she feel for the moment that she was safe.

"He frightens me!" she told herself, "and it is a good thing that I am not in love with Lord Charles, as I am certain he intends by some means or other to break up our 'engagement'."

She sat down on the stool in front of the dressing-table and looked at her reflection.

"Perhaps if he knew who I really am, he might not be so antagonistic," she went on, "he thinks I am not good enough for his precious brother – and Papa would consider that an insult!"

Chapter Five

When dinner, which had been a very talkative and amusing meal was over, the *Comte* said:

"I expect you gentlemen will want to play cards."

There was a murmur of assent from his sons and from Lord Charles.

Speaking to him the *Comte* said:

"As you tell me that you and *Mademoiselle* Venarde are leaving early tomorrow morning, I am going to take your *fiancée* to the picture Gallery. She cannot leave without seeing the portraits of my ancestors."

His children laughed at that and teased him, and Eva said:

"You know I want to look at everything in the *Château* which is the most fascinating building I have ever seen."

"You see there is one person who admires my obsessions!" the *Comte* said to Pierre, who replied:

"We are all as proud as you are, Papa, but we do not say so much about it!"

"Go and play cards, you cheeky boy!" the *Comte* replied.

He drew Eva out of the Salon, and they walked to where, at the end of the *Château* was a long Gallery.

Like everything else, it was beautifully arranged.

The pictures started with the *Comte*'s first ancestors.

Gradually they went round the Gallery until it ended up with a recent "*Tableau de Genre*".

It was of himself, his wife and his children.

Many of the names were familiar to Eva.

The *Comtes* de Chabrillin had been celebrated Statesmen, Courtiers, and Generals.

They had therefore been her heroes since she was a small child.

She was listening attentively to everything her Uncle told her.

They moved slowly from portrait to portrait.

Finally with a leap of her heart she realised she was looking at the face of her mother.

Lizette had been painted when she was seventeen.

Before the *Comte* spoke Eva guessed it was when she had become officially engaged.

She stood looking at the portrait seeing her own eyes, her own nose and her own lips.

The main difference was that her mother's hair was dark.

Also her skin had not the same pink-and-white transparency which was very English.

Because it meant so much to Eva she forgot for the moment that the *Comte* was with her.

She could only look at her mother, feeling almost as if she spoke to her.

Then, as if the *Comte* became aware of her special interest in the portrait, he said:

"This is my sister Lisette, who I am afraid, caused something of a scandal in the family when she ran away with an Englishman."

Eva did not speak, and he went on:

"As you can see, she was very lovely, and I only regret that I did not see her again before she died."

Eva drew in her breath.

She tried to prevent the tears from coming into her eyes.

She had always found it difficult to speak of her mother without wanting to cry.

Now her portrait seemed to be speaking to her.

She needed all her self-control to prevent herself from breaking down.

Then, as if the *Comte* was aware of her attention, he looked at her.

Suddenly there was an incredulous expression on his face.

His head turned from her to the portrait and back again.

Finally, as if he was speaking to himself, he cried:

"The likeness is incredible! I knew there was something familiar about your face, but I could not think what it was!"

Eva gave a little gasp, but before she could speak the *Comte* said:

"Is it possible – can you be Lisette's daughter?"

Eva looked towards the door as if she was afraid somebody was listening.

Then she said pleadingly:

"Please . . do not say . . any more! It is a secret . . and nobody here has any . . idea of it."

The *Comte* stared at her.

"Are you telling me that you *are* my niece, and you are engaged to Lord Charles, but he has no idea you are my sister's child?"

Eva nodded.

"Please . . please, do not . . ask any more . . questions."

The *Comte* smiled.

"Do you really expect me to be inhuman? Now that I have found you, that I must not talk to anyone about it?"

"But . . you must not . . you must not!" Eva said. "If I tell you the reason . . will you swear to me on . . your honour that you . . will not tell . . Lord Charles or . . the Duke?"

"I will promise anything you ask," the *Comte* said, "at the same time, I insist on knowing the whole story."

He reached out and took her hand in his.

Then he looked up at the portrait and said quietly:

"I think it is something your mother would want you to do."

Because he spoke gently and kindly, Eva felt the tears run down her cheeks.

Quickly she wiped them away.

The *Comte* drew her back to the end of the Gallery where there was a comfortable sofa and several chairs.

He sat down on the sofa and drew her down beside him.

"First I must tell you," he said, "how deeply I regret that I never saw your mother after she had run away with your father."

"Mama was . . very sad that she had . . lost her family," Eva replied, "although she was . . ecstatically happy with . . Papa."

"Unfortunately, I was not here when it happened," the *Comte* continued. "I was five years older than she was, and in the Army. Shortly after she ran away I was sent to Africa with my Regiment."

"Mama told me all about . . you and her . . other brothers and sisters. That was why I was so . . thrilled to . . come to see the . . *Chateau*."

"I can understand that," the *Comte* replied. "I thought from the first you were very lovely, and now I know why you appealed to me was because you resemble my beautiful sister."

Once again Eva wiped away a tear, and he said:

"You must not cry, but tell me what has happened to your father and why you are here with Lord Charles?"

It was difficult for her to speak without crying.

Eva wiped her eyes because the tears embarrassed her.

Then she told him how her father had died of a heart-attack.

She related how she had gone to collect his shirt-stud from Leonide Leblanc.

She went on to explain how *Madame* Leblanc had arranged for her to save Lord Charles from having to marry *Monsieur* Bischoffheim's daughter by pretending to be his *fiancée*.

She was not aware that the *Comte* stiffened when she spoke of Leonide Leblanc.

Then when she spoke of *Monsieur* Bischoffheim's intentions he exclaimed:

"I have never heard anything so disgraceful! How dare Bischoffheim attempt to blackmail Lord Charles into marrying his daughter!"

"You will understand," Eva said, "why Lord Charles was trying frantically to avoid the situation. At the same time, he is still desperately afraid that *Monsieur* Bischoffheim will not pay him what he is owed."

"You had no other contact with Leonide Leblanc, except that she was a friend of your father's?" the *Comte* asked.

"She was very kind to arrange that I should be paid so much money," Eva answered, "which means that I can continue to live in that beautiful house which my grandmother left to Mama."

The *Comte* smiled.

"Certain members of the family were very disappointed when they found it was not left to them."

"I was . . afraid they would feel . . like that," Eva said, "but I love it . . too, and I want to be . . able to go on . . living there."

"We will talk about that another time," the *Comte* said. "But *now* I want you to know that you are always welcome here, and I think my wife will prove a better chaperon than the Aunt you are pretending to have with you."

Eva looked at him wide-eyed.

"Do you . . do you . . really . . mean that?"

"Of course I mean it," the *Comte* replied.

"But . . please . . you must not say anything to anyone . . until Lord Charles receives his cheque."

185

"I can understand now," the *Comte* said, "that is the reason why he wishes to return to Paris tomorrow morning."

Eva nodded.

"Very well, my dear," he said, "you must go back with him and as soon as everything is settled, we will meet and talk about your future."

"You are kind . . very kind," Eva murmured. "I know that is what Mama would want . . for me. At the same time . . I do not wish to be an . . encumbrance on you any more . . than . . I would impose myself on my father's relatives."

"As you can see," the *Comte* smiled, "there is plenty of room here and you can certainly use your house in Paris whenever you wish, as long as you take one of my family with you."

He gave a laugh before he said:

"I can assure you they will be only too willing to be your guests. My older children all have a yearning for Paris, and have often complained that there is not enough room for them in my own house."

He patted Eva's hand as he said:

"Do not worry your head about that for the moment, just fulfil your obligation which I can quite understand you must do, to Lord Charles. Then we will have luncheon together the day after you are free."

"Until then you . . promise you will . . say . . nothing to . . anybody?"

"I assure you as a Chabrillin I never break my word," the *Comte* said, "and as your blood is the same as mine, I realise that you cannot break yours."

"I know that is . . something Mama would . . expect you to say," Eva said, "and thank you . . thank you for being . . so kind!"

"I have not had an opportunity of being kind yet," the *Comte* replied, "but I feel I owe you a great deal that I should have expended on your mother."

He gave a deep sigh.

"But regrets are a waste of time, and my only excuse for neglecting Lisette in the past was that my father was a hard man. He never forgave her and for years he would not have her name mentioned."

"But you remembered her," Eva said, "and I am sure it will make her happy to . . know that we have . . met each other . . now."

"I know it will," the *Comte* said, "and never again, my beautiful niece, are you to think you are alone and obliged to seek the help of somebody like Leonide Leblanc."

There was a note in his voice which told Eva how much he disapproved of *Madame* Leblanc.

She thought perhaps it was because she was so theatrical and as her mother would have said, did not look like a Lady.

"But she was very kind to me," she thought, "and I must express my gratitude, although I am not quite certain how."

The *Comte* glanced at the clock over the mantelpiece.

"I suppose we must go back to the others, and it is time for you to go to bed," he said. "There is so much more I want to hear about your mother, and I shall look forward eagerly to our next meeting."

"So shall I!" Eva said.

They both stood up, then the *Comte* bent and kissed her on the cheeks.

"You are very lovely, my dear," he said, "and every time I look at you I shall feel it is like having your mother with us again."

They walked down the Gallery and only when they reached the door did Eva say:

"You will be very, very careful in front of Lord Charles, and the Duke? I am sure they would be shocked at what I have done if they knew I was Papa's daughter."

"Of course they would," the *Comte* agreed, "and it is something which will never happen again. Thankfully it will be over once Lord Charles has been paid."

Eva smiled at him.

They walked in silence into the Salon where the male members of the party were still playing cards.

Some of the women, however, had already retired.

Eva slipped away.

When she was in bed she prayed for a long time, telling her mother how wonderful it was to be in the home she had loved so much.

Now she need no longer worry about the future.

"I know it is . . all due to you . . mama, and of course Papa, who always . . believed that 'something would turn up'. I am lucky . . so very, very lucky!"

When she fell asleep she dreamed she was talking to her mother.

They were sitting together in the Salon downstairs under the crystal chandeliers.

. . . . . .

Eva had told her maid to call her early.

She also thought it would be quicker if she had breakfast in her room.

She had only just finished and was putting on her hat when she was told that Lord Charles was waiting for her.

She could understand his haste to be back in Paris.

As two footmen hurriedly carried her trunk away from her room she ran down the stairs.

There was quite a number of the Chabrillin family to say goodbye to her.

The *Comtesse* kissed her and said:

"I hope when you are married, my dear, you and your husband will come to stay with us. We have so enjoyed having you!"

"Thank you, *madame*. Every moment has been a delight!" Eva replied.

The *Comte* helped her into the Curricle, saying as he did so:

"I feel it will not be long before we meet again, *Mademoiselle* Venarde!"

His eyes were twinkling as he spoke and his fingers pressed hers.

Eva knew that she was amused at the pretence they were keeping up in front of Lord Charles.

"Thank you! Thank you for everything!" she cried

She knew he understood.

As they drove off she looked back to see at least six of her relatives still standing on the steps waving to them.

"They are charming," she thought, "and I love them so much already."

Lord Charles was driving swiftly and exceedingly well.

Eva knew he was determined to reach Paris and bring his business transaction with *Monsieur* Bischoffheim to an end.

Because she was curious she could not help asking:

"You will not say . . anything to him about our 'engagement?'"

"Certainly not!" Lord Charles said. "You are not likely to have any contact with him but if you do, just be dignified and refuse to answer any questions."

Eva thought that might be difficult, but she did not say so.

They drove on.

When they reached her small house he hastily put her trunks down in the hall.

Lord Charles drove away.

He had said as she got out of the curricle:

"I will see you later in the day."

At the same time, he did not say "thank you" which she thought was somewhat unkind.

She only hoped there would be no more difficulties or obstacles in the way of him being paid.

Then she could revert to being herself.

As her Uncle had suggested she could stay at the *Chateau*.

She was so happy at the idea that she wanted to sing and dance.

She ran up the stairs to change from the clothes in which she had driven back as if she had wings on her feet.

She came downstairs again, wearing a gown that Josie had made smart enough for Paris.

It was then she thought that now she should visit Leonide Leblanc, and tell her that everything had gone well.

Leonide had known her father.

She was the only person who would understand how much it meant for her to be accepted into the Chabrillin family.

"I must tell her at once!" Eva thought.

Then she remembered she was not supposed to walk in the streets without having somebody with her.

But when she enquired where Marie was, she learnt that she had gone to market.

She knew that Henri, who was suffering from rheumatism, could only walk very slowly.

Anyway he would have no wish to leave the house.

"What will it matter?" Eva asked, "if just this once I walk alone?"

She hurried off.

Because she was intent on where she was going, she had no idea that anyone had noticed her.

Nor that men turned round to take another look at her.

When she reached Leonide Leblanc's house, it was luncheon-time.

She was aware that she felt rather hungry.

'Perhaps Leonide Leonide will offer me something to eat,' she thought.

When he opened the door the man-servant smiled at her.

"*Bonjour M'mselle*! If you wish to see *Madame* she is in bed and alone."

"I am very anxious to see her," Eva replied, and ran up the stairs.

Leonide Leblanc was in bed, looking more fascinating than ever.

She wore a transparent pink nightgown and pink ribbons in her hair.

"My dear, I am delighted to see you!" she exclaimed. "I have been wondering what has happened and whether you would let me know if everything went according to plan."

"Not quite," Eva replied, "but very well."

She sat down on the chair beside the bed, and told Leonide Leblanc exactly what had happened.

She listened without speaking until Eva had finished, then she said:

"*C'est extraordinaire! Comme un conte de fées!*"

"That is what I thought myself," Eva replied.

"How fortunate that the *Comte* is your Uncle, now the *Comtesse* will chaperon you and find you an acceptable husband."

"I have no wish to marry, at least not for the moment," Eva replied, "and only when I can find somebody as charming and amusing as Papa."

Madame Leblanc sighed.

"*Hélas*, but men like that are few and far between! But now you are safe, and nobody will insult you when they know you are under the protection of the family Chabrillin."

"I cannot think why anyone should want to!" Eva objected, "except perhaps the Duke, who is very curious, and I think a little hostile."

"Forget him!" Leonide Leblanc said. "He will go back to England, you will be in France and never meet him or Lord Charles again."

"Charles is very grateful to you for saving him," Eva said, "I am sure he would never have thought of anything so clever on his own."

"What you are really saying is that he would never have found anyone like you!" Lenoide said, "but now you must forget this little escapade, and do not talk about it to anyone except your Uncle."

"No . . of course not," Eva agreed.

There was a knock on the door and the man-servant asked:

"Do you require your luncheon, *Madame?*"

"Yes, and at once!" Leonide replied, "and *Mademoiselle* Venarde will have it with me."

She looked at Eva and added:

"I have the idea that nobody has asked you to luncheon?"

"Nobody!" Eva laughed.

"Then we shall eat together and after that, we must say goodbye, for you realise you must never tell anybody that you have met me."

"I told my Uncle."

"I expect he was shocked, even if he did not show it."

Eva thought this was very likely true.

She still did not understand why, but aloud she said:

"I shall always remember how kind you have been, and although you say I must not see you, I think Papa would want me to love you and always be very, very grateful that it was through you I found my Uncle."

"I told you it is a Fairy Story!" Leonide said, "and now all you have to do is to live happily ever after!"

They laughed and talked all through the very delicious luncheon which was brought upstairs on elegantly arranged trays.

Then when the meal was finished Eva said goodbye.

"I wish there was something I could give you," she said. "Can you think of anything you would like?"

She looked around the flower-filled room and remembered the beautiful objects d'art she had seen in the Salon.

"You seem to have everything!" she added.

"What I would like," Leonide said, "is for you to send me just sometimes a little momento of what you are doing – the announcement of your Marriage, the printed Marriage Service when it takes place, and of course, photographs when you have them, of you and your family."

"Of course I will send you those things," Eva cried, "and every time I post them to you, I shall remember it here, and all that happened because of you."

Leonide Leblanc held out her arms.

"*Adieu*, my most charming and lovely little friend. Do not forget – you must never say that you have been here in my house. But just remember me sometimes in your prayers."

"You know I will do that," Eva said.

She kissed her affectionately.

She turned back to wave as she reached the door.

As she did so she thought there was something wistful in Leonide's expression.

She took one last look at the orchids which seemed to fill the hall.

She had a glimpse of many more through the open door of the Salon.

Then the man-servant let her out and she walked down the steps and out into the street.

She hurried home, knowing it would be a mistake to linger at the shops.

When Henri opened the door she said:

"I am back, Henri! Has anybody called?"

"No, *M'mselle.*"

Eva ran upstairs to take off her hat.

She was hoping that nothing had gone wrong with Lord Charles's interview with *Monsieur* Bischoffheim.

If it had, she thought she would still have to go on pretending to be his *fiancée*.

That could mean she would not be able to have luncheon with her uncle tomorrow.

"I pray everything has gone well," she thought. "But surely Lord Charles could have let me know by now? Unless once again, *Monsieur* Bischoffheim is keeping him waiting!"

She went downstairs to the salon which seemed very small after the enormous one in the *Château*.

But they were very like each other.

She knew from what her Uncle had said that it was her grand-mother who had made the *Château* so attractive.

Her taste must have been impeccable.

Eva stood in front of a glass cabinet admiring some pretty little Dresden china figures.

She heard the door open.

She turned round eagerly thinking it would be Lord Charles.

To her astonishment, the *Marquis* de Soisson came into the room.

She stared at him incredulously before she asked:

"Why . . are you . . here? What do you . . want?"

He smiled before he said:

"I will answer your first question, which is that, quite by chance I was driving down the *Rue d'Offement* when I saw you come out of a certain house which is, of course, the most famous in the whole street!"

Eva stared at him thinking how much she disliked him.

She also knew by the tone of his voice that he thought he had been very clever in discovering something about her.

"I followed you back here," the *Marquis* continued, "and now, *Mademoiselle* Eva Venarde, we can put out cards on the table, and you can stop deceiving me, however cleverly you have deceived Lord Charles!"

"I do not know . . what you mean," Eva answered, "and as . . my Aunt who is . . chaperoning me is . . upstairs in bed, I must ask you, *Monsieur* to leave . . immediately."

The *Marquis* laughed.

"So that is your little game! Well, my dear, you do not 'pull the wool' over my eyes, and as a friend of Leonide, I assure you you can no longer keep up the pose of being a Social débutante."

"I asked you to leave, *Monsieur*!"

"Which I have no intention of doing, until you listen to what I have to say."

"I cannot imagine that you will say anything I want to hear," Eva said, "and I can only ask you to behave in a proper and civilised manner and leave me alone!"

The *Marquis* sat down on the sofa.

"Now stop playing games," he said, "and let me tell you exactly how I feel. I want you and I intend to have you!"

"I have no . . idea what you . . mean," Eva replied.

She was in fact, speaking truthfully, but at the same time, she was frightened.

There was something in the way the *Marquis* spoke.

Also the expression in his eyes told her he was dangerous.

She was not certain, however, what she could do about it.

She knew that by now Henri would have returned to the kitchen.

Even if she asked his help in turning the *Marquis* out of the house, he was an old man.

He would be incapable of standing up to somebody like the *Marquis*.

She wondered frantically what she should do and as she hesitated the Marquis said:

"Come and sit down like a sensible girl, and hear what I have to say to you."

Because she appeared to have no alternative, Eva did as he asked.

She moved towards a chair as far away from the *Marquis* as possible.

However he made a gesture with his hand towards the sofa where he was sitting.

She thought it would seem childish not to obey him.

She sat as far as she could from him.

He leaned back, very much at his ease with one arm along the back of the sofa.

"You are incredibly lovely!" he said, "in fact when I first saw you, I thought you could not be real, but a figment of my imagination!"

Eva did not answer and he said:

"I cannot think you have been in Paris long, or I would have met you before Craig did. However, if he is the first man in your life, I intend to be the second!"

"I .. I am engaged to be .. married .. to Lord Charles," Eva said.

The *Marquis* laughed, and it was a very unpleasant sound.

"That is what I learnt from Bischoffheim, and quite frankly, I do not believe a word of it!"

Eva looked at him in horror.

He must have upset *Monsieur* Bischoffheim by telling him that she and Lord Charles were not really engaged.

Perhaps that was why Lord Charles had not brought her the cheque as he had promised to do, and the whole deal might be off.

Because the idea was so terrifying, she said:

"Surely, you did not .. say anything so .. untrue .. to *Monsieur* Bischoffheim?"

"As it happens, I do not!" the *Marquis* replied.

Eva heaved a sigh of relief.

"But I watched you and Craig together, and I thought there was something 'fishy' about the whole thing, besides the fact that you got yourself invited to Chabrillin's *Château*."

"I cannot think why you should .. suspect that there is anything .. wrong about our engagement!" Eva managed to say.

"I knew I was right, my pretty one," the *Marquis* said, "and absolutely right when just now I saw you coming out of Leonide's house. Now tell me exactly what your game is! And if you ask me, you are backing the wrong horse!"

Eva made a little gesture with her hand.

"What you are . . saying is quite . . incomprehensible!"

"Nonsense! You understand every word!" the *Marquis* said. "You thought Craig was rich, and you pursued him, and because he is a rather stupid young man he promised you marriage!"

He paused a moment and seemed to leer at her as he went on:

"You will not marry him – you can be quite certain of that – not when his brother finds out about you. So you had better 'cut your losses'!"

What he was saying, and the way he was speaking, made Eva feel bewildered.

Then before once again she could ask him to leave, the *Marquis* said.

"Now what I am offering you is a far better proposition I am a very rich man, and when I get what I want, very generous. I suppose this house is rented, but I will give you one of your own, a carriage with two horses and all the jewels you can put round your pretty neck! What do you say to that?"

He spoke in a flamboyant manner as if he thought she would find what he was saying irresistible.

"I think . . *Monsieur* . . you are . . insulting . . me!"

The Marquis laughed.

"You know as well as I do that you will find it difficult to be offered more, unless you were Leonide, which you are not! Now, come along, let us have no more playing about!"

He reached out his hand towards her as he spoke.

Because Eva realised he was going to touch her, she jumped to her feet.

"Go away!" she said, "go away . . from me! You are . . horrible! Bestial! I refuse to . . listen to any . . more!"

Because she was frightened, she spoke frantically.

Then as the *Marquis* rose she realised how large and powerful he was.

She took a step away from him saying:

"Leave . . me . . alone!"

"That is something I have no intention of doing," he replied. "And let me tell you, I like little birds who flutter and defy me. I find it very exciting to capture them!"

He reached out towards her.

Once again Eva backed away from him only to find there was a chair directly behind her.

It was impossible to go any further.

The *Marquis* put his arms around her and pulled her roughly against him.

She gave a cry, and started to struggle with him.

Attempting to thrust him away with her hands.

She was also moving her head from side to side as she tried to prevent him from kissing her.

"You excite me!" he said in a low, deep voice, which sounded like the growl of a wild animal. "I want you, and by God, I mean to have you!"

It was then Eva screamed.

As she did so she felt his lips, hot and demanding, against the softness of her skin and she screamed again.

Chapter Six

The Duke had not said good-bye to Eva and Lord Charles for the simple reason that he had already left the *Château*.

He had an important appointment in Paris.

He therefore rode across country on one of the *Comte*'s fastest horses.

He sent his luggage and his Valet by road.

When he arrived at the house near the *Bois* he had a bath and changed his clothes.

Having eaten a large English breakfast he left to keep an appointment with the Emperor.

He had messages for Louis Napoleon from the Prince of Wales, and also the Prime Minister.

Then, because they were old friends, the Duke and the Emperor sat talking for over half-an-hour.

The Duke returned to the *Comte*'s house and was sitting at a desk writing a letter when his brother burst into the room.

"I have got it! I have got it!" Lord Charles shouted. "Now there need be no further problems!"

The Duke smiled.

"I gather you were somewhat apprehensive in case Bischoffheim did not pay up."

His brother put the cheque down on the blotter in front of him.

The Duke saw that it was made out for £15,000.

"No wonder you were worried!" he remarked. "How much of this is yours?"

"Nearly £9,000," Charles replied.

"Will that pay all your debts?"

"The most pressing of them. There will however, be a number left over."

The Duke was silent, and Charles looked at him questioningly. Then he said:

"I will pay the rest."

Charles stared at him.

"Do you mean that, Warren?"

"There is, naturally, a condition attached."

"What is that?" his brother asked anxiously.

"That you will leave for London immediately."

"Why?"

"I should have thought that was very obvious," the Duke replied. "Your friend Leonide Leblanc will certainly need some of this, and quite frankly, you cannot afford the women of Paris."

"As it happens," Charles said defensively, "Leonide has never charged me so much as one *franc*."

"Then you have been lucky. But if she sees this amount of money, she will undoubtedly want a present."

"I suppose you are right," Charles said reflectively. "At the same time, I owe her something for producing Eva."

The Duke stiffened.

"What do you mean by that?"

"I was going to tell you once Bischoffheim settled up!" Charles said. "I was given a tip-off that he intended to blackmail me into marrying his daughter!"

"The Devil he was!" the Duke exclaimed. "How could you possibly do such a thing!"

"It is something I have no intention of doing," Charles retorted, "but if I had refused, he would have threatened not to pay the money I had already expended on the horses."

"It is the most disgraceful thing I have ever heard!" the Duke said, "the man is a complete outsider."

"I know that," Charles agreed, "but I had to defeat him at his own game, and it was Leonide who produced Eva like a rabbit out of a hat!"

The Duke did not speak and Charles gave a little laugh before he went on:

"You will hardly believe it, but she made me swear on my honour that I would 'leave the girl exactly as I found her.'"

"What did she mean by that?" the Duke enquired.

"In her own words – 'pure, innocent, and untouched'," Charles answered.

The Duke raised his eye-brows, and his brother said:

"I have kept my word, and I promised Leonide that I would give Eva £500."

He expected his brother to make some comment, but the Duke merely took a cheque from his wallet.

"I will cash Bischoffheim's cheque immediately, at the Bank I use in Paris," he said. "You will take mine for the same amount to London."

"And Eva?" Charles asked.

"I will see to her, and I will also send Leonide Leblanc something she will appreciate in your name."

"Warren, you are a sportsman!" Charles exclaimed, "and do you really mean you will pay my debts?"

"I have said I will pay them," the Duke replied, "but try to be a little more sensible in future. As you can imagine, I have been wondering how you could keep a wife on credit!"

Lord Charles laughed.

"You well know it would be impossible, unless we were happy to live in a tent."

"Well, that at any rate, will be unnecessary," the Duke said in a tone of relief.

"I cannot begin to thank you . . " Charles began.

The Duke looked at his watch.

"If you do not catch the one o'clock train to Calais, I might change my mind."

Charles gave an exclamation of horror.

At the same time, he was laughing.

"I will catch it," he promised, "and drink your health all the way to Dover!"

"Before you go," the Duke said, "you had better give me the address of Eva Venarde."

Charles explained where the house was in the *Rue St Honoré* and the Duke said:

"Let me advise you – on no account tell the story of what has occurred to anybody! It would be a great mistake."

"But I am longing to say that I have 'pulled a fast one' on Raphael Bischoffheim!" Charles protested.

"As I imagine he could be a very vindictive man, and money always speaks louder than laughter, it is something you would regret."

"You are right – of course you are right," Charles agreed, "but I really have got the better of him."

"Then keep it to yourself," the Duke advised.

As Charles went from the room the Duke could hear him shouting for the curricle in which he had travelled to the country.

"He is incorrigible!" he said to himself, but at the same time he was smiling.

He realised even better than Charles did that Bischoffheim was not a man to be trifled with.

He therefore drove immediately to a Bank in the *Rue de la Paix* which was affiliated to his Bank in London.

He paid in the cheque for £9,000 and collected £500 in *francs*.

Then he drove to his Club.

After a light luncheon, the carriage which belonged to the *Comte* carried him to the house in the *Rue St. Honore*.

An elderly servant opened the door.

The Duke stepped into the hall he heard Eva scream.

Without waiting for Henri who, as usual, was moving very slowly, he walked swiftly to the door of the Salon and walked in.

One glance told him that Eva was fighting desperately against the *Marquis* de Soisson.

Neither of them realised that anyone else had come into the room.

Then when Eva gave another helpless, pitiful little scream of an animal caught in a trap the Duke acted.

He sprang forward, catching hold of the *Marquis* by the back of his collar, and pulled him away from Eva.

"What the hell do you think you are doing?" he asked.

For a second both the *Marquis* and Eva looked at him in sheer astonishment.

Then Eva threw herself against the Duke.

"Save me . . save . . me!" she cried and his her face against his shoulder.

The *Marquis* released himself from the Duke's grasp and pulled the lapels of his coat back into place.

"Why are you here? And what has it got to do with you, Kincraig?" he enquired.

"Get out!" the Duke said sharply.

The *Marquis* went crimson in the face.

"I have as much right here as you have," he replied

"I told you to leave," the Duke said.

"And if I refuse?" the *Marquis* asked aggressively.

"Then I am quite prepared to use forceful means to evict you," the Duke said coldly.

Because he did not raise his voice his threat was far more effective than if he had shouted.

He was much taller than the *Marquis*.

There was also an expression in his eyes which had made many men quake in front of him.

With a muttered oath the *Marquis* turned on his heel.

He walked out of the Salon slamming the door behind him.

The Duke did not watch him go.

He merely looked down at Eva who was still hiding her face on his shoulder.

He was aware that her whole body was trembling.

Gently he moved her to the sofa and helped her to sit down on it.

She was very pale, and he was aware that the expression in her eyes was one of shock.

"It is all right," the Duke said. "The *Marquis* has gone, and I doubt if he will come back."

"But . . if . . he does?" Eva faltered, and shivered.

The Duke glanced round the room.

"Are you living here alone?" he enquired.

Because she was so shattered by what had happened, Eva told him the truth.

"Y.yes."

The Duke looked surprised. Then he asked:

"And whose house is it?"

"It is . . mine."

Now the Duke was definitely astonished.

He glanced again at the beautiful antique furniture

"H.how . . could you have . . come just at the . . right moment?" Eva asked in a very small voice, "and . . s.saved me?"

The Duke took the packet of money which he had collected at the Bank and placed it in her lap.

"I have brought you this from my brother," he said. "It is the £500 he promised to pay you."

"Then . . *Monsieur* Bischoffheim has . . given him . . a cheque."

"Yes, that is right," the Duke replied.

Eva was staring at the packet on her lap which she had not touched.

Then she said: "Please . . will you give it back to Lord Charles? I . . I do not . . want it."

"You certainly earned it," the Duke said.

"I am glad . . I did not make . . any mistakes . . but it is . . unnecessary now . . and I would . . rather not be paid for . . what I did."

The Duke looked puzzled.

Then he said:

"You mean you are rich enough to refuse such a large sum of money, or is there another so-called '*fiancé*', in your life?"

"No . . no . . of course . . not!" Eva answered, "but I wanted the money so that I could . . live here in this . . lovely little house . . but now I can go to the *Chateau*."

The Duke stared at her.

"The *Château*? Do you mean where we were last night?"

Eva nodded.

There was silence until the Duke asked:

"Does the *Comte* know that you are a friend of Leonide Leblanc?"

"I told him that I went to her for help because she had been a friend of Papa's . . but he said I was . . not to tell . . anybody . . about her."

"She was a friend of your father's?" the Duke repeated as if he was trying to understand.

Eva gave a little sob.

"Papa . . died in her . . house . . when we were staying here . . and you may think it very wrong . . that I agreed to ⌐. help Lord Charles . . because after I had paid for the . . Funeral there was . . not much . . money left."

Because she was speaking of her father, the tears came into her eyes, and her voice broke.

She felt she must make the Duke understand, and she said:

"I knew if I earned £500 that I could live here for a long time, and pay the servants, but of course, I was lying . . and Mama would have been shocked . . even though . . I was helping . . Lord Charles."

"I am beginning to understand your difficulties," the Duke said in a kind voice, "but I cannot quite understand why the *Comte* has asked you to live with his family."

Eva's eyes flickered, and she looked down before she said:

"I . . I am afraid . . when you met me . . you were told another . . lie about my . . name."

"You mean – it is not Venarde?"

"N.no."

"Then what is your real name?" the Duke asked.

"My father was . . Sir Richard Hillington."

The Duke started.

"Hillington? I cannot believe it!"

"It is true, and we came to . . Paris because Mama had been . . left this lovely house . . by her mother . . who was the *Comtesse* de Chabrillin."

The Duke drew in his breath.

"How can you have done anything so foolish as to stay on here alone after your father died, and also to be inveigled into pretending to be my brother's *fiancée*."

Eva did not answer, and the Duke said:

"Surely you should return to England where you must have relations."

"I have a great many," Eva replied, "but I think they never really . . approved of Mama . . any more than the Chabrillins . . approved of Papa when she . . ran away with him."

"I remembered now hearing that your father, whom I have often met on the race-course had caused a great deal of gossip when he was young," the Duke remarked.

"Papa and Mama . . eloped," Eva said, "when she was . . engaged to be married to a . . Frenchman . . whom the Chabrillins had . . chosen for her."

"It was obviously a very brave thing to do," the Duke said.

Eva clasped her hands together.

"Thank you for . . saying that. Mama was very . . very happy with Papa . . although she . . always felt sad that . . her family would not . . speak to her."

"And now you are going to live with them!" the Duke said reflectively, "and you think that will make you happy?"

"They are very, very kind, and I think the *Chateau* is the most beautiful place I have ever seen!"

"I thought the same," the Duke agreed, "except that I prefer my own house."

"Is it very, very impressive?" Eva asked.

"Very!" he replied.

There was the sound of something being knocked over or dropped outside the door. Eva started!

Once again the terror was back in her eyes.

"S.someone is . . there!" she said. "You do not . . think . . you do not imagine . . ?"

"Leave it to me," the Duke said.

He rose from the sofa and walked across the room.

Going out of the Salon he shut the door and Eva heard his voice speaking although she could not hear what was said.

The terror of what she had felt with the *Marquis* swept over her and she suddenly felt exhausted.

Once again her hands were shaking.

As she thought about it and she could feel the *Marquis*'s hard lips on her cheek.

She had felt despairingly that if his mouth had taken possession of hers he would have dragged her down into something dirty.

It would be something despicable from which she could not escape.

"I hate him!" she thought.

Then as the Duke did not come back she felt frantic in case he had left her.

If he did so and the *Marquis* returned, she would have no way of protecting herself.

She would be completely at his mercy.

She wanted to run upstairs and lock herself in her bedroom.

Yet it was too difficult to move from the sofa.

She could only lie back against the cushions and close her eyes.

For a moment her head seemed to be swimming, and she felt as if she was sinking into a bottomless pit.

The Duke came back into the room.

He walked to the sofa and looked down at her before he said quietly:

"It is all right! It was only your man-servant. I have given him instructions that nobody is to be allowed into the house."

Eva did not answer and the Duke realised that she was on the verge of collapse.

"Listen to me, Eva," he said gently.

With an effort she opened her eyes.

"What I am going to do," the Duke said, "is to carry you upstairs to bed. I want you to go to sleep and I will fetch you later at eight o'clock, and take you out to dinner."

She gave him a weak smile and he picked her up in his arms.

Carrying her very slowly, he went up the stairs.

When he reached the landing he said:

"You will have to show me which is your bedroom."

Eva did not speak.

She merely made a little gesture with her hand and he managed to open the door.

It was a large room which had obviously been used by her grandmother.

It was as elegantly furnished as the Salon and there were miniatures of the de Chabrillins on each side of the mantelpiece.

There was also a portrait of the *Comtesse* when she had been a girl.

There was a likeness to Eva in the shape and colour of her eyes.

The Duke put Eva gently down on the bed.

Then when he thought it unlikely she would make an effort to undress, he pulled a lace and satin cover over her legs.

"Now, go to sleep," he said, "I will tell your servants to waken you at seven o'clock."

She made a little murmur which he was sure was one of agreement.

Then as she lay with her long lashes dark against her pale cheeks he stood for a long time looking down at her.

Only when her breasts moved rhythmically was he aware that she had fallen asleep.

It was a sleep of sheer exhaustion.

He knew that it happened to men after they had been in battle, or in peril on the sea.

They slept dreamlessly from the shock.

The Duke went to the window and pulled the blind half-way down to keep out the sun.

Then with a last look at Eva he went from the room closing the door softly behind him.

He went down the stairs and looked for the servants.

He found Henri and Marie both in the kitchen.

They stood up when he appeared.

He gave them orders clearly and concisely, so that there would be no mistakes.

He then left two golden *louis* on the table and Henri thanked him profusely as he opened the front door.

"*Merci beaucoup, Monsieur, merci!*" he said several times.

"Now, you understand?" the Duke said in excellent French, "No one is to be allowed into the house, except myself."

"*Oui, oui, Monsieur*, your orders will be obeyed," Henri replied.

The Duke stepped into the Chaise that was waiting and drove surprisingly to the *Rue d'Offement*.

He had heard from Eva such a tangled tale that it seemed incredible.

He wanted confirmation of all she had told him.

The one person, he thought, who knew the truth, was Leonide Leblanc.

When he arrived there her man-servant informed him that she had just come home from a luncheon-party and was alone in the Salon.

"Announce me!" the Duke ordered, giving his name.

Leonide was looking, what Eva would have thought, even more theatrical and fantastic than usual.

Her gown was crimson and was obviously a Frederick Worth creation.

The bustle consisted of frill upon frill, ornamented with velvet and lace and a number of silk flowers.

The rows of pearls she wore round her neck were, the Duke thought, worth a 'King's ransom'.

Her ear-rings which matched them had diamond drops the size of olives.

As his name was announced Leonide was obviously surprised.

Then she moved towards him with a grace for which she was famous.

"Is it really Charles's redoubtable brother?" she asked. "I have, *Monsieur*, always longed to meet you."

"The omission can be remedied now," the Duke replied, "for the simple reason that I need your help."

Leonide gave a little exclamation of horror.

"Your brother is not in trouble? Surely, Bischoffheim has paid what he owes?"

"Yes, he has paid," the Duke affirmed.

"Then, please, *Monsieur*, sit down and tell me all about it," Leonide suggested. "I have been worrying in case something should go wrong at the last moment."

The Duke sat down comfortably and crossed his legs.

"I am most gratified to you," he said, "for taking such an interest in Charles and, as I understand, saving him from a situation which might have proved disastrous!"

"I could not imagine, Your Grace, that you would have been very pleased to have Bischoffheim's daughter for your sister-in-law."

"It is something I would have greatly disliked," the Duke said, "and my brother tells me I have to thank you for most cleverly saving him."

"I am glad to have been of service," Leonide said with a provocative smile.

She moved a little nearer to the Duke as she asked:

"And now, what can I do for you?"

"It is quite simple," the Duke said, "I want you to tell me how you met Eva Hillington."

Leonide looked at him as she was trying to read his thoughts.

Then she said perceptively:

"Are you thinking that Charles and Eva have told you lies? It is actually quite simple."

"Then please tell me the truth," the Duke begged.

"Sir Richard Hillington who was an old friend of mine," Leonide said, "inadvertently dropped his shirt – stud when he collapsed with a heart-attack. After he was buried his daughter came to ask me if it was here."

"Her father's shirt-stud?" the Duke repeated beneath his breath. "So that is how you know her!"

"While she was here," Leonide went on, "your brother arrived, having just learnt of Raphael Bischoffheim's intention of making him his son-in-law."

Leonide threw up her hands in an eloquent gesture.

"*Hélas*! From that moment the wheels started turning."

The Duke laughed.

"Of course. That Eva should be Charles's *fiancée* was your Idea. Everybody has always said you are the most intelligent woman in Paris."

"That is what I like to believe," Leonide said, "and now, tell me what has happened to your brother, and of course, to Eva."

"I have sent Charles back to England," the Duke answered, "and he has asked me to give you a present. One of the reasons why I have called is to ask you what I can buy you that you do not already have."

Leonide laughed.

"That is an easy question, when I am asked it by an Englishman."

She looked at the Duke from under her eye-lashes as she spoke, and the Duke asked:

"Well? What is it?"

"What could it be but a horse!" Leonide replied.

The Duke smiled.

"Very well, you shall have one which you will be proud to ride, and I will arrange to send it over as soon as possible."

"*Merci, Monsieur*," Leonide said, "*vous êtes très gentil*."

She moved a little nearer still as she spoke, and her lips were raised to his.

"You must thank my brother when you next see him," the Duke said. "It is his present, not mine."

Leonide was too experienced with men not to understand what lay behind his words.

She rose from the sofa.

"Now you must excuse me if I go to lie down," she said. "I have someone calling on me very shortly, and I also have several parties tonight, which will doubtless go on until very late."

The Duke rose.

"Let me thank you again," he said, "and I know, because you are a wise woman, you will not speak of this to anybody."

"I would not do anything which would hurt either your brother, of whom I am very fond, or Eva, whom I have already instructed to tell no one she has ever met me."   "I can only say again – you are a very wise woman!"

He lifted her hand to his lips and said:

"You shall have a horse on which you will look like the 'Queen of Paris' which you undoubtedly are!"

Having left Leonide the Duke drove back to the *Comte's* house.

As soon as he entered the hall he realised that his host had returned.

He walked into the Study to find him alone.

"Hello!" the *Comte* said, "and how is the Emperor?"

"In bad health and depressed," the Duke replied.

"You mean – the Prussians are making more trouble than usual?"

The Duke accepted a glass of champagne which the *Comte* handed to him and sat down in an armchair.

"If you ask me," he said, "the French are running into a trap, and unless they behave more intelligently than they are at the moment, they will challenge the Prussians which will be disastrous."

"I agree with you completely," the *Comte* said, "it would be absolutely disastrous! Did you tell the Emperor so?"

"His Majesty gave me the impression that he is being advised by too many people, at the same time being pushed by the Empress into a confrontation with a nation she has always disliked."

"Women should not interfere in politics, or in national affairs!" the *Comte* averred angrily.

"At the same time," the Duke went on, "there is quite a number of Frenchmen who think they can ride into battle with a flourish of flags and trumpets and win, just because they are French."

"I know exactly what you are saying," the *Comte* replied, "and somebody ought to do something before it is too late."

"That is just what I thought myself," the Duke said.

They talked until the *Comte* said he must dress for dinner which was the reason why he had come to Paris.

"I am dining with the Prince Napoleon tonight," he told the Duke. "He has been predicting for years that we are playing into the enemy's hands, but no one will listen to him."

When the Duke went upstairs to dress he was looking very serious.

He knew it had been reported that the Prussians had a large well-trained Army on the borders of France.

The French, with their wild extravagance, fascinating women and endless search for pleasure, would if it came to war, be able to put up very little resistance.

"If the French Army is defeated," the Duke told himself, "the Prussians might even besiege Paris!"

It seemed unlikely.

At the same time the two countries had never been compatible.

While the Duke knew their Statesmen insulted each other both privately and publicly.

As he had his bath the Duke was thinking how much the Prussians would enjoy humiliating the French.

He also knew how agonising it would be for the citizens of Paris.

Then he told himself that it was no use worrying over other people's affairs.

Thank God, the British had always had the Channel between them and the Continent.

When he dressed he found his host had already left the house.

But one of the *Comte*'s comfortable carriages was waiting for him.

He drove towards the *Rue St. Honore*, aware that he was looking forward to seeing Eva again.

She was undoubtedly extremely lovely in a very original and unusual manner.

Now he could understand her fair hair with its touched of gold came, like her fair skin, from her father.

It was her mother who had provided her dark eyes.

He had seen her exquisite features in the *Comte*'s children when he had been at the *Château*.

He thought it very remiss that he had not realised then that there was a distinct resemblance between Eva and the *Comte*'s youngest daughter, who was seventeen.

But Eva also had a vibrant personality of which he had been aware from the moment he had first met her.

What he had not been able to understand was that she was frightened of him.

He had thought at first that it was because he had not been told of her engagement to Charles.

She had continued to avoid him and had even run away from him when he had sought her out in the Library.

Then he had known that it was something deeper.

It was fear, he knew now.

A fear which was something sensitive and very different from the terror the *Marquis* had aroused in her.

He knew that even as Eva had struggled with him, she had not fully understood exactly what the Frenchman intended.

The Duke thought that only by the grace of God had he arrived in time.

He had been able to save her from an experience which would have scarred her for life.

When he had carried her up the stairs he had thought how fragile she was.

She had been very light in his arms.

When he put her down on the bed she looked like a Fairy Princess who had fallen asleep for a hundred years.

Then he remembered the tale of the Sleeping Beauty – awakened with a kiss from a Prince.

He knew as he had stood there looking down at her that he had wanted to kiss Eva.

Even if only to reassure her that she need not be afraid.

He was quite certain after what Charles had said that she had never been kissed.

It was extremely regrettable that her first experience of a man who desired her should have been with the *Marquis*. He was a dissolute and somewhat debauched man.

The Duke knew a great deal about him that he had no intention of telling Eva.

He was thinking that she would have to protect herself from him and a great number of men like him.

When she had done so she would lose her elusive innocent charm.

It made her different from the women with whom he usually came in contact.

"I must talk to her about the future," he told himself firmly.

He stepped from the carriage to where Henri was holding open the front door.

He was looking forward to the evening with a very strange feeling in his heart.

. . . .

Eva was waiting for the Duke in the Salon.

As Henri showed him in he saw her jump up from the chair in which she had been sitting.

She took a step forward as if she wanted to run towards him.

Then as if she checked herself, she walked slowly until they met in the centre of the room.

She dropped him a curtsy.

She was looking, he realised, very lovely.

He was not aware that once again she was wearing one of her mother's gowns.

It was one which Josie had admired and said needed nothing to make it more perfect.

She had taken it with her to the *Château* in case they had stayed a second night.

But now it made her look smart enough for a much more important occasion than the quiet Restaurant to which he was taking her.

"Are you feeling better?" the Duke asked.

She looked up at him with shining eyes and said:

"I slept until Marie woke me and now I must apologise for behaving so . . stupidly."

"You were not stupid and it was understandable in the circumstances," he replied.

He saw the pleasure in her eyes. Then she said in a different tone:

"I . . I have something to . . ask you."

"What is it?" he asked.

"It was . . very kind of you to . . escort me out to dinner . . but perhaps it is . . incorrect to be alone with you . . and my Uncle might be . . angry with me."

The Duke smiled.

"It is certainly something which would not be allowed if you were staying at the *Château* with the *Comtesse*. But as you have not yet taken up residence there they have for the moment no jurisdiction over you."

"So I may come with . . you," Eva asked eagerly.

"I shall be very disappointed if you refuse, and we are going somewhere which is very quiet where no one will see us, and no one will gossip about us tomorrow."

"Then that will be lovely!" Eva said. "Papa took me to two Restaurants in Paris when we first arrived, and I was afraid now that I would never be able to go to one again."

"We are going to one where the food is famous," the Duke said, "and I shall be disappointed if you do not enjoy it."

"I shall enjoy every moment," Eva promised.

"Then what are we waiting for?" he asked.

She smiled at him and he thought she seemed almost to float over the floor until they reached the hall.

There was a velvet wrap to put over her shoulders.

When they stepped into the carriage, Eva said:

"This is very exciting for me, but I am sure, because you are so important, that you should be taking somebody out like . . "

She stopped.

The Duke knew she had been about to say "Leonide Leblanc" then realised she had been told not to mention her.

Instead Eva said a little lamely:

" . . the lovely ladies who I have seen in the *Bois*."

"If you are looking for compliments," the Duke said, "I can assure you Eva, you are as lovely in fact, lovelier than any lady I have seen in the *Bois* since I arrived."

Eva gave a little cry of delight.

He thought it was very child-like and very touching

"I want to believe you," she said, "because nobody has . . ever said . . anything like . . that to me . . before."

"Then I am privileged to be the first," the Duke replied.

They drove to the *Rue Madeleine*.

There was a Restaurant near the Church where the Duke often dined when he was in Paris.

It was not fashionable, but the food was outstanding and "*Larue*" was patronised by epicures.

There was a table in an alcove which he knew of old was where one could dine and see but not be seen.

He could tell from the expression on Eva's face as they sat down that she was thrilled with her surroundings

There were comfortable sofa-seats and lighted candles on the tables.

Flowers were very much part of the decor and there was no music.

Eva looked around.

Then as she took off her gloves she said in a very young, excited voice:

"It is . . very thrilling to be here . . with you!"

She looked at the Duke as she spoke, and as their eyes met, it was difficult to look away.

Chapter Seven

The Duke took a long time choosing the food and the wine.

When the waiters had left them he sat back in his chair and said:

"I would be very remiss if I did not tell you that you look lovely!"

Eva blushed.

He thought it was something he had not seen a woman do for a long time.

When the food came it was delicious, and Eva knew her father would have appreciated it.

There were also wines with each course of which she took a tiny sip, but left the rest to the Duke.

Only when they were drinking coffee and the Duke had a liqueur beside him did Eva say:

"I shall always remember this dinner and this lovely place to which you brought me."

She spoke in the same rapt little voice he had heard when she saw something beautiful in the *Château*.

He knew it was completely sincere, and came from her heart.

"I would like you to remember it," he said, "and now Eva, I want to talk to you about yourself."

She looked at him apprehensively.

There was silence as she thought he was choosing his words with care.

Then he said:

"Are you quite certain you are wise in being determined to live in France rather than England?"

"I . . I am sure I would be happy at the *Château* where Mama was a girl," Eva replied.

She looked at the Duke, and she had the idea he was worried.

After a moment he said:

"I feel it is a mistake, as your father was English, for you to live in France."

"Why?" Eva asked.

"Well, two things worry me."

"What are they?"

"The first is that I am quite sure that within a year's time there will be a confrontation between France and Germany."

"Do you mean War?" Eva asked in astonishment.

"I am afraid it is inevitable," the Duke replied.

"I cannot believe it!" Eva cried. "Everybody in France seems so happy! Why should they want to fight the Germans?"

"It is a long story," the Duke said, "but I was with the Emperor today, and I was sure he was being pushed into War by the Empress and the *Duc* de Gramont."

"I have heard Papa talk about it," Eva said, "but I cannot believe they would sacrifice so much when everything here seems so delightful and so luxurious."

"The pleasures of Paris!" the Duke said beneath his breath.

He was thinking as he spoke of the wild extravagance of the Courtesans like Leonide Leblanc, and the vast amount of money that men expended on her.

Eva was looking at him anxiously and he said:

"If there is a War, which will be between the Prussian Army and the French, who are definitely not so well-equipped, I only hope that you are in a safe place."

"A safe place?" Eva questioned. "But I would be in my Uncle's *Châ/teau*."

"Which is less than twenty-five miles outside Paris," the Duke said.

There was silence, then Eva asked:

"Are you suggesting that the Prussians might advance on Paris and capture it?"

"I think," the Duke answered, "it might be besieged."

"I cannot believe it!" Eva whispered.

The Duke had a sip of brandy before he said:

"There is something else I think you have not considered in your decision to stay here."

"What is . . that?"

"It is that your Uncle, being French, would feel it his duty to arrange your marriage."

Eva sat upright in her chair.

"Do you mean," she asked, "that I would have an . . arranged marriage like the one . . mama ran . . away from?"

"Your Uncle would believe it was in your best interests," the Duke said quietly. "As you are well aware, the whole family disapproved of your mother because she married the man she loved."

Eva clasped her hands together.

"I never . . thought of . . that. It was . . foolish of me not to . . remember it."

"She gave a deep sigh.

"You are right . . I must go . . back to England."

"That is what I hoped you would say," the Duke replied. "And I know it is something you will not regret."

Almost beneath her breath Eva said:

"Papa's relatives are mostly . . very old . . and they will . . talk and talk . . about him. I feel I could not . . bear that at . . the moment."

"I can understand what you are feeling," the Duke said, "and if you leave it to me, I will find somebody with whom you can stay when you first arrive . . and who will be happy to have you until you find somewhere you really want to live."

"Could you . . do that?" Eva asked. "It would be very . . very kind . . but I would not wish to . . impose on . . you."

"I assure you, you would not be doing that," the Duke said, "and now, because you have had a long and upsetting day, I am going to take you home."

He saw an expression of disappointment on Eva's face and added:

"I am staying in Paris until the day after tomorrow. Have luncheon with your Uncle and tell him you have changed your mind. Then perhaps you would honour me by again being my guest at dinner."

"Of course," Eva exclaimed. "That will be . . wonderful for . . me!"

Her eyes, which had been clouded, were shining again, and the Duke went on:

"The following day, I will take you back to England. And until I do you must not do anything so foolish as walking about the streets alone."

Eva remembered that, when she had walked to visit Leonide Leblanc, the Marquis had seen her.

She gave a little shudder, and the Duke knew what she was thinking.

"Forget him!" he said.

"I . . I will try to," Eva answered, "but when you told me that my Uncle would . . arrange my marriage . . I thought I might have to . . marry . . somebody . . like the Marquis!"

"All Frenchmen are not so unpleasant," the Duke said, "and you must remember he was not treating you as if you were your father's daughter."

His voice deepened, and it was almost stern as he added:

"It is always a mistake to lie."

"I . . I know that," Eva agreed humbly, "and Mama . . would have been . . ashamed of me!"

The Duke called for the bill and they left the Restaurant.

Outside the carriage was waiting and it was only a short way to the *Rue St. Honoré*.

Eva did not speak.

The Duke, looking at her profile silhouetted against the window by the lights outside, thought she was very beautiful.

'How can she possibly look after herself?' he asked, 'when every men who sees her finds her irresistible!'

It was his experience which told him it was not only because she was so lovely that men would desire her.

There was an aura of innocence and purity about her which Leonide Leblanc had recognised.

While men like the Marquis would instinctively desire her.

The horses drew up outside the little house and as they came to a standstill Eva said in a very small, frightened voice:

"Suppose . . just suppose that . . while I have . . been away . . he has got into the . . house?"

The Duke was aware that the terror was back in her eyes and her hands were shaking.

"I will make quite certain he has not," he said gently.

He told the carriage to wait.

When Henri opened the door he walked into the house beside Eva.

They went into the Salon where there were still some candles alight in the candelabra.

As they did so they heard Henri close the front door and shuffle back to the kitchen.

Eva looked up at the Duke as if she was waiting for him to take the initiative.

He smiled at her, put out his hand and took hers.

"Now, we are going to explore the house together," he said, "then you can sleep without being frightened of anything."

She gave him a shy little smile.

As if she was a child, he took her first round the Salon.

He looked behind the curtains and an attractive screen which stood in one corner of the room.

Then they walked across the empty hall to the Dining-Room.

Small and very attractive, it had an oval table and a marble mantelpiece which the Duke recognised as being 17th Century.

Again he checked the curtains and even looked under the table.

They walked up the stairs to the First Floor.

Here it was much darker and the only light came from the candles in the sconces below them in the hall.

The Duke felt Eva's fingers tighten on his.

He went to the first door which was her bedroom, and opened it.

As he did so there was a crash.

Eva gave a scream and flung herself against him holding on to him frantically.

He put his arms around her.

In the light of one candle by the bed he saw that the crash had been caused by the draught from the window.

This had caused the curtain to billow out and knock down a plant that was on a table nearby.

It was still billowing out, but he was quite certain there was nobody behind it.

At the same time, Eva was so terrified and he could feel her whole body shaking.

"It is all right," the Duke said soothingly.

"It is him . . it is . . him!" Eva murmured. "Save me . . save me again."

She looked up at him pleadingly.

The Duke knew he had never known anyone so frightened.

"I will save you, my darling," he said.

As he spoke he pulled her closer still and his lips were on hers.

For a moment Eva could hardly believe it was happening.

Then as the Duke took possession of her lips she knew her fear had left her.

Instead, something incredibly wonderful was happening.

At first, the Duke's kiss was very gentle, as if he was afraid to frighten her more than she was already.

Then as he felt the softness and innocence of her lips, his lips became more demanding, more insistent.

It was to Eva as if the Heavens had opened. She had been carried up on a shaft of moonlight and was among the stars.

The moonlight seemed to be seeping through her body.

It was moving with an indescribable ecstasy through her breasts and on to her lips.

When the Duke raised his head she made a little murmur because she was losing him.

At the same time, the wonder of it was so overwhelming that she could only hide her face against his shoulder.

"You are quite, quite safe now, my precious," he said, in a voice that sounded a little unsteady, "and I will never let anyone hurt you!"

"I . . I love . . you," Eva whispered.

Once again there was that rapt note in her voice.

When she looked at him he knew there was a spiritual ecstasy in her face which he had never seen before.

"And I love you," he said, "and I have done for a long time."

"For a . . long . . time?"

"Ever since I first saw you, but I thought you belonged to my brother."

"And I . . thought you . . disapproved of . . me," Eva whispered.

"I disapproved of you marrying Charles because I wanted you for myself!"

His arms tightened.

"How could you have tortured me, my darling, by letting me think you would be my sister-in-law, when I wanted you as my wife?"

Eva gave a little cry and it seemed like the song of the angels.

Then she said in a whisper the Duke could hardly hear:

"Are you . . are you . . asking me to . . marry you?"

The Duke smiled.

"How else can I look after you and protect you? You are far too beautiful to be left alone for a moment!"

"I love you . . I love you with . . all of me! But . . I did not understand it was . . love."

"I will teach you about love," the Duke said, "and if any other man attempts to do so – I will kill him!"

Eva looked at him adoringly, and he went on:

"I did not mean to tell you about my love until we knew each other better, and I had taken you back to England."

"Now I . . understand why you . . wanted me to . . return home," Eva said.

"That was the principal reason. At the same time, the two objections I gave you about the War and being a French citizen are very valid."

"I want . . to be English . . and I . . want to be . . with you!" Eva said passionately.

"That is what you will be," the Duke promised, "and if, my darling, you love me enough, we can be married before we return to England."

"I love you . . so much that I . . want to . . marry you now . . at once . . at this . . moment!" Eva said.

The Duke laughed.

"That would be rather difficult, but I will try to arrange it for tomorrow, or perhaps the day after."

Eva put her head against his shoulder.

"You . . are quite . . quite certain you . . want to marry me?"

"I have never wanted to marry anyone before," the Duke said. "In fact, everybody believes I am a confirmed bachelor."

There was silence. Then Eva said:

"Supposing . . when you . . have married me . . you are disappointed . . and think you have . . made a mistake?"

The Duke smiled.

"You are everything I have ever wanted in my wife, and I love and adore everything about you. I also want to know a great deal more."

Eva looked at him solemnly.

"Will you promise to . . teach me to do . . all the things you want me to do?"

"I promise," the Duke said, "but I want you to be just as you are, and your real self."

Eva hid her face against him.

"I am . . so ashamed now that I . . lied."

The Duke knew it was not because she had lied that she had run into trouble.

It was because she had become involved with Leonide Leblanc.

At the same time, if she had not gone to see her to find her father's shirt-stud, he would never have met her.

"Fate moves in mysterious ways, my precious one," he said, "and all we have to remember is that we have found each other, and in the future we will be very, very happy."

"You do not . . think," Eva asked, "that it will be . . a shock to your family that you have . . married somebody . . as unimportant as . . me?"

"I think quite a number of them will have met your father," he said, "in which case, he would have charmed them as he charmed everybody he met."

"That is what I . . like to . . hear you . . say," Eva said, "and perhaps . . I shall be able to . . charm them too."

"I am quite certain you will," the Duke said, "just as you have charmed me."

He kissed her again and went on kissing her.

Now she was travelling on a rainbow into a Heaven she had never known existed.

"It is a heaven of Love," she told herself.

She felt such an indescribable ecstasy that she thought no one could feel such sensations and not die of the wonder of it.

Finally the Duke said:

"I want to stay here, my darling, kissing you and telling you how wonderful you are, but you must go to sleep."

Because she felt so happy, Eva had forgotten her fear that the *Marquis* might be hiding somewhere.

Then as she glanced across the room the Duke said:

"We will just finish exploring the house. Light some candles while I shut the windows."

Eva did as he told her and the extra candles made the room seem warm and glamorous.

The Duke shut the window but before he did so he looked outside.

There was a sheer drop to the small garden.

It was impossible for anybody to climb up, unless they had a very long ladder.

He did not say anything, but pulled the curtains to, and picked up the plant which was lying on the floor.

Then he walked across the room, and taking Eva by the hand as he had before, he took her out into the passage.

They explored the other two bedrooms which were rather smaller than the one in which Eva was sleeping.

There was no one in them.

As they came out the Duke locked the doors on the outside and gave Eva the keys.

"Now you are to lock yourself in," he said, "and I will tell your man-servant that no one – and I mean no one – is to be allowed to enter the house until I arrive tomorrow morning."

"You will not . . forget me?"

"That would be impossible."

The Duke was standing at the top of the stairs and he held her close against him.

Then he said:

"To make things easier for you, my lovely one, I am going to tell your Uncle, whom I shall see at breakfast tomorrow morning, that we are to be married."

He paused to look at her tenderly.

"There will be no point therefore in you having luncheon with him as he had arranged."

"You will tell him I am very . . grateful for his . . kindness?" Eva said.

"Of course I will," the Duke agreed, "but as I want to be with you every minute, we will have luncheon quietly. By that time I shall have a lot to tell you as to when and how we can be married."

Eva gave a little murmur of joy.

Then he was kissing her gently and very lovingly, as if she was infinitely precious.

"Now go into your bedroom," he said, "and let me hear you lock the door, and try to go to sleep."

"I shall say my . . prayers and thank God a . . million times that you . . love me," Eva said.

As if her words moved him, the Duke kissed her forehead.

Then he turned her round to push her gently through the door of her bedroom and shut it behind her.

He heard her turn the key in the lock, then he went downstairs.

He gave his orders to Henri, tipped him because he had stayed up late.

Then he heard the bolts on the front door go into place before he drove away.

His carriage carried him back to the house near the *Bois*.

He knew he was prepared to dedicate his whole life to loving and protecting Eva.

He had never felt like this about any other woman.

He knew how utterly helpless she was without him.

There were terrible difficulties in which she could find herself, not only in France but also in England.

"She needs me," he told himself, "and she is what I need, but never realised it until now."

. . . .

When the Duke came down to breakfast, the *Comte* was already sitting at the table with the Newspaper open in front of him.

"The papers are already working the public up against the Prussians," he said. "I can only hope they will not go too far."

The Duke did not reply.

He had already told the *Comte* his feelings as to what would happen, and knew he had not been believed.

Instead he changed the subject.

He told the *Comte* that he was going to marry Eva.

The *Comte* was completely astonished.

"I had no idea! It never struck me for a moment that you were interested in her," he said.

The Duke smiled.

"I find her completely adorable."

"I agree with you, but of course, I am delighted for one of my most distinguished friends to marry my niece."

"I hoped that was how you would feel," the Duke said, "and now I want your help."

It was the *Comte* as the Duke hoped, who made everything easy for him and Eva to have a secret marriage.

"If the British Embassy get to hear of it," he said, "it will be blazoned over every newspaper in England!"

"That is what I thought," the Duke agreed. "In which case, as you are aware, Eva will be criticized for marrying when she is in deep mourning, and there will be a great many speculations as to why the marriage should take place so quickly."

The two men did not need to say any more to each other.

Both were aware of how unpleasant gossip could be.

The Duke and the *Comte* had worked out what they thought was a perfect plan.

Then the Duke borrowed one of the *Comte* Phaetons and drove to Eva's house in the *Rue St. Honoré*.

She was dressed in one of her prettiest gowns, and was waiting for him in the Salon.

As he came into the room and Henri shut the door behind him she took a little step towards him.

Then she hesitated although she was longing to run to his side.

He smiled and held out his arms and the next minute she was in them.

He could feel her whole body quivering with excitement.

He kissed her until they were both breathless.

Then he said:

"Let me look at you, my darling. Did you sleep well?"

"I slept . . and I dreamt you were . . kissing me."

"That is what I was dreaming too," the Duke replied.

He kissed her again, then drew her towards the sofa.

"I have so much to tell you," he said.

"Which I am longing to hear," Eva replied quickly.

"First," the Duke began, "tell me you have not changed your mind."

Eva laughed, and it was a very pretty sound.

"I was afraid . . you might have . . changed yours."

"That would be impossible," the Duke said.

She lifted her lips to his, but he pushed her a little away from him.

"You are not to tempt me," he said. "I want to kiss you, and go on kissing you, but first you have to listen to what I have planned."

"You are not . . sending me . . back to England . . without you?"

"Do you really think I would do such a thing?"

"I was only . . afraid you . . would think that . . the right thing to do."

"What we are going to do," he explained, "are all the things which other people might think were wrong, but everything that is right for us."

Eva clasped her hands together and moved a little closer to him.

"We are . . going to be . . married?" she whispered.

"A secret marriage which no one will know about for a long time."

"Tell me . . please . . tell me."

"I have worked it out with your Uncle," the Duke said, "who, incidentally is delighted that you are marrying me."

"You are . . quite sure he is . . not angry?"

"Not in the least," the Duke smiled. "He is very pleased to have an English Duke in the family."

Eva laughed.

"What we have arranged," the Duke went on, "is that your Uncle is at the moment having our marriage registered at the *Mairie* so that in an hour's time, you will legally be my wife."

Eva drew in her breath and her eyes seemed to fill her face.

She did not speak, and the Duke went on:

"Because your Uncle has influence, the Mayor will not make the announcement public and everything will be kept secret until we are ready to send a notice of our marriage to the English newspapers."

Eva made a little murmur of excitement, and the Duke continued:

"This evening at six o'clock your Uncle will call for you and take you to the house of one of his friends, who has his own private Chapel."

Eva slipped her hand into the Duke's as if she wanted to hold onto him and he said:

"We will be married by a Priest who is your Uncle's private Chaplain, who will of course never reveal what has occurred."

Eva looked up at him with a puzzled expression in her eyes.

"A . . Priest?" she questioned.

"It was your Uncle who told me that after you were born your mother wrote to her mother, your grandmother and told her that because she had been brought up a Catholic you had been baptised into the Catholic Faith. Then because she loved your father also as a Protestant."

Eva gave a little cry.

"Now you mention it, I remember Mama telling me that a long time ago. I never thought of it again because Mama and Papa always went to an English Church near our home."

She paused before she said:

"Mama loved him so much that she always did exactly what he wished . . and never thought of . . herself."

"Will you do the same?" the Duke asked.

"I will . . always do what you want . . as Mama once said . . love is more important than . . anything else."

"Of course it is!" the Duke agreed, "and the love we have for each other, my beautiful little wife-to-be, comes from God and is greater than any Service or ritual. I believe in all truth, it is part of the Divine."

He spoke very solemnly, and Eva said:

"How can you . . think as I think . . believe as I do? I never thought I would find a man . . who could do that."

"Now you have found me," the Duke said, "and after we are married we will be one person."

"It will be . . wonderful to be a part of you," Eva said, "and I shall always . . remember that you are the . . most important part!"

The Duke smiled.

"That, of course, is what I want you to think, but nothing in the world is more important to me than you!"

He kissed her again and she knew that no one could be more wonderful.

They had a quiet luncheon together, talking about themselves.

When Eva went back to her house she told Henri and Marie she was going to be married.

They were extremely excited and impressed, and promised to keep it a complete secret.

"My husband and I will be staying here tonight," Eva went on, "but tomorrow we are leaving for Venice. After that we are going to Rome and Naples where we will take a yacht which my husband will charter and visit the many places in the Mediterranean."

As she spoke she thought that nothing could be more exciting than to be alone with the Duke.

She also wanted to see all the places about which she had read, but thought she would never have the opportunity of visiting.

But all that really mattered, she thought, was to be with him.

"We are going to have a very long honeymoon, my precious," the Duke had said, "and only just before we return to England will our marriage be announced, without the actual date when it took place. If people assume it was a week or so before then, that is their business and now ours."

He smiled at her.

"Then you will be able to go back home without wearing mourning, so there will be no one saying that you should have waited until after your father's death for a longer time before you took a husband."

"I know Papa would . . want me to marry . . you and would . . think like . . that," Eva said.

"I am sure he would," the Duke replied, "and I know your father would want me to look after you."

"Now I shall feel safe for ever .. and ever!" Eva said, "and I need .. never be .. afraid again!"

"Never!" the Duke agreed firmly.

．　．　．　．　．　．　．

When the Duke left her in her house, on his instructions she promised Henri and Marie that she would increase their wages.

They were to look after everything for her and she would come to Paris as often as she could.

As she was going upstairs wondering what gown she should wear in which to be married, a box was delivered at the door.

It contained a very beautiful wedding-gown from Frederick Worth.

It was so exquisite that Eva could not believe it was really for her.

When she put it on Marie admitted that the Duke had taken one of her gowns away with him.

That was how he knew the exact size of her tiny waist.

The bustle in silver tulle ornamented with diamanté made the gown so beautiful that Eva was almost afraid to wear it.

When she was dressed there was a veil over her hair held down by a wreath of orange blossom.

As she looked in the mirror she knew that all she wanted was for the Duke to admire her.

She knew too that although it would be a small and quiet Service it would be something neither of them would ever forget.

She drove with her Uncle to a huge mansion in the *Champs Elysees*.

When she saw the Duke waiting for her in the tiny Chapel, her heart turned a thousand somersaults.

In evening dress, wearing his decorations as was correct in France, the Duke looked handsome yet at the same time very English.

Her Uncle took her up the sort aisle on his arm.

Then as the Duke took her hand in his the Service began.

It was very short because, although Eva was counted as a Catholic, the Duke was a Protestant.

The Priest said the words in Latin and in French so that they both understood.

When they knelt for the blessing, Eva knew she had indeed been blessed.

She would thank God all her life for letting her find the Duke.

Because he knew it would please the *Comte* the Duke had agreed that they would go back to his house.

There they drank champagne.

The *Comte* said over and over again how pleased he was that his niece was now the Duchess of Kincraig.

"I had intended to find you a husband, my dear," he said to Eva, "but even if I had searched the whole of France I doubt if I could have found you a man more distinguished or more charming . . "

Eva drew in her breath and slipped her hand into her husband's.

She knew he was thinking he had been right in saying that the *Comte* would have considered it his duty to marry her to some aristocrat.

She had been saved from that.

Before they drove away back to the little house, that was waiting for them the *Comte* gave Eva a present.

It was a very beautiful brooch from Oscar Masin a famous Jeweller who had made many lovely things for the Empress.

The Duke knew he had also created some magnificent pieces of jewellery for the Courtesans.

He waited until they were back in the *Rue St. Honore* before he said:

"You have had one wedding present, my darling, and now I want to give you mine."

"But . . I have . . nothing for . . you!" Eva cried.

"You can give me a present which I want more than anything else in the world," the Duke replied, "but I will tell you about that later."

She was not quite certain what he meant.

At the same time, because of the way he spoke she blushed.

He kissed her before he said:

"There are wonderful jewels waiting for you at Castle Kincraig when we arrive home, but this is something very special which is all your own, and which I hope you will always wear."

As he spoke he brought from his coat-tails a velvet box.

He opened it and Eva saw a most exquisite ring made in the shape of a heart.

In the centre was a diamond surrounded by diamonds.

As they glittered in the light, she knew it was the most precious thing she had ever owned.

She kissed her husband and he held her so close that it was difficult to breathe.

"There are thousands more things I want to give you," he said, "but we will have time on our honeymoon to search for treasures and they will always remind us of our happiness."

"Then they will be very, very precious!" Eva said quietly.

The Duke had arranged for dinner to be sent from '*Larue*' where they had dined the precious night.

Henri, helped by a young waiter, served it with a flourish.

They were all dishes, Eva knew, that the Duke had discovered she liked the best.

But it was difficult to think of what she was eating, and she kept thinking how handsome he was.

She knew by the expression in his eyes that he was thinking only of her.

There were sudden silences in what they were saying, and they spoke to each other without words.

. . . .

It was much later that night in the bed which Eva had always felt was too big for one small person.

She moved against the Duke's shoulder and he asked:

"Are you awake, my lovely one?"

"How can I . . ever sleep again . . when I am . . so happy?" Eva asked.

"I have made you happy?"

"So wildly, ecstatically happy that I cannot believe I am . . still alive . . or if I am . . I must be dreaming!"

"You are very much alive," the Duke said, "and darling, we will go on dreaming for a very long time."

Eva pressed her cheek against him.

"Y.you were . . not disappointed in me?" she whispered.

"How can you think anything so foolish?" he answered, "you were perfect and my precious, no man could have a more enchanting wedding present."

"Do you . . mean . . me?" Eva asked.

"Yes, my beautiful wife, I mean you!"

"I . . did not know that . . love could be so . . wonderful," Eva said.

"I . . I did not understand . . that it could be even more marvellous than your . . kisses!"

"Is that what it was?" the Duke enquired.

"There are . . no words to tell you that when you . . loved me you took me into Heaven . . and I think I am . . still there!"

"That is where we will always be," the Duke said, "in our own special secret Heaven, my precious heart, where nobody will ever frighten you."

"I . . love . . you! I . . love you!" Eva murmured.

It was something they both said to each other a hundred times.

But there was no other way in which they could express the glory and ecstasy of their love.

It came from Heaven, it was part of Heaven and would be theirs for Eternity.

The Scent of Roses

AUTHOR'S NOTE

Tsar Alexander II disliked war, but the Empress wanted to reinstate Constantinople as the greatest City in Christendom.

The Russians had an age-old dream of opening the Straits to Russian Ships.

In 1875, Serbia declared war on Turkey and thousands of Russian volunteers poured into Belgrade.

After the uprising in Bulgaria, the terrible reprisals of the Turks were described by a British Diplomat as:

'The most horrendous crime of the Century?'

In Britain the Leader of the Opposition, Mr Gladstone, took up the cause fiercely and the people applauded him.

The Prime Minister, Lord Beaconsfield was, however, conscious that the only country that the Russians feared on their march on Constantinople was Britain.

The Tsar, pressurised by his brother The Grand Duke Nicholas as well as the Empress, finally declared war in the Spring of 1877, which is where this story begins.

What the Marquis suggested as a show of strength actually took place.

The conflict lasted nine months and due to Britain's intervention the Russians never took Constantinople and were denied access to the Mediterranean which they had hoped to reach through Bulgaria.

As Lord Beaconsfield said gleefully to Queen Victoria:

'Prince Gorchakov says: "We have sacrificed one hundred-thousand picked soldiers and one hundred million pounds for nothing!"'

When I visisted Cuzco in 1977, there were still many beautiful 17th Century buildings fading in the sun, bulging out of their frames and being allowed to rot through neglect.

The Virgin in the Rose Garden by Lochner is now in the Louvre in Paris.

Chapter One

Nikola walked across the garden.

She was thinking as she did so how beautiful the house was.

"King's Keep" had been in her family since the reign of Henry VIII.

It had been used as a Hunting Lodge for Queen Elizabeth.

It was, Nikola thought, redolent not only with history but also with the ghosts of the past.

She could understand why her brother loved it more than anything else in the world.

Laughingly she often said to him:

"Any wife, if you ever had one, will be desperately jealous of King's Keep."

"It is mine!" he said fiercely. "Mine, and no one shall take it from me!"

He had talked like that ever since he was a small boy.

Yet now, as she thought about what he was doing so that King's Keep could continue being his, she shivered.

She was expecting him now.

She wondered apprehensively what he would have to tell her.

"How can we go on in this way?" she asked.

She was looking at the house as she spoke.

But it was really a prayer to her mother.

Nikola thought she would understand better than her father how dangerously her brother was behaving.

In a way she could understand.

It was agonising for him to see the house falling into disrepair.

He did not have enough money to keep it as perfect as it had been.

Sir James Tancombe was the 10th Baronet and exceedingly proud of his lineage.

Nikola often thought if King's Keep were taken away from him he would die of a broken heart.

They had very few servants.

She helped those there were almost from the moment she got up in the morning until she went to bed.

If there was a speck of dust, if a piece of furniture wanted polishing, or one of the beautiful old embroidered curtains needed mending, James's eagle eye would see it.

It hurt him as if it was a wound in his flesh.

This morning, because he was coming home, Nikola had inspected all the rooms.

She had made quite certain he would be unable to find anything wrong.

She could still remember the agony in his eyes when a year ago the ceiling fell in one of the bedrooms.

It was after that, they had almost starved themselves.

They had to find the money to repair it.

Then Jimmy, as she called her brother, had said:

"This cannot go on, and I know exactly what I am going to do!"

"What is that?" Nikola asked.

She was not hopeful that he would think of anything really helpful.

Only a week earlier one of their relatives had said harshly:

"It is no use, James, I cannot help you any more, and the best thing you can do is to sell King's Keep. After all, it is only a house!"

Nikola had seen the fury in her brother's eyes.

She knew King's Keep was not just a house to him.

It was everything – everything that mattered.

Everything that was important, everything that gave him a sense of stability.

She could remember when he was young the happiness in his eyes when he returned home from School.

"I am home! I am home!" he would shout.

It was not really his father and mother he had missed. But King's Keep.

She hoped they would not know how shocked she had been when she had realised what he was doing.

He had taken her to stay with an ancient Aunt.

She had been a Tancombe before she married Lord Hartley.

Now she was a widow and very wealthy.

Nikola thought however, it was extremely unlikely that Jimmy would get a penny out of her.

Yet she was sure that was the purpose of their visit.

They had driven down the narrow, twisting lanes which made their journey a tiring one.

All the way there she was wishing they had stayed at home.

It was Jimmy who had suggested they should stay with their aunt.

Nikola knew he hoped to persuade her to give him enough money for repairs.

They were urgently needed on the roof.

Moreover some of the diamond panes of the windows needed replacing, and the floors in several of the main rooms were cracking.

They needed to be relaid with stronger supports.

She thought her brother was going to be disappointed.

His charm which fascinated most women, would be wasted on their Aunt Alice.

She had therefore said rather tentatively:

"You know, Jimmy dear, Aunt Alice is very mean, and Nanny told us the last time we stayed there that there was hardly enough to eat in the Servants' Hall."

"I know that," Jimmy replied.

"She never gives a penny to charity, and Nanny says she even begrudges the flowers she puts on her husband's grave."

Jimmy laughed.

"I thought I had heard all that before, but this is a new story!"

"Then do you really think," Nikola said, "that she will listen to you pleading for money to repair King's Keep?"

"I am not going to ask her for a penny!" her brother replied.

Nikola stared at him in astonishment.

"You are not?" she exclaimed. "Then why are we going to stay with her?"

"I will tell you later," Jimmy replied evasively.

They arrived at the large, rather ugly house.

It stood in a large garden with woods behind it.

The garden was not well kept.

Lady Hartley economised on the number of gardeners she employed.

As they went in through the front door, Nikola noticed that the Butler's coat was almost threadbare.

Even the footman's liveried waist-coat was almost in shreds.

"I cannot imagine," she said to herself, "why Jimmy insists on coming to this depressing place."

Her Aunt was waiting for them in the Drawing-Room.

"Oh, here you are!" she exclaimed when they appeared. "It is nice to see you. At the same time, it makes a lot of extra work for the staff."

"It is too long since we visited you," Jimmy said with one of his charming smiles, "and you know, Aunt Alice, I feel, as head of the family, I should keep in touch with all my relations."

"Personally I should have thought it a waste of time," Lady Hartley said sharply, "but now you are here I suppose you would like a glass of sherry?"

"It is certainly something I would welcome after the dust on the roads," Jimmy replied.

He was given a minute glass.

There was only enough sherry in it to be swallowed in two or three sips.

Nikola, being a young girl, was offered nothing.

She was very thirsty.

She was glad when she went up to change for dinner to drink the water that was in a glass bottle on the wash-stand.

There was not any water for her to drink at dinner.

It was a sparse meal, although the chicken lunch that was the main course came from the Home Farm.

Jimmy was allowed two glasses of a rather indifferent white wine.

He was also given a small glass of port.

He, however, talked charmingly to Lady Hartley, telling her stories of their other relatives.

He also paid her compliments which were obviously a novelty.

She accepted them with a certain amount of coyness.

When they moved into the Drawing-Room he said:

"I never realised before, Aunt Alice, what a vast number of pictures you have, and I am also very impressed by your collection of snuff-boxes."

"I did not collect them," Lady Hartley replied. "Your Uncle

Edward wasted a great deal of money buying things that were of interest only to him."

"Well, they interest me!" Jimmy said. "So I am going to take the opportunity, now I am here, to look at everything that Uncle Edward treasured, as I should do if they were mine."

"I should have thought you had enough 'Treasures', as you call them, at King's Keep!" Lady Hartley said tartly.

"One can never have too much of a good thing," Jimmy replied.

He got up as he spoke and started to walk round the Drawing-Room.

He looked at the pictures.

Then he inspected the collection of snuff-boxes which were in glass-topped cabinets.

He then left the room, explaining that he wanted to inspect some of the other rooms.

Lady Hartley started to tell Nikola of the difficulties of getting good servants.

The extravagance of the younger ones appalled her who preferred to throw away a torn sheet rather than darn it.

Jimmy was away for a long time.

Nikola could not imagine what there was to interest him in this ugly house.

The pictures might be good, but they needed cleaning.

The lack of light did not show them off to their best advantage.

The walls on which they hung were painted with drab colours.

Or else papered with what she thought were extremely dull designs.

When Jimmy returned to the Drawing-Room he congratulated his Aunt on the way the house was kept.

"I see, Aunt Alice," he said, "you expect perfection, as I do. But it is sad to see so many rooms shut up and apparently unused."

"I cannot afford to have a lot of people staying with me," Lady Hartley answered. "What do I want with a lot of chattering magpies, or to be asked to Balls and Receptions which are only for the 'Idle Rich'?"

Nikola gave her a wistful smile.

"I would love to attend a Ball," she said, "and perhaps next year, when we are out of mourning, Jimmy will be able to arrange it."

"If you are thinking of having a Season in London, it is something I am quite certain you cannot afford!" Lady Hartley said.

She did not see the disappointment in Nikola's eyes, but went on:

"A friend was telling me only a few days ago what it cost for her daughter to be a débutante and – would you believe it? – after all the trouble she went to, the stupid girl never received a single proposal of marriage!"

"I . . I suppose her parents . . had hoped that . . by taking her to London . . she would find a . . husband," Nikola said a little hesitatingly.

"Of course they did!" Lady Hartley agreed. "But it does not surprise me that the young women of today find it difficult to get one, seeing that their . . "

Nikola did not listen any more.

She had already heard her aunt's views about the young.

"They are uppish and impertinent!" she exclaimed.

There was no point in arguing.

Of one thing Nikola was quite certain: if she wished to shine in London Society, their Aunt would not assist her in any way.

She would, in fact, not offer to pay for so much as a petticoat, let alone a gown.

She wondered if that was one of the reasons why Jimmy had brought her here.

She could have told him, if he had asked her, that it was a waste of time.

They said good-bye the next morning.

It was obvious to Nikola that their aunt was pleased to see them go.

She thought Lady Hartley begrudged every mouthful they had consumed.

"I hope you will come to see us at King's Keep," Jimmy said politely as they said good-bye.

"It is too far for my horses," his Aunt replied.

As they drove down the drive Nikola said:

"I do hope we shall not have to go there again! The beds are uncomfortable, and mine was short of blankets." She looked at her brother as she spoke.

She saw to her surprise that he was smiling.

"You cannot really have enjoyed yourself, Jimmy?" she exclaimed. "I cannot imagine how Papa, who was always such fun and so very generous, could have such a stingy old sister as that!"

"Nor can I," Jimmy replied. "But do you realise that house is packed with Collectors' items?"

"Do you mean the pictures?" Nikola asked.

"Uncle Edward knew what he was doing when he bought them," Jimmy said, "and they must have gone up in value a dozen times since."

Nikola shrugged her shoulders.

"I cannot see how that helps us."

Jimmy did not reply.

When they arrived back at King's Keep he came into the Drawing-Room.

Nikola, who was repairing a piece of tapestry on one of the chairs, looked up.

She saw that Jimmy had changed his clothes.

He was carrying something in his hands.

"Have you unpacked?" she asked. "There was no reason to. I will do it after tea."

"I have unpacked," Jimmy replied, "because I have something to show you."

He put what he was carrying down on the table.

Nikola got up to walk towards him.

She saw that he was holding two very pretty miniatures and an oil-painting.

"What are those?" she asked.

"I found the picture in one of the upstairs rooms which are shut up and never used," Jimmy replied.

"Upstairs rooms?" Nikola repeated.

Then she gave a little cry.

"You mean . . they are Aunt Alice's? Oh, Jimmy, how could you have taken them away with you?"

"Very easily," he answered, "and I am certain that the old girl will never notice they are missing!"

Nikola gave a cry.

"But, Jimmy, – that is . . stealing!"

"In a good cause," he replied. "The money I will get for these will repair the roof!"

Nikola stared at him in horror.

"But . . you cannot mean . . to sell them? But, Jimmy, you could go to prison for theft!"

"That is a risk I shall have to take," Jimmy replied, "and what is the point of that old hag sitting on a 'gold mine'? She does not appreciate them, and certainly has no intention of sharing them with anybody else."

Nikola could only stare at him.

She thought how shocked her mother would be.

Jimmy was stealing, even if it was for his beloved house.

"And . . the . . miniatures?" she faltered after a moment.

"I found those in a drawer of Uncle Edward's desk in the Study. He must have bought them just before he died, and did not have time to hang them."

He touched one gently.

"They are both over two hundred years old, and there is no reason, if I sell them, why anybody should connect them with him."

"J.Just suppose . . somebody . . guessed they did not . . belong to you?"

"Who is likely to do that?" Jimmy asked. "As far as I can gather from the way Aunt Alice was speaking, she did not encourage any of the family to visit her."

He saw the stricken look in his sister's eyes.

He put his arms round her.

"Now be sensible, Nikola," he said. "We have to save King's Keep, and what I have done in taking these will not hurt anybody."

"But . . it is wrong . . I know it is . . wrong!" Nikola murmured.

"Then I suppose this will upset you," Jimmy said.

He put his hand in his pocket.

He drew out something very small which he placed in the palm of his hand.

It glittered in the sunshine coming through the window.

"What . . is it?" Nikola asked in a frightened voice.

"It is a diamond!"

"Where did you . . get it?"

"From one of the snuff-boxes."

Nikola made a stifled sound of horror but Jimmy went on:

"If, which is very unlikely, Aunt Alice or anyone else notices it has gone, they will just think it has fallen out, perhaps years ago."

Nikola did not speak.

After a moment Jimmy said:

"You will learn that people cease after a time to notice things that are familiar, things that have always been there."

That was true, Nikola was to find in the next few months.

Jimmy sold what he had taken for what seemed to her to be a large sum of money.

She thought he would be satisfied.

It certainly mended the roof and repaired the windows and the floors.

All the time there were workmen in the house Nikola tried to persuade herself that what Jimmy had done was not really wrong.

The money had been spent in preserving something of historic value.

At the same time, she prayed that he would not be punished.

Her mother would definitely have thought of it as a sin.

When the money had all been spent she realised Jimmy was restless.

"The curtains in the hall are faded," he said, "and something should be done about it."

"That is certainly something we cannot afford," Nikola said without thinking.

Then she saw the expression on her brother's face.

She felt as if a cold hand gripped her heart.

"Oh no Jimmy!" she cried. "You are not thinking . ."

But it was what he was thinking.

A week later he told her they were going to stay with another relative.

This one lived in an isolated part of Norfolk.

He was a Cousin who had married a woman very much richer than he was.

Her blood was not as "blue" as his.

The Tancombe family had always suspected that her money came from trade.

They had two rather plain daughters, both of marriagable age.

The moment they arrived Nikola was aware that they considered that Jimmy as the 10th Baronet, was a good matrimonial catch.

The house was certainly in contrast to the cheese-paring and discomfort they had endured with Lady Hartley.

Colonel Arthur Tancombe and his wife lived in the most luxurious fashion.

There were four footmen in the hall and two house-maids to unpack Nikola's small trunk.

There was champagne to drink before dinner.

Different wines were served with every course.

Their cousins both had been presented at Court the previous year.

The Colonel and his wife had given them a Ball in London, and were planning another in the country.

It was only regrettable that they were both exceedingly plain.

They looked, Nikola discovered,their best on a horse.

Jimmy, however, put himself out to be charming.

Not only to the two girls, but also to Mrs. Tancombe.

They were delighted with him.

"Your brother is a delightful young man," she said to Nikola. "I cannot understand why he has not married."

"I am afraid it is something he cannot afford," Nikola replied.

"There are a great number of heiresses looking for a husband," Mrs. Tancombe said rather pointedly.

Later in the evening she confided to Nikola that Adelaide, her elder daughter, had accepted a proposal of marriage.

It was from a man who had nothing to offer her but his family tree.

"There were however, no titles in his family," Mrs. Tancombe explained, "and as he was thirty-nine, we felt he was really too old for Adelaide."

"Much too old," Nikola agreed. "And I do hope she finds somebody she loves."

Mrs. Tancombe laughed.

"My mother always said to me that love comes after marriage, but I was very fortunate, and fell in love with my husband as soon as I saw him."

Looking at the Colonel Nikola thought he had undoubtedly been very handsome in his youth.

Good looks ran in the Tancombe family.

It was just unfortunate that his two daughters resembled their mother.

It was Mrs. Tancombe's money that had furnished the house in such an extravagant manner.

The pictures, however, had been collected by generations of the Colonel's family.

Nikola was not surprised that Jimmy was looking at them with interest.

"It is nice to think you care about such things," she heard the Colonel say to him. "I always wanted a son who would bear my name."

"I am particularly interested in the family portraits," Jimmy replied, "and I see you have quite a collection of early Masters."

"They belonged to my great-grandfather," the Colonel answered. "He bought this house, I have always believed, simply because it had plenty of wall space!"

He laughed.

"Well, he certainly covered it," Jimmy replied.

Escorted by the Colonel, he went from room to room.

In one he noticed there was a collection of small Chinese bowls.

"Where did these come from?" he asked.

"That was another relative, a distant Cousin," the Colonel explained. "He left the collection to my father when he died, but I cannot say I find it very attractive. I prefer the pictures."

"So do I," Jimmy agreed. When they returned to King's Keep he showed Nikola three Chinese bowls.

"This one is Ming, this is Sung, and the last is the Ch'ing dynasty," he told her.

"Are they very . . valuable?" she asked.

"They are unique – priceless!" Jimmy answered.

"And . . you have . . stolen them," Nikola murmured beneath her breath.

"Only from somebody who does not appreciate them! Therefore he has no right to anything so splendid!"

"But . . supposing the Colonel . . notices they have . . gone?"

"It is very unlikely," Jimmy replied. "He is only interested in pictures, and I would be surprised if he has ever counted the bowls or anything else in the house."

There was no use telling Jimmy she thought it wrong.

He went to London the next day.

He came back wildly elated with what he had obtained for the bowls from a Connoisseur of Oriental pottery.

"He told me he had never dreamt of being lucky enough to find such perfect specimens," Jimmy boasted.

"He is . . not going to . . sell them again?" Nikola asked anxiously.

"No, fortunately. He wishes to keep them for himself."

Nikola gave a sigh of relief.

She had been afraid that if a lot of the bowls were put up for sale they might be written up in the newspapers.

Then the Colonel might think they were just the same as some he owned.

She lay awake all night worrying about the Chinese bowls.

But by the end of the year she had grown used to Jimmy taking her to stay with some remote relative.

Only once did they come away empty-handed.

That was because Jimmy had found nothing in the house that was really worth taking.

She had to admit that the improvements to King's Keep made the whole house glow like a precious jewel.

The ancient pink bricks were repointed.

The windows and the door were painted.

Then one by one, the rooms inside were redecorated.

It was beginning to look very lovely.

But Nikola held her breath every time a visitor admired it.

She was always afraid they would wonder how it had all been paid for.

Now as she reached the house she was aware that Jimmy should be back within the hour.

He had gone to London to sell a picture.

He had found it in the last house where they had stayed.

It belonged to a distant relative, Lord Mersey, who was a widower.

He had no children but was, Jimmy said, very close.

That meant, Nikola knew, he had refused at one time or another to lend him any money.

Lord Mersey had been born a Tancombe.

He had become a Peer when after a distinguished career at the Bar and on the Bench he had finally become a Lord of Appeal in Ordinary.

It was quite a large picture.

When he had carried it into her bedroom late at night she had exclaimed:

"But . . you cannot take . . that! It is so big that they will know at once that . . it has gone!"

"It is 17th century, and by Dughet. French artists who studied in Italy are beginning to fetch large prices," Jimmy said in a hard voice.

"W. Where did you . . find it?"

"In the big Servants' Hall which is only used when they have shooting parties."

"Surely the . . servants will see it has . . gone?" Nikola questioned.

Jimmy smiled.

"You under-rate me, my dear little sister! I have replaced it with a eleograph which I am certain they will admire far more than this!"

Nikola drew in her breath.

"It is . . the same . . size?"

"Almost exactly! I found that in a passage on the top floor where no one will miss it!"

As he spoke he wiped his handkerchief gently over the picture to remove the dust.

"This is going to give us the new curtains for the Dining-Room," he said, "and will pay the wages for another man in the garden."

There was a note in his voice which told Nikola it was no use arguing with him.

He was like a man in love.

He would do anything, however disreputable, for King's Keep.

He had brought the picture to Nikola's room because her trunk was already half-packed.

It was ready for them to leave the following morning.

"I have so few things with me," Jimmy said, "that the Valet would notice this picture if I carried it in my luggage."

"I do not want it in mine!" Nikola said quickly.

Even as she spoke she knew it was no use saying that to her brother.

He opened her trunk and lifted out the clothes which her maid had already packed and were neatly folded.

He placed the picture at the bottom.

He then put back the clothes he had taken out.

"Now you pack the rest," he said, "and make quite certain your maid does not rummage about if she puts in anything that has been left until the last minute."

Nikola found it impossible to sleep.

She was so frightened.

But they left without anybody suspecting that they carried away with them a picture.

Jimmy had taken it to London.

She told herself she should not be interested.

Yet she longed to hear what he had obtained for it.

As she entered the house she heard the sound of carriage-wheels outside the front-door.

She did not wait for Butters.

He was suffering from rheumatism and therefore was slow on his feet.

She pulled open the door.

Jimmy stepped out of the carriage in which he had been travelling.

She knew by the expression on his face that all was well.

"You are home! You are home! Oh, Jimmy, I am so glad to see you!" she cried.

He bent to kiss her cheek, then said:

"Yes, I am back, and I have some very exciting news to tell you!"

He walked into the house.

Butters, who had arrived belatedly from the kitchen-quarters, collected his luggage.

They entered the Drawing-Room which overlooked the garden.

"What has happened?" Nikola asked in a conspiratorial tone.

"A great deal," Jimmy replied. "I have obtained a thousand guineas for the picture!"

Nikola gave a gasp.

"As much as that?"

"More important," her brother went on, "we have been invited to stay with the Marquis of Ridgmont, and we are going there next Friday."

"The . . Marquis of . . R.Ridgmont?" Nikola repeated, thinking she had not heard of him before.

"His is one of the largest collections of pictures in the country," Jimmy said, "and it was he who bought the Dughet from me."

Nikola clasped her hands together.

"You are . . quite certain," she said in a voice little above a whisper, "that he did not suspect . . ?"

"No, no, of course not," Jimmy replied. "Why should he? As I told you, the picture was in the Servants' Hall."

Nikola gave a little shiver.

She thought it would be a mistake for Jimmy to become involved with Collectors.

They would know a great deal about pictures, and who owned them.

She had heard her father talk of various of his friends who were knowledgeable about antiques of every sort.

One was a collector of French furniture.

His ancestor had brought a great deal of it back from France after the Revolution.

There was another who had a passion for silver.

He attended every sale of it in London.

He also kept a record of the silver owned by great families.

She felt that as long as James concentrated on obtaining small pieces like the miniatures and even the Chinese bowls, he was more or less safe.

But moving amongst experts was surely a mistake

As if he knew what she was thinking, Jimmy said:

"Oh, do stop worrying! I can feel it vibrating from you."

"I . . I cannot . . help it," Nikola said. "You know, dearest, that if there was the . . slightest suspicion . . that you were a . . thief . . you would . . even if you did not go to . . prison . . be ostracised by everyone including our own . . f.family."

"It is easy to be honest and cautionary when you are rich," Jimmy remarked, "and as I have only stolen from people who do not appreciate what they own I do not feel in the least guilty!"

Nikola sighed.

She could understand her brother feeling like that and how much he wanted money for King's Keep.

He might try to justify what he was doing but it was still stealing.

She knew how unhappy it would have made her mother.

Her father would have been very angry.

"Now stop being like a wet rag and listen to what I have planned," Jimmy said sharply.

"I . . am listening," Nikola said in a very small voice.

"We are going to Huntingdonshire to stay in one of the finest and most magnificent houses in the whole of England! We are going to see pictures that surpass anything that is in the National Gallery or any other Museum!"

"The Marquis has invited you?" Nikola said.

"He has, as I told you, bought the Dughet from me. I hinted, just lightly of course, that I might have some other pictures which would interest him."

"Did he ask you where you got that one?"

"No, of course not," Jimmy said. "I told him I owned it and was only selling it because I was forced to do so."

He gave a little laugh before he said:

247

"He was so impressed when I described King's Keep to him that I know he will want to come here and look at it for himself."

"If he does, will he not realise it could not have come from here?"

"Why should he? I might have kept it in the cellar rather than with the family collection, and I assure you he will pay a very high price for anything else like it."

Jimmy was wildly excited by the large cheque he had brought home with him.

There was nothing Nikola could have done to dampen his spirits.

She only knew that she was worried.

She had what amounted to a presentiment.

It was that however genial the Marquis of Ridgmont might appear to Jimmy, there was something sinister about him.

"I am just . . imagining . . it," she tried to tell herself.

At the same time, the feeling was there, and she was frightened.

Chapter Two

Nikola was arranging some flowers when her brother came into the room.

"We are going tomorrow," he said, "to stay with Aunt Alice again.

"Aunt Alice?"

Nikola turned to stare at him in astonishment.

"That is what I said," Jimmy replied.

"But . . we have only just been there, and you know how you disliked the discomfort and the food."

"I am not going to give you three guesses why we are returning there," Jimmy said.

Nikola started.

"Oh, no, Jimmy!" she cried. "You cannot . . take any . . more of her . . pictures!"

"I have to have some by Friday," he replied, "to take to the Marquis."

Nikola put down the flowers.

She walked to where he was standing with his back to the mantelpiece.

"Now listen, Jimmy," she said. "We cannot . . go on like . . this!"

"We cannot go on without money," he replied. "I have given the order for the curtains and chairs. That will swallow up everything we have in the Bank."

"We can do . . without new curtains," Nikola said beneath her breath.

She knew it was hopeless arguing with her brother.

He would steal the Crown Jewels if it was for King's Keep.

She only thought despairingly that they were sinking further and further into crime.

"I want you to help me," Jimmy said in a determined voice, "and I wish to take Aunt Alice a present."

"I think she will be very surprised if you do so," Nikola retorted.

"It was something I should have thought of doing last time we went there," James went on in a lofty air. "In the East everybody always arrives with a present for their host."

"But we are not in the East . . although I agree it is a . . pleasant custom."

She looked at her brother.

She was wondering if she should go on pleading with him.

She wanted to go on her knees and beg him not to take anything more from that ugly house which depressed her.

She however knew he would not listen, so after a moment she said:

"I cannot imagine anything that Aunt Alice would like in the shape of a present considering, as you said yourself, that the house is full of treasures."

"I was not thinking of pictures or snuff-boxes," Jimmy replied, "but perhaps a dog."

"A dog?" Nikola exclaimed. "You must be crazy! It would need feeding and that would cost her money."

"Then what do you suggest?" Jimmy asked.

Jokingly Nikola said:

"Bessie has three kittens in the kitchen which she wishes to dispose of."

"Kittens!" Jimmy exclaimed. "That is a very good idea!"

"I do not think Aunt Alice would think so, even though they are exceptionally pretty kittens."

Jimmy walked out of the Drawing-Room and along the passage to the kitchen.

When he was gone, Nikola sank down in a chair.

"What am I to do?" she asked. "I know this is wrong, but because it is all for King's Keep, I do not believe a Regiment of soldiers could stop him!"

Every instinct in her body shrank from the idea of accepting their Aunt's hospitality again.

Even though it was reluctant, so that they could steal from her.

She wondered despairingly if there was anything she could do.

Jimmy came back into the room.

In his hands he was carrying a small white ball of fluff.

Despite herself, Nikola smiled.

"They really are very pretty!" she said. "And we cannot keep all three of them."

"Well, this one is going to Aunt Alice."

"I am sure she will refuse it."

"Then we will bring it back with us when we leave the next day," Jimmy said.

He was implying that they would have other things to bring back with them.

Nikola lapsed into silence.

Her brother put the kitten on the table.

It ran up and down looking very pretty as it did so.

"I will take a bet with you," Jimmy said, "that when she sees *Snowball* which is what I intend to call this kitten, Aunt Alice will fall in love for the first time in her life!"

"You are asking for a miracle," Nikola replied.

At the same time she was laughing because Jimmy made it sound so funny.

. . . .

James and Nikola set off the next morning.

Snowball was in a basket which Nikola had padded with some old material in a pretty shade of pink.

She had also tied several bows of satin ribbon on the handle.

It made it look a very attractive gift.

They drove through the dusty lanes as they had done only a short time ago.

Nikola was wishing with all her heart that Jimmy had never realised how large their Uncle's collection of pictures was.

Only when they had driven for a long time in silence did she ask:

"What will you say if Aunt Alice tells you she has noticed that the picture you took was no longer there, and also the miniatures?"

"If you want the truth," Jimmy answered, "as it was the first time I had stolen anything, I was extremely foolish."

"In what way?" Nikola enquired.

"I should have taken a great deal more, and saved myself this second visit. This time, I do not intend to be so stupid."

The way he spoke made Nikola shiver.

She knew that he had every intention of filling the large trunk in which he had made her pack her clothes.

"It is far too big for one night," she had protested.

He did not bother to answer her.

She therefore included several starched petticoats she did not really need.

She knew that they could be crushed down to make room for the pictures.

But on their arrival the housemaids would not think it strange there was so much room in the trunk.

She always loved driving with her brother.

If their object had been different, she would have enjoyed seeing the countryside.

The Spring flowers in the hedgerows were very lovely.

But now, every minute took them nearer and nearer to their Aunt.

She therefore merely felt apprehensive. She was sure Lady Hartley would be suspicious because they had called again so soon.

As usual Jimmy had been determined to get his own way.

He had not given his Aunt a chance of saying that she did not want them.

He had merely, Nikola discovered, written her a letter saying that he was very anxious to see her again.

He hoped they could stay with her overnight.

Otherwise as she would understand, it would be tiring for the horses.

They drove up to the house.

It looked, Nikola thought, even uglier than she remembered.

There was a groom waiting outside with what she suspected was a surly expression on his face.

She thought, like the other servants, he would be resenting the extra work they made for him.

Jimmy, however, was charming to everybody.

He greeted the groom as if he was an old friend.

He told the Butler in his threadbare coat that he was delighted to see him again.

He smiled at the footmen.

Then they walked into the Drawing-Room where Lady Hartley was seated in her usual chair.

She looked, Nikola thought anxiously, very unwelcoming.

"Good-afternoon, Aunt Alice!" Jimmy said in his most effusive manner. "It is delightful to see you again!"

"I am very curious as to why you are here," Lady Hartley said in an uncompromising voice.

"The answer is quite simple," Jimmy replied, "we have brought you a present."

As he spoke he deposited the basket containing *Snowball* at her feet.

"A present . . ?" Lady Hartley began.

Then she looked into the basket and asked:

"What is it?"

It is a kitten called *Snowball*," Jimmy replied. "I suddenly realised after we had left you that it was the one thing missing in the house."

But I do not like pets!" Lady Hartley said firmly.

At the same time she was looking down into the basket.

Snowball had slept peacefully while they were moving.

He was now standing with his paws on the side of the basket.

He looked very sweet against the pink background.

Neither Jimmy nor Nikola said anything.

Then after a moment Lady Hartley remarked:

"It is a pretty little cat. I have never seen a completely white one before."

"*Snowball* is unique," Jimmy said, "and that is exactly why, Aunt Alice, we wanted you to have him."

"I really do not think . . " Lady Hartley began.

Before she could finish the sentence, Jimmy took *Snowball* from the basket and placed him in her lap.

As if she could not help herself, Lady Hartley put out her hands to prevent the kitten from falling over and held him steady.

Then as *Snowball* began to purr, she said as if the words were dragged from her:

"It is certainly an attractive little creature!"

"That is exactly what I thought," Jimmy said with satisfaction, "and it will be company for you Aunt Alice."

Nikola was certain she would say she did not want company.

Then she realised her Aunt was not listening.

She was looking down at *Snowball* with an expression in her eyes Nikola had never seen before.

Jimmy glanced at her meaningfully.

It was no use! Jimmy was always right, and once again he had got his own way.

Butters came in with the usual minute glass of sherry.

Afterwards they went up to change for dinner.

By this time it was obvious that Lady Hartley was completely captivated by the new addition to her household.

"I told you so!" Jimmy said as they reached their bedrooms.

Nikola made a grimace at him, but she felt a little happier.

At least they had "given" something, which was better than just "taking".

. . . .

Later that night Jimmy came into Nikola's room carrying two pictures with him.

She was almost asleep.

She had guessed when she went to bed that he intended to visit the rooms that were shut up.

She had therefore left two candles burning.

Jimmy came into her bedroom.

She saw with relief that the pictures he was carrying were not very large.

He put one down on the bed.

"It is called *A Young Couple*," he said in a whisper, "and it is by Van Leyden."

It was not a particularly attractive picture, Nikola thought.

Yet she had heard her father mention the name of Van Leyden.

She was almost sure that he had been a pupil and admirer of Durer.

She did not speak, and Jimmy showed her the other picture.

"This is by Mabuse," he said, "who was a Flemish painter."

It was a clever portrait of a rather unattractive girl.

But Nikola could see that the gown was brilliantly painted.

So was the cap which haloed her hair and was set on the back of her head.

As if Jimmy was impatient at her not being more enthusiastic, he turned and went from the room.

He left the pictures on her bed. For a moment she could hardly believe he had gone.

Then she thought that as he had not said goodnight he would be returning.

"Surely," she said to herself, "he cannot be collecting any more?"

She got out of bed and put the two pictures into the bottom of her trunk.

She then began to repack the clothes which the housemaids had hung in the wardrobe.

She had not got very far before Jimmy returned.

"You have not .. taken any .. more?" she asked in a whisper.

It was a stupid question.

He was carrying what seemed to her much too large a picture.

He put it down on the bed.

By the light of the candles she could see that it really was very attractive.

"This is called *The Virgin in the Rose Garden*" Jimmy said, "and it is by Lochner. When the Marquis sees it, he will be absolutely delighted!"

"But .. it is .. too big!" Nikola complained.

"It will go into your trunk," Jimmy replied.

"Actually it is only about 20 inches high, but I cannot leave the frame behind."

"N.no .. of course .. not .. " Nikola stammered.

She thought her Aunt would be extremely suspicious if the frame was discovered without a picture in it. Jimmy walked across to her trunk. He removed the things she had packed.

Then he took out the two pictures which she had put at the bottom of it.

For a moment Nikola was not concerned with what he was doing.

She was thinking how lovely the picture was.

It was something she would love to own herself.

The Virgin with the Child Jesus on her lap was seated on a throne.

She wore a very elaborate silken gown billowing out in front of her.

In the background were a number of winged angels.

Two were in flight in the top corners of the picture.

The whole composition was lovely and perfectly executed.

She could understand Jimmy wanting to take it away.

It was, however, impossible to believe that anyone could lose such a treasure, and not be aware of it.

"I knew you would think it beautiful," Jimmy was saying as he came back to stand beside her.

"I am sure it is . . dangerous to . . steal it!" Nikola retorted.

"I doubt if Aunt Alice had any idea it was there," he answered. "You can see the dust is thick on the frame."

He picked up the picture as he spoke.

He carried it across the room and put it very carefully into the trunk.

With surprising skill for a man he packed some of her clothes on top of it.

Then he added the other two pictures.

Nikola was sitting on the bed in her nightgown.

As he finished she knew by the expression of satisfaction on his face how pleased he was with himself.

He came to her side.

"Get up early," he ordered, "and pack everything else before you are called!"

As Nikola did not say anything he went on:

"Fasten the two straps and be quite certain not to leave anything out so that the housemaids open the trunk again."

He was giving her orders, Nikola thought, as if she was a raw recruit.

She realised he was frightened of losing something that would be of such importance to King's Keep.

"All right, Jimmy," she replied in a whisper, "I will do as you say."

He smiled and kissed her.

"You are a good girl," he said. "Sleep well!"

He walked to the door.

He hesitated for a moment, just in case somebody might be in the passage.

She heard him go into his own room.

Then she went to her trunk.

She packed everything she possessed except for the gown she would wear tomorrow, and the nightgown she had on. She put her starched petticoats on top of the trunk.

When it was closed they would be crushed down.

She knew Jimmy was right.

It would be dangerous for a housemaid to see how full the trunk was compared with when she had unpacked it.

When Nikola went back to bed it was difficult to sleep.

She kept thinking how wrong it was to steal anything so beautiful as *The Virgin in the Rose Garden*.

There was something very spiritual about the picture.

She felt when she looked at it, that it vibrated towards her.

She was sure it was the Faith which had been poured into it by those who had worshipped in front of it over the years.

It had become Holy so that it could bless those who prayed to the Virgin.

Although the picture was now hidden in her trunk, Nikola found herself praying to the Virgin.

She asked Her to help Jimmy and prevent what he was doing from being discovered.

It was a very fervent prayer.

She could not help wondering how they could go on indefinitely.

Perhaps coming back again and again to steal pictures from Aunt Alice?

Then making another visit to Lord Mersey and anyone else who had valuable pictures.

"Help us please . . Help us," Nikola prayed.

She thought that the Mother of God holding the Holy Child heard her.

. . . .

Nikola was up and dressed by the time the maid came to call her at eight o'clock.

"You're early, Miss!" she remarked.

"We have a long way to go," Nikola replied, "and I have a lot of things to do when I get home."

The maid smiled.

"I 'spect they'll be waitin' for you," she said. "'Tis always th' same if one goes away. One comes back t' double what was there before one left."

"That is true," Nikola agreed.

She glanced round the room to be certain there was nothing left behind.

The straps on her trunk were secure, as Jimmy had ordered.

When she went downstairs to breakfast she found her Aunt already there. She was feeding *Snowball* with milk in a saucer.

"He slept on my bed all last night," she said to Nikola, "and never woke me once!"

She spoke in the voice of a mother who has just discovered her child is an infant phenomenon.

"I knew he was exactly what you wanted," Jimmy said with satisfaction, "and he will keep you free of mice."

"*Snowball* will have to grow a little first," Lady Hartley replied.

Almost for the first time since Nikola had known her, she laughed spontaneously.

She thought Jimmy had certainly made Aunt Alice happier than she had been before.

The world might think it a poor exchange.

A kitten whose value was practically nil for three masterpieces which were undoubtedly priceless.

But Nikola told herself, no one could put a price on happiness.

"Now remember, Aunt Alice," Jimmy was saying as they left, "*Snowball* should have fish to eat while he is so small, and chicken when he gets a little older."

"Yes, of course," Lady Hartley said, "and I am glad you reminded me."

"He will need a meal in the morning and a meal at night," Jimmy went on, "and I have never thought that rabbit is good for small cats."

Lady Hartley was hanging on his every word.

. . . .

As Jimmy and Nikola drove away she asked:

"How is it you know so much about cats?"

"I do my home work, and I asked Bessie before we left what she gives our cat."

"I have to admit that I have never seen Aunt Alice look so human, or so happy!" Nikola said.

"I have my good points," Jimmy replied.

When they arrived home Jimmy cleaned the pictures as best he could.

He had learnt how to do so from one of the greatest experts in London.

Nikola looked at *The Virgin in the Rose Garden* every moment she had.

She knew that in two days time Jimmy would take it away.

Then she would never see it again.

She felt as if it spoke to her.

It made her feel not only that her prayers were heard, but that the Virgin was blessing her.

"I wish we could keep that picture," she said wistfully to Jimmy."

So do I," he agreed.

Nikola hesitated. Then she said:

"You do not suppose we could change it for one in the house which is not so beautiful? Or perhaps so valuable?"

Jimmy's lips were set in a hard line.

I stole this to save King's Keep," he said. "If I kept it for myself and for our pleasure, I should feel I was cheating!"

Nikola gave a little laugh.

"I suppose in a way, I understand your somewhat twisted principles." Jimmy did not reply, and she added:

"If I had enough money I would buy the picture from you."

"That is what the Marquis of Ridgmont will do!" Jimmy retorted.

Nikola knew it would be a long drive to the Marquis's house in Huntingdonshire.

They could have gone some of the way by train.

It would however, be much more difficult to convey the pictures that way than if they went by road.

Fortunately the two carriage-horses they possessed were young and strong.

As long as they had a good rest after they arrived, the journey would not hurt them.

It was on the Thursday before they left that Jimmy said:

"I suppose, really, I should have told you to buy a new gown to wear."

"A new gown?" Nikola repeated in astonishment.

"Well, the Marquis, being one of the wealthiest men in England, can afford to be very smart."

Nikola looked at him in consternation.

"Are you . . saying that the Marquis is . . young and that he may . . have a house-party?"

"I suppose he is about thirty-three or thirty-four," Jimmy replied, "and it is very likely he will be entertaining his friends."

"I . . I thought he would be . . old . . like Lord Mersey."

It was very stupid Nikola thought, but she had not expected a young man would be a fervent collector of pictures.

It had never struck her that they would not be alone with the Marquis.

It is what they had been with Lord Mersey.

Or else just a small family gathering.

"I had much better not come with you," she said quickly.

Jimmy stared at her.

"Do not be so ridiculous! How could I possibly manage without you?"

"I do not see why not. You are not going to steal from the Marquis, you are going to take him something!"

"I know that," Jimmy said, "but I want you to look sad when I say we must sell things from our own house. Also because you are so pretty, you may prevent our host from asking too many uncomfortable questions!"

Nikola stared at her brother in sheer astonishment.

"You have never said that before!"

"The Marquis of Ridgmont is rather different from the other people we have stayed with," Jimmy replied.

Then mockingly he added:

"I saw old Mersey, ancient though he is, eyeing you, and there is no doubt he thought you were just as attractive as the Venuses he had on his walls!"

Nikola laughed.

"Now you are making fun of the whole thing! At the same time, I have nothing new to wear."

"And I suppose there is no time to buy anything," Jimmy said reflectively.

"Not unless I fly to London on wings," Nikola replied, "or one of the ghosts in the house has a magic wand!"

Jimmy shrugged his shoulders.

"Very well, he will have to accept you as you are, but I wish I had thought of it before."

Nikola thought the same thing.

But she had seldom asked her brother for anything personal.

She knew he always felt she was spending money that should be used on King's Keep.

Now she went up to her bedroom to look at what was hanging in her wardrobe.

She realised how inadequate it was.

Because there had been no money for extravagances, she had made her own gowns.

She was very skilful, but the material had not been expensive.

She would not pretend to herself that she could compete with Frederick Worth.

She had read about him and the other great fashion designers in *The Ladies Magazine.*

"What shall I do?" she asked forlornly. She spoke in little above a whisper.

She was seeing the elegant full-skirted gown worn by *The Virgin in the Rose Garden.*

Her question became almost a prayer.

She was sure the Virgin understood how important it was that she should help her brother.

It was then she thought of the curtains which hung on one of the four-poster beds.

They had been chosen many years before by her mother.

They were pure silk and of the same turquoise blue as the scarab she had seen from Egypt.

"It has always been a lucky colour in the East," her mother had said, "and as your father has put in this room some of his more exotic pictures, I thought it appropriate."

It was a room they used for special guests.

Lately it had remained empty, simply because Jimmy had been unable to ask anyone of any importance to stay.

Nikola knew one curtain would make her a very beautiful evening skirt.

She could fashion herself a bustle and a very pretty bodice out of the other.

The whole question was, did she have the time?

She ran to the bedroom, to take down the curtains.

Then she went down the stairs to the kitchen.

Bessie was seated at the table shelling the young peas that had just been brought in from the garden.

"Mr. James has asked me to have a new gown to wear when we go to stay with a friend of his the day after tomorrow," she said.

"A new gown, Miss Nikola?" Bessie asked.

"An' where's the money t' come from for that, I'd like t' know!"

"I'm going to use the bed-curtains in the Blue Room," Nikola explained.

Bessie stared at her.

"Is there anyone in the village who could help me?" Nikola asked.

"I can cut it out and, as you know, I can sew very quickly, but I do not think I could make a whole new gown in a day and a half!"

Bessie thought for a moment.

"There's Mrs. Gibbons at Honeysuckle Cottage," she said.

"Her made th' new altar cloth for th' Church an' her daughter, who's nigh on fifteen 'as done some repairs t'th' curtains in th' Vicarage."

"Thank you, Bessie," Nikola replied.

"Two hours later Nikola was cutting out the gown on her bedroom floor.

Mrs. Gibbons was arranging her sewing-basket in the window.

By the evening they had the gown tacked together.

By working the whole of the next day until dinner-time Nikola had her gown.

There was still quite a lot to do before the gown was finished to perfection.

But just to look at she had a gown which she thought was as smart as anything that might have come from Paris.

Certainly the colour became her.

Her hair was fair, but it had little touches of red in it, which seemed to be accentuated by the blue of the silk.

It made her skin look very white.

She had cut out the gown, following a photograph she had seen in a magazine.

It had been lent to her by the Vicar's wife.

When it was finished Nikola was rather afraid the décolletage was too low.

She therefore added, which again she had seen in a magazine, a little frill of the same satin round the neck.

It matched the bustle which was made of frill upon frill until it touched the floor.

"'Tis th' prettiest gown I've ever seen!" Mrs. Gibbons exclaimed when she tried it on. "'An' you looks like a picture in it, Miss Nikola, you do, really!"

"'Thank you, Mrs. Gibbons, and I only hope that is what my brother will think," Nikola replied.

It flashed through her mind that it was more important for the Marquis to think so.

Then she laughed at herself.

Whenever Jimmy spoke of him he had sounded very grand and very important.

He would hardly notice anyone as insignificant as herself.

Now she had learnt that he was different from what she had expected, she had asked questions.

She had discovered that far from being old, he was extremely athletic.

He raced his own horses in Steeple-Chases.

Also although Jimmy was rather vague about this, he was a well-known traveller.

"Where does he travel to?" Nikola asked.

"About the world," Jimmy answered vaguely.

"And he still has time to collect pictures?"

"He has one of the best collections in the whole of England!" Jimmy assured her.

"It was of course handed down to him through the generations."

"And he is adding to it?" Nikola asked.

"Obviously," her brother answered, "or we would not be going there!"

"And what else does he do?"

"Enjoys himself!" Jimmy answered. "As he can well afford to do!"

"But he is not married?"

Jimmy laughed.

He has sworn that is something he will never do."

"But . . why?" Nikola questioned.

"Surely he wants an heir to inherit his pictures?"

Jimmy shrugged his shoulders.

"I expect he has been crossed in love, or has an aversion to being shackled. Anyway he is a confirmed bachelor, so it is no use your 'setting your cap' at him!"

"I was not thinking of doing any such thing!" Nikola said crossly.

She was annoyed that Jimmy should say anything so vulgar.

She did not ask any more questions.

She thought when she was alone that the Marquis sounded very awe-inspiring.

At the same time almost inhuman.

"I wish we could go somewhere else," she said to herself.

She knew, however, that her brother was counting every second until he could be with the Marquis.

He was determined to obtain from him a very large sum of money to spend on King's Keep.

Chapter Three

The guests at the luncheon party were beginning to look at the time.

The Marquis thought with relief that he would be able to leave.

It had in fact, been quite an interesting luncheon at the French Embassy.

He had met several friends.

Lady Lessington, with whom he was having an *affaire de coeur* came up to him to say in a low voice:

"Will you dine with me tomorrow evening, Blake? George is going to the country."

"Unfortunately, so am I," the Marquis replied.

He saw the look of disappointment in her beautiful eyes and said:

"But I will see you next week."

There was a smile on her lips as she moved away to thank her host and hostess for their hospitality.

The Marquis watched her go.

He thought that Lady Lessington was undoubtedly one of the most beautiful women in London.

At the same time, he was honest with himself.

The fire which had blazed between them was not burning as brightly as it had.

If there was one thing the Marquis disliked, it was a love affair which flickered away.

Then there was nothing left but a few dying embers.

His reputation for being ruthless came from the fact that the moment an affair began to pall he ended it.

Not only abruptly but sometimes brutally.

Something fastidious within him revolted at accepting anything but the best.

It was what he expected and sought for in everything.

He wanted his houses to be perfect, his estates to be an example to other Landlords!

Naturally his women must be uniquely beautiful.

He had managed through sheer cleverness not to be proclaimed a Roué as many of his friends were.

He was discretion itself.

He protected not only the reputation of the women whose favours he accepted, but also his own.

Lady Lessington left the large Salon, which was on the First Floor of the Embassy building, and descended the stairs.

As she did so the Marquis decided that he would not see her again.

Not intimately, although inevitably they would meet at parties and other functions.

He knew that she would resent and fail to understand his feelings about their affair.

But as he knew he was not her first lover, he was certain she would find another man to take his place.

At the same time he could not help knowing this would be difficult.

Without being conceited he was aware he was outstandingly handsome and also a very ardent lover.

He took as much trouble over his *affaires de coeur* as he did over his horses.

That was saying a great deal.

He climbed into his Chaise which was waiting for him outside and picked up the reins.

As he drove off he wondered, since he had finished with Lady Lessington, who next he would pursue.

She would leave a gap in his very full and busy life.

He needed to have a beautiful woman with whom he could relax.

What was more, he enjoyed the chase of some new and exotic Beauty.

It was in the same way as he enjoyed a good run on the hunting field, or riding in a hard Steeple-Chase in which he was invaribly the winner.

He vaguely remembered noticing a woman with the most striking red hair at Carlton House last night.

Her hair had struck him as being unusually lovely.

It was difficult now to recall her face.

He had no doubt she was beautiful.

He had only to ask the Prince of Wales, who had been their host, to learn who she was.

When he knew more about her he thought he might be disappointed.

For the moment however, it was something to look forward to.

The Marquis turned his horses at Hyde Park Corner towards Buckingham Palace.

He drove them with a flourish down the Mall.

They were a pair he had recently acquired from a friend.

He was an extravagant aristocrat who needed to raise a large sum of money immediately.

The two perfectly matched chestnuts had been, the Marquis thought, absurdly expensive.

At the same time, he had done his friend a good turn.

He therefore did not begrudge the money.

Anyway, the horses were worth it.

He realised a great number of people were admiring them as he drove down the Mall.

The top-hatted men and elegant women walking in the Spring sunshine were staring not so much at himself as was usual, but at his horses.

They would, he thought, be an asset in his stables.

These already contained, in his opinion, the finest horses in England.

The same could be said of his race-horses which he stabled at Newmarket.

He remembered that he had two entered for the races which would take place next week.

He had not yet decided whom he would invite to his house-party there.

He was hoping, because he was not quite sure, that he had not included the Lessingtons.

It was something he would have to find out when he returned to his house in Park Lane.

His Secretary had a note of every invitation he had given or received for the next two months.

He drove across Horse Guards Parade thinking that was the simplest way of reaching Downing Street.

He had been an officer in the Household Cavalry.

He was therefore allowed to reach Whitehall through the gate which was guarded on each side by a trooper on horseback in a sentry-box.

From Whitehall he had only to turn right to be in Downing Street.

Now he began to wonder why the Prime Minister had sent for him.

It had been an urgent message which he could not ignore.

At the same time, it was inconvenient when he had other plans for the afternoon.

"I hope Lord Beaconsfield will not keep me long," the Marquis said to himself.

As a matter of fact he was always delighted to see Benjamin Disraeli who had been raised to the Peerage the year before.

The Marquis thought, as the Queen did, that he was undoubtedly the best Prime Minister England could have at the moment.

Her Majesty had a partiality for Lord Beaconsfield.

Although baptized into the Christian faith at the age of 13, he had been born into a Jewish family.

The Marquis was an astute man.

He had known that despite his eccentric appearance the Prime Minister was exactly the right man in the right place at the right time.

His brilliant brain, his wit and diplomatic tact had already proved him so, even to his critics.

The Marquis drove up to the door of Number 10.

He was shown into the Prime Minister's private Study.

Lord Beaconsfield rose from his desk to hold out his hand.

"I knew Your Lordship would not fail me," he said.

"That is something I hope I will never do!" the Marquis replied. "But of course I am wondering what catastrophe has occurred."

The Prime Minister laughed.

Coming from behind his desk he indicated an armchair in front of the fire.

It was quite a warm day.

There was however a fire burning and the Marquis knew that Lord Beaconsfield had a dislike of the cold.

He had noticed that his skin could look almost blue in the winter.

The draughts in the Houses of Parliament and the fogs coming up from the Thames could make the most warm-blooded Briton shiver.

The Marquis waited now while the Prime Minister put his long fingers together.

It was a characteristic gesture when he was thinking.

Finally he said:

"Her Majesty the Queen has become hysterical!"

If he had expected to shock the Marquis with his statement he did not succeed.

"I presume you are referring to the situation between Russia and Turkey, Prime Minister," he remarked.

Lord Beaconsfield's rather protruding lips twisted in a somewhat sarcastic smile.

"That is true," he answered. "We have been informed that the Russians have almost reached Adrianople, which is only 60 miles from Constantinople."

The Marquis raised his eye-brows.

"Have they really got as far as that?"

"There seems to be no reason to doubt the information," the Prime Minister replied, "and the Queen is furious! For months she has been trying to alert the Cabinet to the danger."

"I gather Turkey is not the main issue," the Marquis reflected. "It is really a question of Russian or British supremacy in the world."

"Exactly!" the Prime Minister agreed.

He gave a little laugh.

"I might have known, my dear Marquis, that you would know as much about the situation as I do!"

"You flatter me," the Marquis replied. "But I have been aware of the Queen's fears, and she was very voluble about them when I was last at Windsor."

The Prime Minister sighed.

"Confidentially she threatens to abdicate!"

The Marquis gave the Prime Minister a questioning look and he went on:

269

"This morning she has written to me saying:

'If England is to kiss Russia's feet, the Queen will not be a party to the humiliation of England and will lay down the crown!'"

"Strong words!" the Marquis remarked. "I very much doubt, however, that Her Majesty would go as far as that!"

"She went on to say," Lord Beaconsfield added:

"'Oh, if the Queen were a man, she would like to go to give those horrid Russians, whose word cannot be trusted, a beating!'"

The Marquis laughed.

"She is magnificent!" he exclaimed. "If she was a man, she could not do better."

"I agree with you," the prime Minister replied. "But what Her Majesty wants at the moment, and so do I, is more information."

Lord Beaconsfield looked straight at the Marquis and there was a pause.

Finally the Marquis said:

"I am beginning to see where I come into this! What do you expect me to do?"

"What Her Majesty wants," the Prime Minister replied, "and what I also require, is first-hand information from somebody who is not already involved in this appalling situation."

"First-hand information!" the Marquis repeated. "How the devil do you suggest I am going to get it?"

Lord Beaconsfield bent forward in his chair.

"No-one, My Lord, is cleverer than you are at finding out the truth."

"I might have been fortunate enough to do that on several occasions in the past," the Marquis replied, "but this situation is very different because Britain is not involved."

"We may have to be," the Prime Minister said simply.

"In what way?" the Marquis enquired.

"We might have to make a show of strength when it is no longer a question of talking."

"What do you want me to do?" the Marquis asked in a resigned voice.

"What I want you to do is to go immediately on a secret mission," Lord Beaconsfield replied, "and find out everything you can."

"Just as simple as that!" the Marquis exclaimed mockingly, spreading out his hands in a somewhat theatrical gesture.

"I know it will not be easy," the Prime Minister admitted, "but the Queen trusts you, and so do I. You speak Russian, and you have an uncanny knack, as you well know, of getting to the root of a problem when everybody else fails."

The Marquis sighed.

"Do you want me to leave immediately?"

"Her Majesty has suggested, and I agree it is the best plan, that you should take the train to Athens," the Prime Minister said, "then cruise on your yacht towards Constantinople, making contact with a number of sources of information which are as well known to you as they are to the Foreign Office."

"I cannot think it will be a particularly pleasant journey you are suggesting to me!" the Marquis remarked.

He was thinking as he spoke of the discomfort of a long train journey across Europe.

As if he read his thoughts, Lord Beaconsfield smiled.

"Her Majesty thought the same, and she has very graciously offered you the Royal coaches which, as you know, are her private property."

The Marquis looked surprised and the Prime Minister went on:

"Her Drawing-Room and Sleeping cars are kept at the *Gare du Nord* in Brussels. They will be attached to the trains which will eventually take you from Ostend to Athens."

"I am of course, deeply honoured!" the Marquis said. "You and Her Majesty must have been very confident that I would not refuse your suggestion of a quiet holiday in the Aegean Sea."

"You have never failed us yet," the Prime Minister said, "and I cannot believe you will do so now."

"Very well," the Marquis said, "and my yacht, as it seems you already know, is in harbour at Gibraltar."

"You can telegraph your Captain to proceed immediately to Athens," the Prime Minister said. "You should both arrive at about the same time."

"Thank you!" the Marquis said sarcastically. "Are you assuming that those who are interested will believe I am taking a holiday just by myself? I should have thought, unless my reputation has deteriorated very rapidly, that both the Russians and the Turks, if they are taking an interest, will find it highly suspicious!"

Lord Beaconsfield laughed.

"Neither Her Majesty nor myself would presume to choose your companions for you," he said. "But I cannot believe that with your reputation, as you have said, you will find it difficult to find some congenial companion with whom you would like to spend a week or two at sea!"

The Marquis did not reply.

He was thinking it somewhat impertinent of the Queen and the Prime Minister to discuss his love-affairs.

He never spoke of them himself, not even with his closest friends.

The Prime Minister's perception was very strong, and he knew exactly what the Marquis was thinking.

He therefore bent forward to say:

"We trust Your Lordship, and we rely on you, but you do realise we want no-one — and I mean no-one — to have any idea why your yacht should be steaming through the Dardanelles and perhaps making for the Black Sea."

"That will certainly make things difficult!" the Marquis agreed.

"It is of the utmost importance there should not be so much as a whisper," the Prime Minister said. "If the gossips were aware of how concerned Her Majesty is about the Russian advance and the Turkish weakness, you know how dangerous they could be."

"What you are really saying," the Marquis replied, as if he was working it out for himself, "is that women talk, however much you tell them not to."

"That is true of most women," the Prime Minister agreed, "and therefore you must find one you can trust."

There was a twinkle in his eye as he said:

"Her Majesty has in fact, said it is a pity you have not a wife."

The Marquis threw up his hands in horror.

"If you and Her Majesty are going to combine in trying to press me into losing my freedom, I shall leave for America!"

The Prime Minister laughed.

"You know, My Lord, you would do nothing so drastic as that! At the same time, be careful whom you choose for, as you are aware, women not only listen on the pillow, but also talk on it!"

The Marquis rose to his feet.

"I can only say that you and Her Majesty are straining my patriotism to breaking-point!"

"On the contrary, we are paying you a very high compliment by sending you on this mission, because we know that no-one else has any chance of being successful."

"I am listening to your honeyed tongue, Prime Minister like a mesmerised rabbit!" the Marquis retorted.

Both men were laughing as they walked towards the door.

"Papers, maps and a new code will be at your house this evening," Lord Beaconsfield said.

The Marquis put out his hand, and Lord Beaconsfield took it in both of his.

"I can only thank you from the very bottom of my heart," he said very sincerely. "I am, as you well know, deeply concerned about the situation which is very different from what I say in public."

"I can only hope I do not fail you," the Marquis answered.

. . . .

Driving home, the Marquis thought that what he had been told to do was something he had never anticipated.

The situation in Eastern Europe had been played down in the newspapers.

Most people in England were not particularly interested.

The Tsar of Russia, Alexander II, had hoped that a recent Conference in Constantinople would provide a peaceful solution.

But the Sultan of Turkey had rejected everything that was suggested.

To the astonishment of the world, two weeks later the Tsar announced that his patience was exhausted and declared war on Turkey.

The majority of people in England including the Members of Parliament remained unmoved.

Both countries seemed a long way away.

If they fought amongst themselves and in their own lands, it did not concern Britain or her possessions elsewhere.

It was like the Queen, the Marquis thought, to be aware before anybody else that Russian supremacy in the Middle East could, in fact, be a great threat to Britain.

By the time he reached his house in Park Lane he had already decided that he could not leave England until Sunday.

He had a great many things to arrange and a large number of appointments to cancel.

Actually he had no wish to go away at this particular moment.

At the same time, something new, something unexpected, was always a challenge.

He could not help wondering whether this adventure, like so many others before would prove dangerous.

Having arrived at Ridge House he sent for his Secretary.

Mr. Grey was a middle-aged man who was as efficient as he was himself.

In a few short words he told him where he had to go and where the yacht was to meet him.

Mr. Grey took down a note of everything he said.

"You will be going to the country today, My Lord," he asked, "as was planned?"

"Yes, of course," the Marquis said. "There are a number of things I want to do at Ridge before I leave."

"You have not forgotten that you have invited Sir James Tancombe and his sister Miss Nikola Tancombe to stay?"

"No, I want to see Sir James," the Marquis replied. "I suppose I have invited some other guests?"

"Lady Sarah Languish, whom Your Lordship will remember invited herself, and on Your Lordship's instructions I asked Lord and Lady Cleveland and Captain Barclay for the weekend."

The Marquis sighed.

For a moment he had forgotten the house-party.

But Grey had arranged everything and at least they would prevent him from worrying unduly about what lay ahead.

"I suppose we shall have something to do on Saturday?" he asked tentatively.

"I thought Your Lordship would wish to try out the new horses that recently arrived from Ireland, and I think Mr. Gordon has planned a small dinner on Saturday night."

It was the way in which the Marquis always entertained his guests.

He therefore nodded, knowing that the details would be carried out perfectly by Grey in London and his counterpart Gordon in the country.

He decided that the main thing would be to get on with the task that had been set him by the Prime Minister.

"I suppose," he said, "it will be possible for me to go abroad on Sunday, and my guests can either go then or stay on until Monday."

"Of course, My Lord," Mr. Grey replied. "I am sure the Prime Minister's secretary will have already alerted Brussels that Her Majesty's coaches will be required? Your Lordship will perhaps find the cross-Channel Steamer less crowded than on an ordinary week-day."

"Very well," the Marquis agreed. "I leave on Sunday morning, and I will of course take Dawkins with me."

Dawkins was his valet who had been his batman when he was in the Household Cavalry.

He was, the Marquis knew, invaluable when he was on a secret mission.

He was quite unperturbed by whatever dangers they encountered at such times.

At four o'clock precisely he boarded his private train which was waiting for him at St. Panrcas Station.

At five thirty it drew up at his private Halt which was only two miles from Ridge.

The Marquis's party from London was accommodated in a private coach which had been attached to another train which left a little earlier.

They were looked after by the Marquis's own servants, and supplied with tea or champagne, whichever they wanted.

The Marquis preferred travelling by himself.

He found the chatter of his guests before they finally arrived in the country spoilt his pleasure in welcoming them to his home.

The first time most people saw Ridge they were stunned by its appearance in the same way as they were overcome by the Marquis himself.

Ridge was enormous but architecturally perfect.

It had been built on a high piece of ground so that from the windows there was a fine view in all directions.

Since they lived in the country James and Nikola had not been asked if they wished to travel to Ridge by train.

They could, as the Marquis was well aware, easily arrive by road.

They had been informed by Mr. Grey that they would be expected any time after six o'clock, and Jimmy had been determined they would not be late.

It had, however, taken them longer than they had anticipated.

He actually turned in at the very imposing drive-gates of Ridge just on twenty minutes past six.

It was Nikola who was overcome first by the beauty of the drive.

The branches of the trees which bordered it met overhead so that they made a green archway.

Then as she saw the house she was speechless.

Never had she imagined a house could be so beautiful.

With hundreds of windows shining in the setting sun it looked like a Palace in a Fairy Tale.

"It is lovely, Jimmy," she exclaimed, "and so enormous! How can one man live in it all alone?"

"The Marquis is not often alone," Jimmy replied.

"I do hope there will not be too many other guests," Nikola said quickly. "I have only one decent gown with me."

"Then you had better wear it this evening," Jimmy replied. "First impressions are important."

Nikola wondered whom she was meant to impress.

She had already made up her mind that nothing she did or said, or the way she looked, would impress the Marquis.

Now she saw his house she knew that he would be surrounded like a hero in a novel by brilliant, intelligent and beautiful women.

Beside them she would be utterly insignificant.

Living alone at King's Keep when she was not helping in the house, she often sat reading in the garden.

The one thing that her mother had insisted upon was that they should have a large Library.

While her father had thought only of his pictures, her mother had bought books.

"We may not be able to afford to travel, dearest," she had said to her daughter, "but that need not make you feel restricted."

Nikola looked at her wide-eyed.

"Why not, Mama?"

"Because, my dearest, you can travel in your mind, and although you may not actually see the countries about which you are reading, you can imagine them, and understand why the people in them behave as they do."

It was something which Nikola began to enjoy when she was very small.

As she grew older books became part of her very breathing.

She quickly learned the languages of the countries in which she was interested.

Her mother found in the village a Frenchwoman who taught her French.

Then there was a School teacher who was proficient in Italian.

He had spent his childhood in that country.

Her education, Nikola thought when she was older, was almost like picking up jewels in a sandy desert.

It would seem there was nothing there.

Then suddenly, quite unexpectedly, there would be a glittering stone.

It turned out to be someone who was ready to teach her Spanish.

Then when she least expected it, she met a Russian girl.

She was a pupil at the School where Nikola attended daily in the Market Town only two miles from Kings Keep.

Her father would drive her there in the morning.

He would then fetch her back in the evening.

In three years she learnt really very little she did not already know.

The exception was the amount of languages she assimilated.

The Russian girl was the daughter of a Diplomat who had incurred the wrath of the Tzar.

He was therefore afraid to go back to Russia.

He settled with very little money in a rather dilapidated house in the Town.

He was a distinguished man and a Count.

Therefore the School which Nikola attended had agreed to educate his daughter for a very small fee.

Even that was more than he could really afford.

He and his family existed on what he could earn by writing articles on Russia.

He also wrote poems which no publishers wanted.

Nikola read them and found them very moving.

She became friends with Natasha.

Because Lady Tancombe felt sorry for the girl she frequently had her to stay at King's Keep.

She was beautiful in her own way.

She was very anxious to learn English.

Nikola was equally anxious to learn Russian.

They took it turn and turn about to teach each other.

Tzar Alexander II finally relented.

He forgave Natasha's father for whatever sin it was he had committed.

Then the family were able to return to Russia.

The two girls said goodbye to each other, both of them in tears.

"I shall never see you again," Natasha sobbed, "but I will always remember you, Nikola."

"As I shall remember you," Nikola said. "So please write to me sometimes, and tell me what you are doing."

They hugged each other.

Natasha went away and Nikola knew, although she did not say so, that something dreadful would happen to her.

It was two years before they learned what it was.

The whole family when they arrived in St. Petersburg had, through some whim or some twist in the Tzar's mind, been banished to Siberia.

The news made Nikola hate Russia and Russians.

She could only pray that she would never come in contact with such terrible people.

She was, of course, not thinking of Russia when she reached Ridge.

She was thinking that only in England could any house look so majestic and not be a Royal Palace.

When she first saw the Marquis she thought he should at least be a Prince.

Because of his good looks and his presence he seemed to stand out from the rest of the party.

On their arrival Jimmy and Nikola had been taken by what seemed to be an Army of servants up to their rooms.

It was suggested they might like to rest after their journey.

There was time before they changed for dinner.

Nikola was shown into a bedroom so beautiful that she felt it would be impossible to sleep in it.

Her brother's room was almost equally impressive.

It was connected to a *Boudoir* they shared.

Nikola was offered tea.

She felt shy of giving so much trouble to the servants and refused.

Only when the footman had shut the door did Jimmy, who was in the *Boudoir* say:

"Do not be so stupid! Accept everything you are offered. You are not likely ever to stay anywhere as grand as this again!"

"I am .. overwhelmed by it all!" Nikola said. "And everything is .. so beautiful!"

"Especially the pictures," Jimmy said.

There were certainly a lot of them on the walls.

"How can he possibly want any more when he has so many already?" Nikola asked.

"He is a Collector, thank goodness!" Jimmy explained. "And because he is a Collector, he will not be able to resist the pictures I have brought with me."

Nikola sighed.

"Oh, Jimmy, it would be so lovely if we were here just for ourselves, and did not have to be frightened in case he is suspicious as to where you got the pictures."

Jimmy laughed.

"When you have met the Marquis, you will find it impossible to imagine him sniffing around the closed up, dusty rooms in Aunt Alice's house!"

Nikola laughed because it sounded so funny.

"Now do stop worrying!" Jimmy snapped. "We are perfectly safe, and all I ask is that I leave here with a large cheque which will all be spent on King's Keep."

That was the only thing that made what they were doing acceptable, Nikola thought for the thousandth time.

When she returned to her bedroom, she found that everything had been unpacked.

She hoped the maid who waited on her had noticed her new gown.

She would certainly be surprised at the other two she had been obliged to bring with her.

She had been trying for months to save a little out of the money Jimmy gave her for the Housekeeping to buy a new day dress.

He had been obliged to buy her a coat for the Winter.

Otherwise, she thought, she would have frozen to death.

But he had grumbled endlessly at the extravagance.

Next Winter, Nikola told herself, she would wear the rugs off the floor rather than ask him for a single penny.

He had received a lot of money for the pictures and bowls he had stolen.

Yet he had not offered her any of it for herself.

He had however, slightly increased the amount she could spend on food.

Yet even if he had offered her some, she was determined to say 'No'.

At the same time, she was wondering how long her shoes would last.

Although she could make her own gowns, stockings and gloves had to be bought.

She had worn out practically everything that had belonged to her mother.

She knew that to a man she might look all right.

A woman would realise at once how shabby her clothes were.

"Anyway," she told herself cheerfully, "I will wear my new gown this evening, and if His Lordship has to see it again tomorrow, he will just have to think that his eyes are deceiving him!"

It all seemed ridiculous!

She was laughing as she started to undress.

Never in her life had she felt so lapped in luxury as she did when her bath was prepared for her in front of the fire.

There were two maids to bring in the hot and cold water.

It came in cans that were polished so highly that she could see her face in them.

'This is an adventure like those I have read about,' she thought.

Then she tried the temperature of the water with her foot.

Chapter Four

The Marquis did not greet his guests as he usually did immediately on their arrival.

He had too many important instructions to give to his Secretary.

He also had to have a consultation with Dawkins his valet, as to what clothes he would require for the journey.

By the time that he learned that all his guests had arrived it was time for him to dress for dinner.

He therefore went straight to his bedroom.

It was only while he was putting on his evening-clothes that he remembered Lord Beaconsfield had advised him to take some companion with him in his yacht.

He knew the only woman he could possibly ask would be Lady Sarah Languish.

She among all the Beauties he had courted recently was unencumbered by a husband.

Lady Sarah was the daughter of the Duke of Dorset.

She had been married when she was very young to a handsome, raffish and more or less impoverished aristocrat.

It had been considered quite a good match from the point of view of status.

The engagement was announced.

The Duke conferred with his future son-in-law's father about the Marriage Settlement.

It was then he realised how very little money there was.

It was too late for him to refuse to allow the marriage to take place.

He could only regret that his very beautiful daughter had not chosen a more eligible husband.

Sarah, who was only just eighteen, was quite understandably wildly in love with Ronald Languish.

He was ten years older than she was and very attractive.

He found her entrancing.

He also enjoyed riding the Duke's horses and staying in the Duke's houses.

When however they were alone in a not very comfortable home of their own, the glamour of their wedding began to fade.

Sarah had been very spoilt by her parents.

She was annoyed when she could not have as many servants as she wanted, better horses and most of all, expensive gowns.

Within a year they began to bicker at each other. Two years after the marriage had taken place they were more or less living separate lives.

It was, as far as Sarah was concerned, the greatest good fortune when Ronald Languish lost his life in a Steeple Chase.

He was riding a horse that was not capable of taking the high jumps that had been erected.

Falling at the third fence, he broke his spine.

Had he lived he would have been a helpless cripple.

The Duke sighed with relief that his daughter was now free.

Lady Sarah had no intention of marrying again.

She enjoyed herself with lover after lover, and at the same time became more beautiful.

She was one of the first of the beautiful women whom the public stood on the seats in Hyde Park to see drive by in her open Victoria.

Lady Sarah met the Marquis.

It was then she decided she would acquiesce in her father's pleading to marry for the second time.

The Marquis as a man was everything she desired.

His wealth and possessions were everything she wanted.

She pursued him relentlessly, but cleverly.

By that time she was far too experienced to make it at all obvious either to the gossips or to him what she intended. She swore, however, that he would be hers.

No one should take him from her.

She was not perturbed by his affair with Lady Lessington. Lord Lessington was in excellent health and Her Ladyship would never face the scandal of a divorce.

Lady Sarah just waited for her opportunity.

She heard from William that he had been invited to Ridge.

She knew this was her chance.

Without appearing to be particularly interested, she enquired of Willie:

"Is it a large party:"

"No, I do not think so," Willie replied. "Only the Clevelands and myself. We are going to try out some of the new horses that Blake has brought, and which he is certain will be the envy of all his friends!"

"That is nothing unusual," Lady Sarah remarked with a laugh.

She, however, had the information she wanted.

The Marquis had invited only a few friends for the week-end, and Lady Lessington was not among them.

She waited until she knew the Marquis would not be at home.

Then she called at his house in Park Lane and asked to see his Secretary.

Mr. Grey came hurrying into the Library into which she had been shown.

Lady Sarah smiled at him.

"Good-morning," she said. "I hear His Lordship is out."

"His Lordship will not be back until this afternoon," Mr. Grey replied.

"Then will you ask him if I can come to Ridge on Friday night and stay until Sunday? I have an engagement in the neighbourhood, and it would be very convenient if His Lordship would let me stay with him."

"I will give His Lordship your message, My Lady, as soon as he returns."

"Thank you," Lady Sarah said, "and if you could send a message to my house, I will be very grateful."

"I will do so immediately I have seen His Lordship, so Your Ladyship should know by this evening."

"You are very kind," Lady Sarah said in a soft voice which all men found fascinating.

She smiled at Mr. Grey and left.

He thought as she did so that she was very lovely.

He was certain his Master thought the same.

At the same time one could never be certain.

As he went back to his office Mr. Grey was thinking of the large number of beautiful women.

All of them had lasted only a short time before the Marquis became bored.

"I wonder what he really wants?" Mr. Grey questioned as he sat down at his desk. Then he told himself that it was none of his business.

. . . .

The Marquis had finished dressing.

He was thinking that if he was going to take Lady Sarah with him on Sunday, he would have to invite her tonight or first thing tomorrow morning.

He was quite certain she would not refuse.

But he supposed any woman would want at least twenty-four hours notice in order to see to her packing.

Doubtless she would want to buy a number of quite unnecessary extras before she undertook such a long journey.

As far as he was concerned, she would help the time to pass when they were in the train.

She would also be a perfect cover if anyone was curious as to why he should cruise from Greece along the coast of Bulgaria.

He took one quick glance at himself in the mirror to see that his tie was straight.

Then he proceeded down the wide corridor which led to the top of the stairs.

He was still thinking of Lady Sarah.

At the same time his eyes were searching the hall beneath him.

Two footmen were very smart in the Ridge livery.

The Butler, his hair just turning white, was waiting to direct the guests into the Drawing-Room.

There were the flags which hung on each side of the marble fireplace.

His ancestors had won them in various battles, in which inevitably the British had been the victors.

As he descended the staircase he glanced also at the pictures.

They had hung in the same place on the walls for over a hundred years.

It was then he remembered with a feeling of elation that Sir James Tancombe was bringing him some more pictures.

He hoped they were as good as the *Duchet*.

If so they would be exactly what he required for the new Gallery he had created in the East Wing.

The original Picture Gallery was full – his father had seen to that!

The new one had involved making several rooms into one large one.

The Marquis was determined that the paintings would be as distinctive and prestigious as those collected by his forebears.

He entered the Drawing-Room to find some of his guests already there.

There were Lord and Lady Cleveland, who were distant cousins of whom he was very fond, and Lady Sarah.

They were all laughing as he proceeded towards them.

Then when they saw him Lady Cleveland rose to her feet.

"Blake, how lovely to see you!" she said as he kissed her. "You know how I adore being at Ridge, which is looking even more beautiful than when I last saw it."

"That is what I like to hear," the Marquis replied with a smile.

He shook hands with Lord Cleveland saying:

"I have been looking forward to seeing you, Arthur."

Then he turned to Lady Sarah.

She was deliberately standing a little to one side.

It was so that he could admire her before he actually reached her.

When he did she held out both her hands.

"Have you forgiven me for thrusting myself upon you?" she asked.

"You know without my saying so," the Marquis replied, "that you are always welcome at any time."

He saw the expression in her eyes and knew how the evening would end.

As if with an effort the Marquis turned back to the Clevelands.

"What were you laughing about when I came into the room?" he asked. "I feel I missed something amusing."

"Very amusing," Lady Cleveland answered.

"Sarah was telling us a very naughty story about George Hamilton, but we have been sworn to secrecy, so I must not repeat it!"

"Except of course, to me!" the Marquis said lightly.

Even as he spoke it flashed through his mind that Lady Sarah should not gossip about the Duke of Hamilton.

He was an older and highly respected man.

If she could gossip about him she might easily do so about other people on matters which Lord Beaconsfield had impressed on him no one must ever mention.

The door of the Drawing-Room opened.

"Sir James Tancombe and Miss Nikola Tancombe, my Lord!" the Butler announced.

The Marquis turned round.

Coming towards him was Nikola wearing the turquoise blue gown she had made herself.

She could not have known that the Drawing-Room was a perfect background for it.

The walls were white picked out with gold leaf.

The Louis XIV chairs and sofas were covered in an almost identical blue to the gown she was wearing.

Everything in the room had been chosen to blend with the furniture.

Even the carpet, was predominantly blue and white.

As she moved towards the Marquis, he thought she was like a piece of the Sèvres porcelain which stood on the mantelpiece.

She also resembled a picture by Boucher in which was incorporated exactly the same shade of blue.

He shook hands first with James.

"It is nice to see you again, Sir James!" the Marquis said. "I am so glad you persuaded your sister to come with you."

Nikola dropped the Marquis a very graceful curtsy.

Then as he took her hand in his he was aware that her fingers were trembling.

It was as if he held a small and frightened bird captive.

As he looked into her eyes, which were large and seemed to dominate her face, he knew again that she was afraid.

Because he wished to reassure her, he held her fingers for a little longer than was necessary.

Then he said:

"Come to meet my friends. We are a very small party."

While he was performing the introductions, Captain Barclay came hurrying into the room.

"I am not late, am I?" he said to the Marquis. "I lost my shirt-stud and had to borrow one of yours."

Lady Cleveland teased him for being so careless and he greeted Lady Sarah.

The Marquis then introduced him to Nikola and James.

He stared at her in astonishment.

"Why have I not met you before?" he asked. "Where have you been hiding:"

"Where I live," Nikola replied, "in the country."

"It is a place called 'King's Keep'," Lady Cleveland interposed. "I have already heard a great deal about it from our host."

"It sounds enchanting," Willie said.

"That is what all the Tancombes think it is," Nikola answered, "but of course, they are prejudiced!"

She found William Barclay easy to talk to.

She was glad she was sitting next to him at dinner.

The Marquis had Lady Cleveland on his right, and Lady Sarah on his left.

It was some time before Nikola was brave enough to look at him again.

She thought that he was even more autocratic and frightening than she had expected him to be.

Sitting at the head of the table, in a carved armchair made in the reign of Charles II, he looked Royal.

At the same time he was vibrant in a way she could not explain to herself.

Jimmy had told her how the Marquis expected perfection.

She decided that he must be very perceptive.

If he was, he was therefore, dangerous.

She thought as she glanced at him at dinner that he had what her father had called an "eagle eye".

"Eagles can see further than other birds," he explained, "and they miss very little. The smallest mouse or rabbit hundreds of feet below them cannot escape."

"He is dangerous! He is dangerous!"

Nikola could feel the words repeating themselves in her mind.

All the time she was talking to Willie, or to Lord Cleveland, who was on her other side, she was pulsatingly aware of him.

The dinner was superb, and so were the wines that accompanied it.

The conversation was witty and amusing.

Because the party was so small they talked across the table as well as to those on each side of them.

In fact, Nikola would have thought it was the most entertaining meal she had ever had.

But there was something like a stone in her breast, which she knew was fear.

"I am being ridiculous!" she told herself as the ladies left the gentlemen to their port. "Why should the Marquis be suspicious of anything Jimmy offers him?"

She looked at the pictures in the corridor along which they were walking.

She knew those that were hanging in the Drawing-Room would have thrilled her father.

"Why should the Marquis want more?" she asked angrily.

"Come and tell me about yourself, Miss Tancombe," Lady Cleveland said kindly.

She was a very considerate person.

She thought perhaps a girl who was so much younger than the rest of the party might be feeling a little shy.

Nikola sat down beside her on the sofa.

"I am overcome by this magnificent house!" she said.

"That is what we all feel when we come to Ridge!" Lady Cleveland laughed.

"I expect its owner is tired of being told how wonderful it is, almost as if it was not real," Nikola answered.

Lady Cleveland smiled.

"On the contrary, I think he expects the compliments, and would be surprised and perhaps irritated if they were not forthcoming."

"My brother is the same," Nikola said. "He thinks King's Keep is perfect, and is astounded if people are not wildly enthusiastic as soon as they see it."

"I suppose most men are like that," Lady Cleveland replied. "Where my husband is concerned, it is horses, and the first thing you have to inspect when you stay with us, is the stables!"

Nikola laughed.

She was feeling less tense because Lady Cleveland was so kind.

The gentlemen came to join them.

The Marquis noticed as he entered the room that the usual card-tables had been erected at one end of it.

He walked up to Lady Cleveland.

"I know, Iris," he said, "you are longing to play Bridge, and Willie and Lady Sarah will join you."

Lady Sarah, who had risen when he came into the room put her hand on his arm.

"I want to play with you," she said softly.

"Perhaps later," the Marquis replied. "I intend now to take Sir

James and his sister to my Study. We will not be long, then perhaps we can have a few hands of Baccarat."

Lady Sarah looked disappointed.

Nikola felt as if the stone in her breast was almost too heavy to be borne.

She was aware, however, there was a light in Jimmy's eyes.

As they walked out of the Drawing-Room with the Marquis he asked:

"Shall I go to fetch the pictures I have brought you? They are upstairs in my bedroom."

"A footman could do that for you," the Marquis replied, "although I expect you would rather carry them yourself."

Jimmy walked towards the stairs and the Marquis said to Nikola:

"We go this way."

They walked down the corridor in the opposite direction from the one they had taken to the Dining-Room.

The Marquis took Nikola into a room which she thought was exactly what a man's Study should look like.

The walls were covered in sporting pictures and over the mantel-piece there was a magnificent painting of a horse by Stubbs.

The sofa and chairs were covered in dark red leather.

As they entered, two spaniels rose from the hearth-rug to greet the Marquis.

There was a flat-topped writing-desk with gold feet and handles.

It had been made in the reign of George III.

A glass-fronted Chippendale cabinet was filled with a number of handsomely bound books.

The red velvet curtains matched the colour of the sofa and chairs.

Nikola thought that once again the Marquis had attained perfection.

"Do sit down, Miss Tancombe," he said, "and I hope you enjoyed your dinner."

"I can say in all honesty that it was the best dinner I have ever eaten," Nikola replied, "but I am finding your house so breath-taking that it is difficult to think of anything else."

"That is what I like to hear," the Marquis said. "At the same time it worries me that you look frightened."

Nikola looked away from him towards the fire.

It was not what she expected him to say, and she therefore had no answer.

"You are very beautiful," the Marquis remarked, "and it is therefore wrong that you should look anything but happy."

She was so astonished at the compliment that she turned to look at him.

Then as her eyes met his she felt the colour flooding into her cheeks.

She looked away again.

"Is it possible," the Marquis asked, "that you find my compliments embarrassing?"

"It . . it is something to . . which I am . . not accustomed," Nikola replied.

"Is King's Keep in the middle of the desert, or are all the men in the neighbourhood blind?" the Marquis enquired.

Nikola laughed.

"It is not as bad as that, but I do not see many young people. James's friends are so intent on admiring the house and the pictures that they rarely look at me!"

The Marquis laughed.

"That is certainly a very sad story!"

He paused before he added:

"When you came into the Drawing-Room this evening wearing a gown which might have been designed at the same time as the room itself, I thought I must be dreaming."

"Now you . . mention it . . I realise my gown is the . . same colour as the china . . and these . . beautiful French chairs."

"Exactly!" the Marquis said. "And perhaps when you bought it, you had a presentiment that you would wear it in this house."

Nikola thought the Marquis would be surprised if he knew she had made the gown herself, and in one-and-a-half days.

However she did not have to answer.

At that moment the door opened and Jimmy came in carrying the pictures.

As usual, when Jimmy was doing anything special for King's Keep he became more animated.

It was as if his whole being lit up.

He spoke not only with his mind, but also with his heart and soul.

He was speaking of the thing he loved best in the world.

The Marquis sat down in an armchair.

He looked, Nikola thought, like Jupiter, King of the Gods, condescending to the mere mortals beneath him.

Jimmy showed him first of all the Van Leyden.

He was clever enough to let the Marquis see for himself the colours of the man's strangely shaped hat and the question in the girl's eyes as she looked at him.

The Marquis did not say anything, and Jimmy then produced the Mabuse.

"This is surely Mabuse," he said.

Now the Marquis sat forward in his chair and exclaimed:

"It is a portrait of Jacqueline de Bourgogne. How on earth did you come by that?"

"I am not certain from where my father obtained it," Jimmy replied vaguely, "but I think it is the most perfect example of his brilliant technique."

"I agree with you!" the Marquis replied.

Then with the air of a magician about to perform his *pièce de résistance*, Jimmy produced *The Virgin in the Rose Garden*.

He propped it against a chair.

The Marquis stared at it.

"A Lochner!" he exclaimed.

"One of the best examples of his work," Jimmy said, "and my sister can hardly bear to part with it."

The Marquis looked at Nikola.

Her eyes were on the painting.

Once again she was praying to the Virgin for help.

There was silence until the Marquis said:

"I think, Tancombe, I should thank you for bringing me three remarkable pictures which I shall certainly be proud to have in my collection."

"I was sure that was what you would feel about them," Jimmy said. "Especially the Lochner."

"It is exquisite!" the Marquis agreed. "I know that once it is mine I shall never want to part with it."

"That is what I feel myself," Jimmy agreed. "At the same time, there is so much to be done at King's Keep, and repairs, as we all know, cost money."

Quite suddenly Nikola felt she could not bear to hear her brother talking like that.

She also knew that they would soon be negotiating over the price.

She felt that to think of *The Virgin in the Rose Garden* in terms of money was an insult.

Nothing so beautiful or so Holy could ever be assessed in pounds, shillings and pence.

She rose to her feet.

"Will you . . forgive me . . My Lord," she said in a very small voice, "if I . . retire to bed? I have a . . slight headache after . . the journey."

"But of course," the Marquis said. "I quite understand, and as it is Friday night, none of us will stay up late."

"Thank you."

She walked towards the door.

Before she could reach it the Marquis was there before her.

He held it open.

"I trust you will sleep well," he said in his deep voice.

Nikola made an effort to smile at him then without replying she moved away down the corridor.

She heard the door close behind her.

The Marquis had gone back and now the bargaining for the pictures would commence.

She was well aware that Jimmy would start by asking a far higher sum than he expected to get.

"If only we could have kept *The Virgin in the Rose Garden*, she told herself, "then I am sure our troubles would have been at an end."

She knew by the expression on the Marquis's face that he had been surprised that Jimmy would sell such a magnificent picture.

Any connoisseur and Collector would want to keep it for himself.

It would have been better, Nikola thought, if Jimmy had brought away something less important.

But it was too late for regrets.

She reached her bedroom.

Because she was inexperienced in staying in grand country houses, she did not ring for the maid to help her undress.

She hung her gown up in the wardrobe.

As she did so she thought how the Marquis had complimented her on its colour.

It was strange that the curtains in the Blue Room at King's Keep should exactly match the Drawing-Room at Ridge.

"That was certainly something Mama did not anticipate when she hung them Nikola thought.

She got into bed, but it was impossible to sleep.

She could only lie worrying about what was happening downstairs.

She wondered what payment Jimmy had obtained from the Marquis.

It was two hours later when he opened the communicating-door from the Boudoir and peeped in.

"Are you awake?" he whispered.

Nikola sat up in bed.

One candle was still alight because she had been almost sure Jimmy would come to tell her what had happened.

He walked towards the bed and sat down facing her.

"What do you think I got?" he asked.

"I cannot imagine," Nikola replied.

"Ten thousand pounds!"

Nikola gave a little cry and put her hands up to her face.

"I . . I do not believe . . it!"

"I can hardly believe it myself," Jimmy said.

"It must . . have been . . what you . . started by asking."

"It was, and His Lordship did not argue."

"It . . cannot be . . true!" Nikola said again.

"It is!" Jimmy assured her. "And now I can do everything I want in the house, and you shall have the new stove in the kitchen you have been fussing about for so long."

"That will be . . wonderful!" Nikola cried. "You are . . quite . . certain he was not . . suspicious?"

"Why should he be?" Jimmy asked.

"It seems strange that he should have agreed to pay what you asked without haggling over it."

"We certainly "haggled", as you call it, over the Daghest and now I am asking myself if I should have let it go so cheaply."

"I think you should . . go down on your knees and thank . . God for what you have . . already received," Nikola replied, "and, Jimmy . . l have . . something to . . ask you."

"What is it?" Jimmy asked in an uncompromising voice.

"Surely . . now that you . . have so much . . this is something you need . . never do again?"

Jimmy got off the bed.

"Shall we say, not for a long time!" he replied.

"I would be happier if you said 'Never'!"

"How can I foresee what will happen in the future?" he asked.

He walked towards the communicating-door.

Nikola knew that he was irritated by her insistence.

As he reached it he said:

"If you want the truth, I am very, very pleased with myself! I think, although you may not say so, that I have been brilliantly clever!"

He did not wait for Nikola to reply.

He went into the Boudoir and shut the door behind him.

Slowly she turned to blow out the candle by her bed.

Then as she lay down she was praying to *The Virgin in the Rose Garden*.

She was giving thanks that the danger she had feared was past.

She could still feel as if there was a stone in her breast.

．　．　．　．　．　．　．

The next morning the sun was shining.

Nikola told herself the fears of the night were over.

The maid who called her said that His Lordship was going riding after breakfast.

Any of his guests who wished to go with him were welcome to do so.

Because Jimmy had praised the Marquis's horses, Nikola had hoped she might have a chance of riding.

She had therefore packed her habit.

It was an old one, but it was well cut because it had belonged to her mother.

Nikola had worn it after she had grown out of her own.

Her mother's jacket, because she hunted, was plainly tailored and fitted Nikola as if it had been made for her.

The stock she wore round her neck was rather frayed.

But she had washed and starched it since the last time she had worn it.

She managed to tie it so that it did not show where it was worn.

She had brought a hat which was not the top-hat worn in the hunting-field.

Nor was it the bowler which had been introduced a few years before.

It was a high-crowned, very attractive hat with a gauze veil.

It was worn, although Nikola was not aware of it, by the 'Pretty Horse-breakers' in London.

They were the women who broke in the horses of the Livery Stables.

Brilliant riders and extremely attractive, they were sought after by the rich "Men-About-Town".

Nikola, however, was not worrying about her appearance as she hurried downstairs.

She entered the Breakfast Room to find three men, including her brother, were there before her.

There was no sign of Lady Cleveland or of Lady Sarah.

The Marquis came in just as she was sitting down beside Jimmy.

"Good-morning!" he said to his guests.

Then he turned to Nikola and asked:

"Are you feeling better?"

"Yes . . thank you," Nikola replied.

"We missed you last night," Willie said, "but your brother managed to empty my pockets."

Nikola heaved a sigh of relief that Jimmy had not lost.

Then she remembered how much he had gained from the Marquis.

"It must have been his . . lucky night!" she said lightly.

"And we are lucky to have you with us this morning," William said gallantly.   "I only hope Blake's horse will not prove too much for you!"

"I should find it very humiliating if it did," Nikola replied.

She found, however, that she was given a perfectly trained and magnificent-looking horse that was easy to handle.

Jimmy had a far more spirited one, which delighted him.

The Marquis was breaking in a stallion that did everything in its power to unseat him.

It was the age-old battle between man and beast.

Nikola thought that no man could look more magnificent or ride more brilliantly.

The Marquis took them to his race-course.

The four men raced each other while Nikola watched them.

The Marquis was the undisputed winner, and Jimmy was second.

As they rode back towards the house the Marquis asked him:

"Are you as knowledgeable about horses as you are about pictures?"

"I would like to think so," Jimmy replied, "but I do not often have the good luck to ride an animal as fine as this!"

He patted the horse he was riding as he spoke.

Nikola wondered if some of the money he had obtained might be spent on new horses for King's Keep.

The two they had were used both for drawing the Curricle and for riding.

They were not in the same class as those owned by the Marquis.

"If we could have just one really good stallion which I could ride when Jimmy is not there," she thought to herself.

Then she started when the Marquis, who must have read her thoughts said:

"I have a feeling, Miss Tancombe, that you are feeling envious."

"Of course I am!" Nikola replied. "You have so much, and we have so little."

"But you have King's Keep!" he said as if he must argue the point.

"Which is a very demanding possession," Nikola replied.

She spoke without thinking.

There was a note in her voice which made the Marquis suddenly aware that she had suffered.

Perhaps she too had made sacrifices for the house which meant so much to her brother.

He was used to being clairvoyant about people, especially when he was "on a mission".

But he had never felt it so acutely before with a woman as he did now with Nikola.

As the Marquis looked at her he thought she was very different from most women.

It was because she was so completely unselfconscious about her beauty.

She was quite unaware of how lovely she looked with her fair hair thrown into prominence by the darkness of her habit.

Also by the black horse she was riding.

Any other woman of his acquaintance after they had been galloping would be smoothing their hair and pulling their habit into place.

They would also be flirting with him with every word they spoke and with every look they gave him.

But Nikola was looking at the house that lay ahead of them.

She was also looking at the lake beneath it and the flowers that grew all around them.

It struck him that her expression was very like that of *The Virgin in the Rose Garden*.

"If an Artist saw her, he would want to paint her in a garden too," he thought, "and of course she is a virgin."

It was a strange thought for him to have.

Then as they rode on, he found himself wondering why Nikola had been frightened the night before.

Why had she left the Study with the excuse of going to bed?

Why had she been praying to *The Virgin in the Rose Garden* as soon as her brother had turned it round?

This was something he had only just thought of, and he was determined to know the answer.

Chapter Five

When they returned to the Castle the Marquis went to his Study.

He knew his Secretary would have a large number of letters waiting for him to sign.

He had just finished a dozen of them when Mr. Gordon came in and the Marquis said:

"I was just wondering, Gordon, where I have heard the name of Jacqueline de Bourgogne."

Mr. Gordon looked puzzled.

The Marquis was thinking it was very strange when Sir James Tancombe had shown him a picture by Mabuse he had known who it was.

There was silence. Then the Marquis said:

"A picture in which she is portrayed was painted by Mabuse."

"Ah! Now I think I remember, My Lord,"

Gordon replied. "It was mentioned in His late Lordship's correspondence."

"Fetch it," the Marquis ordered.

After his father died he had had his very considerable correspondence with other Collectors filed.

It was just in case he wished for details of his purchases at any time.

The name now came to his mind as it was connected with Mabuse.

Perhaps his father had received some information about it which he had read in his letters.

He went on signing his letter.

Only a few minutes passed before Mr. Gordon returned with a large file in his hand.

He put it down in front of the Marquis saying:

"This file, My Lord, contains all the correspondence regarding artists from 'L' to 'M'."

"Thank you."

The Marquis opened the file and turning over the pages found under '*MABUSE*' a letter from Lord Hartley to his father.

He had written:

> "*You said to me when we were in White's Club that you were anxious to acquire a Mabuse for your Collection.*
>
> *I told you that I have his portrait of Jacqueline de Bourgogne. I bought it from a Dealer in Amsterdam whose name and address I have put on a separate sheet.*
>
> *I think you will find him quite a reliable man, and trustworthy. It was in fact this Dealer who was instrumental in my acquiring Lochner's 'The Virgin in the Rose Garden', which is one of the most beautiful pictures I have ever seen.*
>
> *It would be a great pleasure to show them to you if you ever have time to visit my house.*"

The Marquis stared at what had been written.

Then he saw at the end of the letter some words in his father's somewhat scribbled handwriting.

It was so badly written that he had to turn the letter towards the window to read it.

It said:

> "*After Hartley's death got in touch with his widow. She refused to sell anything!*"

The Marquis put the file down on his desk and said to his Secretary:

"Ask Sir James Tancombe and his sister to come here."

Mr. Gordon hurried away to obey his orders.

The Marquis read the letter again, and also his father's note.

A little time elapsed before Jimmy and Nikola appeared.

As they came into the Study, the Marquis was aware that Nikola was again looking frightened.

He rose perfunctorily, then said:

"Will you sit down? I have something to discuss with you." Jimmy took a chair nearest to the desk.

Nikola moved to another one which was opposite the three pictures which had been arranged on the sofa.

'*The Virgin in the Rose Garden*' was in the centre.

299

As she looked at it she had the frightening feeling that it was warning her.

"When I awoke this morning," the Marquis began, "I was wondering how it was that when you showed me the portrait painted by Mabuse I knew it was of Jacqueline de Bourgogne."

Jimmy was listening with his eyes on the Marquis's face, but Nikola was looking at the picture of the Virgin.

It struck the Marquis that once again she was praying.

"I therefore," he went on, "turned up my father's files and found that he had corresponded with Lord Hartley about this very picture."

Jimmy stiffened.

Nikola felt as if she had been stabbed by a dagger.

For a moment it was impossible to breathe.

Very slowly she turned to look at the Marquis.

"I have a letter here which Lord Hartley wrote to my father," the Marquis went on, "and I will read it to you."

He picked up the file and in his clear, deep voice read the letter aloud.

When he mentioned *The Virgin in the Rose Garden* Nikola gave a little gasp.

Clasping her hands together she turned once again to look at the picture.

"Help us . . help us!" she was saying in her heart.

The Marquis finished the letter from Lord Hartley.

Then he read the note his father had made at the bottom of it.

He put the file down on his desk, and looking at Jimmy said:

"Perhaps your explanation, Sir James, is that Lady Hartley changed her mind and sold you both these pictures and the Van Leyden which I have not yet had time to check."

There was a little pause.

Then as Nikola knew that Jimmy was going to try and bluff it out she rose to her feet.

She walked to the desk to stand in front of the Marquis and said:

"Please . . please understand that . . the pictures were . . shut up in a dusty room . . and our Aunt was not . . interested in . . them."

Her voice was hardly audible.

She was very pale.

Her eyes as she pleaded with the Marquis seemed to fill her whole face.

300

"So you stole them!" the Marquis said.

"Lady Hartley is a Tancombe," Nikola replied, "and Jimmy . . needed them so that he could . . restore the house in which the . . Tancombes have lived for . . four-hundred years."

"Nevertheless," the Marquis said in a hard voice,"they were not your brother's to sell, and I imagine that Lady Hartley would not have given them to him had he asked her to do so."

"She would not . . help us even though . . she is very rich," Nikola answered. "Please . . try to . . understand."

"I think your brother should speak for himself," the Marquis said.

Almost as if he had struck at her, Nikola moved away from the desk.

She stood in front of the picture of *The Virgin in the Rose Garden.*

Now she was praying with all her heart that the Marquis would not denounce Jimmy publicly.

"Well?" the Marquis demanded looking at Jimmy.

"Have you nothing to say for yourself?

"My sister has told you the truth," he answered. "I was desperate to restore King's Keep to its former glory and, unless the house was to fall to the ground and we were to starve, I had to obtain money from somewhere."

Jimmy spoke defiantly, and Nikola knew he was fighting for his very life.

There was silence.

Then the Marquis said:

"There are several things I can do about this."

As Jimmy did not ask the obvious question he went on:

"I can of course, send you to Lady Hartley to restore the pictures to her late husband's Collection."

"If you do that, they will just rot in the dust as they were doing before I cleaned them," Jimmy replied, "and no one will see them except the mice."

The Marquis's lips tightened a little cynically as if he thought Jimmy was putting up a good defence for his actions.

Then he continued:

"On the other hand, I can accept the pictures in good faith. In which case, I shall expect you to make reparation for attempting to deceive me."

Without looking round Nikola knew that Jimmy squared his shoulders.

"What do you want me to do?" he asked.

"I realise you have a great knowledge and appreciation of Art."

He paused a moment then went on:

"So in return for my keeping silent about what is unquestionably a criminal offence, I require you to do me service!"

"In what way?" Jimmy asked.

It flashed through Nikola's mind that the Marquis intended to humiliate Jimmy.   She knew in that case he would never agree.

If he refused, then the Marquis might tell Lady Hartley what he had done.

If that happened, she was quite certain the story would be passed round all their relations.

That would mean that Jimmy would be ostracised and decried by every one of them.

Once the story was known to the rest of the family she was quite certain they would talk and talk.

Sooner or later it would be known by a great number of other people as well.

Because the name of Tancombe was besmirched, it would also affect King's Keep.

"That must . . not happen . . it must not!" she cried silently.

"I have had in mind for some time," the Marquis was saying, "to visit Lima, which as you know, is in Peru."

He paused, aware of the bewilderment at what he had just said on the faces of the two people listening to him.

Both Jimmy and Nikola were wondering what this had to do with them.

"And then from Lima," the Marquis went on, "To travel to Cuzco which is thousands of feet up in the mountains."

He stopped speaking for a moment, and then continued:

"It is where, if you remember your history, the Spaniards destroyed 363 Temples built by the Incas, and built in their place 365 Churches."

What he was saying was so surprising that Nikola turned to stare at the Marquis as her brother was doing.

"The Jesuits," the Marquis went on, "had in the 17th century, a School of Painting and their pictures are still hanging in the Churches they built."

He paused, and as they did not speak, he went on:

"Some of these, I understand are for sale, and some, especially those by Basilio Santacruz, are said to be very fine."

Because she could not help it, without really thinking, Nikola moved a little nearer to the desk.

"I intended," the Marquis went on, "as I have already said, to visit Cuzco myself, but now, I think you, Tancombe, should go in my place with a friend of mine, who is extremely shrewd when it comes to money, and knows a certain amount about pictures."

Jimmy drew in his breath.

"You mean – you want – me to buy these – pictures for you?"

"If you think they are worth buying," the Marquis replied.

"Although you will have to leave your beloved house behind, the journey should certainly enlarge your knowledge of the world and of 17th century paintings."

For a moment Jimmy was speechless.

Then he said:

"If I can really do that, then of course I can only thank Your Lordship for being extremely magnanimous and broad-minded."

"When you return," the Marquis said as if he had no wish to be thanked, "we can again discuss the payment for these three pictures, which will be safe in my keeping until then."

Because Nikola was so relieved and knew that her prayers had been answered, her eyes filled with tears.

Then as if the Marquis suddenly realised she was standing near him, he said sharply:

"I have not yet finished. Your sister, who is definitely an accessory to your crime, must also pay a price for my silence."

Nikola's eyes opened wider than they were already.

In a whisper she asked:

"W.what do you . . want me to . . do?"

"I am leaving for Greece tomorrow morning," the Marquis said. "I wish you to come with me as my companion on the journey which will include visits to the Aegean Sea in my yacht."

Nikola felt she could not have heard him aright.

It was Jimmy who said sharply:

"I would like to know, My Lord, exactly what you mean by that!"

The eyes of the two men met and the Marquis said:

"Exactly what I say. It is a long journey, and I would like to have somebody to talk to."

"And you suggest that my sister should accompany you unchaperoned?"

"It does not suit me to have a party," the Marquis said, "and as it happens, no one in England will know where I am or who is with me."

"At the same time . . .!" Jimmy began hotly.

The Marquis put up his hand.

"Your sister will be treated with all . . "

He was about to say "propriety".

Then behind Nikola he caught sight of the picture on the sofa.

" . . as if she was *The Virgin in the Rose Garden*!" he finished.

Jimmy wanted to protest that Nikola should not do anything which would jeopardise her reputation.

Then as if the words were forced from him against his will, he said:

"Very well, My Lord, I trust you."

"I assure you," the Marquis replied, "you will have no grounds for doing otherwise."

Nikola had no idea what they were talking about.

Looking bewildered she said:

"But of course if Your Lordship . . wants me to come with . . you I will do so . . and as James will be away it will be . . very exciting for . . me."

Jimmy pressed his lips together as if he had a great deal more to say on the matter.

Then he knew without words that the Marquis was ordering him to keep silent.

He was in fact helpless to do anything but acquiesce.

"Very well, My Lord," he said, "and when do you wish me to leave?"

"I am leaving here tomorrow morning," the Marquis replied, "and you will come with your sister and me as far as London."

He paused, then went on:

"Where the house-party is concerned, we all have appointments which cannot be cancelled."

"I understand," Jimmy said.

"I hope you do, and let me reiterate because it is important: neither you, Sir James, nor your sister is to tell anybody where you are going or with whom – do you understand? Nobody!"

His voice was harsh as he continued:

"If you do not keep silent as I have told you to do, then I shall not keep silent on a subject which concerns you!"

It was a threat which made Jimmy flush with anger.

"I promise you, My Lord," Nikola said quickly, "that we will be very careful not to do anything you do not want us to do."

Her voice was trembling as she went on:

"Thank you . . thank you for not . . denouncing Jimmy! It is . . difficult to express how truly . . grateful we are!"

She thought as she spoke that Jimmy was appearing very ungrateful.

She could not understand why he was making a fuss about her going to Greece.

Of course it was unconventional for her to go without a chaperon.

But she was sure in the circumstances that the Marquis was not going to treat her as if she were a guest, but more like a servant.

Unlike any other Lady he might have taken with him, he would give her orders.

She would have to do his bidding.

"Now we have settled that you are free to return to the house-party," the Marquis said. "But remember – not a word of anything that has been discussed here, and when we all leave together tomorrow morning, it is because you, Sir James, have a meeting in London."

Jimmy nodded as he went on:

"And I have an appointment which it is impossible for me to postpone."

"We will make no mistakes, My Lord," Jimmy said, "and I will do my very best to find you some pictures in Cuzco which will be good enough to hang in your new Gallery."

Now there was a note in his voice which told Nikola he was excited by the idea of going to a place of which she had never heard.

It was on the other side of the world.

She could hardly believe that she too was going to travel.

Anything would be better than sitting alone in King's Keep worrying about Jimmy.

She went upstairs to change out of her riding habit.

Only then did she realise she had only the few clothes she had brought with her to Ridge.

Somehow she must send home for some more.

She went through the Boudoir to James's bedroom.

She knew he would be changing.

Jimmy had changed, managing as he always did to do so without the help of a valet.

She knocked on the communicating-door and opened it.

As she went in Jimmy said before she could speak:

"I was just thinking, Nikola, that it is rather exciting going to Cuzco. I have heard about the pictures there from Papa."

He stopped speaking a moment, then went on:

"A friend of his had seen them and said they were in a bad state of repair and now that the Jesuits have all gone nobody is interested in them."

"It will be a wonderful experience for you," Nikola replied, "and I am sure it is due to my prayers that the Marquis will not tell Aunt Alice."

"Then you had better go on praying that when I come back he will give me the £10,000 he promised me!" Jimmy said.

He paused for a moment before he added:

"I suppose Butters and Bessie will look after the house all right?"

"Of course they will," Nikola replied, "and I do not suppose I shall be away for long. If nothing else, the Marquis will be back for Royal Ascot."

The worry cleared from James's eyes.

"Of course he will! I am sure he intends that his horse will win the Gold Cup."

"You had better send Butters a note and of course some money," Nikola reminded him.

"It can be taken by one of the grooms, and do you think he could bring back some of my clothes?"

Jimmy laughed.

"His Lordship, for all his planning, has not remembered that! Of course you must have clothes, whatever they look like."

"I suppose if I am to be alone on the yacht with him, they will not matter," Nikola said.

"But if his friends come aboard they may think it rather strange that I am almost in rags!"

Jimmy looked embarrassed.

"Are your things really as bad as that?"

"Worse!"

"Well, that is his business!" Jimmy remarked. "I had better go and ask him now if I can order a groom to ride as quickly as possible to King's Keep.

You must write to Bessie telling her exactly what she must pack up for you."

"If I take many clothes His Lordship will have to send a vehicle of some sort."

"Why not?" Jimmy asked as if he had just thought of it. "Heaven knows the stables are stocked with conveyances of every sort and description."

He put a finishing touch to his tie and walked towards the door.

"Leave it to me, Nikola," he said, "and I promise I will send Butters enough money to last him for at least a month."

Nikola went back to her own room.

She wondered what she should do when she returned to King's Keep if there was no money in the Bank.

Then she told herself there must be some from what Jimmy had obtained for the other things he had sold.

She only hoped the Marquis would never find out about that!

.   .   .   .

While brother and sister were worrying over their private affairs the Marquis was thinking of his.

It was only while he was dealing with Jimmy by sending him to Cuzco that he had remembered his own problem.

He had from the start felt nervous about taking Lady Sarah with him on his mission because she gossiped.

Last night there had arisen another reason for not taking her.

His guests had retired to bed.

Lady Cleveland said she was tired and so was her husband.

The Marquis instead of going to his bedroom had gone to his Study.

He had placed the three pictures on the sofa, as Nikola found them.

He thought as he looked again at *The Virgin in the Rose Garden* that it was one of the most attractive pictures he had ever seen.

There was no obvious resemblance to Nikola.

Yet he found himself thinking of her.

It was as if she was seated on the throne surrounded by small winged angels, her hair haloed by the sunshine.

When finally he went up to bed he decided that, although he knew

Lady Sarah was waiting for him, he was not in the mood for making love to her.

It was only too obvious that was what she expected.

He knew by the way she pressed his hand when they said goodnight that she would be waiting for him to join her.

All during the evening there had been an invitation in her eyes on her lips and in every movement of her body.

It was all a repetition of what he knew only too well was the prelude to the beginning of yet another fiery affair.

"I will think about it tomorrow," he told himself as he undressed.

As his Valet carried away his evening-clothes he got into bed.

He did not blow out the candles.

He usually read for a little while before he went to sleep.

Tonight the book by his bedside which was a somewhat heavy volume on Oriental antiquities, remained unopened.

Instead he found himself thinking of the three pictures he had just acquired.

He was planning where he should hang them in his new Gallery.

He had the feeling that *The Virgin in the Rose Garden* should have a special background.

He was wondering if he should not have it in his bedroom when, to his surprise, the door opened.

It was Lady Sarah.

She was looking very lovely in a negligee that was as transparent as the nightgown she wore beneath it.

It was a deep pink, which was to be expected with her long dark hair falling over her shoulders.

She was beautiful.

Any man would have found her irresistibly desirable.

But for the moment, because she was such a contrast to *The Virgin in the Rose Garden* the Marquis felt cold.

He was in fact, only conscious of a sense of annoyance.

She had broken all the rules in visiting him rather than waiting for him to come to her.

"You have not said goodnight to me," Lady Sarah said in a soft seductive voice.

"I thought you would be too tired," the Marquis excused himself.

"How could I be that, when I was longing for you?" she answered.

She had not moved since she entered the room.

Now she sat down on the bed and very slowly put out her arms to encircle his neck.

"Why should we waste time in waiting for each other?" she whispered and her lips were on his.

. . . .

It was very much later when Lady Sarah left.

She kissed the Marquis passionately before she did so.

The Marquis knew then that even if the Prime Minister begged him to do so, he would not take Lady Sarah with him to Greece.

The difficulty was that if he did not, he would be forced to find somebody in Athens.

He did in fact, have a number of friends who were Greek.

He was sure there would be one beautiful woman amongst them who would be delighted to go with him on a cruise.

But that meant taking on board her husband also and perhaps several other guests.

It annoyed him that he had not been given more time in which to make suitable arrangements.

Yet he knew only too well that when Lord Beaconsfield required something, he wanted it "yesterday".

"Of course I will find somebody," he said doubtfully.

He was, however, absolutely determined that he would not take Lady Sarah.

Now he had decided it would be Nikola, and he congratulated himself on having been very clever.

She was young and she was innocent.

She would therefore make no demands upon him.

She was completely ignorant of the Social World.

There was no reason why their names should ever be linked in any way.

"It all fits so neatly, like a pattern," he thought "that it must be Fate."

He had been trying to visit Cuzco for over a year.

Ever since, in fact, he had learned about the pictures that were falling out of their frames and in which no one was interested.

Then a month ago he had decided to send a man who had bought him some pictures in Vienna.

He was delighted at the idea of the journey to Lima.

At the same time, the Marquis was sure he did not have the "flair" or the instinct which he sensed in James Tancombe.

The two of them combined would make an excellent team.

What they bought would certainly enrich his Gallery.

He was feeling in a very good humour when James came back into the Study.

"What can I do for you, Tancombe?" the Marquis asked.

Jimmy explained that he wished to send to King's Keep for Nikola's clothes.

"I also," he said, "have to instruct the servants to look after the house while I am away."

The Marquis agreed to everything.

"Should there be any difficulties before you return," he said, "I will tell your sister to notify me, and I will send over one of my staff to sort it out."

"That is very kind of you," Jimmy said, "and I suppose Nikola will be back from Greece quite quickly?"

"I sincerely hope so," the Marquis said. "It is extremely inconvenient for me to be away for long."

He paused before he added:

"As it is, I have two horses running at Newmarket next Saturday, and I would have liked to see their performance."

"There are always difficulties when one has to go away," Jimmy remarked.

"That is true," the Marquis agreed.

They walked together back to the room where the house-party had assembled before luncheon.

Nikola was already there.

As Jimmy joined her she gave him a note which he saw was addressed to Bessie.

Taking it Jimmy went from the room to the Secretary's office.

He knew that before they sat down to luncheon that a fast vehicle would have left for King's Keep.

It would be back in the evening soon after they had finished dinner.

. . . .

To Nikola travelling with the Marquis was like stepping into a Fairy Story.

They left Ridge at eight o'clock the next morning before there was any sign of Lady Cleveland or Lady Sarah.

Both Lord Cleveland and Willie, however, came to see them off.

The Marquis begged them to stay until Monday, if it suited them.

He deeply regretted that he had to leave so early.

"Sir James is in the same predicament," he said. "He has somebody of importance to see who will be leaving London tomorrow and therefore they must meet today."

"I will bet the subject they discuss is pictures!" Willie remarked.

"Could it be anything else?" Lord Cleveland asked.

The Marquis picked up the reins.

Nikola waved to the two men until the house was out of sight.

When they left the Halt in the Marquis's private train, Nikola was sure she was dreaming.

There were stewards wearing his livery to wait on them.

While she was not hungry, having recently eaten a substantial breakfast upstairs, Jimmy accepted a glass of champagne.

Later they ate Caviare and paté sandwiches.

Nikola knew her brother was accepting everything on the principle that he might never be offered it again.

Most certainly he could not afford it if he was paying.

When they reached Ridge House in Park Lane, the man who was going with Jimmy to Lima was waiting there.

To Nikola's relief they appeared to get on well.

The Marquis left them while he discussed his trip with Mr. Grey.

An hour after their arrival Nikola had said goodbye to Jimmy.

She was travelling alone with the Marquis to Tilbury.

A cabin on the cross-Channel Steamer to Ostend was at the Marquis's disposal.

As it was a bright sunny day, however, he preferred to walk round the deck.

Nikola read the newspapers and magazines seated comfortably in an armchair.

When they stepped ashore at Ostend she saw the Royal Railway Carriages waiting for them.

It was then that she was unable to contain her excitement.

"Is it .. really true that these belong to .. The Queen?" she asked.

"Her Majesty has most graciously put them at my disposal," the Marquis replied.

Nikola looked around her as if she could not believe her eyes.

The walls of the Drawing-Room were hung with silk *capitonnée*.

There was blue for the dado and pearl grey above, brocaded in pale yellow, with the shamrock, rose and thistle.

Four lights were set into the padded ceiling, while the curtains were blue and white.

An Indian carpet covered the floor.

There was a sofa, two armchairs in blue in Louis XVI style.

The footstool had yellow fringes and tassels.

The Sleeping-car consisted of two bedrooms.

The motif in Nikola's was Japanese with protective bamboo hung round the walls.

Dark red morocco leather covered the wash-stand and the basin.

There was plenty of room for hanging clothes.

When the train started off she went back into the Drawing-Room.

"This is very, very thrilling for me," she said to the Marquis. "In fact, I am quite sure I am dreaming!"

"As we have a long way to go," the Marquis said. "I am afraid you will find it boring before we eventually reach Greece."

Nikola smiled.

"I noticed when we came aboard that there was a large case marked '*BOOKS*'."

"So you are an avid reader?" the Marquis remarked.

"It is only in books that I have travelled so far," Nikola replied, "but I have visited a great number of countries."

Do you consider yourself knowledgeable on Greece?"

"Will there by any chance of our seeing Athens?" she asked.

"I am making no promises," the Marquis replied. "My yacht will be waiting for us, and I think it might be a mistake not to go aboard immediately."

He saw the disappointment in Nikola's eyes.

But she did not plead with him as any other woman would have done in order to get her own way.

He had established from the very beginning that if he wanted to read the newspapers he did not wish to be interrupted.

He therefore raised his newspaper until he was hidden behind it.

Then, because he was curious he looked round it to see what Nikola was doing.

She had moved from the seat opposite him to a chair by the window.

She was looking out.

312

She was obviously completely absorbed by the countryside through which they were passing.

She had removed her hat when she went to her bedroom.

The Marquis thought her profile silhouetted against the window was very lovely.

So was her hair, as the sunshine turned it to little tongues of fire.

Then he congratulated himself that she was keeping quiet.

That was exactly what he wanted on the journey.

When they reached Athens he would tell her what part she had to play.

That was just in case some inquisitive persons came aboard.

He doubted if it would occur to her that those who did call on him would assume she was his mistress.

"That is important," he thought. "People just have to believe that I am having a quiet holiday and that includes both the Russians and the Turks."

Then he told himself it was too soon to start worrying about what would happen.

It could wait until they were at sea.

He returned to reading the newspaper.

. . . .

When it was time for dinner, Nikola wondered what she should wear.

She had told Bessie to send her everything she thought she would need.

But she still had only one decent evening-gown.

She was quite certain that the Marquis would change into his evening-clothes.

"How could he do anything else," she asked herself with a smile, "considering we are at the moment Royalty?"

It was thrilling to think she was sleeping in the Queen's own bed.

It had never struck her for a moment that there was any significance in that the Marquis was just along the corridor.

Dawkins was accommodated in the Day Car.

There was a compartment used by the Queen's Scottish servant who always travelled with her.

In the Sleeping Car which was connected by a short corridor there were only the two bedrooms and a compartment for light luggage.

Dawkins told Nikola that the maids slept on sofas.

"Then it is fortunate we do not have any with us," Nikola laughed, "as they must be uncomfortable."

"Oi'll look after yer, Miss," Dawkins said, "an' don't yer forget t'ask fer anythin' you needs."

"Thank you," Nikola replied, thinking he was a kind little man.

He had unpacked her luggage for her.

Now she looked in the large built-in cupboard which served as a wardrobe.

She thought how shabby everything looked.

Except for her new turquoise gown.

"I can hardly wear that every night," she thought. "And anyway, I do not suppose the Marquis will notice me.'

She put on a white muslin gown she had made herself.

She had not been able to afford enough material to make a bustle.

Instead she wore a sash she had as a child, which made a large bow at the back.

To make it more fashionable she had added a long muslin flounce at each end.

She looked at herself in the mirror.

It did not compare with the very smart gowns which Lady Sarah had worn.

She could not help wondering why the Marquis had not asked Lady Sarah to accompany him on this trip.

She would have looked very decorative and very beautiful in the Royal Drawing-Room.

Nikola did the best she could with her hair.

She tried to achieve a fashionable coiffure.

But little curls would keep escaping.

Finally she gave up trying to brush them straight.

Without looking any more at her reflection she went into the Drawing-Room.

The Marquis looked at her, she thought, critically as she sat down opposite him.

A steward offered her a glass of champagne.

Remembering what Jimmy had said, she accepted it.

The Marquis, she thought, was looking magnificent.

He looked exactly as if he was going to dine with The Queen.

His shirt looked dazzlingly white with just one stud in the centre.

It consisted of a large black pearl.

Nikola had never seen a black pearl before.

She kept glancing at it curiously.

"What has happened to your beautiful turquoise gown which matched my Drawing-Room at Ridge?" the Marquis asked.

There was a little pause before Nikola said:

"As it is the . . only nice gown I have . . I thought I would . . keep it for some . . special occasion."

"And you do not consider that dining with me is one?"

"Yes . . of course . . it is!" Nikola replied blushing. "But as you . . saw it last night . . and the night before . . I thought my appearance might become . . somewhat monotonous."

"It is certainly a very beautiful gown!" the Marquis remarked.

Nikola laughed.

"Why are you laughing?" he asked.

"Because it is really a pair of bed-curtains!"

The Marquis stared at her.

"I do not understand what you are saying."

"When you invited my brother to stay with you . . I had only a day and a half in which to . . make myself something . . decent to wear."

"You made it yourself?" the Marquis asked in astonishment.

"I took the curtains from the four-poster on which Mama had hung them."

"I see you are a very talented young woman!" the Marquis remarked.

He did not make it sound particularly a compliment.

Nikola said apologetically:

"I am afraid you are going to be very . . ashamed of . . me if we meet any of . . your friends. But if it is in the evening . . then I can . . wear the turquoise gown."

"And if it is in the day-time?" the Marquis enquired.

Nikola made a helpless little gesture with her hands.

"Then you will just have to explain that you have rescued me from a desert island where I have been stranded for months, and I lost everything I possessed in a storm at sea."

The Marquis laughed.

"I see you have a very active imagination, Miss Tancombe."

He paused, then he added:

"No, that is wrong. If we are going on this long journey together I must certainly call you 'Nikola', which I think is a very attractive name."

315

"My mother chose it. There are in fact, a number of Tancombes who have lived at King's Keep and were called Nikola, otherwise I would have been christened something different."

"Does your whole life revolve around that house?" the Marquis asked.

"Of course!" Nikola replied. "We have nothing else of any importance, and therefore everything is judged by whether King's Keep does or does not approve of it!"

The way she spoke made the Marquis laugh.

Then he said:

"You are certainly very different from what I expected!"

"What . . did you expect?"

"To answer that question might sound rude," he said. "Instead, I shall find it very interesting to discover how different you are."

"Then do not do it too quickly," Nikola begged. "Otherwise you will be so bored by the time we reach Athens that you may send me back in an . . ordinary train."

The Marquis was laughing again.

When he went to bed it seemed to him that they had laughed a great deal at dinner.

Nikola had an amusing way of saying things.

He could only describe by the same word "different".

He was used to dining with women who flirted with him from the first to the last course.

Their conversation had a *double entendre* in everything they said.

Nikola did not try to be witty.

But he realised that she had thought intelligently about every subject they discussed.

She had an original way of describing things which he found intriguing.

When he asked her if, as she had said at Ridge, her aunt, Lady Hartley, was mean to them, Nikola replied:

"When Aunt Alice dies, she will be the richest person in the graveyard."

Later as the Marquis got into a comfortable bed he thought how fortunate he was not to be travelling with Lady Sarah.

It would have meant all the conversation would have been about Love.

In some form or another it would have lasted from the time they left Ostend until the time they returned.

He had known after he had made love to her on Friday night that he was no longer attracted by her.

Her undeniable dark beauty did not now even arouse his admiration.

The next morning she had behaved in a very possessive manner which he had found embarrassing.

He was furious at the expression in both Lord Cleveland's and Willie's eyes.

He knew they were aware of what had taken place the previous night.

When he had gone up to bed on Saturday night the Marquis's mouth was set in a hard line.

He told himself he would be damned if he would be seduced unwillingly by any woman, whoever she might be.

He had therefore done something he had never done before in the whole of his life.

He had left his own bedroom and spent the night in the Guest-Room on the other side of it.

If Sarah had visited him, as he suspected she would when he did not go to her, he was not aware of it.

He had left the next morning before she could look at him reproachfully.

Now he thought with relief, he was free for at least a short time from all designing women.

Nikola was young and innocent.

She was also too unsophisticated to have any idea of how to pursue a man.

She was therefore, he told himself, exactly what he had asked for a companion.

She would assist him without being aware of it in carrying out the Prime Minister's instructions.

Chapter Six

"Checkmate! I have won!" Nikola cried. "I have won! I have won!"

The Marquis looked somewhat ruefully at the chess-board.

"I must have been asleep," he said.

"Now you are being mean," she retorted. "It has taken me a long time, but at last I have beaten you."

She was so delighted that the Marquis once again found himself laughing.

He had thought it extraordinary that she had made him laugh so much in the train.

Yet since leaving Athens he had been laughing all the way up the Aegean Sea.

It was not that Nikola said anything witty.

Not in the way Lady Sarah or the other sophisticated women he knew would have spoken.

It was simply that she was so young and enthusiastic about everything.

He had learnt while they were still in the train how she spent so much time alone.

It had made her think and reason things out for herself.

It was therefore very exciting for her to be able, for the first time in her life, to air her views.

Although she did not say so, it was something new to be listened to.

Her father had talked to her exclusively about his pictures.

That included talking about various people who had better collections than his own.

Her mother had loved her.

In conversations with Nikola she had tried to make her a sweet, gentle, compassionate woman, which was what her own mother had been.

With Jimmy it was quite hopeless.

Jimmy breathed thought and lived only for King's Keep.

Now, to Nikola's delight, she found herself with a man who was extremely clever and widely travelled.

Because there was no one else, he had to talk to her.

At the same time she was very afraid of boring him.

She tentatively suggested to Dawkins that his Master might play Chess.

She discovered to her delight that the Marquis was considered an outstanding player in his Club.

Nikola had been taught how to play Chess by her father.

They wiled away the long winter evenings at King's Keep.

They would play as the wind whistled outside the windows and there was nothing left to say about the pictures.

Sir Arthur had also taught his daughter at a very early age how to play Backgammon.

It was Dawkins who had prudently brought in the Marquis's luggage both a Chess and a Backgammon board.

"How can you have been so clever as to think of them!" she exclaimed.

Dawkins had grinned.

"Oi knows wot 'is Lordship's like when 'e's bored," he said, "an' I can tell you this, Miss – 'e bores easy!"

Nikola was worried in case she bored him so much that he sent her home alone.

She was so humble about herself that she had no idea that the Marquis found himself surprisingly intrigued by her.

She was so different from what he had expected.

At the same time he was impatient to return to England.

He therefore did not stop in Athens or contact any of his friends there.

Instead he had hurried Nikola from the train down to the harbour.

The Sea Horse was waiting for him there.

The Marquis had found his yacht useful on several missions he had undertaken on behalf of the Foreign Office.

He had therefore installed larger and more powerful engines than any other private vessel afloat.

Nikola was not aware of this.

All she knew was that it was the most splendid yacht she could imagine.

She soon learnt it had the smartest crew, combined with an almost unbelievable comfort and luxury.

The Marquis's Chef was a Frenchman.

This meant Nikola told him, that the food might have come from Mount Olympus.

"In fact," she added, "as it was taken aboard at Athens, it obviously did!"

She felt a little wistfully that she would have liked to see the Acropolis.

She could not understand why the Marquis should be in such a hurry to put to sea.

He thought it was a mistake to make explanations which might make her curious.

Privately he had told the Captain to make all possible speed towards Constantinople.

He had only made one concession in Athens.

It was to send Dawkins, the very instant the train arrived, to buy every newspaper obtainable, regardless of the language in which it was printed.

Dawkins had arrived at *The Sea Horse* only five or ten minutes after the Marquis and Nikola.

He had bought the most extraordinary collection of newspapers.

Those printed in the different languages of the Balkans were several days old.

But they told the Marquis what was happening in the war between Russia and Turkey.

He learnt that the Russians had moved even nearer to Constantinople.

It made him think that if any protests were to come from England they might be too late.

If he was to carry out the Prime Minister's instructions it was extremely important that he find out what exactly the Russians intended.

He had been very careful what he said on the train.

He had no wish to make Nikola inquisitive.

He thought she might ask why he had left England so quickly.

He wondered how he would answer her should she question his purpose in visiting Constantinople at this particular moment.

Then he remembered she was English.

She would know little or nothing about what was happening in the East.

He was therefore astonished when she remarked casually:

"Count Ignatiev, the Tsar's emissary, has with his new Treaty with Turkey proposed a swollen Bulgaria to stretch from the Black Sea to the Aegean."

For a moment the Marquis could not believe what he had heard.

Then he asked sharply:

"Who told you that:"

"I was reading about it in one of the newspapers," Nikola replied. "It stated that virtually the whole of the Balkans is now under Russian control."

"Show me the newspaper," the Marquis ordered.

The newspapers had all been piled on top of a table in the Saloon.

Nikola turned them over until she found the one she wanted.

She handed it to the Marquis who stared at it before he said:

"But this is Greek! Are you telling me that you speak Greek?"

"Not very well," Nikola admitted, "and Papa said my accent was lamentable! But I find it quite easy to read."

"You surprise me!" the Marquis said dryly.

He read the article in the newspaper which Nikola pointed out to him.

He was aware that the Greeks were extremely apprehensive at the Russian invasion of countries so near to them.

He thought however, it would be a mistake to discuss it with Nikola.

He threw the newspaper down and challenged her to a game of Backgammon.

Now the weather was warm.

Nikola wore a thin gown which Bessie had packed for her.

While the Marquis said nothing he realised how worn and shabby it was.

It was Dawkins who said to him in the privacy of his cabin:

"A nicer young lady's never come aboard wi' us, M'Lord!"

The Marquis made no comment and Dawkins went on:

"If yer asks me, it's a cryin' shame 'er clothes be so thread bare. A beggar wouldn't give a 'thank ye' for 'em!"

"I am aware of that," the Marquis replied briefly.

He knew by the way Dawkins looked at him that he was thinking he might have done something about it.

But he knew perceptively that if he had offered Nikola some new gowns, she would have refused.

She was quite unperturbed by them herself.

The Marquis was sure that her mother had instilled in her a very strict sense of propriety.

Carelessly, when speaking of Lady Lessington, whose photograph Nikola had seen in one of the magazines she was reading in the train, he had said cynically:

"She glitters like a diamond, and it is a stone for which she has an insatiable desire."

"Then Lord Lessington must be very rich," Nikola remarked innocently.

The Marquis thought of the extremely expensive necklace he had given Lady Lessington before they parted.

He wondered what Nikola would say if he offered to buy her some jewels.

Then he knew she would be shocked and bewildered by such a suggestion.

She had no idea that Ladies in the Social World would accept any present that was more expensive than a bottle of scent – or perhaps a fan.

Last night after they had dined together, the stars had shone brilliantly overhead.

He had found himself wondering what colour, apart from the turquoise blue of her best gown, would suit Nikola.

He thought it would be amusing to choose her clothes.

He had chosen those of several pretty Ballerinas.

He had also done the same for several of his Social loves to give them an appropriate frame for their beauty.

Nikola had a very unusual loveliness, he thought.

She was also completely unselfconscious about it.

He was quite certain a great number of people would not realise how beautiful she was.

It was like, he thought, seeing a tree stripped of its leaves and being not as perfect as it should be.

He was still thinking of how he would dress Nikola when he was alone in the darkness of his cabin.

It was large and very luxurious.

As she was such a skilful needlewoman, he thought she could more than likely turn the satin bed-cover or the curtains over the port-hole into a gown.

The idea amused him.

Then he thought he would like to take her to Paris.

He would dress her in Parisian clothes which would be as dazzling as her eyes when they lit up with laughter.

Then he told himself he had something more important to think about.

Nikola was just a girl he had brought with him merely as a companion.

Even so, he found himself before he went to sleep thinking of her in a garden of roses.

There were winged angels peeping at her through the flowers.

. . . .

To Nikola, every day was more exciting than the last.

By this time, she was sure that the Marquis had some very important reason for his journey.

Because he obviously did not wish to speak of it, she kept her thoughts to herself.

At the same time she was extremely curious.

Jimmy had spoken of the Marquis as being a great sportsman and a famous Collector of pictures.

He had never hinted at any Political interests or activities.

Yet now Nikola guessed the reason for the Marquis travelling at such speed.

It had something to do with the war between Russia and Turkey.

England was not involved.

But people like the Prime Minister, and perhaps the Queen must be concerned at the way Russia was taking over so much of Europe.

They had, to all intents and purposes, annexed the Balkans.

Now they had turned their attention to Turkey.

As she thought about it, she remembered Natasha's father saying that the Russians always talked about Constantinople as their rightful Capital City.

That was what they were fighting for.

If the Russians acquired it, it would, she thought, unbalance the power in Europe.

323

As they reached the Sea of Marmara it was growing late in the evening.

They anchored in a bay on the North shore.

"I think we should turn in early," the Marquis said soon after dinner.

Nikola gave him a quick glance.

She realised, although he was hiding it from her, that he had a reason for such a suggestion.

They had walked from the Saloon out on deck.

She saw in the light from the moon which was high in the sky that they were in a small bay.

Behind a sandy beach were some low cliffs that appeared easy to climb.

The Marquis was looking at them at the same time as she was.

There was a rough path leading from the bay itself onto the ground above it.

Everything was very silent.

Nikola had expected to hear the distant roar of guns or at least some sign of war.

As the Marquis was obviously waiting for an answer to his remark she replied:

"Yes, of course we should turn in. Do you think we will reach Constantinople tomorrow:"

"I have not decided yet whether I shall call there," he said in an enigmatic manner.

She was well aware what he meant.

It was that he had no intention of discussing the probability of it with her.

She therefore dropped him the graceful little curtsy.

It was what she always accorded him at night and said:

"Goodnight, My Lord. I hope you sleep well, and it is very exciting to have come so far so quickly."

"Goodnight, Nikola," the Marquis replied.

He waited a few minutes for her to reach her cabin and shut herself in.

Then he went to his own.

Dawkins was waiting for him.

He changed quickly from his evening-dress into plain unobtrusive clothes that might have been worn by a well-to-do Russian.

Dawkins gave him a loaded revolver and a sharp dagger-like knife.

324

The Marquis concealed both on his person.

"Now, don't you go takin' no chances, M'Lord!" Dawkins said. "You knows we can't trust them 'Ruskies'!"

"If my information is correct I shall be taking no risks, but merely calling on a friend."

"Oi wouldn't trust any so-called 'friends' in this part of th' world!" Dawkins remarked.

"Do not worry about me," the Marquis answered. "And if anything unexpected happens, take Miss Tancombe to the British Embassy in Athens."

"Don't you go talkin' like that, M'Lord!" Dawkins said, "an' remember – you're more use t' yer country alive than dead!"

The Marquis laughed.

It was the sort of remark that Dawkins always made on such occasions.

He hurried up the companionway.

A boat rowed by two seamen was waiting to take him into the sandy beach of the bay.

. . . .

Nikola heard him leave and knew that he was going ashore.

She thought it was very brave of him.

At the same time it was foolhardy.

Surely the Russians would be watching the coast in case they were attacked by the Turks:

If the information in the newspapers was correct, they had advanced even nearer to Constintinople than they had been before.

One newspaper she had read had hinted that they had reached San Stefano.

Suddenly she was frightened for the Marquis.

She began praying that he would be safe and come to no harm.

It was terrifying to think of him as a prisoner in the hands of men who would not realise his importance.

They could treat him roughly.

They might kill or imprison him.

"He is so magnificent!" she thought. "He is like his great Stallion and I could not bear to think of either of them suffering."

She was praying fervently.

Then the picture of *The Virgin in the Rose Garden* appeared before her.

325

She thought there was the fragrance of roses in her cabin.

She knew The Virgin was listening to her prayer.

Because the view had been so lovely when she stood on deck with the Marquis, she pulled back the curtains over her portholes.

Now shafts of moonlight flooded into her cabin, turning everything to silver.

It was so beautiful.

It seemed impossible that anything so cruel and bestial as war was happening only a short distance away.

Men were killing each other.

Just from the greed to possess more land and rule over more unfortunate and helpless people.

Perhaps in some marvellous way of his own, Nikola thought, the Marquis would help to bring about peace.

The Russians would have to be content with what they already had.

The Turks would cease torturing the Bulgarians.

As she prayed, it made her think of how helpless women were when men wished physically to assault each other.

All that was left for women to do was to pray.

She knew that if the Marquis died, she would feel that she had lost something very wonderful.

He had come quite unexpectedly into her life.

How could she believe that only a week or so ago she had been alone at King's Keep and Jimmy away?

Now she had been transplanted as if by magic into the Sea of Marmara.

There was a belligerent Russia on one side and a defiant Turkey on the other.

"Stop them . . please . . stop them," she prayed to The Virgin. "Let them find peace and, above all, do not let . . the Marquis be in any . . real danger."

Suddenly she heard footsteps running down the companionway and along the passage which led to his room.

To her astonishment, however, instead of opening the door beyond hers, he came into her cabin.

He ran towards the bed.

As he did so she saw with amazement that he was pulling off his coat, then his shirt.

She had been almost asleep, although she was praying for him.

Now she could only stare at him as if she was dreaming.

He kicked off his shoes, flung his clothes under the bed and pulling back the sheets got in beside her.

As he did so he spoke for the first time.

"They are just behind me!" he whispered.

Then he put his arms around her and pulled her against him.

Nikola could hardly believe it was really happening.

Before her lips could move or she could be aware of anything except the closeness of the Marquis, the door opened.

The Marquis was holding her so close that she could not see.

She was aware, however, that two men had entered the cabin.

One of them was carrying a lantern.

It lit up the cabin which was already bright with moonlight.

The Marquis had both his arms around Nikola so that her head was on his shoulder.

Her face was hidden against his neck.

For a moment he did not move.

Then he looked up and asked in a tone of astonishment.

"What the Devil are you doing here?"

His arms slackened slightly, but he still held Nikola against him.

She was conscious that the men could see his naked chest and arms.

"Pardon Excellency!" one of the men answered slowly in English with a very pronounced accent. "We see – man come aboard – this ship and . . "

"A man?" the Marquis interrupted. "Why should that concern you? If my seamen have been ashore, they were, I assure you, doing no harm."

"This not – seaman we see – Excellency," the Russian replied.

"Then look for him elsewhere," the Marquis said sharply, "and get out of this cabin!"

The Russian who had spoken came a little nearer.

Now, by turning her head very slightly Nikola could see him through her hair which was falling over her shoulders.

He was a large, commanding-looking man.

It was clear to her then that the man who had spoken was the leader.

The other who was holding the lantern was his inferior.

The one nearest to the bed had a revolver in his hand.

She could also see the hilt of a dagger at his waist.

327

He was not in uniform, but wore a Russian fur hat on his head.

His dark clothes proclaimed him as a man of some importance.

"I told you to get out!" the Marquis said. "If you want any information about my men, talk to my Captain."

"Your Excellency come – ashore with – me," the Russian demanded. "There – many questions must be – asked by the – Officer in Charge of this – region."

As the Russian spoke Nikola was aware that the Marquis had stiffened.

Because he had raised himself to speak to the intruders her head was a little further down on his chest.

She could therefore hear his heart beating violently.

It was not only with breathlessness as when he had entered the cabin, but also because he was apprehensive.

She was sure there was every reason for him to be afraid.

Quite suddenly she knew what she must do.

To the Marquis's surprise she moved from the shelter of his arms.

She sat up in bed pulling the sheet up over her breasts.

Now she could see the Russian clearly.

She was certain he was a real danger to the Marquis.

She stared at him for a long second as she collected her thoughts.

Then she said angrily in Russian:

"How dare you come here interfering in what is my case! I was sent here by the Third Section and I take my orders from the Chief and no one else!"

She made a gesture with her hand and went on:

"This gentleman fortunately does not understand Russian, but you are making it very difficult for me and I shall report you for incompetence! Go away immediately, and apologise by saying you have made a mistake."

As she continued to speak the Russians stared at her in sheer astonishment.

She went on, her voice sharpening and growing more aggressive with every word she spoke.

Suddenly the Russian seemed to shrival and grow smaller.

"I did not know, Gracious Lady," he said, "that you were here. In fact, we had no idea."

"Does the Third Section have to explain itself to underlings?"

Nikola asked furiously. "You have stumbled into something which does not concern you!"

She paused to give them an angry stare before continuing:

"What has been planned is far too important to be spoilt by an idiotic mistake made by fools who cannot see beyond their noses!"

She used words in Russian which were very rude.

Natasha had taught them to her as a joke.

The Russian to whom she was speaking crumbled.

"Forgive me – I very apologetic – I no idea you were here!"

"Of course you had no idea!" Nikola retorted. "Now stop talking and making things worse than they are already. As I have already said, this is my case, and mine alone, so get out!"

The Russian bowed his head and made a sweeping gesture with his hands.

"Apologise!" Nikola ordered.

"Forgive me – Your Excellency," he said to the Marquis. "It all a mistake – we leave ship – immediately."

He did not wait for the Marquis to reply, but turned and went out of the cabin.

As he did so, Nikola, who was trembling, turned towards the Marquis.

She was suddenly very frightened.

He knew that although the Russians had left the cabin they had not closed the door.

It was the oldest trick in the world to appear to have left but to eavesdrop.

Just in case something worth hearing was said inadvertently, they would listen.

The Marquis was afraid that Nikola might speak.

To keep her silent his lips came down on hers.

For a moment she could not believe it was happening.

She had spoken on impulse and been carried away by her own words.

Only when the Russians left the cabin did she feel it was impossible that she had been successful.

That she had actually saved the Marquis from interrogation.

She knew what this could mean.

The fear of it made her almost collapse.

Then as the Marquis kissed her she did not believe it was happening.

His lips took possession of hers.

She knew it was the most perfect and wonderful thing that could possibly happen.

She had never imagined that a man so overwhelmingly omnipotent would take any interest in her as a woman.

But now, his arms were round her and his lips held her mouth captive.

As his heart beat against her she felt a sensation she had never experienced before.

It was as if the moonlight was moving through her body, into her breasts and touching her lips.

It was so wonderful, so perfect, that she thought for a moment that she must have died.

She was being carried by the angels up into Heaven.

Without meaning to, not only her lips, but also her whole being surrendered itself to the Marquis.

She felt an indescribable ecstasy.

It was the beauty she had seen, felt and heard in the flowers, the trees, the sky.

Yet it was even more wonderful, more perfect.

It was part of everything she expressed in her prayers.

She was not aware that the Marquis had kissed her to prevent her from saying anything the Russians might overhear.

Then he had felt the softness and innocence of her lips.

It became a kiss that was different from any kiss he had ever given or received before.

Vaguely at the back of his mind he heard the Russians moving away down the passage.

Yet he went on kissing Nikola.

It was then he knew that the blood was throbbing in his temples.

His whole body was vividly conscious of her.

The sensations she was arousing in him were an ecstasy that surpassed any feeling he had ever known.

He desired her with every nerve in his body and with his brain.

It was with a superhuman effort that he raised his head.

Then, as if the empty cabin brought him back to reality, he said: "They have gone!"

Nikola did not answer.

She was looking at him with eyes that seemed in the moonlight to be filled with stars.

The Marquis got out of bed.

He bent down and pulled his shirt and his coat from beneath it, and also his shoes.

In a voice that did not sound like his own he said:

"I can only thank you, Nikola, for saving me from what would have been a very unpleasant experience."

"You . . you are . . quite . . certain they . . have gone?"

Nikola's voice came in little jerks from between her lips.

"They have gone!" the Marquis affirmed. "Now you must go to sleep. There will be no further dramatics – tonight at any rate!"

He went from the cabin and shut the door behind him.

"H.he . . kissed me," Nikola whispered to the moonlight, "he kissed me . . and . . I . . love . . him!"

Chapter Seven

Nikola did not feel happy until dawn came.

Until then she was listening.

She was terribly afraid that at the last moment something would go wrong and the Marquis would be taken away.

She was aware, however, that when he had left her he had sent for Dawkins.

A short while later the engines of the yacht had started up.

She heaved a sigh of relief.

Yet at the same time, it was impossible not to listen, just in case the Russians had hidden themselves aboard.

They might try to kill the Marquis while he was unaware that they were there.

She had always hated the Russians for what they had done to Natasha.

Now she knew the Marquis was embroiled with them she was terrified.

She had saved him once, but could she go on doing so?

She wanted to run into his cabin, to find out if he was there.

Then to beg him on her knees to return to England.

Why should he risk his life?

What was happening was not England's war, and therefore not his concern.

Then at last she fell asleep.

． ． ． ． ． ． ．

When Nikola awoke the sunshine was pouring in through the portholes.

The engines had stopped and the quietness made her jump out of bed to see where they were.

One look told her they were in the harbour in Constantinople.

She dressed quickly then ran up the companionway to the Saloon.

She found no one there except Dawkins, who said cheerily:

"'Mornin', Miss! That were a fine 'ow-do-ye-do' last night!"

Nikola realised that he knew what had happened and she asked: "How did those . . men get aboard?"

"There were six o' them," Dawkins replied, "and our two on guard was no match for 'em."

"And . . they have . . all . . g.gone:"

The question came incoherently from between her lips.

"We've left 'em behind an' 'Is Lordship says it's all due to you!" Dawkins replied with a grin.

Nikola drew in her breath.

"Will he . . be safe? Supposing the Turks . . ?"

"'Is Lordship'll be all right," Dawkins interrupted. "'E's sent for a carriage an' an armed guard, so don't you go worryin' about 'im."

He served her breakfast while he was talking and poured her out a cup of coffee.

There were a thousand things she wanted to ask.

But she knew it would be wrong to question the Marquis's servants.

Yet because she was still so anxious, she found it impossible to eat.

After a little while she rose from the table and walked out on deck.

She looked up at the minarets and the dome of a mosque towering above the harbour.

She was praying that the Marquis was safe.

Then her love for him seemed to sweep over her like a tidal wave.

· · · · · · · ·

The Marquis also had very little sleep after what might have been a horrifying experience.

He was also concerned by what he had heard when he had gone ashore.

When he reached the British Embassy, he was received immediately by the Ambassador.

He told him briefly what he had learnt, and it was confirmed by His Excellency.

The Marquis then went immediately to a well guarded room from which a cable could be sent directly to the Prime Minister.

It was now out of date since the British had laid a Submarine Cable which surfaced only at British possessions between London and Bombay.

But the one which ran across Europe to Constantinople was still in use.

The Ambassador assured him that, as far as he knew, the Russians had not tampered with it.

The Marquis therefore sent in a special secret code a cable to the Prime Minister saying:

"SITUATION DANGEROUS, UNLESS BRITAIN MAKES STRONG GESTURE OF PROTEST RUSSIANS WILL TAKE CONSTANTINOPLE. IMMEDIATE ACTION IMPERATIVE."

The Marquis knew that the Prime Minister would understand.

He could only hope that he would be able with the help of the Queen to force the Cabinet to take action.

He then thanked the Ambassador and returned to the yacht.

He saw Nikola waiting for him and was aware of the joy in her eyes that he was safe.

He was however deliberately casual.

He bade her good-morning and went to see the Captain.

The engines started up.

The Sea Horse began to move with incredible swiftness towards the Sea of Marmara.

The Marquis remained on the bridge until it was luncheon time.

When he joined Nikola she longed to ask him what was happening.

He must have known her feelings, but volunteered no information.

She thought it a mistake to try to force a confidence he did not wish to give.

Only when the stewards had left the Saloon did the Marquis say:

"I am interested to know how you can speak Russian, and why you did not tell me you could do so."

Nikola smiled.

"You did not ask me, and as I hate the Russians I am not proud of having learnt their language."

"Why do you hate them?" the Marquis enquired.

She told him about Natasha and the way she and her family had been sent to Siberia.

"And you friend also told you about the *Third Section*?" The Marquis asked.

He had been absolutely astonished at what Nikola had said to the Russians.

He could not have imagined in his wildest dreams that from a quiet unsophisticated English girl.

The most secret police in the world, they were answerable only to the Tzar.

Natasha told her how they were formed by Tzar Nicholas I who put his friend Count Benokendorff in charge.

The Marquis knew this was true.

"And it was they," Nikola went on, "who made the Tzar exile Natasha's father, and I suspect, told him to return to Russia and then sent him to Siberia."

"It must have upset you," the Marquis said sympathetically. "at the same time, I could not believe when I heard you dismiss those men so cleverly."

"I am sure it was . . Papa who told me . . what to do," Nikola replied. "I was very . . very afraid that if they . . took you away I would . . never see . . you again."

"Would that upset you?" the Marquis asked.

She wanted to say that, because she loved him, if he died she would want to die too.

But she knew he would find it embarrassing.

"He . . must never . . never know that . . I love him!" she told herself.

As if the Marquis did not wish to press the question they talked of other things.

Soon he left her to go back on the bridge.

It was after they had dinner together that the Marquis said briefly that he had no wish to talk.

Instead he read one of the books he had brought aboard with him.

It was then that Nikola thought miserably that he was bored with her.

The reason they were steaming so swiftly was that he was eager to return to England.

335

Because it was agonising to sit silent beside him in the Saloon, she went to bed early.

She was very tired, but when she fell asleep there were tears on her cheeks.

. . . .

The next day and the day after made Nikola feel more and more unhappy.

She was near the Marquis, she could see him.

She was aware that every time he spoke to her, her whole being leapt towards him.

But she knew he had withdrawn into himself.

She tried to find the reason.

Finally she decided it must be because he regretted having kissed her and was afraid she might take advantage of the fact.

She walked forlornly round the deck in the sunshine.

All the time she did so she was thinking of the Marquis.

She was wishing she could be beside him on the bridge.

At mealtimes their laughter seemed to have disappeared.

She had the feeling he did not want even to look at her.

"What has .. happened? What have .. I done .. wrong?" she asked.

Her brain told her that the Marquis had come on this voyage for one reason and one reason only.

It was to find out what was the situation between the Russians and the Turks.

He had gone ashore, then visited the British Embassy in Constantinople.

His mission, if that was what it was, had been completed.

Now he could go home.

She was sure he was counting the hours to when he could see Lady Sarah, or some Beauty like her, again.

"He has no further .. use for me," Nikola told herself unhappily. "I am just a .. makeshift companion, and now all he wants is to be .. rid of me as .. quickly as .. possible."

She cried into her pillow.

But she was determined not to be an encumbrance or to cling to him as Dawkins had told her a great many other women had tried to do.

"They're like clingin' ivy, that's wot they be!" he had said when he was tidying her cabin, "an' uses me, they do, if you can believe it, Miss, t' get into 'is good books!"

"How do they do that?" Nikola enquired.

She knew it was wrong to talk about the Marquis to Dawkins.

But he obviously was devoted to his Master and admired him so tremendously.

He was therefore like a protective Nanny or an ancient relation who had always loved him.

Dawkins had grinned at her question.

"Sometimes they slips a few sovereigns into me and," he answered, "an' say:

"If you'll say something nice about me to 'is Lordship, there's more where those came from!"

Dawkins laughed.

"Bribery an' corruption I calls it, but I'd be a mug if I said no!"

"And do you say something nice about them to His Lordship?" Nikola asked.

"I tells 'im wot I thinks is the truth," Dawkins answered, "an' nine times out o' ten, 'Is Lordship agrees with me!"

Nikola told herself she could never be like that.

'I would never degrade myself by bribing a servant to talk about me,' she thought proudly.

One thing was certain, that the Marquis would make up his own mind.

Nothing and nobody would change it.

"He is bored and tired of me," she told herself for the hundredth time.

She felt the tears come into her eyes.

. . . .

The Sea Horse reached Athens in what was undoubtedly record time.

They docked at two o'clock in the morning.

It was only when Nikola woke up that she realised the rush was over.

The noise and tremor of the engines had ceased.

Now everything was very quiet and peaceful.

She knew without being told that they had reached Athens.

It was then she prayed to *The Virgin in the Rose Garden* that the Marquis would not leave as hurriedly as when they had arrived.

"Let him . . stay here for . . just a . . few days," she pleaded. "It would be so . . wonderful to be . . with him . . in Greece."

She knew she felt like that because she thought of the Marquis as a Greek God.

She wanted above all things for him to show her the Acropolis.

He would explain to her what was left of the greatness of Greece when it had altered the thinking of the world.

Then she knew that she was really not so much interested in Greece as in him.

Even to be with him in the train would be an inexpressible joy.

But she felt an agonising pain because every hour every minute took her nearer to the moment when he would say goodbye to her.

After that she would never see him again.

The sands of time were running out.

She knew that even if he was indifferent and bored with her she could at least be near him.

She jumped out of bed.

She had just washed and was beginning to dress when there was a knock on the door.

She guessed it would be Dawkins.

Quickly she put on her dressing-gown before she called out: "Come in!"

Dawkins entered.

"'Is Lordship's compliments, Miss, an' will you put on your bonnet as you're goin' ashore immediately after breakfast."

"His Lordship is taking me with him?" Nikola asked excitedly.

"That's wot 'e said Miss," Dawkins replied. "A carriage is comin' to take you both to th' British Embassy."

He went out and shut the door.

Nikola stared at her reflection in the mirror, not seeing herself, but frightened by a new idea.

Perhaps the Marquis was handing her over to the British Ambassador.

His Excellency could send her back separately while he travelled alone in the Royal Carriages.

Nikola felt that once again the stone which had lain in her breast when she had been so frightened with Jimmy was back.

It was heavy and the sunshine had left the sky.

She put on the gown in which she had started the journey to Tilbury.

She was aware as she did so how shabby it looked.

She had nothing else, and anyway the Marquis would not notice.

"He has .. finished with .. me," she said in her heart.

She felt as if even *The Virgin in the Rose Garden* had deserted her.

She went up to find the Saloon empty except for a steward waiting with her breakfast.

"Where is His Lordship?" she could not help asking.

"'E's 'ad 'is breakfast, Miss an' 'e's givin' orders on th' Quay."

Quickly, because Nikola was afraid of keeping him waiting, she ate a few mouthfuls and drank a cup of coffee.

Then picked up her gloves, she went on deck.

On the Quay she saw there was a very impressive-looking carriage with the Royal Insignia on the doors.

For a moment she could not see the Marquis.

Then she saw him obviously giving instructions to the Second Mate and to Dawkins.

They were standing beside a Hackney carriage.

She walked down the gang-plank and he was waiting to assist her into the carriage from the British Embassy.

They drove off.

When they had gone quite a way in silence the Marquis suddenly said:

"I have something to ask you, Nikola."

She turned her head to look at him and he must have been aware she was nervous.

Also, because she was frightened, her lips trembled a little.

He looked at her for a long moment before he said:

"Do you love me, Nikola?"

It was such an utterly unexpected question that for a moment she could only stare at him.

Her eyes seemed to fill her whole face.

Because she was shy, the colour flooded into her cheeks.

Her eye-lashes flickered as she looked down.

The Marquis was waiting.

Until in a voice that seemed to come from a very long distance and was hardly audible, Nikola murmured:

"Y..yes."

"I thought I could not be mistaken," he said.

He looked away from her.

She thought miserably that now he had even taken away her pride.

Perhaps he felt sorry for her.

That would be even more agonising than loving him without his being aware of it.

They reached the gates of the British Embassy.

Nikola could see the Union Jack fluttered from the flagpole as the Marquis said:

"Do not be surprised at anything I may say in front of the Ambassador. Just agree with me."

She did not understand, but there was no time to ask questions.

The carriage came to a standstill.

An Aide-de-Camp was waiting for them in the open doorway.

As the sentries presented arms he greeted them respectfully.

Then he led them to a room where the Ambassador was waiting for them.

He was a good-looking man with greying hair and reminded her vaguely of her father.

"It is delightful to see you, My Lord," he said to the Marquis, "but I had no idea that you were in the vicinity until I learnt long after you had left that the Royal Carriages were at the station."

"I had reasons for going to Constantinople," the Marquis replied, "and now may I present Miss Tancombe, whom I discovered had no way of leaving that almost beleagured City."

The Ambassador shook Nikola by the hand saying:

"It must have been nerve-racking for you, Miss Tancombe."

Nikola smiled at him and the Marquis said:

"Now that I have brought her safely away, I should be married immediately!"

The Ambassador looked surprised while Nikola was frozen into immobility.

She felt she could not really have heard what the Marquis said.

Then as she stared at him, thinking she must have imagined it, he took her hand in his.

She felt his fingers squeeze hers and as he did so her heart turned a somersault.

She thought the whole room was so brilliant with sunshine that it hurt her eyes.

"Of course, My Lord, your marriage can be arranged," the Ambassador was saying. "I will send for my Chaplain."

"Thank you," the Marquis replied. "And now, as I have several things to discuss with you, perhaps my fiancée could rest in another room."

"I know my wife will be delighted to meet Miss Tancombe," the Ambassador replied.

He smiled at Nikola as he said:

"Let me take you to her."

Nikola looked at the Marquis.

He was smiling and there was an expression in his eyes that she could not interpret.

"Leave everything to me," he said so softly that only she could hear.

The Ambassador had reached the door and was opening it.

There was, therefore nothing Nikola could do but take one last look at the Marquis, then follow him.

They walked a little way to what she realised was the private part of the Embassy.

The Ambassadress was in a comfortable and attractive Sitting-Room.

The Ambassador introduced Nikola saying:

"This poor young lady has been incarcerated in Constantinople and only rescued by the Marquis of Ridgmont."

He smiled before he went on:

"He has asked that they should be married as soon as I can find my Chaplain. I am sure in the meantime, my dear, you will look after her."

"But of course!" the Ambassadress replied. "How exciting that you are to be married here! It must have been very frightening being in Constantinople with those awful Russians coming nearer and nearer every day!"

"It was . . wonderful to be with the Marquis," Nikola answered.

"And now you are to be married! It is very romantic!" the Ambassadress exclaimed.

Then as her eyes took in Nikola's appearance she said:

"I suppose, my dear, you have come away with very little luggage?"

"Very little," Nikola replied truthfully.

"I am sure we can do something about that," the Ambassadress remarked. "Now let me think – I have two daughters and one of them is, I am sure, about your size."

As she realised what she was going to say, Nikola clasped her hands together.

She knew she wanted above everything else to look beautiful for the Marquis.

Yet how was it possible to do so in a gown she had worn for four years and was, she was aware lamentably out of fashion?

"Come upstairs with me," the Ambassadress was saying.

Nikola was now even more certain than before that she was dreaming.

. . . .

When the Ambassador returned to the Marquis, he said:

"My wife will look after Miss Tancombe, and let me, My Lord, congratulate you! She is certainly one of the most beautiful young women I have ever seen in my life!"

"That is what I think myself," the Marquis replied.

"And now tell me," the Ambassador went on, "What is happening in Constantinople?"

"I thought perhaps you had later news than I have," the Marquis replied. "We steamed here with all possible speed. When we left, the fate of Constantinople hung by a thread!"

The Ambassador smiled.

"Then I have good news for you," he said. "I heard only this morning that Admiral Thornby has been instructed to take his six battleships stationed in Besika Bay through the Dardanelles."

The Marquis sat back in his chair.

"That is exactly what I hoped would happen!" he exclaimed.

"It will certainly bring home to the Russians," the Ambassador said, "that Britain is to be considered in any further action taken by the Tsar, and will expect to be consulted about the terms of an Armistice."

"I hope you are right about that!" the Marquis said.

"If you ask me," the Ambassador went on, "and I have been very closely in touch with these things, the Grand Duke Nicolas is aware that the Russian Army is in no condition to fight a war with England."

The Marquis thought with satisfaction that his cable had woken up the Cabinet.

THE SCENT OF ROSES

"I am told on good authority, and I am sure you will be able to confirm it," the Ambassador was saying, "that Russia has an empty treasury and an exhausted Army."

The Marquis did not reply and after a moment the Ambassador said quietly:

"I am not going to ask you, My Lord, what part you have played in this, as I am sure you will tell me to mind my own business. But we have every reason to celebrate the fact that Russia will not take Constantinople, and that you are to become a married man."

. . . .

It was an hour later when Nikola came downstairs with the Ambassadress after having been told twice that the Chaplain was waiting for her.

"Let him wait," the Ambassadress said when the second summons arrived.

"Perhaps . . the Marquis . . will be . . angry," Nikola said a little nervously.

"He too can wait," the Ambassadress replied. "I know, my dear, he will think it worthwhile when he sees how lovely you look."

Her reflection in the mirror told Nikola that she was a very different person from the one she had seen on her arrival.

The Ambassadress had found her a white evening-gown belonging to her second daughter.

It fitted her so well that only one safety pin was necessary to tighten the waist a little.

A very lovely gown of soft chiffon, it had a bustle that flared out in a cascade of frills which ended in a little train on the ground.

The chiffon which draped Nikola's shoulders was sprinkled with tiny diamanté.

It made her look like a flower with dew-drops on the petals.

The Ambassadress's maid had arranged her hair in a fashionable manner.

As they had no wedding-veil they made one out of some yards of tulle which had been bought to trim a gown.

The softness of it made Nikola look ethereal.

The veil was held in place by a small tiara of diamonds which belonged to the Ambassadress.

"Now you really look like a Bride!" Her Excellency said with delight.

The maid opened the door and they walked slowly down the stairs.

An Aide-de-Camp gave her an admiring glance, then hurried to open the door into the Drawing-Room.

The Marquis and the Ambassador rose to their feet as Nikola entered.

She walked shyly towards them.

When she reached the Marquis he looked at her for a long moment before he said:

"That is exactly how I wanted you to look!"

"And that is what I wanted you to say!" the Ambassadress cried.

"The Chaplain is waiting," the Ambassador reminded them.

The Marquis walked to a chair at the side of the room.

Nikola saw that on it there was a bouquet of flowers which must have arrived when she was upstairs.

As the Marquis put it in her hands she saw that it was of roses.

She knew he had chosen it because of the picture of *The Virgin in the Rose Garden*.

She looked at him gratefully, and there was no need for words.

There was an expression in his eyes which she had never seen before.

It made her feel as if she reached up to touch the sky.

Then the Marquis offered his arm.

The Ambassador went ahead with his wife and they followed behind them towards the Chapel.

It was built out at the back of the Ambassy.

When they arrived the Chaplain was there in his surplice waiting to perform the Service.

Someone unseen was playing softly on the organ.

As the Marquis took Nikola up the aisle she felt her father and mother were near her and were aware of how happy she was.

The Chaplain read the beautiful words of the Marriage Service.

The Marquis placed on Nikola's finger his signet-ring.

To her it was the most valuable gift in the whole world.

With it he gave her a Heaven she had never dreamt she would enter.

They knelt for the blessing.

As they did so Nikola felt that it was her prayers to *The Virgin in the Rose Garden* that had brought them together.

Incredibly, unbelievably, the Marquis loved her!

As they left the Chapel she thought it would be an anticlimax to the beauty and sanctity of their marriage if they had to have luncheon in the Embassy.

To her joy, the Marquis took her to the front-door.

Outside she could see there was a carriage waiting.

"All our good wishes go with you both for your future happiness." the Ambassador said.

"I am very grateful to Your Excellency for everything," the Marquis replied.

The Ambassadress kissed Nikola.

"You are a very lucky girl, and the Marquis is a very lucky man," she said. "You will be one of the most beautiful Peeresses England has ever seen!"

"I only . . wish that was . . true," Nikola said.

"Send my tiara back with the carriage when you reach your yacht," the Ambassadress said, "but please keep the gown as a wedding-present."

"Do you really mean that?" Nikola asked.

"I ought to have given you a silver rose-bowl," the Ambassadress laughed, "but I feel this is more practical and my maid has also packed for you some day dresses, nightgowns and slippers."

"How can I thank you?" Nikola cried. "I am so very, very grateful."

She kissed the Ambassadress again before she got into the carriage.

The Marquis joined her and they drove away.

He took her hand in both of his and raised it to his lips.

"I do not . . believe . . this is . . true," Nikola murmured.

"It is true," the Marquis replied, "and I will tell you about it when we reach *The Sea Horse*."

The seamen had been busy while they were away.

The yacht was now decorated with flags and bunting.

Bunches of flowers were tied to the gang-plank.

They were piped aboard.

Then the crew, led by the Captain, gave them three hearty cheers.

The Marquis thanked them before he took Nikola into the Saloon.

It was then she remembered the Ambassadress's tiara.

The Marquis took it gently from her head and gave it to Dawkins.

He hurried back down the gang-plank to hand it to the coachman.

Then as Nikola took off her tulle veil, the yacht started to move.

Before they had left the harbour the steward had brought in their luncheon.

It was a light meal, but at the same time it was all the things Nikola liked best.

It was impossible however, to think of what she was eating.

She was only vividly and exclusively conscious of the Marquis sitting beside her.

He told her about the British Battleships steaming through the Dardanelles.

Although he did not say so, she knew he was responsible for them doing so.

"He is so . . clever and so . . wonderful," she told herself. "How can he . . love me?"

When they had finished luncheon and were alone, the Marquis said:

"I have a lot to talk to you about, my darling, and as I do not wish to be disturbed, I think we should go below."

If he had asked her to climb up a rainbow to Heaven, Nikola would have agreed.

She still could not believe that what had happened was real.

As they went down below she thought that at any moment she would wake up.

She would find herself alone in her cabin.

The Marquis did not take her into her cabin as she expected.

Instead he opened the door of his own.

She went in, then stood transfixed by what she saw.

The whole place was decorated with flowers.

Only as the scent of them fragrant on the air seemed to envelope her, did she realise they were all roses.

There were roses of almost every hue.

But the ones that encircled the back of the bed were white.

"How . . could . . you have thought of . . anything so lovely?" she exclaimed.

"How could I think of any other flower where you are concerned?"

the Marquis asked. "I know, my precious, you have been praying to *The Virgin in the Rose Garden* ever since I have known you, and most especially when I was in danger."

"That is .. true," Nikola agreed, "but .. I thought that .. "

She looked away from him.

"You thought – what?" the Marquis asked.

" .. that you were .. bored with me," she whispered.

"Bored?" he exclaimed. "It has been an indescribable torture not to hold you close to me and kiss you after we had left Constantinople."

"Then .. why?" she asked, "why .. were you so .. distant? I .. I do not .. understand."

The Marquis put his arms around her and they sat down on the side of the bed.

"My precious," he said, "when I kissed you because I knew the Russians were listening outside, I knew that I loved you as I have never loved a woman before."

He pulled her a little closer.

His lips moved over the softness of her cheek before he went on:

"I knew, too, that you felt the same rapture that I did, and that we were meant for each other since the beginning of time."

"Why .. why did .. you not .. tell me so?" Nikola whispered.

"Because, my precious, I brought you on this journey for my own convenience, as a companion."

He paused to smile at her before he continued:

"I never imagined for one moment that I would fall in love with you. When I did, I knew you were everything I wanted in my wife."

Nikola made a little murmur and hid her face against his neck.

"As my wife," the Marquis went on, "I wanted you exactly as you were – pure, holy and untouched until I could put a ring on your finger and know that you were mine."

"H.how could I have .. guessed what you were .. feeling?" Nikola murmured.

"What I was feeling was a wild and violent desire to kiss you and to awaken you to the wonder of love. But I knew you would think it wrong until we were actually married."

Now Nikola understood.

She thought no man could have been more sensitive or more intuitive of what she might have felt had he done so.

"Now you are mine," the Marquis said in his deep voice, "and this, my precious, is what I have been waiting for. I shall no longer have to lie awake at night because I need you."

He paused a moment and then went on:

"I did not dare to look at you in case I kissed you as I wanted to until I could no longer think, but only feel."

"I .. love you! I .. love .. you .. .!" Nikola breathed.

She knew they were the words that had made her cry every night.

She had thought she would never be able to say them aloud.

"As I love you!" the Marquis said.

She had looked up at him as she spoke and now his lips came down on hers.

He kissed her at first gently, as if she was infinitely precious.

Somehow the sanctity of their marriage was still with them.

Then there were little flames of ecstasy throbbing within him.

He knew Nikola was feeling the same, and his lips became more possessive.

She felt that she melted into him.

She was so bemused by the wonder of what he aroused in her that she was hardly aware when he drew her to her feet.

Gently he undid the back of the chiffon gown she had worn for her wedding.

He lifted her onto the rose-encircled bed.

Only as he did so did she realise that she was naked.

Shyly she pulled the sheet over her breasts.

Then the roses seemed to come nearer.

The scent of them intensified and the Marquis was beside her.

He drew her into his arms.

She felt his heart beating as violently as it had when the Russians had threatened him.

But now it was beating with love, not with fear.

She looked up at him and he thought it was impossible for anyone to look more beautiful.

"Am I .. really your .. wife?"

"That is what I am going to prove to you, my lovely darling," he answered, "but I am afraid of frightening you, as you were when I first saw you."

"I was .. frightened then because Jimmy and I had .. done something .. wrong," Nikola answered, "but .. this is right!

348

I know we have been .. joined together by God .. and of course .. by *The Virgin in the Rose Garden* who protected you from the Russians."

"She brought you to me," the Marquis said, "and when we hang the picture in our bedroom at Ridge, we can look at it together and realise how blessed we are."

Nikola gave a little cry and put her arms around his neck.

"You understand? Oh, my wonderful .. magnificent husband .. you understand!"

"What I understand is that I have been looking for you, although I was not aware of it, all my life," he answered. "Now that I have found you, I will never let you go. You are mine, Nikola, mine completely and absolutely and I will love and worship you unto eternity!"

Then he was kissing her.

Kissing her wildly, demandingly passionately.

She felt her love become a flame which quickened and joined the flame within him.

It carried them high into the sky.

They were part of the sun, the moon, the stars, and also the roses which came from God.

. . . .

It was very much later.

The sun had lost its strength and soon darkness would cover the world.

"I .. love .. you!" Nikola murmured.

She had said it a hundred times before, although the words always seemed to be new.

"You are perfect!" the Marquis said.

He knew it was perfection he had never expected to find in any woman.

He added with a little smile:

"I have one present for you, but you will have to wait until we reach Paris for the rest."

"We are .. going to .. Paris?" Nikola asked.

"To buy you a trousseau, my precious, and it will be very exciting to dress you so that you look even more beautiful than you are at this moment!"

Then he laughed and said:

"Actually I prefer you with nothing!"

Nikola blushed.

"You are . . making me . . feel shy," she said accusingly.

"I adore you when you are shy," the Marquis said.

He pulled her closer to him.

Then as if he must finish what he was saying he said:

"Now you have some pretty clothes to wear we will stop in Venice."

"Oh, I would . . love . . that!" Nikola exclaimed.

"The Royal Carriages will meet us there and this time there will be no lobby between you and me."

"We will . . be . . together in the . . Queen's bed," Nikola murmured.

"As long as I can make love to you, it does not matter where we are," the Marquis replied.

His hand was on her breast but he remembered what he had promised her.

"Let me give you your first present."

He bent down and picked up something off the floor.

Without Nikola realising it, he had brought a newspaper from the Saloon.

It was "The Morning Post," a week old.

The Marquis had folded the pages.

As he handed it to Nikola there was one piece of news in the centre which he obviously wanted her to read.

She took it from him, wondering what it was that could concern her.

Then she read:

"TRAGEDY OF A DISTINGUISHED PEERESS

Lady Hartley, the widow of Lord Hartley of Melcombe, was killed in a tragic accident which happened near her home in Essex.

Driving in her carriage drawn by two horses the shaft broke and injured one horse, sending him wild. The two animals galloped down a steep hill with the coachman unable to stop them, and crashing into a narrow bridge at the bottom of it, turned the carriage over. The coachman escaped with a few injuries and slight concussion.

Lady Hartley was however crushed by the vehicle and died

a few hours later after she had been taken to a neighbour-ing house.

Before she died, however, Lady Hartley made a new Will. She left her white cat Snowball, her house and all her possessions to her nephew Sir James Tancombe 10th Baronet of King's Keep, Hertfordshire.

Sir James is at present abroad and the Solicitors are making every endeavour to get in touch with him."

Nikola read the story to its end, then gave an audible gasp.

The Marquis was watching her.

Then suddenly she laughed.

"*Snowball!* It was Jimmy who gave Aunt Alice *Snowball* and that is why she has left him everything she possessed!"

She laughed again.

"You do see, my wonderful husband," she went on, "that after all, Jimmy has not stolen *The Virgin in the Rose Garden* because it is now his!"

"That is something I shall contest very forcefully!" the Marquis replied. "It is ours, my darling, and we will never allow anyone to take it away from us."

"Yes . . it is ours," Nikola agreed.

She threw the newspaper down beside the bed and lifted her face to her husband's.

"It is . . ours!" she said again. "And now I need not feel . . guilty about it, for the . . scent of roses will fill . . our house with love . . and our . . children will . . be as . . happy as we . . are."

"Our children?" the Marquis asked softly.

Nikola put her cheek against his and whispered:

"I want to give . . you a son who . . will be as . . wonderful and as . . handsome as . . you."

The Marquis held her so tightly that she could hardly breathe.

"I want that, my precious," he said, "and daughters who are as perfect as you. But for the moment, I can be content that we are together and you are mine!"

He looked at her lovingly as he said:

"Mine, my precious, innocent, perfect little wife, and nothing else is of any consequence."

As he spoke Nikola saw the fire in his eyes.

Then he kissed her.

There was a fire on his lips which ignited the flames that were already burning within her breasts.

Once again it carried them up into a Heaven where there is always perfection for anyone who seeks it.

It is the Heaven of Love.